It could happen to anyone, thing—life, plans, hopes, dre your life can change even he ..., ...king them to depths you never thought possible. But can you love again after such a loss? Fully? Completely? Can one love be compared to another love, or are we given only one chance? Blow that and it's over . . . James C. Magruder's timeless work, *The Desert Between Us,* explores this question without frivolity, yet with heartfelt emotion, with honesty, and with a story that will leave you breathless . . . and full of hope.

—Eva Marie Everson, CEO, Word Weavers
International, Bestselling Author of *Dust*

Too often we forget the depth of our love, becomes the depth of our loss, once the object of our affection is ripped away. *The Desert Between Us* isn't just for those who have suffered the devastating loss of a loved one. It's for anyone who's facing the pain and uncertainty of life. If you're struggling to see the path forward, Jim is your guide. He's done a fabulous job, "keeping it real" while at the same time introducing a shot of hope into even the darkest of nights. This book encouraged me and I know it will be a blessing to you as well.

—Larry Dugger, Bestselling author of *When
Good People Make Bad Choices*

James C. Magruder pulls no punches on the depth of grief we feel when we lose a loved one. He captures the feeling when the air hisses from our lungs—that time when one physically feels as though the ache of loss will take their own life. *The Desert Between Us* is a moving and yet gut-wrenching story filled with tenderness, wisdom, and ah-ha moments that you won't want to miss. A must-read.

—Cindy K. Sproles, Bestselling Author of *This is Where It Ends*

Losing a loved one is difficult. Losing the love of your life is devastating. In *The Desert Between Us,* author James C. Magruder takes readers on a journey of love and loss, while masterfully weaving in hope and healing. The story grips you from the first page, and it doesn't let go until the very end. This beautifully written book, with its believable characters and carefully crafted dialogue, touched my heart in a way I never expected. It caused me to hold my husband a little closer and be grateful for every moment we share together. I believe readers, especially those who have experienced a life-altering loss, will find wisdom in Magruder's words, and be encouraged to love again.

—Michelle Medlock Adams, a multi-awarding author of more than 100 books including *Fly High: Understanding Grief with God's Help*

In the words spoken about the main character of *The Desert Between Us,* author James C. Magruder is a musician with words, and boy did he make this story sing! Main character Chase Kincaid gains membership to a club no one wants to join when he tragically loses his wife of nine years. Magruder vulnerably explores the depth of his character's heartache through interactions with the son he's left to raise and a possible new love interest. Magruder's writing stirs the reader with good reason – he too joined a grief club no child should have to experience, and that wisdom and understanding offers hope on the pages of *The Desert Between Us.*

—Julie Lavender, award-winning journalist and bestselling author of *Children's Bible Stories for Bedtime, Strength for All Seasons: A Mom's Devotional of Powerful Verses and Prayers,* and *365 Ways to Love Your Child: Turning Little Moments into Lasting Memories*

In *The Desert Between Us*, author James C. Magruder tackles the deep waters of grief and love; both of which aren't possible without the other. With warmth and compassion, Magruder writes from the heart, his words honest and raw. For anyone who has lost a loved one—the pain is real, but you are not alone. May your journey through these pages be a part of your healing."

—Amanda Flinn, author of *Yoga Baby*
and *God Made All Your Feelings*

Love is the force that drives all of us—the need to love and be loved. In *The Desert Between Us*, James C. Magruder does an amazing job of answering the universal question—is it possible to love again after loss? Get ready for an emotional ride through a journey of loss, grief, hope, and restoration. A beautifully written and touching story that will tug at your heart and renew your faith.

—Dejah Edwards, author of *Shattered Innocence*
and *The Christmas Welcome Sign*

Tragic loss of a loved one steals your peace. Regardless if the thief is death or divorce, the loss is unplanned, unkind, and breaks the hearts of young and old. Add another loss—words. What do you say to a young son when his mother dies? What can you say to bring peace to him and to yourself? In *The Desert Between Us*, James C. Magruder delivers realistic scenes packed with wisdom and sensitivity. He speaks the truth in love. After all, great love yields great grief—and as the author reminds us—feeling is healing.

—Dr. Donna D. Kincheloe, DNP, RN, author of *A Life Just Like Mine: How God & Nursing turned Past Pain into Present Peace*

Can we love again after loss? It's a big question. To experience the loss by death or divorce shakes us to the core. The love that should have lasted a lifetime is ripped away, leaving a gaping wound. Learning to love again is a perilous journey. Because love is risky. It makes us vulnerable to hurt and pain and loss. Magruder captures this in all its angst and beauty. I found myself smiling through the tears as he inspires us to believe again in the healing power of love."

—Peggi Tustan, author of the *Real Life Blog;* Moody Radio Cleveland *Pause for Prayer Team*

THE
DESERT
BETWEEN
US

James C. Magruder

END GAME
Press

The Desert Between Us

End Game Press books may be purchased in bulk at special discounts for sales promotion, corporate gifts, ministry, fund-raising, or educational purposes. Special editions can also be created to specifications. For details, contact Special Sales Dept., End Game Press, P.O. Box 206, Nesbit, MS 38651 or info@end-gamepress.com.

Visit our website at www.endgamepress.com.

Library of Congress Control Number: 2023951494
Hardcover ISBN: 9781637971987
Paperback ISBN: 9781637971291
eBook ISBN: 9781637972045

Cover by Dan Pitts
Interior Design by Typewriter Creative Co.

Published in association with Andy Clapp of the Cyle Young Literary Elite, LLC.

Printed in the United States of America
10 9 8 7 6 5 4 3 2 1

DEDICATION

I dedicate this book to my parents,
James H. Magruder & Rosemary J. Magruder.
Married seventeen years.
Six children.
Separated by my mother's premature death
for forty-three years
until
my father's death.

~

And to my wife, **Karen B. Magruder,**
who not only inspires me to write,
but every single day gives me
the one gift I need most
to write:
Time.

~

Karen, may you always think
of this novel as a
love letter — to
you.

A TRIBUTE

To my sister, **Kathii,** who suddenly lost her husband, **Bill,** and to my cousin, **Maureen,** on the passing of her husband, **John,** and to cousin **Jesse Magruder,** who prematurely lost his beautiful wife, **Brianne.** To cousin **Kelly Kuglitsch,** who said goodbye to her remarkable husband, **Paul,** much too soon.

I pray someday you may all love like that again.

CHAPTER 1

July 2016

The sun hadn't cracked the horizon, and already Chase Kincaid had a strange sense of dread as he padded barefoot across his Malibu hotel room to the window.

Where did this sudden anxiety come from, and how did it find him today, of all days? Friday, July twenty-ninth. Just another summer day for the rest of the world, but his ninth wedding anniversary. The feeling he tried to brush away hung like morning mist. While his wife, Aimee, lay asleep, he quickly dismissed it—not because it wasn't real, but because he feared it was.

They had celebrated their ninth anniversary a day early with an overnight stay at their favorite getaway. Chase would sleep better tonight when reunited with Clay, their six-year-old son. Normally self-assured and optimistic, Chase stuffed his feelings before Aimee woke. A cup of coffee and a hot breakfast would diminish the dread, like the sun diffused fog.

~

As the two cruised north on US 101 toward their home in Santa Barbara, Aimee leaned forward and turned on the radio.

"Oh, I love this song."

"You love every song," he replied, smiling.

She sang along and gazed out the window at the Pacific and the Santa Ynez mountains as they drove along California's coastline. Chase loved these about her—spontaneity and a soft but beautiful voice she was too humble to share with the world. "It's a voice to sing in the shower, not the choir," she used to say. He stopped trying to convince her a long time ago that she belonged on stage, not backstage. In his life, his heart, she lived on center stage.

They neared a bottleneck, a tapered channel recently nicknamed "The Squeeze" because of the narrow road caused by construction and three tight driving lanes bordered by temporary four-foot cement walls on both sides. With no shoulders to pull over onto in an emergency, it was a death trap.

They entered The Squeeze at a higher speed than he liked because the traffic behind and alongside him pressed in. Two hundred yards into the channel, Chase heard the passenger seat creak and Aimee let out a gasp. Quickly glancing her way, he tried to maintain control of the vehicle in the fluctuating traffic patterns.

"Hon, I'm doing the best I can to navigate here. Don't panic. I know it's cramped, but if I stay focused, I can ..."

Her body convulsed and vaulted forward.

"What's wrong, honey?" He kept his eyes glued to the twisting road in front of him.

She didn't answer and grasped her chest with both hands.

He glanced her way again.

Her face flushed, and she stuttered. "My chest ..." She sucked a breath. "Something's wrong ... like ..."

Chase finished her sentence. "Like two years ago when you had that—heart attack?"

"Yes ... same ... symptoms ..." She struggled to catch her breath.

"The cardiologist was supposed to fix that with the stent." Chase gripped the steering wheel tighter and tried to speak calmly. "Take the nitro and the baby aspirin in your purse. Then lower the seat back so you don't get dizzy."

She dug in her purse, found the aspirin, and swallowed it before placing the nitro tablet under her tongue and reclining her seat.

She waited a minute. "Chase, it's not working. I feel light-headed ... chest pain." The fear in her voice caused his palms to sweat.

Perspiration beaded on her forehead, and his body temperature rose.

"I ... don't ... feel ... good." She slurred her words.

His eyes darted to the rearview mirror. Behind him, the driver hugged his bumper. On the right, the car ran parallel to him, its driver lost in his own world. On the left, a semi-trailer hemmed him in. Sandwiched in the middle lane, and with no shoulder, the oblivious commuters surrounded him as traffic slowed to a crawl before coming to a complete stop.

Pulling over was impossible. Locked in by vehicles, he pounded on the horn in frustration. No one could move. Gridlock. His fingers grew stiff, and his stomach rolled as Aimee gasped again.

"Chase ... pain ... running down my left arm."

"I'm calling 911." He dialed with his thumb.

The dispatcher answered immediately. "911. What's your emergency?"

"My wife's in distress. She's short of breath, feeling faint, chest discomfort, pain shooting down her left arm. But we're stuck in traffic."

"What's your location?"

"We're northbound on 101 just past the Mussel Shoals exit, near Carpinteria. She needs an ambulance, but the northbound lanes are now a parking lot."

"Sir, I can dispatch an ambulance not far north of you. I'm notifying them of your location."

Aimee clasped Chase's right hand—her only mode of communication now. Squinting as though in agony, she squeezed his hand tighter. Chase glanced at her, released his seatbelt, and ran around the car to the passenger seat. He screamed at the driver across from her. "I need a doctor. Now!"

The man got out of his vehicle, glanced at Aimee, and ran from car to car for aid.

"Hold on—Aim." His voice cracked again. "Help is on the way."

Each minute was precious now. As he yanked open her door, she collapsed and slid out of the shoulder harness toward him. Sweat beaded on his brow and his hands trembled as he released her seat-belt. He carefully pulled her out of the car, placing his jacket under her head as he laid her on the concrete. A crowd swarmed.

"Stay with me, Aim."

Her eyes turned glassy. No response.

Two cars behind him, an off-duty firefighter arrived with an Ambu bag and a small oxygen tank. "My name is Aiden. I'm an EMT. I can help."

After informing Aiden of what he had told the dispatcher, he relayed to the dispatcher that an EMT was now on the scene.

As the onlookers encircled them, a doctor emerged from the crowd. Aiden took her blood pressure while the physician checked her pulse.

"Blood pressure is eighty-four over fifty-two."

"And there's no pulse," the doctor added. "She's cyanotic. Start CPR."

Chase bit his lip, paced, and watched in horror while the dispatcher kept him talking. Sensing she was trying to keep him on the phone and out of the way, he ended the call to focus on the scene unfolding before him.

"She's turning blue!" a bystander shouted.

Aiden and the doctor worked faster, applying compressions and breathing.

Bending over Aimee, the doctor checked her breathing and pulse again. He wiped his forehead, glanced up at the sky, and then slowly turned to Chase.

Sirens wailed in the distance, but they would never arrive in time.

After several chaotic minutes, the doctor shook his head at Aiden. They ceased rescue efforts.

Leaning back on his haunches, Aiden glanced at the doctor and said, "Want to call it, Doc?" Exhaling hard, the physician glanced at his watch. "Time of death, 10:17 a.m."

Chase gasped as the doctor stood and placed his hand on his shoulder. "There's nothing more we could have done."

The ambulance arrived in the southbound lanes, and the EMTs ran across the highway. When they realized they were too late, they stood in silence, and the crowd dispersed.

Aiden grasped his bag and the portable oxygen tank. "I'm sorry—I'm so sorry." His words reinforced the finality of the outcome.

Chase threw his head back and screamed. His legs collapsed. Landing on his knees, he crawled beside the only woman he had ever loved.

Cradling her in his arms, he rocked her. Sobbing, he rocked faster. After what seemed like an eternity, he collected himself, wiped his tears with his palm, kissed her on the lips one last time, and whispered, "I'll always love you, Aim."

He lowered her back to the pavement. Aiden returned from his truck with a blanket. Chase stood and stepped back.

Aiden raised his hand to address the remaining gawkers. "Okay, everyone, please return to your vehicles."

The doctor led Chase away from the scene as Aiden covered her body. Chase felt faint.

"You don't look good," the doctor said.

His knees buckled.

The doctor caught him. "You all right, son?"

Heart racing. Numb. Chase tried to speak. His mouth was chalk, his words wedged deep in his throat. After a moment, he cleared it and spoke in a soft, shaky, halting voice. "No, Doc—my wife ... just died ... and I think ..."

The kind, nameless doctor put his arm around Chase's shoulders and waited for him to finish.

Chase swallowed hard. "... and I think—I just died with her."

CHAPTER 2

Almost Two Years Later

Chase sat on his patio with a glass of sweet tea and a book at his modest Santa Barbara home overlooking the ocean after yet another futile day wrestling to write his second novel. The fading sun turned into a golden globe, painting the sky orange, and started its peaceful descent below the horizon on this Friday evening.

Now more than ever, he understood why writing a successful sequel to his bestselling debut was like chasing the wind. "Better to scrap it and try something completely different," he told himself.

Less criticism and comparison if I start from scratch or switch genres. Like all authors, Chase understood sequels typically suffocated under the crushing weight of expectations and critical reviews. He questioned why he would put himself through that scrutiny. Yet his agent highly recommended it.

Chase loved to write—he always had. It came naturally, and he liked the way it relaxed him.

"It's who you are," his father, David Kincaid, once said. "You're a musician with words—you can make any story sing—and I love the sound of the music you write."

Chase worked out of his home as an executive speechwriter and advertising copywriter—it paid the bills while he strived to grind out novels. Aimee had planted the idea in his head of being a novelist. It was one more thing he loved about her. She'd nudged him to reach for the stars when he was perfectly content living with his feet flat on the ground, as long as it was with her.

Before switching to the publishing industry a few years back, he had worked in advertising as a copywriter. In publishing, he specialized in marketing books and writing captivating promotional material and back cover copy for fiction. Working in New York taught him the ins and outs of the literary business and gave him the confidence to throw his hat in the ring and take a shot at crafting a story before transplanting himself on the West Coast, becoming a freelance writer, and working for himself.

Chase loved Santa Barbara for its slower pace of life. The tranquility allowed him to write with greater clarity. The city suited him and his family. Yet he returned to Santa Barbara for another reason—personal history.

His grandfather, Joseph Kincaid, had lived here, where Chase would often visit him as a boy. His grandmother died before he was born, and he loved his grandfather. The magic between them never faded, but the old man had passed while he was away at college.

When Chase was young, he believed his grandfather could do no wrong. After reaching adulthood, he wondered if he had placed his grandfather on a pedestal, or if that was a throne where all grandparents lived in the minds of their grandchildren.

For decades, Chase had magazine articles published, and about a year ago he hit pay dirt when he landed an agent and his first novel won the lottery by landing on the New York Times Best Sellers list.

However, one regret haunted him. If only he had written it sooner. Aimee had never seen it published. Now he struggled to find his voice for his sequel and questioned whether his bestseller was a fluke, a lucky break, dumb luck, or all three.

Listening to the rhythmic sound of the surf, he feared what all new authors fear—having only one book in him.

"Chase, don't fight it—just finish the sequel. Don't be a one-hit wonder," his agent, Ed McCabe, often reminded him, especially as the deadline loomed for his second novel.

Ed was a revered agent, but Chase sometimes questioned his motives. He was never sure if Ed respected his writing or sought every opportunity to make a buck. Chase couldn't shake the feeling that Ed was pushing him to finish the sequel only to collect the second half of the advance.

I'm far from a household name. I need to amass a body of work, hope lightning will strike twice, and trust Ed to increase the odds of that happening.

Chase leaned back in his patio chair and let his thoughts wander out to sea as the gulls screeched and circled overhead. It was just shy of two years and an unthinkable number of sleepless hours since Aimee had slipped away and left him and Clay, who was now eight, to fend for themselves. Later this month would be their eleventh wedding anniversary. *Thirty-three is too young to die,* he reasoned. *Much less of a heart attack. How does that happen, and how is it fair?*

First her father, now her.

Swiveling in his chair to face the ocean, he picked up the book he had placed on the patio table—*Message in a Bottle* by Nicholas Sparks. The similarity to his life struck him. As he gazed at its pages, he started daydreaming of better days while waiting for Clay to arrive after having a late dinner at the home of his school friend, Fernando. The two were close, and Fernando had been there for Clay after his mother died. Chase was grateful his son had someone to talk to.

The scenic view absorbed him. Santa Barbara was easy to love, and he loved it for many of the reasons everyone flocked to central California—sun, sand, beaches, cool breezes, cloudless blue skies, and the way palm trees punctuated the sky like art. The sunny and warm weather made every day feel like Groundhog Day.

That's the blessing and the curse of living in Santa Barbara. Every day is picturesque, but you pay for it—and it's exponentially more expensive than a sunshine tax.

For Chase, the weather wasn't the only thing that was like

Groundhog Day. The gaping hole in his heart made every day feel like a rerun. He was learning to adapt, but it felt like an infinite process.

Although he made good money as a freelance executive speechwriter, and he had received a generous advance on his bestseller, he could only afford to live on the ocean in his modest three-bedroom house for one reason. It was long paid for, and he'd inherited it from his late aunt several years after she had inherited it from his grandfather.

Aunt Mary never married and was a caregiver for her father in the waning years of his life. His grandfather had left the home to her since he had only two children, and Chase's father had no mortgage and was living in Santa Clarita, about an hour and a half southeast of Santa Barbara. A prominent architect, Chase's father was reasonably wealthy. Aunt Mary, however, was another story. She was a local librarian.

When Chase was young, she enjoyed reading to him and fueled his love of books. Aunt Mary always said, "The best place to park is behind an open book." She had always been kind to Chase and put the home in his name shortly after being diagnosed with ALS five years ago. Complications from the progressive disease would take her two years shy of her five-year prognosis.

Aimee had adored Aunt Mary for her compassion, her unassuming way, and inner contentment. The quaint home offered spectacular ocean views, and Aimee loved it. "Chase, this is a writer's home," she would say. "Your inspiration is on the other side of every window."

Chase would smile and nod, knowing where his true inspiration rested.

"Funny," he whispered to himself, "how things are so much more enjoyable when we define the terms, and intolerable when we don't. I had loved being alone—but I hate being lonely."

At thirty-seven, he had dated little since losing Aimee, except for a couple of ill-fated blind dates set up by his best friend, Jack Simmons, who had suffered an agonizing divorce four years ago.

At Jack's incessant urging, Chase also tried online dating with mixed results. High-tech relationships worked for some people, but not for him.

"I'm hoping for chemistry and connection," he told Jack. "Online, I feel neither, so far."

The online dating model just didn't fit him. He struggled at the thought of glamor photos and understated flaws. Chase was a simple man, this he knew, and he believed he could tell if a woman was right for him just by an engaging conversation, a warm laugh, one afternoon of chilling together, and a look in her eyes.

Chase stood and walked to the far edge of the patio overlooking the ocean. He ran his hand through his hair and closed his eyes, letting a cool sea breeze wash over him.

Since Aimee passed, not a day went by without Chase thinking of her and remembering her devotion to him, her playful sense of humor, her unique laugh, and the way she loved Clay. Most of all, he simply missed the way she looked—and the way she looked at him. Aimee was beautiful, with sandy blonde hair, penetrating sky-blue eyes, high cheekbones, and a poise that was a gift. She was the girl next door—and *that* was all he ever wanted.

"There are few things in life where there are no second chances," his father would say. "This is one of them—at least for me."

Chase walked back to his chair, sat, and thumbed through the Sparks novel on the table, noting the pages he had previously highlighted in yellow that ran parallel to his life, before being distracted by another memory—and questions.

Can I learn to accept the possibility of being alone—and Clay living in the same vacuum I did when my mother died?

"Better to live with the memory of the one you couldn't live without than to risk living with the wrong person," his father told him the first year after losing Aimee. He had intended to console him, not confine him. Chase had unconsciously adopted this philosophy—and the resulting paralysis.

My father was a decade older than me when he lost my mom. So if I follow his philosophy, I could live in this lonely, emotional desert ten years longer than he did.

Chase took a sip of his sweet tea before gazing at the blue sea. Two questions nagged him the most. Would Clay struggle as much as he did to fill the void of going through life without a mother? And was Clay destined to live his father's life—*like I did?*

CHAPTER 3

Chase was still lounging on the patio when Jack greeted him as he walked around the corner of the house to the backyard.

"There you are," Jack said, raising an eyebrow and displaying a playful grin. "I saw your Jeep in the driveway, but you didn't answer the doorbell, so I figured you were out here again."

Chase smiled. "Is there a better place to chill?"

"Can't beat the view."

Chase motioned to the cushy swivel patio chairs. "Take a load off. What's up?"

"Nothing. Just wanted to stop by and see what you're up to this weekend."

"Haven't thought about it yet. When Clay gets home, I'll see what he feels like."

"How's the little guy doing? Any better? I know it's been what, almost two years now, since you lost Aimee, right?"

Jack was referring to Clay struggling the last two years. Jack was no stranger to pain after barely surviving his bitter divorce. Chase was there for him through it all, and for the last two years, Jack had more than returned the favor. Clay had even started calling him Uncle Jack.

Chase slipped his hands behind his head and stretched his legs. "Nothing seems to make sense anymore."

Sliding into his chair, Jack gazed at the ocean and turned to Chase. "You talking about Clay or yourself?"

"Honestly?"

"Yeah."

"Both."

"Where's Clay now?" Jack swiveled his patio chair around to face the house, then back to the ocean.

"He's having dinner at his friend Fernando's house and then playing video games. It's Friday, so I told him he can stay later than usual. Fernando's mom will drop him off."

"Is he in summer school again?"

"Yep. Again." Chase nodded and spoke in a soft, compassionate tone.

"How's he doing this time?"

"Better, but not great. Seems he's still easily distracted and lonely. His teacher—Miss Taylor, I think her name is—sent home a note a few weeks ago. She says he's having trouble concentrating and if it continues, she'd like to meet with me."

"Does his teacher know what he's been through?"

"I doubt it." He paused, sat up straight, and crossed one leg over the other. "Aimee died when he was in first grade, so I didn't mention it to his third-grade teacher. I didn't want this following him around like it did me when I was a kid. So I didn't mention it— but I've thought better of it and I intend to let his teachers know. It might be in his records."

"Makes sense. Poor guy. He's been through a lot." Jack inhaled the fresh ocean air.

Chase could hear the empathy in his voice. It's what made Jack such a loyal friend. He always empathized with people despite his propensity to tease them. Empathy with a twist of humor—it was a strange dichotomy that coexisted in Jack's appealing personality.

"I feel for the kid. He's lost his mom and has no siblings to cushion the blow or add perspective," Jack said. "He's traumatized alone—with no peers to tell him he'll be all right."

Chase nodded but didn't say a word, just gazed over the water at the distant horizon.

"You know what that's like—you went through the same thing when you lost your mom." Jack paused. "You sure don't want him turning out like you." A smile cracked along his lips.

Chase turned to face Jack, clasped his hands together, then exhaled hard. "And that's exactly why I worry about him going through it. I remember what it's like to feel lost as a kid."

Jack nodded. "It's frightening, yeah?"

"Yeah. Imagine what it's like to feel lost for a couple of years. For me, the worst part was to appear normal, but feel hopeless. It was like having a black hole in your heart. This mysterious void that no one else could see—or feel—and you're left to cope alone. As a twelve-year-old, I didn't have a clue how to fill it. I suffered in silence because I didn't know how to survive."

"That's not exactly the way your father tells it."

"My father had to deal with his own grief. How could he possibly understand mine? I believe he tried initially, but he then defaulted to thinking what worked for him would work for me, but I'm wired differently."

"Your dad always acts like he understood what it was like for you. He's told me in passing that you did just fine all those years. 'You weathered the storm together.'"

"Don't hold that against him, Jack. Think about it. He was trying to figure out how to cope with grief too. When he felt himself healing, he hoped I was too. He tried to keep everything together, but ..."

"But what?"

"He didn't fully understand childhood pain. He tried, but he couldn't feel it from a kid's point of view," Chase explained.

"Have *you* ever told him how you felt?" Jack reached over and poked him to make his point.

Chase paused and changed the subject. "Hold that thought. Can I get you something cold to drink?"

"Just a Coke."

Chase walked to the house and brought back a Coke for Jack and one for himself. They popped them open together.

"Where were we?" Chase asked as he sat.

"I asked if you ever told your dad how you felt as a kid when you lost your mom."

"Why would I? That was a long time ago. Doesn't matter anymore. That stays between us, Jack. Please never mention it to him or anyone else. Agreed?"

"Why?"

"It's ancient history. No need to dig up what's buried. Do you understand?"

Jack raised his palm. "Okay, fine."

"You say that, but you've let things slip out in the past when you argued with my dad."

"I was just going to bat for you."

Chase raised his voice to make his point. "Jack, I'll say it again. Please never mention to my dad how much my mom's death messed me up as a kid."

"Roger that. But you should level with him. You're still carrying that stuff around, and now, on top of it, you've lost your wife."

Chase shifted his weight in his chair. "I know, but I've dealt with the loss of my mom. Besides, I should be over her by now."

Jack's eyes widened. "Over her? Really? Who do you think you're talking to? It's me, remember?"

"That kid buried that baggage. I put it to bed years ago."

"You trying to convince me—or yourself?"

Gulls squawked as they made graceful arcs in the blue sky, and Jack took a long slug of his Coke.

"Neither."

"Good," Jack said, "because I'm not buying it—and neither is your twelve-year-old self."

Chase laughed. "What, you're a psychiatrist now?" He stood and walked a few steps toward the ocean before stretching, then eased himself back into his chair.

"No, just saying that you got some things in your life that still need—fixing."

He smiled and wagged his finger at his friend. "That's the mechanical engineer in you, Jack. You think you can fix everything. It's not that easy."

"Look, like it or not, I can see right through you. And you've got some things to fix. You could see through me when I was going through my divorce with Julie. And you called me on it. We've got too much history together, pal. It's the blessing—or the curse—of friendship." Jack swiveled in his chair to face Chase. "By the way, how's that other thing going?"

"What other thing?"

"Your relationship with your mother-in-law?"

Chase raked his hand through his hair with the sea breeze. "Oh that. Honestly, I've been avoiding Joyce because it hasn't got much better."

"She still blames you for Aimee's death?"

"Let's just say she thinks if I had done things differently, Aimee might be here today. As you know, Aimee died of ventricular tachycardia. She had a family history of fatal cardiac arrhythmia, the same heart condition that suddenly claimed her father's life. I've talked to several physicians since her death, and they all agree CPR infrequently works on this condition. It may have helped, but likely, she still would have passed."

Shaking his head, Jack said, "So Joyce can't give it up. How are you going to fix that?"

"After two years, I may never fix it." Chase stood, glanced at the grill, and turned to Jack. "What are you doing for dinner?"

"Nothing. What you got in mind?"

"Clay will be home late. Let's throw some steaks on the grill and eat here on the patio."

A smirk came across Jack's face. "Twist my arm."

~

Chase and Jack walked back to the house. Once in the kitchen, Chase grabbed some asparagus, yellow squash, and zucchini from the fridge and handed them to Jack.

"Rinse, slice, and season these. There's olive oil in the pantry, second shelf. I'll grab the spices for you. The aluminum foil is in the third drawer on the right. We'll get the veggies started on the grill before we throw on the steaks."

Chase pulled the fillets from the fridge, unrolled the butcher paper, set them on a plate, and seasoned them before carrying them to the patio. While Jack seasoned the veggies, he fired up the grill and allowed it to preheat. He gave the veggies a ten-minute head start before placing the fillets on the grates. Chase loved the sizzle as they seared.

"O'Doul's?" he offered.

"Sure."

When Chase returned, he handed a bottle to Jack and set the timer on his phone to turn the steaks and veggies. They sat in silence on the patio facing the ocean, drank their beverages, and enjoyed the view and the cool breeze.

Without looking at Jack, Chase broke the silence. "I buried that twelve-year-old kid several years after my mom died."

Jack raised his eyebrows and swiveled in his patio chair to face him. "That's a shame."

Chase spun his chair toward him. "Why?" He paused. To dampen the surprise in his voice, he kept his tone gentle. "Why would you say that, Jack? You know how hard I've been working to forget the trauma. A twelve-year-old shouldn't have to go through that."

"You're right, a young kid should never have to go through that."

Chase glanced out to sea and turned to his closest friend. "Then why did you say it's a shame that twelve-year-old kid is no longer around?"

Jack smiled. "I guess it's because that twelve-year-old kid could really help an eight-year-old I know."

Chase felt the sting of what Jack said. Jack never pulled punches, and it was just another thing Chase admired about him. He always told the truth and left it up to you to be burdened by it—or better off for it.

The alarm went off on Chase's phone. Setting his beverage down, he raised the grill lid, turned the fillets, and flipped the veggies with tongs.

"Anything I can do?" Jack paused and smelled the aroma of sizzling steaks punctuating the salt air.

"Yeah, grab a couple of plates, utensils, napkins, and salt and pepper from the kitchen. I think you know where everything is."

"Roger that."

After turning the steaks, Chase lowered the lid and reset his alarm. Jack placed the plates on the patio table.

When the alarm went off again, Chase turned off the grill, placed the veggies and steaks on the plates, and brought them to the table. They sat and raised their bottles.

"To friendship—and better days," Chase said.

"To friendship and better days. Cheers." They tapped the necks of their bottles together.

They ate in silence for a few minutes.

Jack broke the stillness. "Before we change subjects, just one last question about your past because we haven't talked about it for a while. Since you believe your twelve-year-old self no longer exists, how is your current self dealing with the loss of Aimee?"

Chase cut another piece of his steak and placed it in his mouth, considering his answer. He needed time to ponder the question. "Even though it's been two years, I'm still healing, as you would expect. It's not something you ever get over, right? But I've started a new routine that's helping me heal."

Jack wiped his face with his napkin. "Really? What's that?"

"I write about it."

"You write about it?"

Chase lifted his bottle and took a sip. "I journal."

"You *what?*"

"I journal about it."

Jack leaned forward and smirked. "So you keep a diary?"

"No, a journal."

"Diary, journal, what's the difference?"

Chase cut his veggies before answering. "A diary is like a running log of your life. You write entries daily."

"So you don't write in your journal daily?"

"Not usually. But sometimes. Depends how I'm feeling."

"And you benefit, how?"

"I typically write in my journal only when I've got something to think through."

"Like the loss of Aimee?"

"Right. And how I'm going to live without her—long-term."

Jack leaned back in his chair and sipped his drink. "Hey, you could just talk to me, pal. That way, you wouldn't have to write anything down."

"I know, and I do talk to you. But sometimes I need to…"

Jack finished his sentence. "Talk to yourself."

"Yeah, so I can figure things out."

They were quiet for a moment. The patio was like a piece of paradise for them. The house sat in front of it, the ocean in back, and an expansive oak tree shaded the yard with branches that stretched like fingers pointing toward the azure water.

"May I ask what exactly you write in your journal?"

Chase toyed with him. "You can ask, but I won't tell you. Not yet."

Jack put his beverage down and settled into a more comfortable position in his chair. "Fair enough. But I'm here if you need me."

"As you've always been."

"Do you find answers when you journal?"

Chase turned to him and grinned. "I thought you said you had only one last question."

"Sorry, but we haven't seen each other lately. That's why I stopped by without calling first."

"You usually stop by without calling." Chase playfully punched his friend on the shoulder. "Yes, sometimes I find answers when I write in my journal."

Jack smirked. "So it's kind of like therapy?"

"Partially. But it's more than that. Journaling helps me *see* how I feel by allowing me to pour my feelings literally on the page, where I can view them in broad daylight. And when I can *see* them, it helps me figure out what to do about how I feel."

"So you're saying—for you—journaling is its own healing balm?"

"I'm saying, for me, pain is the inspiration, writing is the outlet. I'm trying to turn an emotional process into a logical one. Does that make sense?"

"I guess." Jack squinted as he considered the wisdom in the statement. "But it sounds like journaling is just venting. And that's good."

"No, it's not venting, because it's not about anger—it's about pain. Journaling is more like processing and then discovering how to heal. Anyway, when I scrawl everything on a page, I can sort it out. And that gives me hope to move on without Aimee. Besides, even if I were to vent a little, that's confronting my feelings, right? Something you've always encouraged me to do."

"Okay, you've got me there," Jack conceded.

"Let me put it the way an engineer like you will understand it,

Jack. It's sort of like reverse engineering. Once something's disassembled, you can analyze it, understand how it works, and try to put it back together."

Jack laced his fingers and slipped his hands behind his head, then turned to Chase. "If this has been such a struggle for you these past two years, think how Clay feels."

Chase nodded. "You have *no* idea."

Jack bristled.

Chase caught himself. "Oh, Jack. Sorry. Of course, you know what it's like. I know how painful your divorce was. Not sure why I said that. I'm a little self-absorbed right now."

Jack changed the subject. "How's your second novel coming? Did you decide if you're going to write a sequel or go in a completely different direction?"

"Still not sure. Ed wants me to write a sequel, so I'll attempt it, but I'm not feeling it—at least not right now." Chase stared at his beverage. "I lost more than Aimee when she died."

"What else?"

"Inspiration. Novelists always write for something—or someone. Not that we need inspiration every day, but there's usually a source of motivation in a writer's life that propels him or gives him purpose."

"I get it."

Chase spoke in a whisper. "I just don't feel compelled to write like I did when she was alive." With these words, he knew he had just admitted something he had locked inside himself for almost two years.

After taking another sip, his friend responded. "I can't say I understand writers, but I know what you mean. It makes sense that you need a person—or a purpose—in your life to get your muse back. Just don't tell your agent that."

"I think Ed already knows."

"What have you got so far?"

"Not much. Maybe a rough idea of where I want to go, but little else."

Jack stretched his legs in front of him. "I can't help you with Ed, but I can tell you Clay is now your inspiration—and he even looks a lot like Aimee. He may be as close as you're ever going to come to restoring your inspiration or sense of purpose."

Chase listened to Jack and let it settle in. Wasn't two years of grieving enough? For twenty-four consecutive months, he'd felt frozen in place, like wet skin on dry ice. He dreaded the prospect of going through life alone—he'd had a similar tour of duty as a young boy. And thankfully, his father had pushed him to move forward.

Jack broke his train of thought. "You mentioned journaling is helping you heal and giving you a sense of hope again. Maybe journaling will give you hope for something else."

"I'm listening."

Jack gazed out at the horizon, then turned to his friend. "Hope for finding that twelve-year-old kid again. So he can encourage you—and help Clay."

CHAPTER 4

About an hour after Jack left, Fernando's mom dropped off Clay later than expected.

Sleepy from the car ride, Clay stumbled toward his room. Chase walked with him, helped put on his pajamas, and made sure he brushed his teeth before climbing into bed. Clay's eyes were heavy as Chase gave him a hug, kissed his forehead, and helped him say bedtime prayers.

"Good night, little man." He turned on the nightlight and flipped off the overhead light. Clay was breathing heavily before Chase reached the door.

As Clay drifted off to sleep, Chase stood in the doorway, staring at the smooth features of his face, and marveled—as he always did—at how much Clay resembled Aimee.

"The miracle of genetics," he often said to himself. Jack was right. Clay was as close as Chase would ever come to having Aimee alive, the nearest thing to finding inspiration and purpose again. Clay was reason enough for Chase to write again.

He turned off the lights in the house except in his office, where he sat on the couch. Grabbing his leather-bound journal, he opened it and stared at the blank page. Closing his eyes, he wondered where his thoughts would guide him tonight, as it was his custom to write in his journal before turning in when his heart was heavy and his mind was clear.

His thoughts drifted back to Aimee. Her presence was palpable. In his mind's eye, he gazed at her sky-blue eyes, the gentle contours of her face, her perfect eyebrows, her engaging smile and vivacious personality that energized a room. Her flowing hair made her look like royalty when she wore it up and a professional model when she wore it down.

Most of all, he loved her humble spirit. To Chase, there was nothing more beautiful than an attractive woman who didn't know it. And wasn't that the epitome of the proverbial girl next door?

Tears welled in his eyes, but he wiped them with his palm before they could run down his face. Wiping them away somehow made him feel stronger, more in control. Many nights he sat here and never scratched out a syllable. The words had refused to come. Tonight would be different. When he opened his eyes, he exhaled and then poured his heart on the page.

~

Is anyone ever the same after they lose someone they love? I mean, really the same? People die—but grief doesn't. It fades, but it lies in wait to strike when you least expect it—when you're driving down the road, making an important presentation, taking a relaxing shower, or drifting off to sleep. You never see it coming.

It's been just shy of two years since we lost Aimee. I've missed her terribly on her birthdays, Thanksgiving, and, of course, Christmas. Yet hardest of all has been the emptiness Clay and I feel on his birthday—a boy should never be without his mom on his birthday.

~

Love remains a mystery to me, especially the second time around. True love doesn't seem elusive the first time because, well, we find it so naturally. I met Aimee at a supermarket when we were in high school. She was standing across from me in the produce aisle squeezing an avocado. A chance meeting. A clever line. Some quick chemistry. A flirtatious moment. A first date. A second date. A relationship. After college, I popped the question and started spending my life with my best friend.

But what do you do when fate ruthlessly separates you forever? It's a question I may ask myself for the rest of my life. Why is it so difficult for me to even consider loving again? Why do I struggle with feelings of betrayal at the mere thought? Just how do I love again? In the same way? To the same depth? Is it possible to achieve the same connection, or to be as compatible?

Nothing seems to come naturally the second time around. Jack challenged me to give online dating a fair shot. It never works. At least, not for me. Internet profiles replaced chance meetings. Lame blind dates replaced casual conversations. No clever lines. No chemistry. And no ripe avocados. Just contrived smiles, clumsy conversations, and lukewarm romance.

I've learned loving someone the second time around—really loving them—and having them love you in return is not a guarantee, it's a gift.

I've often wondered why some couples seem to love each other with all their heart and soul and see life through the same lens while others drift aimlessly in uncharted waters.

As a young man, I never thought I would ponder such things. Yet I do. The reason is simple. I've loved a woman, one woman, with all my heart, married her, and suddenly lost her for eternity. And that leaves me with two questions I must answer about love if I'm going to reclaim my life—and find victory.

If I believe Aimee was the only one for me, can I love once more? Or will I secretly and inevitably always hold something in reserve for her, the woman I gave my heart to first?

This I must know if, unlike my father, I'm going to grant myself permission to love again.

CHAPTER 5

It was a beautiful Saturday morning in Santa Barbara. Chase had never taken the predictably beautiful weather for granted. It made central California one of the most desired locations to live in America.

He woke early again, an enduring side effect of grief, to a half-empty bed and the sting of a loneliness so deep it cut to the bone. Rising early gave him time to think before Clay would wake and come looking for breakfast.

The sky was changing from orange to baby blue as the sun rose. Opening the fridge, he grabbed two eggs, broke them over a hot skillet, and fried two of them while the bacon sizzled on the back burner. After popping down two pieces of wheat toast, he grabbed the grape jelly from the fridge so Clay could spread it on his toast when he woke up.

When he flipped the eggs, he heard Clay pad into the kitchen barefoot, right on schedule. Clay's body clock would wake him most Saturday mornings without fail.

"I'm hungry." He wiped one eye and climbed up onto the bar stool.

"Coming right up." Chase slid the eggs from the frying pan to a plate, forked two pieces of bacon from the back burner, and placed the bacon and a piece of toast on his plate.

Clay reached for the jelly.

"What would you like to do today, buddy?"

He scratched his head. "Could we go to the wharf and ride a tandem bike?"

Chase hesitated. While he enjoyed Stearns Wharf, he wasn't in the mood for the city's most popular tourist trap.

He noticed Clay's eyes widen and a smile curl on his face at his own suggestion.

"Sure," he said. "Sounds like fun." He didn't sound convincing, but he knew how much Clay enjoyed the ocean and the buzz of activity.

Clay licked some jelly off his finger. "Can we eat there too?"

"Let's do it. I'll make our lunches, and we can eat on the beach."

Chase opened a new loaf of bread, spread peanut butter on two slices, and reached for the jelly Clay had set down. "Do you want to steer or ride on the back of the tandem?"

Clay smiled with anticipation. "Can I steer?"

"Why not? We can go right after you finish your list of morning chores." When Chase finished making the sandwiches, he placed them in plastic bags, then packed them along with two small bags of potato chips, juice packs, chocolate chip cookies, and napkins in brown paper lunch bags before tucking them into his backpack.

After Clay finished brushing his teeth and getting dressed, he started his weekend chores of dusting his room, vacuuming, making his bed, and putting his clothes in the laundry room. Chase then conducted his Saturday morning single-parent tradition—a quick walk-through of Clay's room and the family room, which sometimes doubled as Clay's video arcade and entertainment center.

Chase made a habit of inspecting Clay's room every Saturday, knowing his son was getting off easy with a weekly inspection. Yet it was a lesson he'd learned from his father to hold Clay accountable and teach him to take ownership of caring for his room. Chase's father had held him to a higher standard—a daily inspection. If his bed-making skills did not pass muster, he would have to make it again. The same applied to Clay—but just on Saturdays.

If Aimee was alive, they would have raised the stakes. Yet as a single parent, he cut him some slack. Chase believed in the adage, "Rules without a relationship lead to rebellion."

Better to build a relationship than fuel rebellion.

The goal was for Clay to pull his own weight and feel, even as a boy, that he was contributing to his family. Chase remembered how his boyhood chores made him feel more grown up and feel a little better about himself—and about losing his mother.

"I'm ready, Dad," Clay said as he put on his Dodger baseball cap.

"Okay. Nice work cleaning your room today, buddy. Let's go."

Chase drove southeast on State Street, all the way to the ocean and the wharf. He headed north on Cabrillo Boulevard, then parked on the street before renting a tandem bike. Together they pedaled north toward East Beach.

Cabrillo Boulevard was an idyllic seaside spot in Santa Barbara. Weekends bustled with activity. Joggers, walkers, kite flyers, and bikers crowded the beach path. Chase and Clay took the biking path north toward the Santa Barbara Zoo. With the wind blowing through his hair, Chase admired the pristine beach, lush landscape, and tranquil gardens. When they turned around, the striking view of the wharf stretching into the ocean stunned him.

After they rode for an hour, Clay asked, "When do you want to stop for lunch?"

"Whenever you're hungry. It's almost noon."

Clay glanced over his shoulder at his father again. "I'm hungry now."

"Why am I not surprised?"

"Where should we stop?"

"How about that special spot we've stopped at before among the cluster of palm trees just before the wharf?"

"Okay." Clay stood to pedal the bike in a strong headwind.

Approaching the palm trees, Clay pulled over and held the bike upright, allowing his father to dismount first. Chase lifted his backpack out of the front basket before laying the bike on its side and finding a shady spot to picnic. Chase handed Clay his brown paper bag, grabbed his own, and sat alongside his son.

"Do you love peanut butter and jelly sandwiches as much as I do, Dad?"

Chase winked at him. "They kept me alive when I was a kid."

"Really? Why?"

"Without your grandma to cook for us, your grandpa and I didn't always eat the best."

Clay took a sip of his fruit drink. "I could live on peanut butter and jelly sandwiches too."

Chase smiled and patted him on the head. They ate in silence, enjoying the natural beauty of the beachfront. Chase looked out over the water and reflected on how often they had picnicked on this beach when they were a family of three. Then Clay broke his concentration with a question he didn't see coming.

"Do you still think about Mom?" he asked as he took another bite of his sandwich.

"Every day," he admitted. Chase had stopped talking openly about Aimee over the last year, hoping silence was synonymous with healing. Talking about her, even with Clay, was akin to ripping off a scab. *All that does is start the bleeding again.* It was the same mistake his father had made with him—hoping grief would dissolve if buried. Grief, Chase knew, had a way of bubbling to the surface when ignored. They needed a relief valve.

Chase believed he was becoming like his father in this dimension too. If he failed to confront and release his own feelings, how could he possibly help his son with his grief?

Clay's eyebrows narrowed as he thought. "What do you miss most about her?"

Chase bit his lip. "I don't know." It was a fair question, but he wondered how far he should allow this conversation to go. He deflected by answering with another question. "What do you miss most about her?"

Clay thought for a moment, then smiled. "I miss her teasing you."

"Really? That's what you miss the most? Why?"

"Because it made me laugh. And then I could tease you too."

Chase brushed Clay's hair off his forehead. "You saying you two loved to gang up on me?"

"Yeah, and we always won."

Clay did not grasp the emotion he'd just stirred within his father. Like waves pounding into the shore, Chase felt a rhythmic flow of memories. Aimee was still there—he could feel her. He could see her smile again. Hear her laughter, feel the warmth of her embrace.

Why did she have to die?

Gazing out over the water, he stifled a tear, then turned to Clay and hugged him. "Yes, you two always won."

Clay's voice became softer. "Teasing you made me feel like we were a family."

Raising his son's chin with his finger, he looked him in the eye. "Do you feel like a family now?"

"Sort of. But…" His voice trailed off.

"But something's missing?"

"Yeah." Clay sipped his juice pack until it was empty.

Chase stared into Clay's blue eyes, another place he routinely found Aimee. "I feel it too—every day."

The skin between his eyes wrinkled again. "Will it always feel this bad, Dad?"

It was a question Chase had asked himself a thousand times growing up. He wasn't sure how to answer his grieving son, and it helped him better understand his father's struggle to help him as a boy.

"Someday it won't hurt as much," he said, reaching for his son's hand. "Someday you will only remember the good things. God has a way of letting the hard things fade away and the joyful things find a permanent place in our memory—and that will make you happy again."

"Like Mom teasing you?"

"Yeah, like Mom teasing me."

Clay sniffled and wiped his nose with his napkin. "There's something else I miss about her."

"What's that, buddy?"

"I miss her touch. Like you just did when you brushed my hair out of my face. I liked it when she would mess up my hair. Hug me. Tickle me."

"Don't I do all those things?"

"Sometimes." He paused. "But not like Mom."

"How come?"

Clay shrugged. "I don't know. Because you're not Mom, I guess. It just doesn't feel the same. She used to hug me more."

Chase's stomach tightened with the revelation of another failure as a single dad. "Don't I hug you when you need it?"

"Sometimes, but ..."

"But?"

"Mom used to hug me for no reason. She just knew when ..." Clay's voice faded.

"I get it. Moms are special. They just know how to make us feel ... loved. Dads, well, we just do the best we can. Grandpa did his best with me, and I'll do my best with you. Promise. I'm not too good at the single-parent stuff."

Clay ate his last few potato chips and crumpled up the bag. "You're doing pretty good, Dad."

Holding his breath, he waited for the exception.

Clay reached into his brown paper bag for a cookie. "It's okay, Dad. You don't have Mom's superpowers."

Chase laughed. "Superpowers?"

"Yeah. She always seemed to know what I was thinking."

"Clay, dads don't have those superpowers. I hope you understand I can't be both a mom and a dad to you. It's tough enough to be a father."

Clay looked up at his father. "I know. It's okay. But could we do more stuff together?"

"Like what?"

"I don't know. Stuff. It just feels better being together than being alone. Especially since after we lost Mom, we also lost Queenie and Ginger."

Chase took the last bite of his peanut and jelly sandwich. Life had been empty for him too. After losing his wife, they lost their two rescue dogs Aimee had brought home. Queenie, a black Labrador, was ill from the beginning, and Aimee couldn't stand the thought of her dying alone. Ginger, a border collie, was Clay's dog and ran into the street where she was hit by an SUV that never stopped. Thankfully, Clay hadn't seen it happen. They loved their dogs, and the loss only made the hole in their hearts wider and deeper.

Chase's schedule also kept him busier than he wanted to be as he brainstormed his novel, drafted executive speeches for his clients, and created ads—not to mention, managed his own business.

"Sure. We can do more stuff together. Let me think about what that could look like." He recalled the loneliness he felt coming home from school years ago when his father was still at work. Chase remembered how empty hours needed filling and how, as a boy, seclusion had often forced him to replay his mother's death in his mind on an endless loop. Chase finished his drink and recollected how activity fueled healing in his early life.

～

That evening after Clay was in bed, Chase sat on the patio enjoying the breeze off the ocean and thinking about how he was failing as a father. He realized there were times he had emotionally abandoned

Clay to deal with his grief alone. It wasn't intentional, but his father had made the same mistake with him, so he should have known better.

As clouds rolled across the evening sky, he laid his head back on his soft patio chair, hoping he could reconnect with the one person who could help him recall what Clay was going through now—his twelve-year-old self. Closing his eyes in the moonlight, he let his mind drift back to the week of his mother's passing.

~

It was the first Saturday following his mother's funeral. David Kincaid had found Chase lying under his bed, clutching a blanket and pillow. Chase resorted to this hiding place after losing his mom. It provided a strange sense of security. It was his fort, his escape, and it made him feel safe from a world he no longer understood. A life that made little sense.

When his father walked into his room, all Chase could see were his ankles, his white socks, and the dirty tennis shoes he had worn to cut the grass. The bed creaked as he sat just above him. He didn't call out to his son because he must have known Chase was lying just beneath him, like he had most afternoons this week. Instead, he sat and talked to him in soothing tones.

"What's going on under there, Chase?" David rubbed the back of his neck and waited for an answer.

"Just thinking."

"What are you thinking about?"

"Mom."

Neither one of them could think about anything else. A few days ago, cancer caused their worlds to collide, then collapse.

"What about her?"

His father had tried many times to get him to talk about her this past weekend, but he wasn't ready.

Chase swallowed hard. "What are we going to do now?" He buried his face in his blanket.

"Do you want to come out from under there and talk about it?"

"No," he stammered. "I can talk from he-here." His tears and his stutter embarrassed him. At twelve, he knew he was too old to cry.

To his surprise, his father got on his hands and knees, turned over on his back, and slid under his bed beside him. Rarely the emotional type, his father put his arm around him and pulled him closer. Chase realized no matter what his father would say next, it wouldn't matter. Already he had done what Chase needed him to do—he touched him and made him feel loved, something he wondered if he would ever feel again.

His mother's touch had been powerful, profound, and frequent. Chase didn't expect his ex-Marine father would make a habit of hugging him, but today, it was all he needed.

Clearing his throat, his father said, "Okay, well, I'll tell you what we're going to do now. We're going to move forward—every day. Slowly, but forward. And we're going to keep living our lives, doing the things we enjoy. We're going to promise ourselves that we will live the way mom would want us to live, which is to be happy."

Chase's voice cracked, and he felt himself cave, which he didn't want to do in front of his father. "How do I move forward if I feel left behind?"

His father's voice was steady, so Chase almost didn't notice a tear form in the corner of his eye and slide down the side of his face and behind his ear. "I don't know. But we'll figure it out—together."

He wiped his eyes with his blanket. "Will I turn out different from how I was supposed to be?"

Facing his son, David ran his hand through Chase's hair the way his wife, Grace, used to. "No. You won't turn out different. You'll turn out just the way God intended you to be. Trust me."

His words carried hope and warmed his son's heart. Chase desperately wanted to believe his father.

"Dad, how can I be the same without a mother?"

The room fell silent. David pulled his son closer—and squeezed.

CHAPTER 6

S ierra Taylor loved to run, especially on a Sunday afternoon when the city was still alive and full of energy.

A star runner on her cross country teams in high school and at the University of Southern California, she never tired of the exhilarating runner's high—especially when running in a picture-postcard setting like Santa Barbara. The city was a self-contained paradise with spectacular views stretching 110 miles along California's Central Coast.

She only ran for fun now and often stopped along the way to enjoy her surroundings.

Forfeiting the pounding pace of San Francisco, she opted for the slower pace of Santa Barbara. Neither city was optimal on an English teacher's salary, but an inheritance after her father's unexpected death a few years ago helped her find a downtown apartment she could afford.

She never expected much from her father—and he delivered. The inheritance was the sole exception. Growing up, every time she tried to get close to him, he would find a reason to pull away, leaving her feeling abandoned yet again. She didn't understand his attitude, sometimes letting her in, other times pushing her out of their relationship. She wanted a mentor, but she got a role model of what she never wanted from a man—love from a distance.

When she landed her current teaching job at Peabody Elementary School, they informed her a principal's position may open soon, and they would consider her based on the breadth of her administrative experience. She was tracking a similar opportunity in Phoenix.

With instrumental music playing through her earbuds while she ran, she often thought to herself that when God created Santa Barbara, He realized He had just created His inspiration for Hawaii.

Sierra alternated her running routes depending on her mood. Today, she opted for the city. She ran, directly toward the ocean, amid the flurry of activity on State Street.

Dodging an oblivious shopper exiting an eatery, Sierra reflected on why she ran.

Why not? she thought. *Where else is every day a perfect day?* She didn't run just for a runner's high—she ran to restore serenity. To collect her thoughts, evaluate her goals, and pick up a few misplaced pieces of her life—or, if she were honest, shattered pieces. Running was not merely exercise for her. It was a place she could go to slow down time, listen to the roar of her life, and make sense of it.

Today, she thought about her father and the two days of his life that had scarred hers. The day he learned his volatile attitude had a name, and a diagnosis—bipolar disorder. On a good day, when she was a teen, he told her things would get better.

"I won't pull away anymore," he promised. "We will always be close." But the second day came when he pulled away permanently. When he took his own life—and shattered hers.

So much for trust, she thought.

After she ran under the viaduct, she could see Stearns Wharf, the oldest working wooden wharf in California. She was fond of the city's history and the eclectic array of restaurants, wine tasting rooms, gift shops, and ice cream parlors on the wharf.

When she reached the Cabrillo Boulevard, instead of turning left toward East Beach, as she usually did, she ran directly on the wharf, careful not to trip on the wooden walkway's uneven planks. She had once rolled an ankle that way. The wharf was a place to cool down. Here she would often pause and let her mind wander while she stretched.

Today, while resting at the end of the wharf, she saw a man who looked similar to her former fiancé. She thought she had loved him, but she ended the relationship at the Santa Barbara Shellfish Company restaurant, next to where she stood now.

She wasn't sure why, but she allowed the memories of the night she broke up with him to whisper to her while she stretched her legs on the wooden railing.

~

His name was Merritt Michael Patterson III—and with a name like that, "I should have known better," she often said.

At first, he seemed legit—buttoned down, sincere, the genuine article, and he looked the part. Jet black hair. Hazel eyes. Handsome. Broad shoulders and two impressive initials after the high-brow name—MD.

Merritt was an emergency room physician at the Santa Barbara Cottage Hospital, a Level I trauma center. For a small town of about ninety thousand residents, this facility had five hospitals and medical centers, twenty-one specialty care clinics, and fifty-five specialties. You might say he had arrived.

Sierra met him when she rolled her ankle running on the wharf and wound up in the ER. It was just a minor sprain, but his extra attention and gentle touch made her blush.

He noticed her reaction, and it generated enough stimulus for him to ask for her phone number. After a few days, they met for coffee. "It's my way of making a house call," he teased.

None of this was typical for her. In a weak moment, she accepted, and so began a whirlwind romance that took her by surprise when she let her guard down.

She prided herself on not being swept off her feet, but this happened when she felt vulnerable, and it was easier to go with the flow than question his motives or keep her guard up. Coffee led to dinner, dinner to dating, and steady dating led to a proposal eighteen months later. Against her nagging little voice, she accepted the proposal, but not without reservations.

Jennifer Adams, Sierra's closest friend, initially encouraged the relationship. It wasn't her fault. Jennifer was unaware of the red flags Sierra experienced but didn't talk about.

"What are you afraid of?" Jennifer would say. "Hey, you love teaching kids. He loves treating patients, especially kids. Seems like a nice guy—handsome, a respected physician, and he appears to love you." That was the qualifying phrase that rung in Sierra's ears—*appears* to love you.

Sometimes with Merritt, Sierra couldn't differentiate between what appeared to be true and what was true. Once they'd been dating for a while, she would notice him flirt with servers when they went out to dinner, but didn't all guys do that?

She knew she should have trusted her gut when she met his parents. For the longest time, he delayed introducing her to them. In retrospect, Sierra wondered if he wanted to make sure he had set the hook first.

Merritt's parents, Merritt II and Glenda Patterson, came from means, and it didn't take long after exchanging pleasantries for Glenda to share the family pedigree of higher education, boards they served on, and how their wise investments led to their enviable net worth. After doing so, she raised her eyebrows and cocked her head, as if to invite Sierra to share her breeding. She didn't bite. Instead, she paused and waited for Merritt to step up and defend her or diffuse the situation. When he intentionally looked away and pretended not to hear, Sierra thought for a minute and then responded with a question. "Tell me, Glenda, what do you think is the truest measure of one's net worth—dollars and cents or content of character?"

Glenda lifted her nose in the air and cocked her head away from

Sierra. "Are you insinuating that I ..." Her voice halted, and she paused—attempting to guilt Sierra into an apology?

Once again, she didn't take the bait.

When Merritt drove to dinner at the Santa Barbara Shellfish Company on the wharf that night, Sierra remained silent. She could feel the heat rising and had hoped he would address it head-on and take her side. It was too much to hope for, and the handwriting was on the proverbial wall.

"Did you feel it was necessary to insult my mother like that? After all, you just met her."

Sierra turned red, a shade lighter than her lipstick. "Insult her? Don't you think she insulted me first by setting me up like that?"

"What are you talking about? She simply *shared* our family background and inquired about yours."

This was the moment she could no longer deny Merritt didn't have a clue. "Really? Is that how you saw it? Merritt, she wasn't *sharing*—she was *comparing*. She was verifying whether I was worthy of the patented Patterson image."

Merritt turned left toward the restaurant. "You're overreacting. She was just looking out for me now that we're ... getting serious."

Sierra touched her throat and raised her eyebrows. "Looking out for *you?* She was interrogating me. If we're going to be together, don't you think she should look out for *us?*"

Merritt shook his head. "Don't turn this into a mother-in-law thing."

"That's right. I just met her, and she's already assessing my value to make sure I'm good enough for her baby boy. She's talked to me in the same tone in the past over the phone before I ever met her."

Merritt rolled his eyes. "That's not fair."

"It is fair. And it will probably end badly for me."

"You're blowing this out of proportion—as women usually do."

Sierra glared at him. "Excuse me?" She clenched her teeth. Her lips set in a straight line. She made a mental note that the balance of this conversation could be a defining moment—or the beginning of the end of their relationship. It depended on how Merritt played it. The ball was in his court. He could take the shot—or take a pass.

He passed—and it didn't surprise Sierra.

"Look, let's drop it. You just met her. I get it. You made a mistake, but in the future, show my mother a little respect."

She stood her ground. "Respect is a two-way street, don't you think?"

Merritt drove over the bumpy wooden planks on the wharf before they arrived and parked in front of the restaurant. Sierra sat seething. He wisely paused and waited for her temperature to fall. If a mistake was made tonight, she wanted him to make it, not her. She chewed on the inside of her cheek during the awkward silence and waited for him to respond. Her question hung in the air.

The entirety of their relationship flashed before her. She recalled what she knew—and didn't know—about him. She knew he loved practicing medicine. Add sun, sand, and surfing. Not much else. She wasn't certain if he loved her, but she was certain he loved something else: nurses—or at least flirting with them.

Late one morning, on her birthday, she had hoped to surprise him by picking him up at the hospital and taking him to lunch. She found him in the hallway with a young nurse reviewing a chart. Sierra stopped down the hall. From where she stood, she could see the nurse had eyes for him. The body language, the look, the giggles, all dead giveaways. Merritt ate it up and offered her a casual compliment—and a well-rehearsed pickup line. Sierra recognized it. He had used it on her when she sprained her ankle. Then he invited the nurse to join him for lunch, but the kicker was when he asked for her phone number.

Sierra turned and left the building. Merritt never knew she was there. She didn't confront him. Instead, she hoped to bring it up at a better time. Now, she figured, was as good as any.

"Let's eat outside tonight," he said. "We'll have more privacy that way."

The hostess led them to a patio table with a black and white checkered tablecloth and black cloth napkins rolled into gold holders.

Once seated, Sierra suggested they have a drink first, knowing she may not be hungry after they talked. When the server arrived, they ordered a glass of wine, and she told him they would order dinner a little later.

Merritt made small talk until the server returned with their wine. After taking a sip, he picked up the conversation where Sierra had left it in the car, never suspecting the issue on her mind had now transitioned from his mother's behavior to his.

"Yes," he agreed, "respect is a two-way street, but I don't think my mother was being disrespectful. I think she was just making conversation—and wondering what you had to contribute."

Sierra frowned. "Contribute? Your mother sounded more interested in my financial portfolio than me."

He looked at the sky and let his head hang back. "There you go again—overreacting."

"I'm not overreacting. I just need to know, really know, what I'm getting into."

"What's that supposed to mean? Are you having doubts about us?"

She shifted her weight and took a sip of her wine. "I'm just not sure anymore what I'm getting with you—or your parents."

Merritt reared back in his chair. "Sierra, what's going on?"

"I stopped by the hospital to surprise you the other day."

"When?"

"On my birthday."

"Your birthday?"

"That's your first problem." She glared at him as she swirled the wine in her glass and licked her lips.

"I didn't see you this week."

"That's right. Because I left right after I saw you."

"What? Why?" Merritt looked confused and leaned forward.

"You were with a nurse."

Merritt swallowed. "Okay—makes sense. I'm a doctor. I work with nurses."

She folded her arms across her chest. "From what I could see, you weren't working."

"Oh, really? What was I doing?"

"Flirting."

"What? I'm sure I wasn't flirting." His face turned red to match his wine.

"Why did you ask for her phone number?"

Merritt's mouth dropped. Another couple stepped onto the patio and sat with their backs to them. A server poured the couple a glass of water.

Sierra stiffened. "You have only one shot at the truth, Merritt— and this is it."

He wiped his forehead with his hand, inhaled, and sighed. It was enough for Sierra.

"It's not what you think. Sometimes, we need to contact nurses when they are off duty to come into the ER when we're busy."

"I wasn't born yesterday. You were not scheduling work. You were scheduling a rendezvous."

Merritt gave her a blank look. "Why would you even stop by the hospital that day?"

"Don't change the subject. I wanted to take you to lunch on my birthday."

He cleared his throat. "You shouldn't stop by unexpectedly like that. Besides, shouldn't I be taking you to lunch for your birthday?"

"How could you if you don't know when my birthday is?"

He touched his eyebrows with both hands. "Sierra, why are you doing this?"

She looked away, then locked her eyes on a server across the patio, pouring a cup of coffee. She waited until the cup was full before staring directly at Merritt. "Answer the question."

"Okay, I forgot your birthday." He paused. "I thought this was about my mother."

"It's about both."

"Why the sudden problem with me and my family?"

"Because, if I'm honest with myself, I don't fit in—and now no longer want to."

She slipped her engagement ring off her finger and placed it on the table. Although she was the one pulling away for the first time, she couldn't ignore the sinking feeling in her gut that she was the one who had been abandoned again.

She stared at him. "Let's not kid ourselves. Our relationship doesn't stand a chance. We want different things. I want a life with someone who loves me—really loves me. Someone who values the truth, someone I can trust. You want to play the field—which means I play the fool."

"Are you saying it's over, just like that?"

"Just like that." Sierra reached for her bag and stood. "When you've lost trust, you've lost everything. I'll take an Uber home."

Merritt stood, threw his napkin on the table, tipping over his wineglass, and raised his voice as she walked out. "Really? That's it? Is that all you have to say?"

Stopping, she pivoted to face him. "No. How was your lunch with that nurse—on my birthday?"

Stunned, and aware the other couples were staring at him now, he sat—barely noticing his wine run over the edge of the table and onto his khaki pants.

CHAPTER 7

Recalling her relationship with Merritt altered Sierra's mood. After she finished stretching her legs and trunk at the end of the wharf, she didn't feel like running. Instead, she wandered through the gift shops. She walked past Longboards Grill, Char West, and the Deep Sea Wine Tasting Room and headed to the Great Pacific Ice Cream Company.

After reliving that day with Merritt, I deserve some ice cream. Besides, it had been a while since she had rewarded herself after a run.

The line at the ice cream shop weaved outside the store. When she got in line, she noticed a man about her age standing across from her, leaning against the wharf railing overlooking the ocean. His head was down, and he was reading a novel. When the line advanced, she moved closer and glanced at the title. *The Bridge Between Us.* She'd read that novel last year and remembered how deeply it had resonated with her. While she couldn't remember the author's name, she could not forget how it made her feel.

The customers shuffled forward, and she leaned toward the man to read the author's name on the front cover.

Looking up, he caught her staring. He smiled. "Hey."

Embarrassed, she responded, "Hey." Then she glanced at the open sea, hoping he would lose himself in his book again to diffuse the awkward moment. Almost impulsively, she added, "That's a great book, brilliant actually."

"You've read it?"

She returned a smile. "Last year."

"So you liked it?"

"Actually, I loved it. Made me look inside myself and think about life in a deeper way. You might like it if ..." She didn't finish her thought. When the line advanced, she followed, getting closer to the storefront.

"If?" he asked. It was her cue to complete her thought.

"If"—she hesitated—"if you like love stories." The minute she finished her sentence, she realized how foolish it sounded. She flushed. "Sorry. Guys don't read love stories. So maybe you won't like it—but your wife will." She noticed he squinted and now wore a pained expression, so she glanced at his ring finger. No ring. *Did I just say something wrong?*

When the line wound near him, she noticed how handsome he was and how he spoke in soft tones. She changed the subject. "So what's a guy doing reading a love story, on a wharf, outside of an ice cream shop, on a Sunday afternoon?"

He recovered quickly and laughed. "You sound like a detective. I'm waiting for my son to retrieve our ice cream cones. He's in line somewhere ahead of you. And I'm not actually reading the novel. I'm scanning it."

"You're scanning a novel? What, you a speed reader?" She hoped he would laugh again.

A smile graced his tan face, and he spoke with a tenderness she couldn't ignore. "No. I've already read the novel—several times, actually. I'm just scanning it for things I would do differently."

The line moved quickly now, and he joined her in the line since they were fully engaged in this conversation.

"You read love stories? Didn't think that was a guy thing," she teased.

"Sometimes."

"Did you find any author errors in this novel?"

"None glaring. But I would have done a few things differently."

"Really? You're an aspiring author, then?" She realized she was enjoying the conversation and wondered if it was because he was an author and she was an English teacher—or if it was something else.

"Sort of. I look for flaws so I can learn from them." They walked side by side now as they approached the entrance of the ice cream shop.

"Do you hope to write a novel someday?"

"A second novel, actually. My hope is the one I'm writing could be as good as this one." He peeked at the book cover.

She turned to him and smiled. "I love it. You set such a high standard for yourself. I don't remember who wrote it, but that novel is a bestseller. It's a worthy goal to put yourself in his company."

"That's what I've heard," Chase said.

"It's something to strive for," Sierra responded. "By the way, I'm not sure it's true, but I heard *The Bridge Between Us* was the author's debut novel."

"It's true. It was my first attempt. And I got lucky."

She turned to him. "*You* got lucky?"

He smiled. "Yeah. Real lucky."

"May I see this?" She wedged the novel out of his hand and glanced at the author's name before flipping it over. She stared at the photo, then at him. She stepped back. "*You* are Chase Kincaid?"

"Sort of appears that way."

"Really?" She looked at the photo again. "You *are* Chase Kincaid. I thought you looked familiar."

She saw kindness in his eyes. He slipped the novel from her grip. "Yep. That's my name right here on the front cover and my photo on the back, so I guess it must be true. I admit it's not the best picture—but it's me."

She winced and clenched her teeth. "Well, I've completely embarrassed myself. Can we start this conversation over?"

"Sure."

She cleared her throat and was suddenly formal. "Mr. Kincaid, I loved your debut novel."

"Well, thank you, but I think this has suddenly become too formal. We're making this too complicated." Extending his hand, he said, "Hi, I'm Chase Kincaid. It's nice to meet you."

She took his hand and replied, "Hi, I'm Sierra Taylor." She looked into his eyes and wondered if he noticed she held his hand longer than she should have.

Before their conversation could continue, Clay interrupted them. "Dad, here's your cone. Oh, hi, Miss Taylor."

Chase glanced at them. "You two know each other?"

"She's my summer school teacher, Dad."

She placed her hand on her chest. "You're Clay's father? Really? I didn't know. Actually, I've been wanting to talk with you."

Chase cut her short. "Say, Clay, would you save that table over there for us? Miss Taylor and I will join you in a minute after we get her cone."

Licking his cone, Chase wrapped a napkin around it. Sierra was next in line. She studied the menu board and placed her order with the teenager working behind the counter before turning to Chase. "I've been wanting to contact you because I've noticed some things about Clay that aren't improving. I should have contacted you long before I sent home the note, but I've been dealing with several other discipline issues in class, and the principal and I felt it best to deal with them first."

"I got the note you sent home with Clay a few weeks ago." Chase looked away and returned a glance at Sierra. "I'm not sure you know this, but my wife passed away almost two years ago, when Clay was in first grade. It's been rough on him."

She brought her hand to her mouth. "Oh, I'm so sorry. I didn't know he had lost his mom. And I'm sorry for your loss." She thought for a moment. "I should have checked his file before contacting you. That's on me. This helps explain a few things."

"Such as?"

"His behavior in class. Clay is a little withdrawn. Sometimes nonverbal. But I think you just explained why." Sierra paid for her cone and walked with Chase toward the table where Clay sat. "May I call you this week to discuss this further, privately?"

"Sure. My contact information is on file with the school."

"Right, so we don't have to talk about this now. Let's just enjoy Clay now."

They sat together at the picnic table alongside Clay, and she noticed Chase visibly relax, increase eye contact, and focus on her. While it resonated with her, she didn't read too much into it.

"What have you been doing when you're not in class this summer, Clay?" she asked.

"Nothing."

She turned to Chase. "Typical boy answer."

"This is everyday life raising a boy," Chase added with a smile. "Clay, tell Miss Taylor what you've done this summer."

Clay's forehead wrinkled for a moment. "We went hiking in the mountains. Um, we went to two of the Channel Islands, I don't remember which ones. We went swimming at Leadbetter Beach, and yesterday we went tandem bike riding and had lunch by the bike path."

"Sounds like you're having a wonderful summer. Maybe I should have you write about it before summer school is over."

He grimaced at her. "Okay." After he finished his cone, he wiped his sticky hands on his shirt. "Dad, look at the pelicans over there by the fisherman. Can I go see the fish he caught and put in his pail?"

"Stay where I can see you."

"I will."

Sierra looked at Chase. "You've got a good kid, Mr. Kincaid, and you appear to be a good father."

"Thanks. Please call me Chase." He looked out over the water from the center of the wharf, then faced her. "That's kind of you to say. This single father thing isn't easy sometimes. I never know if I'm doing the right thing. Aimee kept all of us so ..." He searched for the right word. "Centered."

"I'm sure it's tough being a single parent."

"I feel like I'm floundering a bit, having lost my best friend, my feedback loop, and so much more."

"Sounds like you had a special marriage."

"Sometimes I think I was the luckiest man alive. But nothing lasts forever, right?" Chase cleared his throat. "How about you, Miss Taylor? Do you have a family?"

"Now who's being formal? You can call me Sierra—when I'm not in school. Plus, doesn't it seem awkward to be formal at the beach?"

He nodded. "It does, doesn't it?"

"To answer your question, no. I'm not married. I was engaged once, but, thankfully, that was the closest I came to being married. Or at least, to marrying him. It would have been a mistake."

Chase ran his hand through his hair in the gentle breeze, then looked at her. She looked away, then back at him. His eyes were tender and innocent, and it warmed her. She wondered if it was more an illusion than reality.

Sierra glanced at Clay, now fully engaged talking to the fisherman. The old man bent over, uncovered his bucket, and showed him his catch.

"You know, it must be nice writing novels."

Chase grinned. "It's hard work. Hemingway once compared writing novels to wrestling alligators or opening a vein. Why did you say it must be nice?"

She tucked a loose strand of her hair behind her ear. "Well, in your fictional world, you can create perfect couples, situations, and settings—and then bring them all together."

"True, but it's not really that easy."

She licked her cone and turned to him. "It's easier than in our nonfiction world, don't you think? In the real world, some people you love often pull away from you. In the fictional world, you pull them together. Every ending can be a happy ending."

He blinked twice, furrowed his brow, and seemed to study her. She wondered what he was thinking. "My characters have flaws too. They have to figure out their world just like we do."

She wiped her hands with her napkin and countered, "Yes, but by the end of the book, it's problem solved and happily ever after, right? At least, most of the time."

Licking his cone before it dripped, he said, "That's why I was scanning my book earlier. I was looking for my mistakes—like simple conclusions to complex problems. I don't want to write a sequel with a Hallmark ending. My goal is to write about fictional characters facing real-life issues. If I identify my mistakes, I can do a better job writing about complicated relationships."

She listened intently as he took a breath and continued. "I think there should be some truth in fiction, don't you? One of my favorite authors said, 'When we understand someone else's story, we come to better understand our own.' And that's true in nonfiction and fiction."

She nodded, thought for a moment, and realized he spoke from a position that challenged her to think deeper. There was something authentic about him.

When their eyes met, she responded, "Makes sense. I haven't always put the words truth and fiction together in one sentence." Glancing at her phone, she checked the time. "Well, I better get going. I need to run back home. It was so nice to meet you, famous author Chase Kincaid."

"And you too, Miss Taylor, third-grade teacher extraordinaire."

They laughed as they stood.

"I'll contact your office next week, and we can discuss my concerns about Clay in class in more detail."

Chase nodded. "I work alone out of my home, but yes, have your people contact my people."

She laughed. "Your people?"

"That was my life once in the publishing industry in New York. Now 'my people' refers to just me. When you call, I'll answer the phone."

She smiled. "Good to know. Well, until then."

∼

When Sierra jogged off, Chase realized something had just happened as he gazed at Clay with the fisherman.

He had noticed—finally noticed—another woman since Aimee. Her almond-shaped dark brown eyes, her smooth skin, her thick brunette hair pulled tight into a ponytail, and how easily her lips parted to yield a bright white smile. Her jogging suit graced her fit figure, and he had perceived something else—the faint smell of the perfume Aimee wore. It stirred him. For a fleeting moment, he asked himself if Sierra resonated with him because she embodied something familiar—a piece of his past—or a gateway to his future.

It also registered with him that their conversation was not empty chatter like previous conversations with women over the last two years. No obligatory pleasantries or mundane chit-chat. It had felt like life after death. Love after loss. A pulse that warmed the body, relieved numbness, and restored feeling—*any* feeling. Finally, he sensed hope—hope that life not only could go on, but it could also be meaningful again.

Clay broke his train of thought when he returned to the table. "Dad, you should see the fish the fisherman caught."

"They must be really biting today, hey?"

"Yeah." The skin wrinkled between Clay's eyebrows. "Dad, do you like my teacher?"

Chase's stomach tightened. "What makes you think that?"

"Nothing. She's my favorite teacher. She's nice to me, so I like her. Do you like her too?"

Chase relaxed and exhaled slowly. "Sure, Clay. I like your teacher too. She seems nice."

~

Later that evening, when Clay was asleep, Chase sat out in the warm summer air surrounded by the patio lights and tiki torches. Reflecting on the events of the day, he thought about meeting Sierra and his conversation with her. He didn't know what it all meant, but he knew one thing. If only for a moment, he had felt alive again. His heart was beating—and it felt good. Clay gave him a reason to see her again. Yet if he was honest with himself, he had another reason to see her.

Beneath the moonlight and the torches, he opened his journal and wrote.

~

I met a woman today. Her name is Sierra. When I talked to her, something happened, or at least I think it did. I felt an uptick in my pulse. It wasn't much, but just enough to confirm I'm not dead. She is Clay's summer school English teacher, so I need to be sure this doesn't get complicated. Clay comes first. Besides, whatever I felt today was probably nothing—and I'm sure she didn't feel a thing.

We had a cone on the wharf together. Maybe it's just me, but ... my ice cream never tasted so good.

CHAPTER 8

Monday morning came early.

Chase was up, half asleep, hair disheveled, and working on breakfast. He whipped the scrambled eggs into a bowl while bacon sizzled in the skillet on the back burner. They had become comfortable with their breakfast routine—scrambled eggs, hash browns, and bacon on Monday, pancakes and fruit on Tuesday, yogurt or toaster waffles on Wednesday, grain cereals and an English muffin on Thursday, Clay's choice on Fridays, and whatever on weekends.

Life was a routine now.

They both found comfort in the familiar, security in repetition, but they allowed themselves the flexibility to mix it up anytime. A routine allowed Chase to operate on autopilot, instead of thinking, feeling. While he didn't enjoy his perpetual state of numbness from losing Aimee, he capitalized on its primary benefit. After all, he said, "If you're numb, you can't feel pain."

Pouring the eggs into the hot skillet, he waited a moment to flip them with a spatula. Clay walked out of the bathroom and approached the breakfast bar, looking as ruffled as his father. He stretched both arms over his head before sitting. Chase poured him a glass of orange juice, knowing he seldom talked before he was fully awake. The apple didn't fall far from the tree.

Turning the eggs to keep them from sticking or burning, Chase felt his inadequacy. Cooking did not come naturally to him. The kitchen was Aimee's domain. She was the family chef, and she'd spoiled him. Even as a teenager, she could outcook her mother—and that was no minor achievement.

Aimee particularly liked to bake. Chase recalled how she would throw her hair up in a bun, roll up her sleeves, and in her jeans and flip-flops, she would litter the counter with flour and bake bread, brownies, cookies, and pies. She once won two blue ribbons in the county fair for her pies. Whenever Aimee baked, it was Chase's cue to settle into his den and write. They also enjoyed the added benefit of the sweet aroma wafting through the house. One more way she made it feel like home. Now, every time Chase attempted to cook, he felt the vacuum.

He scooped a portion of the scrambled eggs onto Clay's plate, added a piece of bacon, and placed it in front of him before refilling Clay's juice glass then serving himself. Sitting alongside his son, he didn't make much conversation. *Typical for two hungry men.*

Clay finished first and helped himself to another piece of bacon.

"If you're done, please put your dishes in the sink, jump in the shower, and make your bed. I've got a few things to do before I take you to school."

"Okay. Can Fernando come over and play after school?"

"I think so. If it's okay with his mom."

"She doesn't care."

"All right then. Did you finish your homework last night?"

"Yeah, but you didn't check it over."

"I'm sure it's fine. Get ready now. We don't want to be late—again."

The last two words hung in the air. *Late again.*

It had almost become part of their routine. Chase knew it was his fault as much as Clay's, but he should know better. He had some work to do rearing him, this he knew. It was easy to grow weary, to feel overwhelmed. Paying bills, cutting the grass, helping with homework, cleaning the house, grocery shopping, home and car repairs, and laundry—his personal Mount Everest.

Add his job and his writing career. While he loved to write, there were inflated expectations and killer deadlines. It was a world where, if excuses lived, careers died. There was only one clock, and the client owned it.

Besides advertising deadlines, there were his publication deadlines for articles and novels. Now that he was enjoying some success with his first bestseller, the timelines were tighter, hopes higher, demand greater.

If he wanted book deals, he had to write faster to create a book series, his agent told him. "Readers want more out of an author than one book. If you write a series and your first book is successful, you have an automatic audience. It's no longer just about the quality of the writing—it's about the size of the platform. Like it or not, it's a numbers game now."

The pressure was a blessing and a curse. It kept him so busy writing—or noodling ideas—every day that he had little time to ponder his loss, and because he didn't, he wasn't sure he grieved Aimee completely or in the right way, if there was a right way to grieve. Both he and Clay had grieved separately, out of sync, so instead of the loss binding them together, Chase feared it may drive them apart.

He hadn't had long, meaningful talks with Clay about losing his mother, what it meant to him, and what it would mean to them from now on. They never had the "why bad things happen to good people" father/son talk. In retrospect, he was handling this crisis in lockstep with his father. In the deep recesses of his soul, he harbored some resentment against his father for the way he managed, or failed to manage, their grief. *Now I'm becoming a replica of my father.*

After Chase dropped Clay off at school, he returned home and walked to his office, which he affectionately referred to as "the den." It was an old term, he knew, but it had a warm feel to it.

Knowing he could have tagged this spare bedroom as his home office or studio, he opted for something a little less presumptuous. Besides, he had once vowed to never take himself too seriously if he was successful. To Chase, a den carried the implication of a cozy place where he could both work and relax. A place to crank out ad copy or novels, and then stare out the window at the ocean.

Often, people misunderstood the life of a freelance writer. Except for Jack, many of Chase's friends acted like the *free* in "freelance" meant he had free time, so he was available to lend a hand. In reality, the freelance life required discipline. Chase was writing from five until six o'clock in the morning. Quick starts generated momentum. At six, he started breakfast and woke up Clay so they could eat together. Then he helped Clay get ready for school before dropping him off.

In the morning, he attacked creative work. After returning from taking Clay to school, he would write again from eight o'clock till noon on his second novel—although he was struggling, and he knew it. He couldn't pry the words out with a crowbar. He was tentative, dry, and unsure of where he wanted the story to go.

Whenever he hit the wall on the novel, he would edit ads, corporate brochures, and executive speeches he had drafted the day before, hoping the cross-pollination of ideas would help him overcome writer's block. His client work came easier to him. When he was stuck writing the novel, he would craft nonfiction articles for publications.

Afternoons were for mundane work—returning emails, building his social media platform, continuing to market his first novel, working with Ed to schedule book signings, and if time permitted, prospecting for additional freelance work to maintain cash flow during the dry periods that were inevitably part of the book publishing business. To Chase, the life of a freelance writer was anything but free.

Friends would often ask him, "How do you get inspired to write every day, and what do you do if you're not inspired?"

Chase would laugh and ask, "Are you inspired to go to work every day? And if you're not, do you stay home?" After he made his point, he would add, "Inspiration is nice, but if I only worked when inspired, I would starve and so would you. You don't find inspiration, it finds you—and when it does, it's usually when you're already busy at work."

Although Chase knew this was true, he never needed inspiration to write more than now. Inspiration followed discipline, but what did you do if you lost your discipline? Losing his wife stifled his discipline to write. When Aimee was alive, he had something to write for. It wasn't that he wrote to please her. It was more than that. Because he had a family who loved him, he naturally felt inspired to work. It was subtle but steady—and he knew he derived his purpose and his passion from his wife.

When Ed or the managing editor pressed him on his deadlines, he would cop out with the typical excuse—writer's block—but it would be only a matter of time before Ed would call him on it. They both cut him some slack because of his loss—and he never wanted sympathy to be an excuse.

Chase poured himself another cup of coffee, settled into his den, and reviewed his work for a few corporate clients. Satisfied with the edits he had made on Friday, he let the copy cool for another day. Change to: Leaning back in his swivel chair he stared out the window. The breeze filtered through the room. His gaze surveyed every wall and settled on a photo of Aimee resting on his bookcase. It was a candid of her washing his car. She loved to wash his car for him. Hair up, wearing a powder blue sleeveless blouse and blue jean cutoffs with tan legs, bare feet, and soapsuds on her chin below a grin that was part mischievous, part flirtatious. A touch of makeup she didn't need.

"She was so beautiful," he whispered aloud.

From where he sat in his den, he had a clear view of the patio, the towering oak tree his grandfather had planted, and the ocean beyond it.

On the wall above the couch hung a series of inspirational quotes by authors he admired, the finest ever to put pen to paper. Writers who changed or influenced the course of literature—Hemingway, Faulkner, Fitzgerald, Emerson, Thoreau, Poe, Steinbeck, Dickinson, Whitman, and Wilde. He would often gaze at them and, with the resulting energy, take his writing to the promised land.

Pulling out his novel—his sequel—he couldn't help but notice the incomplete outline and the scant manuscript. Nothing of significance written. Worst of all, he didn't like what he had written. He would start over. Ed was right about writing a sequel first, this he knew. So he would attempt to write one. He was aware, though, that he would write through discipline and not passion, as his heart was on a different path. And if his heart was somewhere else, he feared the writing would ring hollow.

One principle he'd learned from writing speeches was that if the speechwriter didn't like his work, the client didn't either. Chase still hadn't signed a contract for a sequel with the same publisher of his debut novel, even though they were offering Ed a three-book series. He wasn't about to let Chase sign until he had shopped the sequel with a few large publishers, although the managing editor at his current publisher was also turning up the heat. "You don't want to leave money on the table."

This was the part of the business Chase hated. Like most artists, he desired to create the product, not sell it.

The rest of the morning, he drafted rough outlines for two approaches to his second novel—one was a sequel, and the other was a new standalone novel with new characters and a new setting that could become the first book in a three-book series.

～

At noon, he cooked hamburgers on the grill and relaxed and ate under the umbrella at the patio table. Chase loved simple things, and a good hamburger with all the fixings and an ocean view were hard to beat.

By mid-afternoon, he was cranking out email correspondence when his phone rang. It was Sierra. His pulse quickened at the sound of her voice. Today, she had a professional demeanor, unlike their casual conversation on the wharf yesterday. She spoke in a tone that sounded like they had never met.

"Mr. Kincaid?"

"This is Chase."

"Hi, it's Miss Taylor, Clay's summer school English teacher."

"Hi, Miss Taylor." He followed her sudden formality.

"I wanted to follow up on our conversation yesterday and set up a meeting with you to discuss the concerns I have about Clay."

Chase wondered if, based on her tone, her boss was in the room with her. "Thank you for calling, Sierra. May I call you Sierra?"

"Yes. I'm sorry. I just thought I shouldn't be presumptuous, so I …"

Chase cut her off. "Sierra, it's fine. No need to explain. Look, I'm not a formal guy, so never feel you have to be. Just call me Chase unless we're at your school."

"Okay then. Chase, are you available to meet tomorrow at two o'clock in the afternoon at my school office? I think we only need an hour. We should be done by three o'clock, so you'll be here when Clay finishes for the day."

"I'll be there."

"Perfect. My room number is 223. I'll see you then—Chase."

He smiled when she emphasized his name. "I'll look forward to it, Sierra." He paused. "It will be nice to see you again." He held his breath, knowing, in some small way, he had just put himself out there. She now had the advantage, and he was vulnerable.

She paused for a moment. "I enjoyed having ice cream with you yesterday—and I look forward to seeing you again too." He sensed the warmth in her voice once more. The formality had melted.

~

After Chase picked up Clay and Fernando after school, he returned to his den to clean up a few projects while they played in the backyard where he could see them. Sitting at his desk, he itemized his to-do list for the balance of the week.

When he quit early for the day, he leaned back in his chair and glanced at the plaques gracing his wall.

At the end of a grueling day, he often paused from writing and gazed at the wisdom adorning the wall. Authors now long dead—their words alive—inspired him to hone his craft, and like all writers, to elevate his audience above the mundane to the sublime.

His eyes landed at an all too familiar place again—on the one author quote that once had inspired him and now haunted him. It was a gift from Aimee when he struggled to write his first novel.

> *"There are all kinds of love in this world,*
> *but never the same love twice."*
> F. Scott Fitzgerald

CHAPTER 9

Shortly after Chase returned from dropping Clay off at summer school on Tuesday, he poured himself a cup of coffee, walked to his den, and opened a window to allow the sea air to waft through the room. Pulling up his office chair, he sat and reviewed the two concepts he had been considering for his second novel. The phone rang as he continued to flesh out outlines for both ideas. It was his agent.

"Chase. How are you?"

"Good, Ed. You?"

"Fine. Look, I don't have a lot of time. I just wanted to reach out again and check in on the progress of your second effort. How's it going?"

"It's going—slow," Chase replied and offered nothing more.

"When will you have a completed manuscript for me to review and shop?"

"Not sure. What's the hurry?"

"You know how it works. Publishers are looking for a finished manuscript and another idea right behind it. Most authors have a second book in their back pocket when their first strikes gold. I don't want you behind the curve."

Chase put the call on speaker, laced his fingers behind his head, leaned back in his chair, and gazed out his window to the backyard and the ocean in the distance. He changed the subject. "By the way, what's the status of the contract offer on my second effort from my current publisher?"

"Frankly, they're lowballing us—and pressuring me to pressure you to sign. So I'm stalling. If you can get me a full manuscript of book two and a concept for book three, I'll pitch it as a three-book series to your current publisher *and* shop it," he said. "I'd like to create a bidding war. How'd you like to follow up your bestseller with a new contract and an advance for two more?"

"An advance would be nice. What kind of marketing support can you guarantee as a part of the deal?"

"Let's not get ahead of ourselves. I need to know what I have to sell before I sell it, right? The more we offer them, the more they may offer you. Besides, you still need a larger platform. That will give you more leverage. What have you finished so far?"

"I've got a synopsis and three sample chapters of a sequel, and I'm still working on a concept for a standalone I prefer to write instead of the sequel."

"That's all you've got?"

Chase paused. He swore he could hear Ed blinking incredulously on the other end.

"I'm also fleshing out an outline for the standalone novel."

"Chase, I think we need to give publishers what they want—more of the same—while you have momentum. As we've discussed, they want a sequel to *The Bridge Between Us*."

"Ed, I'm writing the sequel, but honestly, I'm still not comfortable writing it. I want to avoid the comparison trap. My career is too young to survive the wrath of an overeager critic desperate to make a name for himself. I'd rather introduce my audience to a new story with captivating new characters, an alluring setting, and a contemporary theme. I'm not comfortable with a continuing story that picks up where the first novel left off. I feel like I need to do something different."

"Send me the three sample chapters and a synopsis of the sequel. Then I'll talk it up to a few editors I trust. We can talk about your standalone idea later. Sound fair?"

"It's fair, but I'm just not comfortable with it, Ed."

Ed cleared his throat. "Chase, I hear you, I really do, but you need to trust me and understand that, at this stage, I have a better idea of what's best for your career than you do. You have a window of opportunity here—and windows close quickly."

Chase leaned forward in his chair. "I need to trust my instincts too. Look, I get it. I need an agent. I respect and value your experience and your point of view. But, right or wrong, I'm trying to own my career. And my gut is telling me something different."

Chase heard footsteps and assumed Ed was pacing around his office pondering his response. "Look, I'll be honest. I trust my twenty years of industry experience more than I trust your gut. I know what works. There's a roadmap for success in publishing, and I'm trying to keep you on the path."

Staring out his window, he glanced at the sea and the wind blowing between the trees. "Ed, okay. I'll make the sequel a priority, but understand I'm simply not comfortable with it. I'll attempt both. I think that's fair."

Now Chase could hear Ed tapping on his keyboard and wondered if he was pulling up his calendar. "How much time do you need? I need a product I can sell if you want to capitalize on your fifteen minutes of fame."

"Let me get back to you."

Ed paused and took a breath. "Don't let your window of opportunity close because you're trusting your digestive system instead of your agent."

"Roger that."

When Chase hung up, he knew Ed was right. The search for the next original voice was relentless. And agents wanted writers with a velocity to their writing who had amassed a large body of work and had a unique voice to cut through the clutter.

In fairness, Ed was no different—and in a perfect world, he

should have expected Chase to have a second book written when the first one had launched. Chase didn't have a large body of work in the pipeline. His platform was mediocre but growing, and he had lost his inspiration when he lost his wife.

Success had caught Chase by surprise. His first effort was an overnight success, so his back pocket was empty—nothing to offer voracious readers for their appetite for America's next beloved storyteller.

It wasn't easy to admit to himself, much less to Ed, that after Aimee's death he had not only lost his inspiration, but he'd also lost his literary voice. This writer was floating aimlessly like a piece of driftwood. He never wanted to be branded a one-hit wonder. It was obvious what that label would mean—no agent would touch him.

Chase spent the balance of the morning thinking through the story arc of both a sequel and his new standalone idea—an idea that would bring the world new characters, setting, circumstances, and theme. He felt Ed could sell this new concept in the same genre as *The Bridge Between Us*.

Chase believed in this approach and in taking a stronger stand managing his own career. He realized Ed didn't make money unless Chase did. Like most authors, he was reluctant to yield total creative control, but he needed balance. It was Ed's job to push him—he just wasn't mentally ready to be pushed.

Chase had lost track of time and missed lunch as he continued to draft his ideas. When he checked his phone, it said one twenty, so he wrapped up what he was doing and slipped a notebook and a few pens into his portfolio to prepare for his meeting with Sierra. Before leaving, he grabbed an apple from the fridge and finished it before slipping out the front door.

While driving to the school, he wondered what Sierra would say regarding Clay's continuing problems—and if he was doing something wrong as a father. Clay hadn't been the same since he lost his mother. Needing to take a few summer school classes underscored his problem with distractions and not keeping up.

When Chase turned into the parking lot, he was ten minutes early, so he pulled over and thought for a moment, remembering how he struggled in school when his mom died. He recalled the feeling of repeating a grade—of feeling displaced, of his friends moving on without him. The feeling of being lost and disillusioned, with no way out. In those days, his school didn't have the programs available today. Kids often coped alone.

When he walked up the stairs, the door to Room 223 was open. Sierra sat at her desk, her hair cascading over her shoulders. Her appearance struck him. She was correcting papers when he knocked on the door.

Looking up, she smiled and waved him in. He felt the warmth of her smile. "Thanks for coming, Chase."

"Thanks for reaching out." Approaching her, he sat on the opposite side of her desk.

"Well, let's jump right in. First, let me tell you Clay's a good boy, a pleasure to have in class. He has a soft heart, and he's friendly and cooperative."

"Thank you. He's a good kid."

Sierra continued. "But he's distracted, has trouble concentrating, and has a tendency to withdraw—especially lately. Naturally, this affects his performance in the classroom. It's like he's somewhere else. Sometimes he stops communicating. On the playground, he occasionally isolates himself from others, except from his friend Fernando."

Chase nodded. "Yeah, Fernando is his buddy. He has been good for Clay."

"Yesterday, you told me he lost his mom almost two years ago. Our records show that, and as I told you, I should have responded to this much sooner. This explains his behavior."

She glanced down at her notes, then at Chase. "Clay continues to have trouble concentrating. I'm not a grief counselor or a social worker, but I know that with a significant loss, kids often have trouble concentrating on anything other than their loss. Tell me something. Is he still having trouble concentrating on his homework?"

Chase scratched his chin and thought for a moment. "Now that you mention it, I suppose he gets distracted. He takes a long time to finish his homework and his chores. But don't all eight-year-olds have a short attention span? I had hoped he would be almost over this by now."

She leaned back. "We all grieve differently. He could struggle with concentration for an extended period. It's not unusual. Does he show anger, sadness, or loneliness regularly at home?"

"Not really. I noticed he gets frustrated easily when things don't work out for him. I've also noticed we've both been more easily irritated over the last few weeks."

"Any reason?"

"I have a hunch. I think we're both anticipating the second anniversary of his mother's death at the end of this month—July twenty-ninth. But back to your question, he doesn't display much anger, sadness, or loneliness at home. Sometimes he talks to me openly, but he often keeps to himself."

"Does he talk to anyone else?"

"Well, he plays a lot of video games at home with Fernando. They seem to talk to each other a lot."

She nodded. "I've noticed he spends most of his free time here with Fernando too. That's good. He needs someone to feel safe with—someone he can open up to who will understand how he feels. Does he have any difficulty sleeping?"

"Not that I've noticed. In the first year after losing his mom, he had nightmares for a while. I think he's sleeping well now. How are his grades in your class?"

She lifted a water bottle to her lips and took a sip. "He's doing better, but he's still lagging. It's clear to me something's bothering him. Sometimes he falls asleep in class, so he may not be sleeping as well as you think. I'll watch for additional symptoms."

Chase shifted his weight in his chair. "So where do we go from here? How do I—we—help my son?"

"Well, I'd like our social worker to talk with him. Her name is Jennifer Adams. She's both my closest friend and my colleague here. I'll brief her on our meeting today. She will evaluate Clay, and after her evaluation, she will put a plan together to address his needs to get him back on track. We can start the plan now and run it into the next school year as needed."

"I like the sound of that."

"You'll love Jennifer—sorry, Miss Adams. She's well credentialed, with bachelor's and master's degrees in social work, but best of all, she really loves kids. I'll have her call you. How does that sound?"

"Great. There's nothing worse than feeling lost after losing your mom. Been there. Done that."

Her back straightened. "Oh. You lost your mom as a boy too?"

He gave a crooked smile. "One of life's ironies. By losing my wife, I'm living my father's life, and now my son is living mine. Strange, isn't it?"

"I'm so sorry, Chase." She paused for a moment and touched her lips. "Seems we have something in common. I lost my father a few years back—in the worst way."

His eyes widened. "Oh, now I'm sorry. You mean he …?"

"Took his own life? Yes. He was bipolar, not that it makes it any easier."

"If I may ask, how did you cope?"

"Not very well, actually. I felt so abandoned. But I had—have—someone I can talk to. Jennifer has talked me through more than one tough day over the years. She was instrumental when my dad died."

She quickly recovered and changed the subject. "May I ask, did you struggle in school because of your mom's death?"

He lowered his head and rubbed his hands together. "Yeah. When I look at Clay, I see myself. But I was twelve, so I may have felt the full impact of my loss. It kind of messed me up as a kid. Because he's four years younger than I was, I thought that would insulate him from the pain of the loss. Maybe I was wrong."

Sierra jotted notes on her pad as Chase talked, then looked up. "Let's see what Miss Adams has to say. She's dealt with a lot of this in her career. She'll bring a fresh perspective and develop an action plan with the help of a school support team."

"Who is on this support team?"

"Miss Adams will lead the team, but it will also include our principal, me, and, if needed, outside resources, like additional counseling. In Clay's case, I don't think he'll need outside services."

"Is there anything I should do in the meantime to help him at home?"

"Just keep him on task with his homework and try to spend more time with him. I think he really needs you now. Is there anything you can do together? You know, to give him more opportunities to verbalize his thoughts and feelings to you. I'm sure Miss Adams will stress that. Clay needs an outlet."

"He's been asking me to spend more time together. I'll try to do that."

"In the meantime, I'll talk with Miss Adams and have her call you and set up an appointment."

He felt compelled to call her by her first name, so he took a shot. "Thanks, Sierra." He noticed she paused. "Or should I call you Miss Taylor here?"

She appeared to consider his question. "In school, call me Miss Taylor. If I ever see you outside of school, Sierra is fine."

Chase wondered if her comment was an invitation to see

her again or if she meant he would likely only see her regarding this issue.

She put her pen down. "Questions?"

"I don't think so. Do you have questions for me?"

She leaned back in her chair. "Just one—on an unrelated subject."

"Go for it."

She wore a sly smile. "Sunday, when I first met you on the wharf. You rarely see an author reading one of his own books. Are you sure you weren't admiring your own work?" She winked at him.

He laughed. The question surprised him and made him feel more comfortable. Pushing his chair back from her desk, he assumed a more relaxed position.

"No, I wasn't admiring my work, despite appearances." He smirked.

"I thought all artists admire their own work."

"Maybe painters do—or sculptors. Writers, not so much."

"You're saying Hemingway didn't admire *A Farewell to Arms?*"

"Doubt it."

"Fitzgerald didn't admire *The Great Gatsby?*" She was quizzing him.

"Probably not."

"Melvin didn't admire *Moby Dick?*"

"Not likely."

"And Faulkner didn't admire *The Sound and the Fury?*" She leaned forward now, as if to challenge him.

He crossed one leg over another. "My, you're well-versed in literature."

"Well, I *am* an English teacher, and, of course, I've read the masters of literature in high school, college, and beyond. They were the best in their time."

Chase grinned. "Faulkner may have admired his own work. He had a bit of an ego."

"I find your premise interesting, but still a little unbelievable."

Lifting both hands, he conveyed his innocence. "Look, it's just my opinion, but I seriously don't think writers admire their own work."

She raised an eyebrow. "You honestly believe Hemingway didn't admire *A Farewell to Arms* or *For Whom the Bell Tolls?*"

"Hemingway certainly had an ego too—and his success was enviable. But it's my theory he didn't admire his own work. For example, what if I told you I wrote forty-seven endings to my novel? Would you think I admired it?"

"No. I'd think you were unhappy with it—at least the ending—forty-six times. But I know where you're going with this."

"I'm sure you do as a Hemingway fan. As you probably know, he wrote forty-seven endings to *A Farewell to Arms*. I'd say that's a good example of an accomplished writer never being fully satisfied with his work, wouldn't you? It doesn't mean he didn't like the work. I'm just saying, in principle, writers don't admire their work—because they're never satisfied with it. If he was alive today, and he had the chance, I'd bet he couldn't resist writing a forty-eighth ending."

The custodian interrupted Chase. He raised his eyebrows and made a hand gesture indicating he would return soon to clean Sierra's classroom. She simply nodded, and he left.

"You're saying even if you guys write a bestseller, you're never completely satisfied with it?" Sierra asked.

"'You guys'? Really? Are you throwing me in the same company as these legends and Pulitzer Prize winners?" He grinned like he'd just achieved membership in an exclusive club.

"For the sake of argument, yes."

"Well, thank you for the kind words. I think as writers, we rarely admire our work because of what we *see* when we read it."

She leaned back, folded her arms across her chest, and played along. "What do you *see?*"

"Flaws."

"You mean errors? Typos?"

"No. Flaws."

"What flaws?" She took the cap off the water bottle on her desk and took another sip, waiting for him to continue.

"You know, the narration could be smoother. Dialogue tighter. Description richer. Subplots deeper. No head-hopping. And, of course, the big one, show don't tell."

"So when you scan your books, you're always looking for flaws instead of appreciating the work for what it is?"

"Yes, often. That's what I was saying when I met you on the wharf. I'm searching for errors or mistakes—so I don't replicate them in the next novel. That doesn't mean I don't enjoy the book. It's just that I'm always looking for other ways I could have said it. You can always turn a phrase better."

She furrowed an eyebrow. "Are you saying for the rest of your writing career, you'll never admire your own work—no matter how commercially or critically successful it is?"

"Probably."

"That's a shame, really."

"Why's that?"

She glanced at him, and he wondered if she felt the connection he did. Her voice was soft. "Because I admire it."

Wanting the meeting to end on the note that had just stirred something within him, he stood. Following his lead, she rose.

Chase exhaled. "Well, that's what should matter most to an author, isn't it? That the readers, not the writers, admire the work? After all, we write for you."

Sierra nodded and walked him to her classroom door. She looked contented, like she enjoyed his company. "I'll have Miss Adams call you."

"Thanks, Miss Taylor." He winked at her. "I appreciate this more than you know." It was all he said.

~

At three o'clock, when he walked to his car with Clay in tow, the scent in the air was familiar and carried him back to another time and place—when he had lost his mom. The desperation he'd felt as a boy swept over him, and he knew he'd never fully verbalized his feelings to his father. As Clay buckled his seatbelt, Chase wondered what his son had buried and if he didn't have the words to set himself free. Being his father, he knew he must navigate his way back to his son's eight-year-old heart.

Jack was right. Chase's twelve-year-old self needed to connect with Clay.

When he opened his car door, he slid behind the wheel, pulled the door closed behind him, and started the Jeep. As he buckled his seatbelt, it occurred to him that when he drove to the school, he had felt like a drowning man. Now, finally, Sierra had thrown him a life preserver. With her help, he and Clay might now be able to swim to shore—together.

~

Later that evening, when Clay was asleep, Chase processed the events of the day and grabbed a pen and his journal before plopping on the couch in the den. Playing some instrumental music, he wrote.

~

I met with Clay's teacher today. She's nice. Very nice. She's concerned about Clay's lack of concentration and communication, and his tendency to withdraw from others. It felt like déjà vu.

He's still grieving the loss of his mom, she said. I suppose it shouldn't surprise me. I struggled longer.

I learned today that Sierra is acquainted with grief too. She is no stranger to feeling abandoned, either. It also became apparent that

I'm missing some of Clay's cues, subtle, non-verbal cries for help—or at least, for my attention. It's my fault. I'm too busy managing my business and too preoccupied trying to figure out my next novel so I don't land on the heap of one-hit wonders.

I'm not sure I can be successful in every area of my life. Perhaps I have to decide in which area I am most willing to fail. I could survive a failed advertising business, and I could justify failing as an author. But could I ever forgive myself for failing as a father?

It's funny. As an author, I'm always editing my work, eliminating errors, and striving to write better. Maybe I need to edit my life too. You know, eliminate errors and live better. Not just for me—but for Clay.

Sierra says I need to be an outlet for him and give him "more opportunities to verbalize his thoughts and feelings."

Guys are not very good at "verbalizing their thoughts and feelings." I never remember seeing or hearing my father cry after my mother's death. Not saying he didn't—just never saw or heard him.

He did the "guy thing"—stuffed his feelings. That was a flawed strategy. A road to nowhere. The road I'm on.

It's important to spend more focused time with Clay. I regret that I've been so consumed by my own life and grief that I haven't helped him cope with his. It's one more way I'm living my father's life, mistakes and all. I'm not doing it intentionally, so my dad probably didn't either. It's a simple fact—grief throws us off our game.

I read somewhere that "hope is music to the soul." I need to be a source of hope to Clay. And Heaven knows we need more music in our lives.

CHAPTER 10

As Chase lay in the dark early Wednesday morning, the large red numbers of his digital alarm clock shined like a beacon and informed him of the bad news—it was 4:07.

Chase could sleep another hour, if he could sleep at all. Not today. It was one of *those* mornings. They were sporadic, but he had labeled them "memory mornings." They were the mornings where everything reminded him of Aimee—and his loss. Once his mind got rolling, it wouldn't stop. His thoughts would land in rapid succession, like planes at LAX.

Although the bedsheets had long lost their smell of Aimee's perfume, Chase could swear in the middle of the night or just before dawn he could detect a faint scent of it on his pillowcase.

His position in the bed reminded him he was still sleeping on *his* side. Aimee's side remained empty, as though she were on vacation and would return home soon. He had never moved to the middle of the bed. He wasn't completely sure why. Perhaps he was avoiding changes that reinforced the finality of his loss. That's why Aimee's clothes still hung in the closet.

Occasionally, he would stand in the closet and stare at her clothes. Her scent was fading, but he had hoped if he closed his eyes, an outfit would transport him back to an occasion where she wore it. Maybe then he might recover a forgotten detail—her teasing him during a double-date, the sound of her laughter during a romantic comedy, her sense of wonder as she gazed at the stars, her cry at a close friend's funeral, her gentle conversations with Clay on date night to help him overcome his fear of a new babysitter, the feel of her sliding her smooth, warm hand between his fingers during the vows at a wedding, and how a dress and heels accentuated every curve. On memory mornings, he was the air traffic controller, and he permitted all thoughts to land, believing every rediscovered detail brought her closer to him.

Often, he recalled how she had gotten up before him and padded around the house barefoot in her pink pajamas before making breakfast for them. She would pull her hair back in a ponytail, a few stray strands falling on her face before she tucked them behind her ears. *She was beautiful in the morning,* he thought to himself. So natural, with no makeup required. She was all he ever needed—all he ever wanted.

And Aimee was so good with Clay—patient, kind, encouraging, and loving. He treasured the way she let Clay lean into her on the couch and stroked his hair, and how it made Clay feel loved and secure. It was something he had wished for as a boy—the loving touch of a mother. His grandfather was right. He used to say, "You can copy many things in this world, but not *duplicate* them. There's a difference."

Feelings of guilt, betrayal, and comparison kept him from dating with the proper frame of mind. Dating after Aimee had always been unfair to his date and meaningless to him—dry runs to nowhere. Empty attempts to lift him out of the dumps. Dating didn't move him forward—it had the opposite effect, convincing him that finding love, true love, was as much a matter of chance as a matter of choice. Make the wrong choice and you may have lost your chance.

Lying in the stillness, he remembered how this had been the most difficult time of day for him as a boy. After his mother died, the early morning darkness had suddenly taken on new meaning—separation and uncertainty. Like Clay, he had wondered how he was going to live without his mother. How would he make it through life without ever seeing her again? He remembered thinking he would never hug her again. She would never hug him. A mother's loving touch lost forever.

In the morning's stillness after his mother's death, he had asked questions similar to the ones Clay was asking now. Would his life ever be the same again, or was it on a new trajectory? How would his life be different? How could he possibly be the same person without her influence, her guidance, her touch?

His father sent Chase to school a day or two after his mother died, refusing to let his son drown in his own grief. "I'll keep Chase moving forward by simply keeping him moving," he once said.

Now, as the early morning light peeked through his window shade, Chase stretched and sat on the edge of his bed to shake off the memories and get going. Yet one final thought glided into his airspace. It was one that especially troubled him. Despite these intermittent memory mornings, and his intense love for Aimee, he had not cried since the week she had died. It was as if he had made a subconscious pact with himself. After all, if his father rarely cried after losing his wife, should he?

CHAPTER 11

L ater that week, when Clay was at summer school, Chase was busy with his advertising business. The diversity of creative work thrilled him. Every day was different. On Monday he wrote a capabilities brochure for an environmental firm, on Tuesday he generated headlines and wrote body copy for an ad for a Fortune 500 company introducing fashionable new sports apparel, and on Wednesday he crafted the first draft of a speech for an executive of a running shoe company. Today, Thursday, he focused on his literary career as he edited the first three chapters of his sequel and revised the synopsis to appease Ed.

When he completed the final edit, he turned his attention to an alternative idea for the standalone novel. His phone rang, breaking his concentration.

"Hello."

"Hi, Mr. Kincaid?"

"Yes."

"Hi, this is Jennifer Adams, the social worker at Peabody Elementary School."

"Oh, hi, Miss Adams."

"Sorry it's taken so long to get back to you. I wanted to observe Clay's behavior in the classroom a little more and follow up with Miss Taylor before I reached out to you."

"No problem." Chase raked his hand through his hair then grabbed a pen and a pad of paper.

"Is now a good time to talk?"

Chase looked at the clock hanging above the authors' quotes on what he had dubbed his Inspiration Wall. "As good as any. I've been looking forward to your call."

"Good. Well, my observations are like Miss Taylor's. I noticed Clay was frequently looking out the window, often searching for things inside his desk, and seemed to overreact to some of the other students' actions. Sometimes he appears to be low on energy and lays his head down on his desk several times a day. These are not terribly unusual behaviors for a child who's lost a parent, but they seem to interfere with his learning."

"Okay, good to know."

"By the way, please accept my condolences regarding the loss of your wife. I can't image what it's like to lose a spouse."

"Well, thank you. I appreciate that." He glanced at a far wall in his office where his advertising awards hung, hoping they would deflect his attention from the pain of her last sentiment.

"Clay is a good boy, and it's obvious there's structure and stability in his life."

Jennifer's voice was tender, and Chase heard the kindness in her soft tone, and it relaxed him.

"Thank you for your kind words. We both feel a little displaced, and honestly, we're still trying to find our way." Chase walked out of the den and sat on the patio where he could be more comfortable. "It appears we all agree on the diagnosis, but where do we go from here? How do we help Clay?"

"That's what I'd like to cover with you today. Before I do, has Clay recently or in the past verbalized to you how he feels about the loss of his mom?"

"When Aimee died almost two years ago, we used to talk about it occasionally. Eventually, we realized the more we dwelled on it, the more unhappy we became. We slowly stopped talking about it unless he felt lonely or had a random question. I should have done a better job of helping him grieve, but frankly, I didn't know how, especially when I was grieving myself."

"I certainly understand that. The reason I ask is it's important for Clay to share and verbalize his feelings about losing his mom. Anything you can do at home to encourage that will help him feel normal again."

It was the last thing he wanted to do. Dig up old wounds. Peel the scab again. But it was the right thing to do. *Why does the right thing to do always feel like the wrong thing to do?* "I can do that. Miss Taylor suggested the same thing."

She took a breath and tapped her pencil on the desk. "When a child loses a parent, it feels anything but normal. Verbalizing helps restore a sense of normalcy. That's important for Clay. This might be why he withdraws—he's not just sad, he doesn't feel complete. His friend, Fernando, also lost a parent to divorce. I'm sure that's a big reason they're buddies—they're in this together, and it makes them feel normal."

Chase leaned forward to take it in. "That makes sense. Clay never mentioned Fernando's parents got divorced. Now I understand why they spend so much time together."

"Yes, I'm sure they're holding each other up. I suspect they feel normal when they're together."

"Good to know. I'll be more deliberate about getting Clay to talk with me about how he's feeling. And now I can also tune into Fernando." Chase cleared his throat and rubbed the back of his head. "Did Miss Taylor mention I went through the same thing as a child?"

"No, she didn't. She would never violate your privacy."

"Yeah, Clay and I are living parallel lives."

"Then you know how important it is to share your feelings with the surviving parent."

Chase stood and paced around the patio before stopping to look out over the water. The ocean view and cool, gentle breeze always cleared his head. "Not really. I didn't have this type of support at my school back in the day, and my father believes less is more regarding conversations about feelings. My father is like his father, from the Greatest Generation. Why share your feelings when you can stuff them? Please don't misunderstand me—my father is a great man. A kind man. He just believed moving forward meant moving on. He learned it from his father."

"I get it."

"My father talked openly with me about the loss of my mom for a while. But when he started to heal, he assumed I did. But we were out of sync emotionally. I was healing slower. When he was ready to move on, I was still coping."

She was quiet for a minute, and he wondered what she was thinking. "Did you stop talking about it altogether?"

"No, but over time, I think he believed revisiting grief was reliving it. And there came a time when he wanted me to stop reliving it. He used to say, 'There are better days ahead. Let's move forward—not backward.'"

She was quiet, and he felt he was being heard.

"Miss Taylor mentioned you would put together a team with a plan to help Clay, right?"

"Yes. I've assembled a school support team for him. The team will include the principal, Miss Taylor, a school psychologist, and me. If needed, we can pull in outside resources, but I don't think that will be necessary."

"What will you be doing for him, specifically?"

"There are a few things. First, I'd like him to join a group of kids in similar situations so he doesn't feel like he is going through this alone. This will help him feel connected instead of displaced, and it will create opportunities for him to talk through his feelings after hearing other kids do the same."

Chase sat in his patio chair and swiveled to catch sight of a bird landing in the oak tree shading him. "Fantastic. What else?"

"We have an art therapy class I would like him to take part in."

"Is that where you use art to help him better express himself?"

"Exactly. We'll have him draw a picture of the person he lost. It opens the door for us to ask questions like, 'Where were you when your mother died?' This will encourage Clay to express how he feels about his loss. It also will reduce his inhibitions as he discusses his art."

"I like this idea. I wish I had something like this when I was a kid. Anything else?"

"Yes. I'd like to get you involved at home."

"Of course. What can I do?"

"Well, for starters, you could read some books on death and grief together. The local library has a list of children's books written on this subject to support single parents. I can email you a list of titles."

"Perfect. Thank you."

"There's also a summer camp Clay could attend for a week. It's called Camp Cope. Clay may not need it, but it's an option, so I thought I'd mention it."

"Sounds interesting. What would he do there?"

"It helps kids cope with their loss in a relaxing, non-threatening setting. It would also introduce him to practical coping techniques, and it would use a series of exciting activities to help him feel normal again. Since it's a camp, Clay can swim, enjoy crafts, take part in individual counseling, if needed, and just have fun. Does Clay like to swim?"

"Are you kidding? He's part fish. Can you send me dates and details on this camp? I'm not sure it will fit into our summer, but I'd like to know more."

"I'd be happy to. There is one more thing you could do to help Clay."

"What's that?"

"As I mentioned before, it's important to help him talk freely about his feelings so he doesn't feel alone. A good way to do this is to find a special project to do together—something he likes—that will help you bond."

Chase nodded in agreement from his patio chair, wishing he had the same chances as a child. "I will come up with something. Miss Adams, you've been very helpful. Anything else?"

"That's really it. Of course, ask Clay if he needs help with his homework, and get in the habit of checking it each day so he feels like you're in this together. That will also help get his grades up. Questions for me, Mr. Kincaid?"

He thought for a moment, then asked the first thing on his mind. "When will this program start?"

"There are a few things we can do this summer, then the balance of the program will occur during the new school year. We will notify his fourth-grade teacher in the fall and add him or her to the team."

"Okay. Do you have questions for me, Miss Adams?"

"Just one."

"Shoot."

"How are *you* doing? If you don't mind me asking."

"I'm …"

Chase hesitated. Outside of family and close friends, no one had asked that question in a long time—and he realized he didn't really know how to answer it. No standard lines. No quick quips to deflect and move on.

She surprised him by how patiently she waited for his response. Most people weren't kind enough to ask, but when they did, they were uncomfortable with his answer.

"Thank you for asking. I learned long ago that people are much more comfortable asking about your problem than listening to your answer. It's so much easier to ignore someone's pain than to comfort it, don't you think?"

"I agree, but I'm not uncomfortable asking—or listening."

Chase smiled to himself. Her candor was unexpected—and refreshing. "Fair enough. Let's just say I'm learning to forge ahead, to reassemble the fragments of broken dreams. I'm just missing the glue, if you know what I mean."

"You mentioned earlier that you and Clay are living parallel lives with similar losses. I'm not a grief counselor, but my mother was. One thing she used to talk about was the fog of grief."

He wrinkled his forehead. "The fog of grief?"

"Yes. It's how grief affects our ability to think clearly or concentrate—and how that fog can linger, and we get lost in it."

"Tell me more. What are you saying, exactly?"

"I guess I'm wondering if you feel your fog has lifted or if it's still hazy. Maybe, like Clay, you might benefit from talking about it."

Chase suddenly felt vulnerable. Exposed. Awkward—like the camera shifted from the leading man to an extra uncomfortable with the spotlight. His shoulders tightened. "Thanks for your concern. I haven't talked to many people about it except for Jack, my best friend. He has been a tremendous help. I think I can handle it myself now. Besides, I have to be strong for Clay."

She was silent for a moment, and he wished he could see her expression. "May I say something that might sound strange at first?"

Chase looked out over the ocean, then leaned back in his chair to brace himself for what might come next. "I'm listening."

"If you haven't done so already, it's important to share your grief. Not with just one person. As I mentioned, sharing grief helps you not feel so alone. Sometimes we can heal ourselves with our own words."

"I'm not sure what you mean."

She paused. "I'm just saying that when we discuss what's going on deep inside, we begin to understand our feelings. And while

I recognize it's important to be strong, I remember as a young girl overhearing my mom telling one of her clients on the phone that sometimes it's more important to be weak than strong."

He scratched the back of his neck. "Sounds contradictory."

"She used to say, 'Regarding grief, you'll survive longer as an open book than a sealed vault.' I think she was right."

He raised an eyebrow. "How's that?"

"An open book lets people in. It allows people to approach you, to encourage you, to come alongside and support you. A sealed vault is, well, sealed. Nothing gets in or out. You eventually run out of air. You smother—alone. I speak from experience. I needed to take my mother's advice and open up after my divorce. Thank goodness I had a friend like Sierra."

"And she is grateful to have a close friend like you. She mentioned in passing that you helped her cope with the death of her father. She didn't say much, just that you really helped her."

"That was a really tough time for her. Emotionally, her father was in and out of her life. She struggled with his constant pulling away until he died. She felt so abandoned. I was happy to help her through it because, as a social worker, I help so many young kids with the same feelings. It brought us even closer together."

"Okay, I get it. Better to be an open book than a sealed vault. Besides, who wants to run out of air?" If it wasn't for Jack, Chase would have smothered long ago. "I need to think more about that. I admit it's been getting a little hard to breathe lately."

She continued, and her concern impressed him. It had been a long time since a stranger showed any interest in his loss. "I don't want to overstep, but after you lost your wife, did you ever seek professional grief counseling?"

"No." It was all he said. Chase had considered grief counseling only once—but had passed. He couldn't imagine himself sitting around a circle and spilling his guts to total strangers about how much he loved his wife. After all, it was a private matter.

Counseling helped *some* people, but not him.

Instead, all his life, Chase listened to the little voice in his head that told him he could handle this alone—like his father. Yet he was never sure if he was hearing the voice of wisdom, denial, or false bravado. Deep down, he knew God should play a major role in his recovery, but when his father shut God out, he closed the door, too.

Jennifer disrupted his train of thought. "Well, like I said, I don't want to overstep. I just thought if you opened up, you could cut a path for Clay and counsel him if he faces similar struggles as an adult."

She was quiet for a minute, and Chase sensed she knew he was uncomfortable. "I will send you the list of books on death you and Clay can check out at the library, a brochure for Camp Cope, and phone and email contact information for everyone on Clay's school support team."

Gratitude swept over him with the cool breeze. "You don't know how much I've appreciated this phone call and your concern for Clay—and, frankly, for me. I look forward to working with you and your team."

"Likewise. Well, I'm sure you have things to do, so I'll let you go. Have a nice day. We'll talk soon," she said, and she signed off.

～

Chase stood on the patio for a moment and thought about what had just happened. He walked back into his den to proofread the first three chapters of his sequel for Ed once again. Although his mood had completely changed, he finished proofreading his edits and emailed the chapters and synopsis to Ed before drifting back to his conversation with Miss Adams.

She was right about Clay—and about him. Both had kept too much bottled up. Like tea kettles, they were letting off just enough steam before boiling, but it wasn't enough. They needed a relief valve. And Chase needed to start verbalizing to more people how he felt about losing his soulmate.

Later that evening, after the two played video and board games together, Clay went to bed and Chase sat on the couch in his den thinking about when he would tell Clay about his conversation with the social worker today and the plan to help him confront and conquer his grief. Spending focused time with Clay would help them share their feelings. Reaching for his journal on his desk, he cracked it open. Tonight, the words came easily and flowed across the page.

~

I talked to the school social worker today, Jennifer Adams. She's Sierra's close friend and colleague. She was right. Jennifer loves kids—even big kids, like me. I could see it, or more accurately, hear it, in the way she talked about Clay. It wasn't her words as much as her tone. Funny how sometimes you can hear compassion before you feel it. Jennifer cares about my son—and his father. We now have a team and a plan to help Clay. I feel good about it now. Clay won't drift hopelessly like I did as a boy.

Jennifer went a step further. She challenged me to consider talking to a grief counselor about my life. She called it like it is—I'm a "sealed vault." Okay, maybe I need to open up and talk more to be "healed by my own words." It makes sense, I guess. But I wonder if the benefits of grief counseling fall under the category of "too little, too late" for me.

I read somewhere that "if you change nothing, nothing will change." So I have a decision to make. If I'm going to build a future for us, besides getting help for Clay, I need to get help too. Maybe I've been floundering in the fog of grief for too long.

One thing has become clear. Lifting the fog in my life will begin only if I'm willing to lift it.

CHAPTER 12

W hen the weekend arrived, Chase stepped out the patio doors in early dawn. The air was warm, but the breeze was cool. Another benefit of living in Santa Barbara. Even when the air temperature rose, the coastal breeze was always cool, so residents were always comfortable.

The birds were singing as the sun came up. "One of God's fringe benefits," his grandfather used to say. "Their song reminds us there's always a reason to be happy. A bird singing is like a man whistling. Try to be angry and whistle. Take a lesson from the birds."

Oh, how Chase missed him. His grandfather was the only person who understood him in those turbulent teenage years when he rarely understood himself. "Understanding is one thing Grandpa does better than anyone else," Chase used to say. "He gets it—he gets me."

Wish I could talk to him now.

Walking out to the backyard, he bent over and picked up the basketball lying in the grass. He positioned himself behind his home-made three-point line, a wavy arc he'd fashioned with a paintbrush and an old, tacky gallon of paint.

The basket sat atop a rusty metal pole next to the garage. The net, if you could call it that, had seen better days. It hung limp and torn after being battered by the ball for the last two years. Once his passion, shooting baskets was now a catharsis. Once exercise, now therapy. The condition of the net spoke to the frequency of his therapy sessions.

He dribbled twice before releasing the ball. It hit the back of the rim and rolled forward, curving around it twice, like walking a tightrope. It stalled on the rim in perfect balance and teetered before it fell through. Chase smiled. "That's three-zip, Jack," he said, beating his old friend again in the one place he could always defeat him—his imagination.

Shooting along the three-point arc in four-foot increments, he strived to take his game up a notch—to keep Jack at bay in one-on-one competition. Both prized these friendly contests, were equally aggressive on the court, and were ruthless about collecting the spoils of victory—bragging rights or a cold beverage.

After snagging a rebound, Chase moved right, then left, then drove to the basket, remembering how he had out-maneuvered opponents in the high school state championship game.

Chase never sought to be the hero. Contributing was all he wanted. Content to assist, he didn't need to score. That was Jack's job—he was the team star. Setting up his next shot, he let his mind drift back to that championship game twenty years ago.

~

Aimee was in the crowd, along with her mom, his father, and everyone who meant anything to him, not to mention half his hometown, as this Cinderella team surprised and confounded teams that failed to take them seriously.

In the final minute, the game was tied. As the point guard, Chase was the general on the court. It was his job to direct his team to victory by finding the open man or creating an opportunity for a shot. With the state championship on the line, he felt the weight of expectations as he pushed the ball past half court. Setting up the offense from the three-point line, he drove toward the basket. When the defense descended upon him, he sailed a no-look pass across his body to the open small forward. With the clock winding down, his teammate caved under pressure and refused to shoot. Instead, he passed to Jack. A defender who had stuck like glue to the team's star player slapped the ball out of Jack's hands.

Reaching for it as he dove to the floor, Jack tipped the ball to Chase, who extended his arm to grab it, settled in, and fired off a shot. The ball seemed to slow in the air, hanging there long enough to raise his blood pressure, and for Chase to realize tonight he could be the hero—or the goat. The ball rolled off the rim. An opponent grabbed the rebound.

With the game still tied, Chase ran back down court with thirty seconds left. He spotted Aimee in the bleachers. She was nodding and clapping. Confident. No disappointment. She gave him a thumbs-up as if to say, "You've got this. We've got this."

He felt invincible again.

The opposing point guard brought the ball down. Chase pressed him and leaned in to go for a steal. The opponent turned away, evading Chase and pushing the ball forward. Chase found his blind spot on his other side, reached in, stole the ball, and raced down the court toward his basket. Now double covered, he passed to Jack, who set up for a shot just behind the three-point line. A defender blanketed him. Jack had a split second to decide—attempt a shot in coverage or pass the ball to Chase, now open and breaking for the basket. They had practiced this a thousand times. Any points would put them in a position to win with seconds left.

Jack passed to Chase, who drove in for a reverse layup and was fouled as he shot. The ball rolled in. The basket counted. Ahead by two and standing at the free-throw line, Chase fixed his eyes on the basket, dribbled three times, and put the ball up. *Swish.* The cheers were deafening.

With nine seconds on the clock, Chase's team led by three points. The opponent passed down court to set up a three-point shot to tie the game. When the shooting guard released a fadeaway jumper, Jack blocked his shot. The opponent recovered again, and the small forward took a final desperation shot near the three-point line. His shot bounced between the backboard and the rim before falling in. The crowd roared. A whistle blew. And the opposing team celebrated tying the game.

Suddenly, pandemonium. The refs met at the point of the shot. Did the player have both feet behind the three-point line? The crowd fell silent, the refs conferred, and a state championship hung in the balance. Time stopped. Tension grew. With their hands on their hips, the players paced the court. Finally, a decision was rendered.

On the last shot, the opposing player had one foot in front of the three-point line. Two points, not three. The crowd erupted. Chase's team had won the game by one point—and a new star was born.

He glanced up at Aimee. Both hands covered her mouth. She nodded, clapped, cried, and gave him a look only he could interpret. "Win or lose, that's my man."

It was an offering, and he received it. Tonight, he saw something in her that transcended the moment. *Hero or goat, Aimee's with me, behind me, beside me.*

~

Today, his last shot in the backyard bounced off the backboard to him. Dribbling the ball from hand to hand, he thought about the subtle message she sent him that night with nothing more than a nod, a look, and a few tears. She was *there* for him—with him—and outcomes didn't matter. It felt like a vow. She was so much bigger than the game.

~

That night two decades ago, at seventeen, before celebrating the victory, he sensed something deep within him—he loved a girl, and she loved him. They were young, yes, but it was real.

Somehow, he knew life's victories or defeats could never change that.

CHAPTER 13

Later that morning, just before noon, Jack popped over unannounced, which had become his modus operandi. Back in the day, Aimee hadn't fully appreciated Jack's free spirit and habit of unexpected visits, but Chase loved them—especially now.

Jack relaxed Chase with his informality. There was something refreshing about it. "Friendship doesn't need an appointment," he would say. "Besides, if you could see me coming, you would have the advantage."

Chase once equated Jack with comfort food. "There's nothing fancy about it, but it always makes you feel at home," he would say. "Like tomato soup and a grilled cheese sandwich."

Jack rang the doorbell and walked in. The doorbell was all the warning Jack ever gave him. Chase was in the kitchen when Jack found him.

"Dude."

Chase turned to him. "Hey, Jack, what's up?"

"I was in the neighborhood and thought I'd stop by and see if you and Clay would like to grab a burger at In-N-Out."

"Actually, I was just going to grill some burgers for Clay and Fernando. I promised Clay he could have Fernando over for lunch because he's been spending so much time over there. Want to join us?"

"Sweet. How can I help?"

"I bought groceries yesterday and made the patties, so just set the table. I'll throw the burgers on the grill soon after Fernando arrives."

"Kitchen or patio table?"

"Patio," Chase said.

The first year after Aimee's death, Jack made a point of swinging by at least every week to see if Chase "needed anything." He knew that was code for making sure he was keeping his head above water in the sea of grief. Chase would smile and say to himself, "Comfort food. That's what you are, Jack."

It wasn't always this way. During Jack and Julie's divorce four years ago, when Jack needed compassion, Chase was the comfort food. He stopped by unannounced to make sure Jack still had a pulse and wasn't retreating into the isolated world of regret. Jack hadn't seen it coming. A younger model replaced him. A wealthier model. More self-absorbed. Willing to trade family for fulfillment. Kids for comforts. Fun appealed to Julie and was the real reason she didn't want to have children. "Kids are cute, but too much work. She traded babies for the beach."

Jack and Julie were once on the same page, but now they were not on the same planet.

He was certain he wouldn't have survived without Chase and Aimee to lean on. Chase loved Aimee's optimism—and she knew the secret of raising Jack's self-esteem a few degrees just above the crushing weight of anxiety. She would invite him to dinner and dispense the proper dose of hope to lift him above the relentless cycle of doubt and the prison of despair.

"Dad, Fernando will be here any minute," Clay interjected as he walked into the kitchen.

"Okay, we'll start the grill when he gets here. Jack and I are going to get everything ready."

Grabbing four plates out of the kitchen cabinet, Jack glanced at Clay. "Hey, what's going on, Little Buddy?"

"Nothing. My friend's coming over. We're going to play basketball after lunch."

Jack smiled and crossed his arms. "Cool. You guys any good?"

"Pretty good."

"Think you could beat your dad and me?"

Clay grinned. "Yeah. We could probably beat you."

"Oh, really?"

"Yeah. You guys are old."

Jack's jaw dropped. "Old guys, huh? We were pretty good, back in the day."

"Every old guy says that. Besides, back in the day was before I was born. Even my dad said that was a lifetime ago."

"True, but the court is the same, the basket height is the same, and the game is essentially the same."

Clay laughed and pointed at Jack. "But you're not the same. Your skills aren't the same. You're old, like my dad."

Jack raised his eyebrows. "You want to make a little wager?"

Before Clay could answer, the doorbell rang. Clay ran to answer it. It was Fernando. When they entered the kitchen, Jack was placing the plates, utensils, napkins, salt and pepper, ketchup, mustard, and relish on a tray to carry to the patio table.

"Fernando, this is my dad's friend, Jack. Sometimes I call him Uncle Jack."

Jack extended his hand. "Nice to meet you, Fernando."

"I was just telling Uncle Jack we could beat him and my dad in basketball."

Fernando nodded and smiled. "Yeah, we should be able to beat two old guys."

Jack leaned back against the counter. "Like I said, you guys willing to make a little wager?"

Fernando was a handsome eight-year-old with deep brown eyes, a bright smile, and a playful nature.

Chase looked over at Fernando. "Hey, man, how you doing?"

"Good."

"You hungry?"

"I'm always hungry."

"Want to help me light the grill, Fernando?" Chase walked out to the patio and toward the grill, and his young protégé followed on his heels.

"This will be fun," Fernando said.

Chase explained the steps to light the gas grill. "Do you want to light it?"

His eyes widened. "Yeah."

"Okay, follow the steps I just showed you, and I'll put the burgers on after it warms up a bit."

Fernando lit the grill while Jack brought out the plates, cups, utensils, napkins, salt and pepper, and the condiments. Clay ran over to the small basketball court and picked up the ball.

"Fernando, let's practice before the game," Clay said.

Fernando ran to join him, and they began taking free-throw shots. While Jack set the table and Chase seasoned the burgers and placed them on the grill, David Kincaid walked around the house to the backyard.

Chase hadn't seen his father for a few weeks but was always happy to see him. "Hey, Dad."

"Hey, Chase. Hi, Jack."

"Hey, Mr. K."

David Kincaid had moved to Montecito, just a five-minute drive from Santa Barbara. It was a town for the rich and famous. If you were a star-gazer, you might find movie stars wandering the quaint city. As an accomplished architect, Chase's father had made a name for himself designing luxury homes for a clientele who, despite the multi-million-dollar price tags, could purchase them as second homes or for storage space.

"What are you up to, Dad?"

"We're starting another home here next week."

"For anyone famous?" Jack asked.

"No, just affluent." David sat on a patio chair and Jack sat across from him. "I just had another site visit with the builder and home-owner and made a few modifications to my blueprints. It's been a while, so I thought I'd swing by and see my favorite grandson."

"Your *only* grandson," Chase emphasized. "Join us for lunch? I've got plenty of burgers here," he said as they sizzled on the grill.

"I don't want to intrude."

"Dad, you're not intruding. Clay has his friend, Fernando, over, and Jack is, well, like family."

When the elder Kincaid shot a glance at Jack, he smiled and raised his eyebrows twice, accepting his christening as an adopted son, much to David's chagrin.

"Dad, all we're having is burgers, chips, some store-bought potato salad, and garden variety coleslaw, which is always hit or miss. We'll be ready in fifteen minutes."

"Yeah, *Dad*—it'll be ready in fifteen minutes," Jack said to get a rise out of him.

David's demeanor changed. "I prefer Mr. Kincaid, if you don't mind, Jack."

"Okay, cool." Jack was always taking his temperature.

Chase's father didn't like Jack. He knew it, and Jack knew it. They just didn't know why. There was an unspoken tension that had seemed to dwell just under the surface for several years. Chase suspected his father did not approve of Jack's lighthearted nature and sense of humor—too glib.

Flipping the burgers, Chase noted, once again, the awkwardness simmering between his father and his best friend. To diffuse the tension, he offered a diversion. "Jack, will you grab the potato salad and coleslaw from the fridge and bring out the hamburger buns? I have cold drinks for everyone here in the cooler." Clay was taking a jump shot when his father glanced at him. "Clay, we'll eat in a minute."

When Jack brought out the buns and other items, Chase asked

everyone to take a seat at the table. He flipped the burgers once more before placing them on a serving plate and bringing them to the table.

Among men, it always took much longer to make lunch than devour it. They enjoyed their lunch, the view, and the casual conversation. Chase noted Clay and Fernando's hearty appetite and remembered the hunger of youth—the voracious appetite of a growing boy and how nice it would be to burn calories faster at this stage of life.

Jack tested some new jokes on an eager audience of two eight-year-old boys. A couple landed, and a few brought groans. "A laugh or a groan is success," Jack boasted. "I'll take what I can get. You're an easy crowd." He beamed.

After lunch, Chase, his father, and Jack relaxed on the patio while Clay and Fernando shot baskets to warm up for the game.

"Are you ready to play now, Dad?" Clay dribbled the ball.

"Not yet, champ. Give us old guys a little time to let our lunch settle."

Fernando laughed and turned to Clay. "Hey, we got this—if they need to rest after eating a hamburger." Clay passed the ball to his friend. He took a shot and nailed it. "I hope we never get that old."

Clay shouted to his father, "Dad, are you and Grandpa going to talk about boring stuff again?"

"Yep. Lots of boring stuff, first."

Chase turned to his father and Jack and lowered his voice. "Actually, I have a few things I'd like to talk to you about—and they're not boring. In fact, I'd appreciate both of your opinions."

David leaned forward. "What's on your mind, son?"

"I'll get to the point. As you both know, since Aimee died, Clay has been struggling in school and now summer school."

Before Chase could continue, his father interrupted him.

"Sometimes these things take a while, Chase. It'll pass, just like it did with you."

"Dad, that's just it. It didn't really pass for me, at least not as fast as *you* thought it did. And now I know it won't pass for Clay. I got him some help—and that's what I want run by you two."

"What kind of help are you talking about?" Jack asked.

"Well, for starters, I've talked to his teacher, Sierra Taylor, and the school social worker, Jennifer Adams. Clay is still frequently staring out the window, searching for things in his desk, and over-reacting to other students."

"Sounds like a normal kid to me," David said.

"There's more, Dad. He's low on energy, he lays his head down on his desk often, and he even sleeps in class sometimes."

David cut him off. "Again, it all sounds normal for an eight-year-old, Chase. He seems fine now. Look at him playing with Fernando."

Fernando juked around Clay and made an easy layup and mocked Clay's defense. Clay faked left, then right, before sinking a jump shot to tie the score.

"Dad, some of these behaviors at school are not normal. His teacher and the social worker tell me he often disengages with his classmates and plays alone on the playground except for Fernando. I can tell something is wrong when he gets quiet or when he acts out at home."

Jack was tentative, but he repeated his question to allow Chase to continue. "What kind of help are you getting Clay?"

"Well, both at school and at home, we're going to get Clay to verbalize his feelings about losing his mom. The school has assembled a support team for Clay ..."

David raised a finger to stop him. "A support team?"

"Yes, a support team."

"Isn't that going overboard?"

Chase took a breath and was patient with his father. He had been here before in his own life. "I don't think so. They will invite him to join a group of other kids going through the same thing so he will feel normal again—so he doesn't feel like he is alone in this."

It didn't take long for the elder Kincaid to register his discomfort. "I'm not sure how this plan will help him. Really, Chase. Why rehash it? Clay knows what happened. I see no point in making the poor kid relive it. When your mom died, did you want me to remind you constantly of it and force you to talk about it?"

"Well, no, but ..."

Chase knew as Jack watched this drama unfold, he was likely wondering if his role was to listen—or referee. Jack caught on and created a diversion and a conduit to allow Chase to get this off his chest. "What else are you going to do for Clay?"

Chase turned from his father to Jack, realizing what his friend was doing. "The social worker talked about art therapy. Everyone in the group will draw a picture of the person they lost."

Chase's father interrupted yet again. "Chase, I'm sorry—I'm not trying to be negative. I love Clay, but I'm not convinced this is going to benefit him. This program could work, or it could drag him through the mud again. He's been through enough. You didn't have any of this stuff when you were a kid, and look at you—you turned out fine."

Chase bit his lip and raised his voice slightly. "Dad, the art therapy will encourage Clay to express himself and what he is feeling so he can feel normal again. Frankly, I wish I'd had some of this help because I buried my feelings—like you did—and I almost smothered under the weight of it. I wasn't fine. I was drowning, and I didn't have the courage to tell you I didn't know how to swim."

David stiffened. "What? You weren't drowning, son."

"Dad, you don't know how I was feeling. Like you said, you rarely asked. We barely talked, and as I grew up, you often told me, 'Time heals all wounds.' It wasn't your fault. I'm not blaming you. In fact,

I admired you. I still do." He exhaled hard. "I'm just saying I needed more help than you thought—and you were coping with your own grief. I get that."

His father's face flushed, and he looked away.

"Sounds like a brilliant plan," Jack interjected.

Chase took advantage of the moment of silence to continue. "There are some children's books dealing with death and grief that I'm going to pick up from the library. This might help Clay, too. I hope it will get us talking, and maybe he will open up to me more. The social worker also talked about a special camp for kids in crisis. It helps kids overcome grief. It's called Camp Cope, or something like that."

Jack nodded. "I like that idea."

Chase glanced over at Clay to make sure he wasn't listening. He and Fernando were engrossed in a game of horse.

"He'll be with other kids struggling with the same issue, and there will be opportunities to swim, fish, camp, do crafts, and stuff like that to help him talk about his loss and understand death is a part of life. With the other kids, he'll realize he's not alone. It could be good for him. I don't know if he will go to camp this summer, but I have an open mind."

David leaned forward in his chair and shook his head. "I want to be supportive, but I can't help thinking it is too much to put on him. Aimee died almost two years ago. He's coping with it, and now you're going to force him to confront it all over again."

Chase ignored the comment and continued. "Clay has been asking me to spend more time with him. The social worker thought it would be a good idea to do a special project together."

Jack stretched his legs. "What kind of project?"

"Not sure. Jennifer just thought it would give us more focused time together and it would give him more opportunities to verbalize his feelings to me. I love the idea of doing something special together. That's why I wanted to talk to both of you. Any ideas?"

David looked away, still resisting the suggested grief plan Chase described.

Jack thought for a moment, then posed a question. "When you lost your mom as a kid, what did you do when you were sad?"

"I don't know. I guess I tried to escape."

"Why?" Jack probed.

"To run from my situation—forget about the pain."

David now leaned back in his chair and listened intently.

Jack continued, "Where did you escape to?"

Scratching the back of his head, Chase thought for a moment. "I escaped to my fort. What did you do as a kid when you were sad?" Chase asked Jack.

Jack smiled. "Me? I did what most kids did. I usually ate something. Candy bar. Cookie. Chips. Coke. Didn't matter. Snacks are excellent medicine. Sorry, I'm not much help."

"Any ideas, Dad?"

Deep in thought, David looked at his hands and gently rubbed them together before he spoke. "I remember the forts you used to build in the backyard. You would take my extension pole for painting and tie it to the back of two lawn chairs. Then you would throw a blanket over the pole and stretch out the sides to pitch a tent before weighting the edges with bricks, toys from the sandbox, or my half-empty paint cans. You loved it."

Chase noticed his father softened at the memory.

He whispered, "I remember, Dad. I felt safe there. Not sure why, but I needed my space. But what can Clay and I do together?"

Jack looked around the backyard, beyond the patio, basketball hoop, oak tree, and fire pit to the ocean. He broke the silence with a laugh. "I've got it."

"What are you thinking, Jack?" Chase cocked his head and waited for Jack's big idea.

"Look toward the ocean," Jack said.

They glanced at the far end of the yard.

Chase was perplexed. "Yeah, so?"

"What do you see?"

"The ocean?"

"Before that?"

"Basketball court?"

"What else?" Jack stood and waited in anticipation.

"Firepit?"

"You're getting warmer—no pun intended."

"The oak tree my grandfather planted?"

Jack beamed. "It's perfect."

"What are you talking about, Jack?" David stood to see what he might be missing. Chase now stood next to them.

Suddenly, the light went on. Chase and Jack turned to each other and shouted in unison, "A treehouse!"

After a moment, Chase sat and leaned back in his chair and laced his fingers behind his head. Jack and David sat and swiveled toward Chase.

"We can all do it together," Chase said. "The three of us, plus Clay and Fernando. And it'll be good for their friendship. Besides, look at what we have right here—an engineer, an architect and ..." He stopped short.

Jack finished his sentence. "And ... a writer."

They all laughed together.

"Two out of three ain't bad," David added.

When Clay and Fernando heard them laughing, they interjected. "You old guys ready for a game?"

Jack nodded and turned to Chase. "You ready to show the lads how it's done?"

Chase glanced at the kids. "You're going down, son."

Clay and Fernando simply laughed at their weak attempt to talk trash.

"Bring it on," Clay said.

"Yeah," Fernando chimed in, "let's see if you guys got game—any game."

CHAPTER 14

Working in his home had its advantages.

No commute. That meant Chase started faster and was a more productive writer. By midweek, Chase had written three destination brochures for the Santa Barbara Visitor Center promoting the area, finished an executive speech for one of his business clients, and completed a rough draft of a corporate capabilities piece for the architectural firm that employed his father.

Ed was phoning him again. Chase had let several calls go to voicemail, so he felt obligated to take this call.

"Hello, Ed."

"Hey, Chase. I read the first three chapters of your sequel."

Chase held his breath, knowing this was the "love it or loathe it" moment between authors and agents. "And?"

"Not your best work. What's going on?"

It was a "loathe it" moment, so, embarrassed, Chase bought time. "What do you mean?"

"The writing is flat—dull—pedestrian. Are you okay?"

"I don't know what you're talking about."

Ed cleared his throat and took on a more professional tone. "Chase." He paused, as though for effect. "You've lost your voice. The writing is stale, unimaginative. You don't sound like the bestselling author who wrote *The Bridge Between Us*."

Ed was right, and Chase knew it. The work was flat, and he had lost his passion. While he could admit it to himself, he struggled when Ed called him out on it. If he were honest with himself, he'd known it before he emailed the draft. He wasn't sure why he thought he could get away with it—and Ed knew why he was off his game. Chase respected him for not bringing it up.

"I can't present this, Chase. Should I be worried about you?"

Chase rolled his eyes. "No. You're overreacting."

Ed let the air clear, likely hoping Chase would listen to him. "You'll have to rewrite it."

"I can't rewrite it."

"Then this will be tough to shop with major publishers—unless you're now satisfied with just any publisher. Is that where you want to go with your career? We want to raise the standard, not lower it. Don't compromise your talent, Chase."

"Then don't shop it."

"What?"

"Don't shop it."

"Do you want me to represent you?"

"Yes, definitely, but I don't want you to represent *this* work." Chase stood and walked around his home office, hoping to generate more energy to speak with greater conviction. He did not want to alienate Ed, but he wanted to make his point. He softened his tone to negotiate a compromise. "Ed, I understand what you're saying, and I definitely want you to represent me, but would you consider representing my alternative idea for a standalone book first? I'll write the sequel to *The Bridge Between Us* second. Is that fair?"

Ed listened and spoke plainly. "I think you're going to compromise your young career, and we're going to lose momentum."

"I understand the risks. Just let me send you an elevator pitch for something I'm passionate about."

"I don't have a good feeling about this, Chase. I'll think about it, but in the meantime, rework the first three chapters to the sequel."

"Done."

"And one more thing, Chase."

"What's that?"

"When you rewrite the first three chapters of the sequel, write it like Chase Kincaid would write it."

Chase sighed. "Fair enough."

When Chase hung up the phone, he stared out his window overlooking the patio, the large oak tree, and the ocean. He replayed the conversation in his mind. Deep down, he knew where Ed was coming from. A sequel combined continuity and momentum to ignite his platform and fuel his young career. Besides, his alternative idea was still half-baked, and his inspiration had died when Aimee did.

He furrowed his brow. On one hand, he felt he must write what tugged at his heart. On the other, he had to write for commercial success. *The key is to find a balance between artistic expression and commercial success.*

The trick was to balance his point of view with Ed's. He knew from working in the advertising business that good marketing was as important as good writing, so he vowed to himself that he would rework the first three chapters of the sequel. *In a perfect world, Ed will be able to sell my standalone novel first and have the sequel in his back pocket—rather than the other way around. Not realistic, but I can hope.*

~

Late that afternoon, after summer school had concluded for the day, Chase had an appointment with Sierra, Jennifer Adams, and the school support team to discuss the launch of Clay's plan. The efficiency with which Jennifer conducted the meeting and the commitment expressed by the principal and team members as they completed the program timing, implementation, and follow-up impressed him.

When the meeting concluded, he felt he had Clay on a positive track.

In the corridor after the meeting, Jennifer pulled him aside. "I was wondering if you've considered my recommendation about seeking grief counseling."

The gentleness of her tone and the compassion in her eyes moved him.

"If you're interested," she said, "I think you could benefit by talking with an associate of mine." She opened a file she had tucked into her portfolio and handed him a business card. She didn't push it but recommended an initial consultation. "His name is Dr. Mark McAllister. He's a smart guy. I think you'll like him. He's very casual. It'll be like talking to a friend."

In the deep recesses of his heart, Chase knew he needed someone to talk to, but he wasn't completely comfortable with the notion of a counselor yet. *Just what would I say to this guy? And how can he possibly understand how I feel—if I don't? Besides, despite this guy's credentials, if he's never been through this himself, how much help can he be?* Right now, Chase had his own ideas of who he would like to talk to most. Someone who could see inside his soul.

Sierra was already back in her classroom. She sat at her desk, correcting papers. Clay was at Fernando's house for the afternoon and dinner. Approaching the doorway, he knocked on the frame. She looked up and smiled. He felt it warm him.

"Hey," he said.

"Hey. Can I help?"

"Yeah, I think so."

She put her pen down and motioned to her guest chair. "What's up?"

"I wanted to talk to you about something. Something Jennifer Adams suggested I do."

"Okay."

"Are you done for the day?"

"Essentially. Why?"

"I was wondering if we could talk"—he looked around the room—"somewhere else?"

"What were you thinking?"

"Can I buy you a cup of coffee? I know a quaint little place directly across the street from the wharf. It's new. It's called Zoe's. Nice place to talk. And there's a walking path across the street along the ocean in case we ..." He stopped himself.

"Go on."

"In case we ... have time for a walk later."

"Coffee and a walk at the end of a day sounds nice," she said. "Let me pack up a few papers to bring home. Meet you there?"

He nodded and returned a smile.

~

After Sierra parked and walked to Zoe's, she found Chase sitting at a table on the deck under a blue umbrella. The deck carried the fragrance of freshly cut wood. The wicker furniture featured comfortable pads. Plants and bright floral arrangements added a splash of color, a sweet scent, and a cozy atmosphere.

Sierra looked over at the seating area on the deck. "I love the ambiance. This is really nice." She said this in her usual upbeat tone.

Chase stood and motioned to his chair. She turned to face the ocean and sat as he pushed in the chair for her. "Thank you," she said, impressed by the gesture.

"You're welcome. Now you can enjoy the view. What can I get you?"

"How about a tall iced white chocolate mocha?"

"Be right back."

His timing was good. No one was in line, but customers were coming through the front door. Chase placed his order and grabbed a few napkins before waiting at the end of the coffee bar. When he returned, he handed Sierra her drink and sat across from her. They took a sip before he spoke. "Thanks for meeting with me."

"My pleasure." She glanced at the surroundings. "Beautiful location. I like it here."

"Yeah. Me too. It relaxes me—which is what a coffee shop should do, right?"

"And throw in an ocean view."

"If you're not careful, the sound of the waves will put you to sleep after a long day."

She nodded. "Is everything okay with Clay?"

"Yep, he's fine. I just wanted to get your opinion on something else."

"Okay." She took another sip of her white mocha to give him a chance to collect his thoughts.

When a cool breeze off the ocean blew through her hair, he leaned forward and placed both hands around his cup. "First, thanks for recommending that I talk to Jennifer Adams about Clay's situation. She's outstanding, and you were right, she's compassionate. I think she connects with Clay and clearly wants to help us."

"Jennifer loves kids."

"It's obvious. I like the plan your team pulled together for Clay. He's in excellent hands, and I'm pumped about you launching it next week. Now that I have all the details, I'll explain it to him soon."

"I think it will make a big difference. He's such a sweet boy."

"He is. I appreciate you saying that. Jennifer approached me with another suggestion."

"Oh?" As another couple stepped out on the patio, Sierra heard the screech of a coffee grinder in the background.

"Well," he stalled.

"Another suggestion for Clay?" she asked.

"No. Not Clay—me. That's why I wanted to run it by you and get some feedback."

She raised her eyebrows and took another sip of her coffee. "Interesting. Go on."

"She thinks I could benefit from talking to a grief counselor."

"Really?"

"Yeah. I wanted a second opinion. She's your friend and colleague, and since you're helping Clay with the same issue, I thought it would be good to get your thoughts."

"You and Clay are sort of a package deal?" She smiled, leaned back in her chair, and crossed her legs. "You're wondering if I think you should talk to a grief counselor?"

"Yes."

She paused for a moment. "I guess it depends."

"On what?"

"On whether you think you're still grieving. You said you lost your wife, what, almost two years ago?"

"Yeah. It'll be two years next week—July twenty-ninth."

Sierra looked directly into Chase's eyes—and he had nowhere to run. "Do you think you're still grieving, Chase?"

He took another sip of his coffee and cleared his throat. "I don't know. What I mean to say is, I don't fully understand grief. I still feel the loss, if that's what you mean. I miss Aimee terribly. But I know I need to move on. If not for me, for Clay."

Sierra pulled her chair closer to the table. "May I ask you a few questions?"

"Sure, that's why I'm asking your opinion."

She leaned in. "My questions may seem personal."

He took another sip of his coffee. "Go for it."

Two teens stepped out onto the patio, giggling after getting a sugary iced coffee drink.

"How often do you think about Aimee?"

"Every day. Not a day goes by …"

She smiled a half smile and shifted in her chair. "Have you dated much since you lost her?"

"I tried dating after the first year."

"And?"

"Disaster."

"Why?"

"I wasn't ready. I compared everyone to Aimee. They never had a chance. No one measured up. Jack thought I should at least try dating—it might help me move on, he said."

"Jack?" She took a moment to sip her mocha.

He clarified the relationship. "He's my best friend. He's helped me through this. I was there for him during his ugly divorce a few years ago. He's been there for me now."

"You said it's been almost two years. Any inclination to date now?" She looked for a way to make the question sound more casual than personal.

He hesitated for a few seconds before answering. "Yes, some, if—if the right person came along. Why do you ask?"

He had just put her on the spot.

She took a slow sip of her coffee. His question hung in the air for what seemed like a minute before she answered.

Sierra glanced at the ocean across the street to avoid direct eye contact. "I'm no counselor. I guess I was trying to gauge if you are mentally moving on with your life, or if you're still paralyzed by grief."

"I don't fully understand grief. Jennifer thinks I could still be grieving."

"Did she say why she thinks you're still grieving?"

Chase chewed the inside of his lip. "She didn't really say I was grieving—exactly?"

She removed the lid from her coffee and traced the rim of her cup with her forefinger. "Then what did she say—exactly?"

A middle-aged man with thinning red hair stepped onto the patio, sat across from them, and opened his laptop. She hoped he would pop in a pair of earbuds.

"Jennifer said she was concerned that I'm caught in the fog of grief. That means ..."

She softly interrupted. "I know what it means."

"Anyway, she felt it would be good for me to *share* my feelings and *verbalize* to others how I feel." He made air quotes with his fingers.

The man with the laptop popped in earbuds after sipping his coffee.

"Share your feelings? Verbalize?" she echoed.

"Yeah. Her words."

She smiled. "Yep. It's how we talk in our profession. Jennifer's right, but sharing your feelings or verbalizing your thoughts is not something dudes do, is it?" she asked with a wink.

"Ya think?" A breeze and the smell of salt washed over them. "Do you have time for a walk?"

"Sure."

"Let's take the path across the street along the ocean."

"I have a better idea," she said. "Let's walk on the beach."

~

When they reached the shore, Sierra stooped and slipped off her sandals.

"You really meant a walk along the beach," he said.

"It's not a walk on the beach if you don't get your feet wet. Like so many things in life, to enjoy an experience, jump in with both feet." She paused, reached in her purse, grabbed a hair band, and pulled her hair back in a tight ponytail as he slipped off his sandals.

"Okay, now we're ready for a *walk* on the beach," she said.

"Let's do it."

She glanced at him as they strolled. "Where did we leave off?"

"I was saying Jennifer implied that by sharing my feelings—or *verbalizing* them—I stand the best chance of finding my way out of the fog of grief. She also recommended I consider talking to a grief counselor, Dr. Mark somebody. What is your opinion of her suggestion?"

She hesitated, considering his question. "I'd say don't put the cart before the horse."

"What do you mean?"

"I mean, you don't need a grief counselor if you're not grieving."

"True, but I think Jennifer thinks I'm still grieving."

Sierra stopped, turned to him. "What matters most is what you think. Just be honest with yourself."

"Do you think I'm not being honest with myself?"

"I'm not close enough to you—or the situation—to know. But what I know is, two years is not necessarily a long time to grieve, and you seem confused—which is normal after such a tragic loss."

"You think I'm confused?"

She listened to the waves breaking at the shore before answering. "I think grief can confuse us."

"How do you mean?"

"Well, sometimes we just go through the motions when we're grieving. We run on autopilot, so we conclude we must be over it because … we're still functioning. Yet we're only functioning at fifty percent. Grief can affect our ability to think clearly."

Chase stopped and looked out over the ocean.

She waited for his reaction.

"I'm not functioning at one hundred percent, that's for sure. And I'm definitely struggling to write my second novel—or at least, to write it well. Truthfully, I'm confused about what I should write at all, and my agent knows it."

She processed his comment as they walked. "It's just my opinion, but I believe we grieve the most when we're in private—completely alone. When we're with other people, we can act like we're not grieving—and by deceiving others, we deceive ourselves."

"Yes, but ..."

She cut him off. "Chase, if you're unhappy when you're alone, then I think you're still in the grieving process. If you can admit that, you have the best chance to open up and honestly share your feelings with others, including a grief counselor. Does that make sense?"

"It does."

A gull squawked as it flew overhead.

"How do you feel when you're alone?"

Chase stopped again. "I'm not sure how to answer that question."

She didn't challenge him. Instead, she offered him a safe zone by gently touching his arm. "Chase, I'm a safe place." It was all she said. It was all she had to say to start the painful process of lifting the fog that had engulfed his life.

"Sierra, if I'm honest, I'm afraid," he whispered. "Sometimes when I'm alone, I feel the grip of fear. I feel isolated. Deserted. Left behind."

As they continued to stroll, she touched his arm again. It was enough to fuel his courage to open up.

"What do you fear most?" she asked.

"I fear all the 'empties' in my life."

She looked at him. "Empties?"

Glancing at the beach before him, he let his words fall into the sand. "The empty house, the empty bed, the empty chair at the kitchen table, the empty passenger seat in the car. Then there's mail with her name on it, the silence in a vacant living room where our conversations and laughter once lived. I fear a closet full of memories, her favorite shoes—and where she left them by the back door. They're still there." When he took a breath, their eyes met. "How's that for *verbalizing*?"

"It's a start." She stifled a tear. "You're still grieving. Admit it to yourself—and share it with others, like you just did with me. Don't fight it or deny it. Release it. Set it free."

"I'm a dude. I'm not sure how to do that."

She held his arm longer this time. "Start by giving yourself permission to grieve."

He smiled. "I'm afraid I've duplicated my father's mistakes."

They walked for a moment in silence and listened to the waves whisper over the sand.

"Well, there are at least two things you don't need to be afraid of, Chase."

"What's that?"

"Don't be afraid to see the grief counselor—Dr. Mark McAllister— to figure this out. He makes sense of life when life makes little sense."

"And the second thing?"

"Don't be afraid to cry, to have a good—long—cry."

He nodded. "I did that once—right after Aimee died."

She paused and smirked. "Really? Once?" Her eyes widened. "Tell me something. What on earth makes you think once is enough?"

CHAPTER 15

Later that evening, Chase had dinner alone on the patio as he waited for Clay to return from Fernando's home.

While he waited, he strummed a few chords on his guitar, tightened a few strings, and played. Softly at first, until he found his rhythm, then with greater confidence.

An accomplished guitar player, he once dreamed of being a singer/songwriter. While he could write songs, the challenge was giving voice to them. He was not quite a lead vocalist, and he knew it. As he strummed, he remembered when he was discouraged, his father once said, "Son, you'll find your voice, if not in music, then in literature. You have something to say. You'll find a way to say it."

Settling back into his chair, he swiveled from side to side, finding comfort in the memory. It was moments like this that he felt the most like himself. Aimee used to love hearing him strum his guitar and play a familiar tune. She would sing along from another room.

When the kitchen light went on, he knew Clay was home. Grabbing his guitar and his dinner plate, he went inside. After greeting Clay and fending off his request to play video games, he set him on his course. Clay whined for a few minutes before he began his usual routine—finishing homework, taking a shower, and getting ready for bed. When he hopped in the shower, Chase recommitted himself to *his* routine—reviewing his homework, noting errors, and later discussing them with Clay—before their other ritual.

After Clay put on his pajamas, he shuffled out of his bedroom with a towel and continued to dry his hair. "What kind of ice cream do we have?" He finished wiping his face and ears with the towel.

Chase was sitting at the kitchen table and answered without looking up. "Salted caramel, orange sherbet, and cookies and cream."

"I'll have cookies and cream. What are you going to have?"

"Orange sherbet."

"The usual. It figures, Dad."

"We're creatures of habit, Clay. Speaking of habits, let's review some of your homework and study habits. I found a few punctuation errors you need to correct on your English paper."

"Okay, can we have the ice cream first?"

"Don't you think we should do our work first and have dessert second?"

"I do my best work on a full stomach, Dad."

A smile curved into a smirk on Chase's face. "You're getting a little too clever for a third-grader. Okay, let's have the ice cream first. There's something else I want to talk to you about, anyway."

"Are we going to talk about fun stuff?"

"Some of it's fun stuff. The other part is school stuff."

Chase walked to the fridge, opened the door, and pulled out their treats. Scooping them into two bowls, he brought them to the kitchen table, where Clay waited for him.

"Here you go, buddy." Chase sat alongside him, and they savored their treats together. "Before I go over your homework with you, I wanted to talk to you about ... well, let's call it a special program. It starts for you at school next week."

"What kind of program?" Clay took a spoonful of his ice cream.

"Well, it's a program to help you do a better job in school. It'll help get your grades up." Chase took a breath. "And it will help you not be so sad about Mom."

Clay licked his spoon. "How will it do that?"

"You'll be in a special group—with other kids who have lost a parent, so you don't feel so alone."

Clay was kneeling on his chair, then turned to sit up straight.

Chase ate a spoonful of his sherbet. "What about Fernando?" Clay asked. "Will he be in the group so he doesn't feel so alone?"

"I don't know. His mom will have to look into that. You'll also be in an art class where you can draw pictures about how you feel. Then we can talk about it. There's also a summer camp you can go to if we have time this summer. It's called Camp Cope."

"What will I do there?"

"Fun stuff."

"Like what?"

"Like swimming, hiking, crafts, and games." Chase slipped his arm around Clay's shoulders and pulled him closer. "And I'm going to do a better job of helping you with your homework every night."

"Every night?"

"Yeah, every night."

"You've never helped me every night."

"I know. Even dads don't do a good job sometimes. I'm going to get better."

"You're still a great dad," Clay assured him. "You still always get me ice cream."

"Thanks, buddy. Do you have questions about this program I explained to you?"

"No."

"You ready to go over your homework? Then I want to talk to you about something else."

Chase spent the next half hour reviewing Clay's homework with him, explained his punctuation errors, and showed him proper English usage. When he had finished, Clay brushed his teeth and climbed into bed. Chase tucked him in and lay beside him to talk after they had prayed together.

As he lay atop the covers on his son's bed, Clay asked him a familiar question.

"I still don't understand why mom had to die. Why did she?"

"I don't know." Chase paused and swallowed hard. "Maybe God needed her more than we did."

Clay scratched his head, considering his father's suggestion. "How old is God?"

"How old? I don't know. Why?"

"Well, if He's younger than eight years old, maybe He needed her more than me. If He's older than eight, then I needed her more than Him."

Clay's comment took Chase's breath away, like a gut punch. He scratched the back of his neck to collect his thoughts. "I think we're just going to trust him on this one, buddy."

"How can I trust him? Why should I?"

"Because you trust me when you don't always understand why I do something, right?"

"I guess." He furrowed his brow. "Will we ever get used to Mom being gone? Because I'm not used to it yet."

"I'm not sure," Chase answered from his heart without thinking and suddenly wished he could take it back.

"Fernando says he doesn't think he will ever get used to his dad being gone."

Chase pulled the covers up to Clay's chin. "What happened to Fernando's dad?"

"Nothing. He just left. Fernando doesn't know why. He said it might be because he broke a window at home playing baseball."

"He broke a window? I don't think his father would leave for that."

"Well, he left right after it happened. Fernando says he must not love him anymore because the window cost a lot of money."

Chase lifted Clay's chin to make eye contact. "He left then, but I don't think it was because Fernando broke a window."

"Then why?"

"I don't know. It's complicated."

Clay squirmed under his sheets and fluffed his pillow behind his head. "Why is everything complicated for adults? It's just a window."

"I'm sure there's a different reason."

"Would you ever leave me?"

Chase's eyes widened, and he exhaled hard. "No. Why would you ever think that?"

"Because I almost broke a window once."

Chase sat up straight. "Clay, I can replace a window. I can't replace you. You're my life, Little Buddy. I don't want you to worry about me leaving you—ever. Am I clear?"

"Yeah. But what if something happens to you? What would I do? Where would I go? We don't visit Grandma Joyce as much anymore."

Chase nodded. "I know. That's more my fault than hers. We can fix that. I just need some time. But don't worry about something happening to me, all right? I'll have a plan to take care of you."

"Will you tell me the plan so I'm not scared?"

Clay triggered Chase's memory of just how afraid he'd felt when he lost his mom.

"Absolutely," Chase said. "For now, I just want you to stop thinking about this. Everything is going to be fine."

"Okay. Maybe I'll dream about Mom again tonight."

Chase relaxed and lay beside him again. "Do you dream about her a lot?"

"Yeah."

"Are they happy dreams?"

"Yeah. She teases you a lot—but she's always trying to find her way home."

Chase scratched his cheek. "From where?"

"I don't know. But she's lost."

Chase raised his brow. "Do these dreams frighten you?"

"No."

"Do you remember them when you wake up?" Chase hoped his son's dreams faded away at dawn.

"Most of the time I remember them."

"But you don't think about them at school, right?" Chase wasn't sure if he was trying to convince Clay or himself.

Clay brought his blanket to his lips. "I think about them more at school."

Chase squinted and asked, "Why do you do that?"

"So I can figure them out. I don't want Mom to feel lost. Besides, if I figure it out and dream about her again, I can tell her how to find her way back to us."

Chase now knew dreams were at least one distraction affecting Clay at school.

"We can talk about this more later. You need to get some sleep." Chase sat on the edge of the bed.

Clay turned onto his side to face his father. "Dad, you said there was something else you wanted to talk about. Something fun."

"Oh, yeah. Do you remember when you said you wanted to be together more? I have an idea how to do that."

"How?"

"When I was a boy—and was missing my mom—I built a fort. Somehow it made me feel better. Safe. It was mine, and it made me happy again."

Clay now sat up in his bed. His eyes widened. "Are we going to build a fort?"

"Yep. But not just any fort."

"What are we going to build?"

"A treehouse."

Clay squealed. "A treehouse? Cool! Can Fernando help?"

"Of course. And guess what? Grandpa and Jack are going to help too. Because Grandpa is an architect, so he knows how to design houses, and Jack is an engineer, so he knows how to build what Grandpa designs."

Clay laughed. "And you're a writer—so you won't be much help."

"Thanks, pal. That's what they said."

"When can we start?"

"Next week. Grandpa is going to draw up plans, Jack is going to take some measurements and spec materials, and I'm going to gather tools and order lumber and supplies. How does that sound?"

Clay threw his arms around his father's neck and squeezed. Chase waited for a verbal response. Clay didn't say a thing.

He just didn't let go.

～

Chase turned out the light, closed Clay's bedroom door, and walked to his den. Reaching for his journal on the bookcase once again, he opened the leatherbound book and picked up a pen.

～

After almost two years of searching, I think I found my son tonight. He was with my twelve-year-old self.

I found them both in the same place: a treehouse.

CHAPTER 16

When Saturday rolled around, Chase and Clay met with his father and Jack at Zoe's to plan the treehouse and compile an inventory checklist of tools. After ordering their coffee, they sat on the patio overlooking the ocean alongside the table where he had met with Sierra. The memory of being with her warmed him.

Clay enjoyed a juice pack and a snack while they discussed their approach to the project.

"I inspected the tree this morning," Chase said. "There are several dead branches we need to clear before we can build the platform."

His father took a sip of his coffee and opened his portfolio. "I have some sketches here. Before we look at designs, how high off the ground do you want the platform?"

"Eight feet, maybe ten."

"Do you want the platform to go all the way around the tree?" Jack asked.

"No. I want it to face the house so I can keep my eye on him from my den when I'm writing. Dad, what do you have for designs?"

"I've got a couple of ideas, depending on if you want just a basic design with a railing surrounding the platform or a clubhouse set back on the platform."

Clay stood and chimed in. "We need a clubhouse, Grandpa. So we can play in the treehouse even if it rains."

Jack smiled. "Doesn't rain much in Santa Barbara, sport. But I agree. I think you need a clubhouse."

Chase rubbed his hands together and glanced at Jack. "Great idea. I just need to see Clay from my den when I'm working." He turned to

Clay. "I like to know where you are when you're playing outside, especially if there are neighborhood kids in the treehouse."

David raised his cup but before taking a sip. "If we build the clubhouse, we can add large windows, if you wish. That will address your concerns about visibility. It's more complicated, but we can make it happen. Let me show you some rough drawings now and we can revise as needed."

The elder Kincaid shuffled through papers in his portfolio and laid out his sketches on the table before them. They huddled around the table and reviewed the plans for thirty minutes, discussing the complexities and potential costs.

"I made a partial list of tools we might need," Chase said. "I have many of them, but we'll need a jigsaw, a circular saw, and I'm sure we'll have to rent a fencepost auger to set and level the support posts."

"I have a circular saw and jigsaw." David added them to his list of tools to bring.

"We'll also need three-foot levels, a speed square, and a chalk line, and I've got those," Jack added. "To adjoin the joists to the railings, we'll need special brackets. I can find those online or at a hardware store."

David raised a design and held it to his chest so all could see. "This design has a clubhouse, windows, and a rope ladder facing the house."

Clay interrupted, "I love a rope ladder."

David continued, "And it has a slide on the ocean side."

"Cool. I want a slide too."

His grandfather pulled him close. "You sound like an excited homeowner. Anything else you want?"

Clay wore a mischievous look. "A bathroom?"

"Okay, that's enough. I think we're done here." David smiled.

"This one is my favorite." Clay pointed to the design his grandfather had held.

"Why am I not surprised?"

Jack clapped his hands. "We have a winner, Mr. K."

Clay threw his arms around his grandfather's neck and buried his head in his shoulder.

The trio continued to discuss the treehouse design, and Chase got up, entered the coffee shop, and ordered another cup. Walking back out to the patio, he stopped for a moment and let the scene before him play out.

Clay hadn't been this happy since his mother was alive. Chase's father, son, and best friend were now laughing together, enjoying the spoils of victory. It wasn't lost on him that the building process had already begun—and they were constructing more than a treehouse. In their own way, they were helping him rebuild his life.

CHAPTER 17

It had been a good weekend. On Saturday, the treehouse design plan was Clay-approved, David removed dead branches with a chainsaw to install the base platform, Jack took critical measurements and ordered specialty brackets and heavy-duty platform attachment bolts, and Chase purchased lumber, nails, screws, and concrete mix and rented a fencepost auger to drill fencepost holes for the platform support beams.

After church on Sunday, and together with Clay and Fernando, they installed the treehouse platform attachment bolts and set the four-by-four vertical support beams in concrete. Later that week, after the concrete had cured, they would secure the horizontal beams running from the tree to the vertical supports and install the two-by-twelve-inch floor joists to bear the weight of the decking. If all went according to plan, over the next week they would lay the deck to complete the platform. Once secured, they would install portions of the railing before constructing the clubhouse, the slide on the ocean side of the platform, and the rope ladder on the opposite end, facing the house and Chase's office windows.

Early Monday morning, Chase reminded Clay that his special program would begin at school today.

"Do I have to go?" Clay's tone shifted from a question to concern.

"Yes, you have to go. But remember, you'll meet kids who have been through what you've been through. And the program will include art projects, and I'll be getting some books from the library that will help us learn how to talk about how we feel when we both have bad days or bad dreams, okay? You'll be fine."

"Can Fernando come?"

"I think you'll be okay without Fernando."

"I know, but Fernando might not be fine without me."

Chase wondered if Clay was spending so much time with Fernando not because he needed it, but because his young friend did.

He dropped to one knee and hugged his son. "I love the way you look out for your best buddy."

"He looks out for me too, Dad. Like Uncle Jack looks out for you."

Clay's comment caught his father by surprise. The simple truth of it moved him.

"That's right," he said. "Friendship is a gift, isn't it?"

"It's like an invisible gift, Dad."

"How's that?"

"You can't see friendship, but you can feel it."

"You're right, buddy. You often feel it more than you see it. Now, let's get you to school before we're late."

After Chase dropped off Clay at school and before he started writing his novel and working on corporate projects for his clients in LA, he knew there was something he must do.

Make the call to Dr. Mark McAllister, the grief counselor.

Funny how I sell words for a living, and I'm at a loss for what to say to the doc. Just make the appointment with his secretary. You won't have to talk with him for weeks. Plenty of time to figure out what to say.

After he dialed the number, the phone only rang twice before a male voice that sounded kind and efficient answered it. Chase relaxed a bit.

"Ah, yes, I'm calling to make an appointment with Dr. McAllister."

"Very good, and this is?"

"Chase Kincaid. You come highly recommended by—"

"Jennifer Adams," he replied before Chase could finish his sentence.

"How did you … ?"

"I'm Dr. McAllister. Jennifer is a friend of mine. She told me you might reach out. Please call me Mark."

His quiet nature appealed to Chase, and it calmed him. *It will be like talking to a friend,* Sierra had told him.

"Dr. McAllister, I didn't think you would pick up the phone."

"Well, I'm in early today before our receptionist. Would you like to schedule an appointment?"

"Yes, but there's no hurry, since I know you're busy. Any time in the next few weeks would be fine."

"Let me check my schedule."

Chase paced his office while he waited.

"How about after lunch today? Will that work?"

Chase was stunned. He had banked on having a week to figure out how to talk to a grief counselor. "Ah, sure, ah, that will work."

"I had a cancellation called in late Friday. I can plug you in."

"Well, thanks. Better sooner than later," he said, startled by his sudden about-face.

"Do you have my office address?" Dr. McAllister asked.

"I have your card, and I'm familiar with the area."

"Good. Then I'll see you at, say, one fifteen today?"

"Perfect. Ah …"

"Questions?"

"No, well, just one. How do I prepare for this meeting, session, whatever you call it?"

"No prep. Just bring yourself. Your past will answer all my questions. And let's not call it a session. Let's just call it an appointment."

Chase blinked a few times. He was already getting comfortable with this guy. Yet he thought about the remark that his past would answer all of Dr. McAllister's questions. While he knew it was true, it sounded ominous.

"Okay then, I'll see you at one fifteen."

"Until then."

When he hung up, he felt like things were happening too fast. Yet Dr. McAllister made him feel calm. *And isn't that what you want from a grief counselor?*

Chase spent the morning completing copy for a new apparel catalog before drafting an elevator pitch for his standalone novel. He hoped it would help him convince Ed to follow his direction and abandon the idea of a sequel to *The Bridge Between Us.*

Before driving to see Dr. McAllister, he warmed up leftover lasagna in the microwave for lunch and thought about what he was about to do. Maybe this was why his father handled his feelings alone. It was so much easier to bury your feelings than to reveal them.

When he pulled up in front of Dr. McAllister's office, he was still having second thoughts.

Am I embarking on the road to recovery—or spinning my wheels down a dead-end road?

CHAPTER 18

C hase had taken just a few steps inside Dr. McAllister's office before being greeted by the receptionist halfway across the room. She was an attractive woman with auburn hair that cascaded across her shoulders. Fashionably dressed, she appeared to be about his age. When he reached her desk, he identified himself.

"Hi, I'm Chase Kincaid. I have a one fifteen appointment with Dr. McAllister."

"Welcome, Mr. Kincaid. Please have a seat. He just got back from lunch, and he's expecting you. Give him just a minute, and he'll be right with you."

She smiled, and he noticed her beautiful green eyes. He glanced at her nametag.

"Thank you, Melissa." Somehow it felt comfortable calling her by name. *There's always something soothing about the familiar.*

Sitting at the far end of the room, he glanced across the office at the photos on the wall, presumably of the three doctors who practiced at the clinic. As he looked around the room, he shot glances at the other patients, studying their body language for telltale signs of fractured lives—like his. Most appeared normal. One woman stared at the floor and tapped her heel. She vibrated like a tuning fork. A young man in his mid-twenties sat across from her and flipped through a magazine like a speed reader. The magazine was a prop— he was bored, or it was a vain attempt to mask his preoccupation. An elderly woman sat with her Chihuahua, pulling it close to her chest and petting it lovingly, occasionally kissing the top of its head, and muttering under her breath.

Chase wondered what they could observe about him. Certainly, he telegraphed signs that all was not right in his world. A smirk crossed his face.

We're all open books. Even if we don't know what people are going through, they're easy to read.

Chase wasn't happy being there, but he acknowledged the office was cozy. The wall across from him was Cream City brick. The furniture, although modern, was attractive and comfortable, and the wall hangings of serene landscapes warmed the room. Melissa walked over and brewed a fresh pot of coffee despite the hour.

Open windows on both ends of the suite allowed a cool Santa Barbara breeze to waft through the office. Chase noticed how it calmed him. His grandfather used to say, "I feel closest to God when I'm outdoors." The gentle breeze let the outdoors in, so he relaxed and settled in his chair before leaning forward to grab a magazine from the coffee table beside him.

As he flipped through the pages, he heard his name. "Chase Kincaid?" Near the receptionist's desk stood a handsome, well-dressed middle-aged man with dark hair and a mustache. No white coat. He scanned the room.

Chase approached him without a word. The man smiled, turned, and led the way to another room. Chase followed silently. When they arrived at the doorway, he stopped short and gestured for Chase to enter first.

Upon entering the room, to break the ice, Chase said, "Dr. Livingstone, I presume?"

Dr. McAllister chuckled. "Not quite. I'm sorry, I should've introduced myself at the receptionist's desk. I'm Dr. Mark McAllister. How are you, Mr. Kincaid?"

"I'm good, I think. I guess we'll see if you agree with me after we finish today."

"Great. Why don't you have a seat, and we can chat."

Chase shot a glance around the room and took a seat in a brown Naugahyde leather chair next to a matching couch. *No way am I lying on that couch.*

"Can I get you a cup of coffee? Or something to drink? Water?"

"No, I'm fine."

"Okay. I've heard a lot about you." Dr. McAllister took a seat across from him and opened his tablet. "Jennifer Adams is a good friend of mine, and she referred you."

"That's right. She thought we should meet and maybe you could help me, if I need help?"

Looking at his tablet, Dr. McAllister crossed one leg over another. "Well, look, why don't you recap for me what brings you here, and I'll see how I can help. I am fairly casual, so if you wish, you can call me Mark, Doc, or Dr. McAllister. Whatever you're most comfortable with."

Chase smiled. "Thanks. I like that because I'm just a regular guy."

"Good. May I call you Chase?"

"Please do."

"Jennifer tells me you have an eight-year-old son."

"Yes, his name is Clay. He lost his mom, my wife, about two years ago."

"Would you like to tell me more about that now?"

Chase took a breath to consider how to answer. "Ah, that's right."

"Okay, where would you like to start?"

Chase recounted the details from the heart attack to Clay's lack of concentration in class.

Dr. McAllister wrote on his tablet for what seemed like a minute. Then he looked up from his notes. "And Jennifer tells me you believe you could benefit by talking with a grief counselor? Do I have that right?"

"Yeah, that's what she thinks."

He smiled. "What do you think?"

Chase looked away, ran his palm through his hair, but leveled with him. "Honestly, grief counseling is all new to me. I'll admit I'm grieving the loss of my wife, and I'm not very good at it, but—I'm fully functional, yet I think about her every day. And I'm not sure what the right way to grieve is, or if there is a right way. Doc, I don't want to waste your time, and I don't have a clue what your services cost—much less if my insurance covers this visit."

Glancing up from his tablet, Dr. McAllister nodded. "I understand. Let's not worry about costs and insurance today."

Chase was perplexed. "Well, there must be a cost for this consultation."

Chase couldn't tell if the doctor smiled or smirked. "Then let's not call it a consultation."

"What do you mean? What should we call it then?"

"Why don't we just call it a conversation?"

Chase looked relieved and settled back in his chair. "Okay. Thank you, I guess."

Dr. McAllister shifted his weight and altered the angle of his tablet. "You mentioned you don't know if there is a right way to grieve. Let's start there. Do you think there is a proper way to grieve?"

"Not sure, but there must be easier ways than what I'm doing—hopefully shorter ways."

"Chase, you may have some misconceptions about grief. Everyone grieves differently, and it can take years—no matter how you do it."

"This entire process feels so unnatural to me." As Dr. McAllister recorded a note on his tablet, Chase glanced around the room, noting the medical degrees on the wall, the aquarium behind Dr. McAllister with tropical fish flitting back and forth, and the grandfather clock in the corner with its gentle ticks and the rhythmic swings of the pendulum. He wondered if it would relax him, like hypnosis.

"Okay, let's back up. Let's add a framework to grief. Grief is a normal and necessary process. There are no rules and timeframes, but there are coping techniques. I'm sure you're familiar with the Kubler-Ross model of grief. You know, the five stages of grief?"

"I've heard of them—denial, anger, and three more."

"Yes, it starts with denial because you can't believe the loss has happened, and you're in shock. Anger follows. That's the 'why is this happening to me' phase. You can be angry at the situation, yourself, or even the deceased for leaving you."

Chase nodded. "I've been through the denial stage. Anger, too. I was angry at myself for not doing more to save Aimee. My mother-in-law, Joyce, is still angry with me. What's the third stage?"

"Bargaining. This is when we want to make a deal with God to bring her back. Or we make the 'if only' or 'what if' statements. Perhaps the most common bargain with God is 'I will never be angry at my wife again if you'll let her live.' We want to get our life back to normal—so we bargain. This usually happens before the loss, before it's too late."

Chase wiped his face with his hand and scratched his chin. "I think I've been through the first three stages during the first year and a half. I think the same may be true for Clay."

"The last two stages are depression, followed by acceptance. These two stages are self-explanatory. What's important to understand is that all five stages are not linear. You can go through them in any order, or even return to a previous stage."

"I think that's already happened. When I think I'm through the depression stage, a single thought, memory, or even a scent can send me backward."

Dr. McAllister paused and tapped his stylus on his tablet. "That's normal. Tell me something. Do you think you've given yourself permission to grieve, or have you resisted it the past two years?"

"I think I'm handling my grief the way my father did. To answer your question, in most cases, I'm not giving myself permission to grieve. I'm holding back, like he did."

Dr. McAllister nodded. "If you remember nothing else today, remember it's okay to grieve—it's normal, and it is necessary. You don't have to feel guilty or ashamed about it."

Chase glanced at the floor, then at him. "Easier said than done."

Dr. McAllister locked in on his eyes. "True, but you need to let yourself *feel* your loss. You can't *think* your way through it, you must *feel* your way through it. Not everything is logical. Have you honestly let yourself *feel* your loss? Or would it be more accurate to say you've prevented yourself from feeling the depth of it?"

Chase slowly rubbed his hands together. He had heard this before. "When people are trying to heal—or simply survive—they don't intentionally rip off the scab to *feel* how much it hurts. I think after a tragic loss, we're all in a self-preservation mode. That's where I'm at—Clay too. I guess we're trying to dull the pain, not heighten it."

Dr. McAllister sat up straighter and wrote on his tablet again. "You make a good point, but you can't ignore deep wounds."

"No. But you can stifle them. When I was growing up, my father lost my mother when I was twelve. I rarely saw him cry. Instead, he was a tower of strength for me."

"Really? Do you think that tower of strength was good for you?"

"Yes, at first. We kept moving forward—no wallowing."

"Why do you think his approach to grief was good for you?"

Rubbing the middle of his forehead, Chase closed his eyes. "My father was an excellent role model."

"Of what?"

Chase winced at the question. "Of strength."

"I don't doubt your father's strength, but don't you think you can be strong by confronting your grief?"

"Strength through weakness? That's counterintuitive." He swallowed hard. Dr. McAllister had hit on something that had troubled him for years, but he'd never known how to address it with his father—or himself. "I'm not sure *how* to give myself permission to grieve. I'm sure my father never did."

"Chase, you must not wait for your father to give yourself permission to grieve. You must do it. There's an old saying, 'You can heal it, if you can feel it.' It's by releasing your feelings that you heal. When you release your feelings, they release their power over you. Does that make sense? There are also coping mechanisms or techniques you can use."

Chase shrugged. "Coping mechanisms? What kind?"

"Like keeping a journal of your feelings."

Chase relaxed and sat back in his chair. "At least I'm doing something right."

"Do you keep a journal?"

"Yes."

"That's a start." Dr. McAllister's phone rang. He reached into his pocket, glanced at it, silenced it, then put it back in his pocket and shifted his weight. "Listening to music can also fuel the healing process, Chase. Using art as an outlet can help communicate your feelings and relieve some of the stress of grief."

"My son Clay is using art therapy at school for the same purpose."

"Good, I think he will benefit from art therapy. It's effective for children," Dr. McAllister said. "Coping mechanisms also include exercise programs."

"I need to work out more."

The doctor set his tablet down and gestured with both hands. "Sharing—or verbalizing your feelings—with someone you care about can go a long way to help you overcome your grief."

"A friend recently told me that—and my best friend, Jack, has been my sounding board for the last two years. I'll attempt to be more open with a few others too."

"May I make a spiritual recommendation?"

"Sure. Actually, I'd appreciate that."

"Okay, spiritual coping mechanisms include prayer and Scripture reading," Dr. McAllister said. He paused a moment. "Reading Scripture can be especially healing. Let me ask you this. Have you ever thought about writing a letter to God about how you feel about the loss of your wife? Or have you considered writing a letter to Aimee about how much you love her and miss her? This has been helpful to my other faith-based clients."

Chase spoke in an uncertain tone. "What would I do with the letter after I wrote it?"

"Well, first, the benefit is not in what you do with it—the benefit is in writing it. Second, you could read it to her at her gravesite—or just talk to her there. It would also serve as an element of closure—a reminder that you addressed your loss. Did you say the two-year anniversary of her passing is next week?"

"Yes, July twenty-ninth."

"That's an ideal time to do this. Do these coping techniques make sense to you?"

"They seem like practical ideas, Doc. I've definitely got to get back to exercising and reading my Bible. I've neglected both."

"The main idea is to express how you feel. Some people have even tried scrapbooking or reading novels where the main character emerges victorious after a battle of grief. Of course, you could simply have a good, hard, cleansing cry."

Chase squirmed in his chair and rubbed his hands together at the suggestion. "Sierra, Clay's summer school teacher, mentioned that."

Dr. McAllister folded his hands in his lap. "Tears are healthy—they release tension. Most men are afraid of tears because they think they're a sign of weakness. I would argue that tears can be a sign of strength—strength to confront, cope, and carry on."

He tapped his index finger against his lip. "As I've said, I'm afraid I've approached grieving using my father's formula. Stuff it. Forget it. Move on."

"How's that working for you?"

"Let's just say our 'no more tears' policy doesn't work."

"Poor strategy?"

"Awful. Please understand. I don't fault him. Generations cope with grief differently. Some are better than others."

"You can't heal when you bottle everything up. Eventually, you need to uncork it. Your tears have the power to help heal you—and your son, when he sees you cry. It gives him permission to cry. Something your father never gave you. My concern is you're duplicating your father's 'no more tears' strategy with Clay, right?"

Chase rubbed his face with both hands. "Like father, like son, I guess."

Dr. McAllister casually changed the subject and talked about Chase's career, his novel, and some of his goals. Chase relaxed, and he no longer heard the clock ticking.

Looking at this watch, Dr. McAllister set his tablet on a table beside him. "We're almost out of time. Let me ask you this. Do you think you would have been better off if your father would have shown more emotion with you—maybe even cried with you?"

Chase ran his hand over the back of his head and down his neck. "Yes, I think so. I never really had an outlet—a relief valve."

"Think Clay needs a relief valve?"

"Absolutely, I'm just not sure how to—you know, cry with my son."

Dr. McAllister leaned toward him. "Start by having a deep conversation with him about his mom after doing something fun together. Let it come naturally. Don't force it. See where it goes. Sometimes emotions lie on the surface—they're not buried deep. A little nudge will start the flow. It may surprise you."

Chase was quiet for a moment. "We're building a treehouse together."

"Really? Sounds like there will be lots of bonding time—in a safe space."

Sensing his session was over, Chase stood. Dr. McAllister rose with him.

"This all makes sense. Thank you for fitting me in, Doc. Where do you suggest we go from here? Should we meet again?"

"That depends."

"On what?"

"On you. Why don't you give Clay more focused attention and see what happens? And voice your feelings to people you care about. If you need me, you know where to find me. Over the years, I've learned people often find healing in uncommon places. I'd say you two might have the best chance of finding healing—shall we say—out on a limb."

They laughed together before walking to the receptionist's desk, where Chase thanked him.

"By the way," Dr. McAllister said, "just a reminder—it's not your father's responsibility to give you permission to grieve, it's yours."

When Chase stepped outside, he felt something he hadn't felt in two years. He could breathe deeply again.

～

Later that evening, after dinner, Chase and Clay went bike riding by the wharf and out for ice cream. It occurred to him to make this a tradition this summer—to focus on his son.

After they talked and Clay was in bed, he slipped his journal under his arm, walked to his favorite recliner in the living room, and turned on the reading lamp. After settling in, he let his pen speak for him.

～

It was a good day today. I met with Dr. McAllister, the grief counselor Jennifer Adams recommended. Nice guy. He made me feel relaxed—normal—and gave me some things to act on. I have to feel my way through grief, he said. "I can heal it, if I can feel it." He's right. Like my father, I'm bottled up. I need to pop the cork. Clay and I need to find a relief valve together.

It was just one conversation, and not much has changed yet, but I see more clearly now.

And isn't that the beauty of hope—it lifts the fog?

CHAPTER 19

After Chase returned home from church on Sunday, and while Clay played with the neighborhood kids, he spent half an hour studying his Bible and reflecting on the sermon before he loaded the dishwasher, started another load of wash, and wrote three to-do lists so he could hit the deck running on Monday morning. One list was for his business writing, the other for his sequel and the standalone novel, and the third to complete construction of the treehouse.

Through it all, he felt something troubling him today, like an undercurrent. It wasn't clear at first, but it came into focus when he remembered the date at breakfast. Clay was too quiet—too preoccupied, and uncharacteristically withdrawn. Chase was certain Clay could feel it, too.

It wasn't the day—Sunday—it was the date, July twenty-ninth, but the date would change his day completely. Instead of working on his sequel and, later, the standalone novel, he would take Dr. McAllister's advice and visit Aimee's gravesite.

After pouring himself a cup of coffee, he placed both hands around the cup and brought it to his lips. Sipping slowly, he turned to look out the kitchen window at the progress of the treehouse. The moment he turned, someone standing behind him startled him. He stepped back.

It was Aimee—drinking from her favorite coffee cup. He blinked hard and then again. She was still there in her pink pajamas.

"Aimee?"

No answer. Instead, she took another sip. Setting his cup on the counter, he believed she would be gone after he rubbed his eyes. She was still there and walked barefoot across the kitchen and sat at *her* place at the table.

Chase knew what was happening to him. He glanced at the counter by the toaster, where he had placed Saturday's mail. He fanned through it again. Three vendors addressed junk mail to Aimee. At the sight of her name, his chest tightened, his back stiffened, and he couldn't swallow. This wasn't the first time. It was the mail, always the mail, that made her seem alive again. She would be home soon, looking for it. It was why he hung onto it for so long. To throw it away was to have her die all over again.

Turning toward the kitchen table, he closed his eyes, thinking if she was no longer there when he opened them, then he knew why his mind was playing tricks on him. If she was still there, he would dispel the hallucination by speaking directly to it.

He opened his eyes slowly. She raised her eyebrows and took another sip of her coffee. "Aimee, you're not really here." He picked up his cup and wrapped both hands around it.

This time she answered him, and it shook him to the core when he heard her voice again.

"Are you sure, hon?" Her voice was sweet and kind—as it always had been. It sounded like … well … her.

"I'm sure you're not really here, Aim. If this isn't a hallucination, Dr. McAllister probably has a medical name for it."

"Who is Dr. McAllister?"

"He's a grief counselor."

She brought her cup to her lips again. "Really? Why do you need one of those?"

His throat tightened. "Well, let's just say it's been really hard letting you go."

"You've always been so strong."

"Not since you've been gone. A man never really knows how

strong he is until he's lost something. Until he's alone." Tears welled in his eyes, but he mustered the will to prevent their escape. "Aim, nothing is the same anymore. Two years ago, everything changed for us. I miss you so much. If I could have you back for—just twenty-four hours."

She looked at him with the soft, understanding eyes he remembered. "What could you possibly do in twenty-four hours, honey? You can't *do* much in one day."

He walked closer to her to activate his other senses, hoping this could be real. "No, but you can *say* so much in one day."

She crossed one leg over the other and raised her cup without taking a sip. "What would you say that you haven't already said?"

"I would say everything a man needs to say when he knows he has only one day left with his wife. Everything would be on the table. Nothing missed, forgotten, or—withheld."

She smiled. "Chase, I know you love me—well, loved me."

"I've said I love you—but I never told you *why*. Women crave details, and I left them out." Glancing out the window to compose himself, he turned, faced her, and fixed his eyes on hers. "I would tell you I love the way you make me feel like I can conquer anything, just by the way you stand beside me arm in arm, how you inspire Clay and help him believe in himself, the way you tease me and I know the motive behind it is to spark joy, laughter, and a deep sense of family.

"If I had just twenty-four more hours, I would tell you I love the way you put others first, yourself last, the way you sing around the house, how your laughter lifts my spirits, how good you look in a dress with heels. I'd tell you how much I love it when you wear your hair up, and how even the smell of your perfume reminds me of the good times we had. And I would tell you I've loved no one—like I love you."

She stood, walked to the stove, and leaned her back against it. "So why didn't you tell me this when I was—?"

He cut her off. "If I had just one more day with you, I would tell you how much I enjoy the way you pad around the kitchen every morning barefoot in your pink pajamas, like now. I would confess you are my rock, my anchor, and I derive most of my strength from you. With just one more day, I would make sure you knew I feel *your* love. How it inspires my writing, drives me forward, and gives me courage to fight for what we believe in."

He took a quick breath. "With just one more day, I would tell you I love how you forgive me for my mistakes, stupid *guy*-remarks, and insensitivity."

She wore a silly grin and gazed at him. "Would you tell me you're sorry for saying I looked fat in that old blue dress?"

Chase rubbed the back of his neck. "You still remember that?"

"A woman will always remember that."

"I thought I covered that by asking for forgiveness for all my stupid guy-remarks."

She winked at him the way he remembered. "Okay, I'll let it slide."

"Twenty-four hours, Aim. You don't know how often I've wished for just another twenty-four hours with you. There's so much still to say."

Folding her arms across her chest, she looked stunning to him, so naturally beautiful. "Then let it out. Just say it, hon." It was a term of endearment she often used for him. It was so common he usually let it pass.

Not today. Today he heard it. Felt it. And let it move him. If only he could pull her closer to him—but he didn't know if he was already dangerously close to the boundary separating reality from illusion.

"I was going to say all this later today—at your gravesite." His last word dangled in the air, and he wondered if it would break the spell. She didn't flinch.

A sense of reality swept over him, and he spoke to it. "It's too late to say these things now, Aim. You're not here anymore." He looked at the floor. "It won't do you any good now."

When he glanced at her again, she smiled and whispered, "Too late for me maybe—but not for you."

Taking the last sip of his coffee, he turned and placed the empty cup on the counter behind him. "Now you sound like Dr. McAllister," he said, but as he pivoted to face her, she was gone.

$\sim$

Chase spent the better part of the day processing what had just happened—or what he thought had just happened.

After his conversation in the kitchen, he knew it was time for Clay to talk to his mother. Clay needed to release the relief valve—like he just did.

CHAPTER 20

While driving to the cemetery, Chase tried to approach the subject that had been on his mind all day. "Hey, buddy, I thought we would go …"

"To see Mom," Clay said before he could finish.

"Yeah, how did you know?"

"She died two years ago today, right? I remember. And you have that look on your face."

"What look?"

Clay glanced out his window at the scenery before turning to his father. "That sad look you get when you're thinking about Mom too much."

"Sad look? Could we ever think about Mom too much?"

"No. But you get sad a lot."

"Really?"

"Not in front of people, or when you're writing, but when we're alone sometimes."

Chase nodded. "Okay, I'll have to fix it."

Clay looked at his father with wide eyes. "My teacher says she thinks Mom wants me to be happy, like when she was here."

"Sierra—I mean, Miss Taylor said that?"

"Yeah, and so did Miss Adams. Besides, that's what you and Grandpa have always said too, right?"

"That's right, buddy. I guess I've been using my sad face more than I thought. I guess I've got some work to do."

"It's not a bad thing, Dad. It's just …" Clay stopped short.

Chase looked at him and then back at the road. "It's just … what?"

"It's just that when you're sad, I'm sad. You said we're in this to-gether, right?"

"Right."

"Then if I even think you're sad, I'm sad. Because, if we're in this together, how can I be happy if you're sad?"

Chase faced him, found his innocent eyes, then returned his gaze to the road. "I'm sorry. Trust me, I'm working on this."

Clay paused and looked out the window while his father drove in silence.

"Even the sign in your den reminds you to be sad."

"What sign?"

"The little one in the middle of your wall."

Chase thought for a moment. "Oh, you mean the one by F. Scott Fitzgerald?"

"I don't know. It's the one that means you can't be happy again."

"Do you mean the one that says, 'There are all kinds of love in this world, but never the same love twice'?"

"Yeah, that one."

Chase chewed the inside of his lip. "You think I'm making myself sad because I have that sign?"

"Are you? It seems like it—because you stare at it so much."

Chase realized his son had just seen through him. "I suppose you're right. It's one more thing I'll have to take care of, I guess. I stare at it because it was a gift from your mom."

"I know, but I don't think she wants it to make you sad."

"No. She wants us to be happy."

"You said you're doing other things to not be sad? What other things?"

"I'm talking to a person who knows how to make sad people happy. His name is Dr. McAllister. It's what he does."

Clay scratched his head. "What kind of person makes sad people happy? Is he a clown?"

"No …" Chase hesitated and wondered if he'd said too much. "He's like a doctor."

"There are doctors to make sad people happy?"

"Yeah. It's complicated."

Clay looked away again, and the two of them were quiet for a moment. A sense of peace washed over Chase as he realized he was connecting with his son. He waited for Clay to continue.

"Is it like how you make me happy when I'm sad—and how Uncle Jack makes you happy when you're sad?"

"Yeah, it's sort of like that."

Chase made a left turn and drove up a hill to the cemetery. The road snaked around, and he parked in front of a large oak tree that had served as a landmark to find Aimee's headstone among the sea of granite. While walking to the gravesite, he placed his hand on Clay's shoulder.

"What are we going to do here today?" Clay asked in a tender tone that betrayed the strength he had shown in the car.

"I'll pray and thank God as usual for the gift your mom was to us—and then I'll give you some time alone with her to tell her how you feel."

He looked up at his father. "You usually do that for us."

"Yeah, but I think you're old enough to tell her how you feel now."

"What should I say?"

"Whatever you feel in your heart. Say as much or as little as you like. No rules. Just talk to your mom like she's here."

They stood over the grave in silence for a moment. A breeze washed over them, and along with it was the emotion of a lost loved one. Chase felt the stillness stir his heart, and he remembered how deeply it had gripped him as a boy standing over his mother's grave with his father so many years ago.

Placing his arm around Clay, he offered a simple prayer from a grateful heart.

"God—thank you." His throat tightened and reduced his words to a halting whisper. "Thank you for giving us Aimee. She was an incredible wife and life partner. A wonderful mother. An encouraging friend. She brought us life—and laughter. She was a rock. An anchor. All we ever wanted—everything we needed." He hesitated and wiped a tear with his thumb. Taking a breath, he pulled his son closer to his side. "Thank you for giving her to me—and for her—giving life to Clay. She was a gift. God, we miss her ..."

A tear cascaded down Clay's cheek. His father stepped away and walked back to the car, close to the gravesite, leaving his son to talk with his mother. Chase leaned his back against the front passenger door of his Jeep. From this distance, Chase could faintly hear his son talking to his mother—and he realized he would remember his words forever.

~

"Mom," Clay began, "I miss you, and I'm sorry I haven't talked to you more. Don't worry, I think about you every day at school, usually before and after recess, when I'm most happy. I dream about you a lot. Not as much as before, because Dad says we have to move on. He says it's okay to move on because when we do, we'll still take you with us."

Clay cried and Chase took a step toward his son, then paused as he heard him continue.

"I'll always take you with me, Mom. I promise. I'm doing better in school. I'm helping my friend Fernando. He's my best friend, and he lost his dad. Not because he died, but because he wanted a new family. Dad said he would never leave me, so we don't have to worry about that. Fernando asks me a lot about you. I like it. It doesn't make me sad—because he helps me remember you by talking about you."

Clay wiped his tears away. "Mom, I'm forgetting *some* things about you. They're not big things. I remember the sound of your voice and your laugh, but I'm forgetting things you told me you like. I'm sorry." He lowered his head to collect his thoughts.

"I miss you the most in the mornings. Not sure why. Dad signed me up for a program with kids that have only one parent. I heard a teacher say it's so I feel normal. I hope it never feels normal without you.

"Dad is doing better, but I have to check on him a lot. He pretends to be happy sometimes, but he doesn't sing in the shower like he used to, and he doesn't goof around as much. Don't worry, I bike ride with him and we go get ice cream so he doesn't get too sad. We even promised we would take care of each other, so you don't have to worry. Uncle Jack makes him laugh, and Fernando wants to play with me, even if I'm sad."

Clay turned toward the car, then faced the gravestone. "Oh, one more thing. We're building a treehouse in the backyard. Grandpa designed it, Jack knows how to build it, and Fernando and I are helping Dad nail it together. I think it makes Dad feel better to have something to work on." He paused for a moment. "It makes me feel better to work on it too. Mom, I love you and I miss you really bad. That's all for now."

Clay walked to the car. Chase opened the door for him, then walked around the Jeep, opened the door, and jumped in. He patted his son on the knee, then started the engine. They were quiet as they drove out of the cemetery.

After several minutes, Clay broke the silence with a question. "Do you think Mom heard me?"

"It's hard to say, buddy."

"Do you think God heard me?"

"Absolutely."

"Okay, maybe He'll tell her."

Chase smiled and rubbed Clay's shoulder. "Buddy, the important thing right now is—do you feel better after talking to her?"

"A lot better."

"Me too. For now, maybe that's enough. Feel like some ice cream?"

⁓

Late that night, Chase was tired. His conversation with Dr. McAllister still rang in his ears, a constant reminder of things to think about and act on. Walking into his den, he glanced at his Inspiration Wall, punctuated with the famous author quotes. His eyes fixed on the one in the center of the wall—the Fitzgerald quote Clay said made him sad.

In the soft glow of his den light, he lifted the plaque off the wall and ran his fingers over it, tracing every word. In a whisper, he read it aloud one last time. *"There are all kinds of love in this world, but never the same love twice."* He tucked the sacred gift from his wife inside the bottom drawer of the desk—then shut it.

When he was ready to surrender to sleep, he forced himself to collect his thoughts, pick up his journal, and scrawl just a few lines before closing the book on a complex but intriguing day.

⁓

Today, I thought I saw Aimee. In the kitchen. In her pajamas. The pink ones. Barefoot. She looked gorgeous, healthy—and so alive. I told her what I would say if I had just twenty-four more hours with her. She blushed, smiled, and gave me that look—that intimate look that always rewarded me for a compliment or for being vulnerable and honest with her. She reminded me I need to express myself more. "Then let it out. Just say it, honey," she said. Even she wants me to vent, or verbalize, or whatever you want to call it.

I took Clay to the cemetery today to give him a chance to talk to her—to grieve in his own way—and open the door, even if only a crack, to help us both communicate more on matters of the heart.

I know there's probably a medical explanation for what I think I saw in the kitchen today. But I don't need one. And I don't want one. Maybe Aimee wasn't really here. Maybe it was my subconscious or the mail that arrived addressed to her this week. Or maybe I was just talking to myself. And I may never know if I actually saw her.

But there's one thing I'm sure of. I heard her—loud and clear.

CHAPTER 21

On Saturday morning the following week, Chase stared out his bedroom window at the blue light before dawn.

With only one thing on his schedule, he looked forward to seeing Jack and his father, yet again, to tackle building the treehouse. They had momentum now. The project was progressing well and becoming a joyful obsession for a grandfather, father, and son. Clay and Fernando would join in later today, tweaking David's original design. Last weekend, Fernando had suggested hanging a tire swing under the treehouse, plus an escape rope they could slide down to complement the rope ladder on one end and the slide on the opposite end of the platform.

Chase made himself a cup of coffee as Clay slept and reviewed the architectural plans his father drew up, noting how much they'd completed, materials on hand, supplies yet to order, and loose ends to tie up. He was excited about giving this project, and his son, his full attention today before Clay and Fernando would have another sleepover at Fernando's house.

His mind drifted to Sierra, wondering what she would do today, knowing she loved long runs to clear her head and give her space. There was so much he wanted to tell her, including his talk with Dr. McAllister, the progress building the treehouse, and how this project affected his relationship with both his father and son. Then there was his talk with Aimee in the kitchen. Should he even tell her? Would she think he was crazy? And of course, there was Clay verbalizing his feelings to his mother at her gravesite. There was so much he wanted a woman's perspective on. Recently, he would have dismissed these thoughts. Today, he felt a strange compulsion to share them with someone who cared—and who he cared about. Or at least, he hoped she cared about him.

After Clay woke up and they finished breakfast, Jack and David arrived within ten minutes of each other. David was ten minutes early. Jack was punctual. Chase wondered whether this made Jack feel like he was late. *One more straw to break the camel's back.*

"Hey, Dad, hi, Jack. Thanks for being so punctual. How about a cup of coffee and a team meeting before we start?"

"Sounds good." David turned to Jack.

Jack nodded. "I'm in."

Jack poured a cup and handed it to David before pouring one for himself. They headed to the patio table where they could view their progress on the treehouse and discuss the plan of attack for the day.

"Dad, where should we start? I want to get as much done as possible today. I'd like to turn the corner on this project this weekend so Clay and I can climb up there and have some fun." Chase winked at Clay, who smiled and nodded.

David pointed to a blueprint. "We've secured the platform. The railing is around three of the four sides, so we can use the open side to hoist materials up on the platform. I'd say we can construct the frame of the clubhouse and the roofline. Once we install the plywood on the roof, we could lay the tar paper. With so little rain, I doubt we need shingles at this point. That'll save some money."

Chase agreed and walked toward the building materials. "If you and Jack can start hoisting the materials up, I'll measure for proper placement of the clubhouse on the deck. Once we lay out the clubhouse frame and bolt it to the platform, Jack can cut and attach that old barnwood I collected to the frame as siding. The barnwood is not straight, so it will leave peek holes for Clay, and I will see movement in the clubhouse from my den window so I know where he is."

Chase lifted his coffee mug to his lips and sipped. "I checked our supplies earlier. We may not have enough tar paper, Dad. I'll make a run to the hardware store this morning."

"We won't need it till this afternoon, Chase. Plus, by that time, we will have a growing list of what we forgot to buy."

Jack tightened his tool belt. "Mr. K., on what sides of the club-house do you want to cut in windows?"

David rolled open his rough blueprints on the patio table. "Let's consider the front of the treehouse the ocean side, thus the back is the side that faces the house and Chase's den. So we'll put a large window on the back so Chase can see Clay from his den while he's writing. We'll have small windows on the other two sides for natural light and, of course, a large window on the ocean side next to the front door."

"I love it, Dad. What do you think, Clay?"

Clay glanced at the blueprint. "Can we put a counter along the window on the ocean side for our soda and snacks?"

David smiled. "I think we can arrange that. I have some old stools so you can sit outside, lean on the counter, and have a soda facing the ocean."

Jack laughed. "Next thing you know, Clay will ask for a wet bar!"

Chase grinned. "Yeah, it's time Clay learned the first rule of business. If it isn't in the budget, it isn't happening."

David glanced at his grandson. "Don't listen to them, just talk to me, chief. I'll get you what you need."

Clay gave his grandfather a thumbs-up.

David turned to Chase. "I didn't plan on glass windows because the climate is so fair. Instead, we can find some cheap shades he can roll down if it's windy or cool. Take measurements, then add shades to your materials list, Chase."

Clay stood next to his grandfather and looked like he was trying to make sense out of the blueprints. David put his hand on his grandson's shoulder.

"What else do we need to make this treehouse the ultimate fort, chief?"

Clay scratched his head. "Well, you have a front door, lots of windows, a rope ladder, a slide on the opposite end, an escape rope to slide down for fast getaways, and a tire swing. Is there a secret trap door by the escape rope or will there be a circular hole in the floor like firefighters use at a fire station?"

Chase and Jack looked at each other and grinned. "We completely forgot to cut a trap door into the platform for an escape rope," Chase said. "I'll add hinges to the list for my run to the hardware store."

"Don't know what we were thinking, Clay." David looked over his drawings again. "Of course. We need a secret trapdoor. I think that will be safer than a large circular hole in the floor."

Jack laughed. "Yeah, Clay, if you have a hole in the floor, girls could get in. I'd go with a trap door you can lock."

Clay's eyes widened. "Yeah, we don't want girls to get in."

The older men laughed, recalling clubhouse rules from their childhoods.

David took another sip of his coffee and placed his pencil behind his ear. "Guys, I think we have our marching orders from the chief. Let's get to work and finish building us a treehouse."

～

Chase hoisted two-by-fours and the barnwood for the side boards to Jack on the platform while David measured and drew a plumb line for Jack to bolt the foundational boards for the clubhouse. Using scrap wood, Chase taught Clay how to use a hammer and a power drill to fasten boards together so he could assist them when they attached the side boards to the framework David and Jack were completing.

Initially, Chase worried about Clay getting under foot, but soon realized it wasn't Clay getting in his grandfather's way. Jack was.

Chase was never sure why his father always had no patience for his best friend, so he often took Jack's side. After working in the scorching sun for four hours, Chase realized this might be the project where he could find out why his father struggled with Jack.

"I think there is a better way to do that, Jack," David said.

"I'm sure there is. There's always a better way to do things, but don't you think this way will do?" Chase knew Jack wasn't cutting corners—he was just being efficient, practical, and cost-effective. "After all, we're building a treehouse, not the Taj Mahal."

The skin between David's eyes wrinkled in tight rows. "A job worth doing is worth doing right, don't you think, Jack?"

Jack smirked. "Indeed, but as an engineer, I know there's more than one way to skin a cat. Or I wouldn't be much of an engineer."

"But as an architect, usually there is a preferred way that typically makes the most sense, saves the most money, and makes the client happy."

With a backyard project this involved, there were bound to be a few disagreements regarding the best way to build the treehouse, what to do first, and the proper division of labor. Egos could flare suddenly, and David's resentment of Jack ran like a river—steady, with an undercurrent. The past few years, it wasn't so obvious, and today it didn't run hot, more like an irritating low-grade fever, the kind that you don't feel, yet you sense something is wrong.

At noon, when Chase sensed that even the cool Santa Barbara ocean breeze couldn't cool their rising temperatures, he broke for lunch.

"Hey guys, let's take a break. I ordered sub sandwiches, chips, and beverages. I put everything in the cooler under the treehouse. Help yourselves."

"Dad, can Fernando and I eat our lunch in the treehouse?" Clay asked.

"I thought you two guys might like to bring your lunch and ride along with me. I'm going to run to the hardware store. Seems to me, there's an ice cream shop nearby. You can eat in the Jeep."

"Come on, Fernando. You'll like this ice cream place."

"Cool." Fernando stuffed his soda in the back pocket of his shorts and grabbed a sub from the cooler.

Jack and David sat at the patio table between the treehouse and the house. Walking to them, Chase said, "Guys, enjoy your lunch. I'm running to the hardware store to grab the materials we discussed this morning. Clay and Fernando are riding along. I'll be back soon. Help yourselves to a sandwich, chips, and something to drink."

Chase hoped lunch, a cold beverage, and the serene view would diffuse simmering tempers.

～

David took a bite of his sub and twisted the cap off his beverage. Jack glanced out over the ocean and wondered if they would sit in silence or if he would have to break the ice. It was no accident that Chase took Clay and Fernando with him. It was his way of giving Jack a private moment with Chase's father. Jack knew what Chase was doing. It came from a long history together of standing in the gap for each other.

Jack opened a bag of chips and took a bite of his sandwich before taking a sip of his O'Doul's. There was only one way to break the ice, and that was just to break it—and you could only do that with a quick strike. So he took a swing, a direct hit.

"You don't seem to like me very much, Mr. K. Any particular reason?"

David lifted an eyebrow and pushed his chair away from the table to expand their proximity. "What makes you think I don't like you?"

"Really, Mr. K.? Must we go back that far? Let's just agree you don't care for me and, at a minimum, cite examples from today. Everything I've tried to do has not been good enough for you. What gives?"

"We just approach our work differently, Jack. I'll admit, as an architect, I am a bit of a perfectionist. Things have to be measured. Twice. Everything must fit. Precisely. No guesswork. No errors. Errors are costly." He took another sip of his drink.

Jack was ready to respond. "I'm not buying it, Mr. K. I'm an engineer. I approach my work with the same accuracy as an architect. Same precision, less ego."

David's face flushed, and he sat up straight in his chair. "So now this is about ego?"

"Actually, it's about more than that, but if this conversation is going to be productive, we'll have to put our egos aside. Both of us. I'm direct, and we don't have all day, so I'll tell you how I see it, and you can fill in the blanks."

"Jack, you don't have to waste time with your theories. I'll tell you how I see it, how I've always seen it. In a nutshell, I have a problem with the way you carry yourself."

Jack crossed his arms. "Here we go. How do I carry myself?"

"Everything is a joke to you. Everything is amusing."

"So you're referring to my sense of humor?"

"If that's what you want to call it. You take nothing seriously."

Jack rolled his eyes. "I take everything seriously. My sense of humor may be flippant to diffuse the tension in a situation. Humor helps me cope and restores a sense of perspective."

David shook his head. "I find humor a strange way of coping with serious things."

"But at least it's *coping*. And just what serious things are we talking about here, Mr. K.? The most serious thing that happened today was using a two-by-four instead of a two-by-six."

"I'm not referring to today."

Jack looked out over the ocean as a pelican glided in a graceful arc, took a sip of his beverage, and then faced David. "Just what are you referring to?"

"Two years ago, Chase's wife died. Four years ago, you divorced yours. The losses may both be painful, but they're different."

Jack set his beverage down, and his back stiffened. "Really, how's that?"

"Chase *lost* his wife. I heard you *traded* yours in."

Instinctively, Jack balled a single fist—and just as quickly released it, knowing who he was talking to. Sweat beaded on his forehead. "Excuse me? With all due respect, I don't think you are aware of the circumstances of my divorce."

"No, but do I have to be? Honestly, Jack, if I heard right, you once told Chase your ex-wife was dead to you. Who would say that to a man whose wife was dead? And who would say that about a woman they once loved?" David's voice cracked.

Jack's temper flashed, but he remained calm, remembering how often Chase had told him how his father adored his mother and how devastating it was for both of them to lose her. "Mr. K., if you understood the context of my comment to Chase, you might arrive at a different conclusion—a more accurate one, like Chase did."

David wiped his hands with his napkin. "I seem to have already arrived at a conclusion."

"That much is clear." Jack cleared his throat. "By the way, my wife, Julie, left me for another man after she cheated. I never saw it coming. I had always been faithful to her. She said she didn't love me anymore, maybe never did." His voice softened. "How does that happen, Mr. K.? Especially when my love for her never changed? I would like to think I loved her as much as you loved your wife."

David looked away, then back at Jack. "I don't know, Jack." He added, "I'm sure, like everything else, it's complicated."

Their eyes met. "Look, it's true I said she was dead to me, but I didn't mean it."

"Then why would you say something like that?"

"Because I'm a guy. A young guy, who says stupid things

172 | James C. Magruder

sometimes when I'm mad or rejected—or dumped for someone else for no apparent reason. Maybe it was self-defense."

David pulled his chair closer to the patio table across from Jack. "How so?"

"I said she was dead to me because when she walked out the door that night, I felt I was dead to her—and I died first." Jack leaned in and spoke with conviction. "Mr. K., Aimee *has* died. Nothing will change that, but something will make it easier."

"What do you mean?"

"Set your son free. Set him free to cope with Aimee's death in his own way—not your way. He deserves that—and so does your grandson."

David stood and walked toward the ocean as the breeze washed over him before he turned to face Jack again.

"Chase has handled Aimee's death gallantly. I don't know what you're talking about."

Jack walked toward him. "I realize this is none of my business, but because it involves Chase and Clay, I'm going to lay it all on the table for you."

"Go on."

"You have coped with your wife's death in your own way—and that's fine. But don't expect your son to grieve the loss of his wife the same way you did—by simply moving forward like it never happened. It happened, and Chase hasn't taken the time to fully grieve Aimee, not with you as a role model to stuff it, not talk about it, and march forward."

"I don't know what you're seeing, Jack, but obviously I'm not seeing the same thing. I think Chase is doing fine with Aimee's death—just like he did with his mother's."

Jack shook his head. "Well, since you brought it up. Chase still occasionally struggles with his mom's death."

David glared at him. "What do you mean?"

Jack shook his head. "Never mind. I've said too much. You should talk to your son—*really* talk to him. Better yet, *listen* to him."

David frowned, and his face flared red. "What are you trying to say—and where are you going with this?"

Jack raised his palms. "Nowhere. I shouldn't have said anything. Just talk to your son someday—soon. Besides, the issue for Chase and Clay now is how to grieve and cope with Aimee's death."

"He appears to be doing fine. What am I missing?"

"Appearances can be deceiving. He's still trapped in the cycle of never moving on from Aimee—and never disappointing you. What you're missing is that he's grieving the way you did—dismissing his feelings and believing that's enough."

David looked at their progress on the treehouse and then back at Jack. "What am I supposed to do about that?"

"Give him permission to grieve his way. Set him free."

David appeared to mull his advice, and Jack hoped he would consider that it came from a man his son considered his best friend.

David walked back to his chair, sat, hung his head, and rubbed his hands together. Finally, he spoke in a tender tone that revealed a regretful heart. "Just exactly how do I set him free?"

"Share your pain and your struggle when you lost your wife. Chase once told me he rarely saw you cry over his mother's loss. If that is all a boy sees, he grows up thinking his father is Superman—or men don't cry. And when he's a man, well, his father is still Superman—and that still makes him feel weak."

David had become contrite, and Jack could sense it. Ego melted. Anger buried. Heart soft.

"Jack, how could Chase possibly benefit now by talking about how I could have done a better job grieving the loss of his mother? He's a man now."

"You're missing the point, Mr. K. That ship has sailed. Chase doesn't need a role model of how to grieve the loss of a mother. He needs a role model on how to grieve the loss of a wife." Jack stood near the patio chair David sat in and looked out over the ocean. "By the way, although your circumstances differ from mine, you somehow have it in your head that since I'm divorced, I screwed up. Yet you, Chase, and I have something in common."

David glanced up at him. "Go ahead, say it."

"All three of us lost the woman we loved, and despite the reasons, we will all live our lives without her forever."

David nodded but didn't reply.

"Whether you lost your spouse from death or divorce, it doesn't matter, Mr. K. In the end, pain is pain."

David's cheeks were pink, and he looked away, unable to face him now. Still leaning forward, eyes to the ground, he hunched over in his swivel chair.

Jack continued, slowing his pace as memories gripped him. "In one sense, I know what it's like to have my wife die. Do you know how tough it is to be dead to your wife—when you're alive?"

David listened and sat quietly.

"Imagine bumping into her at the grocery store and never being acknowledged," Jack said. "Imagine being invisible. Having your history expunged. Feeling discarded. Or seeing your replacement holding her hand when you're still in love with her."

Jack stopped for a moment to compose himself, then paced along the edge of the patio. "Pain is a strange beast, Mr. K. Does it really matter *how* we arrive there? You and I have taken different roads to the same destination. We've had different accidents, but the same injuries. Pain is pain. Loss is loss, right?"

David sat quietly. Jack wondered if his words were cutting through David's preconceived notions.

"Do you know what the hardest part of a divorce was for me, Mr. K.?"

Birds cackled overhead and flew into the large oak tree near the patio as a breeze blew through their hair. "No, tell me."

"I not only lost someone I loved—I lost my identity. We live in a couples' world, and I no longer fit in. I doubted even my strengths. Insecurity set in. Eventually, I became emotionally paralyzed, fearing loss again."

David glanced up at him. "How did you cope?"

"Verbal diarrhea."

David smiled, and Jack felt the tension ease. "Say that again."

"Verbal diarrhea. I talked about it constantly—to everyone. That's one difference between Chase and me. He bottled his pain. I shared mine—with anyone I trusted to listen. I let people in—to let the pain out."

Jack walked to the treehouse, climbed the ladder, and resumed attaching barnwood boards to the side of the clubhouse frame. David leaned forward, cupped his hands, and buried his face in them.

"What have I done?" he whispered as Jack looked on. "What have I done?"

~

When Chase and the kids returned from the hardware store, Jack was nailing barnwood to the north side of the clubhouse. David had finished cutting a hole in the clubhouse's floor for the trapdoor. Now they just had to measure, cut, and install the trapdoor with the hinges Chase bought. Chase sat at the patio table and laid out the materials to assemble the trap door, and he set about his work to fashion it. Occasionally, he glanced at his father and Jack, noticing they were quiet.

I wonder if they had it out while I was gone.

When Jack offered an idea, his father was listening more than talking, agreeing with Jack's approach, and exchanging a few laughs along the way.

Chase smiled. *Something must have happened while I was away.*

By late afternoon, with the clubhouse frame finished and many of the sideboards attached to strengthen the frame, Jack laid the tar paper on the plywood roof recently bolted in place. David excused himself and prepared to leave for an appointment.

"Chase, I've got to run now, but I can stop by tomorrow. We still have to install the escape rope and a few other things."

"Dad, I thought about it over lunch, and I would feel better about putting shingles on the roof," Chase said. "We get little rain, but when we do, I don't want to risk the roof rotting prematurely even though we're going to attach tar paper. I want the treehouse to last a while. Clay is only eight and will play in here for several more years."

"Fine, let's talk about that later. I'll call you tomorrow." David looked over at Jack. "See ya, Jack. Nice work today."

"Catch ya later, Mr. K."

After David left, Chase climbed up on the clubhouse roof to help Jack roll out the tar paper and staple it in place. "What was that all about?"

Jack continued to staple the edge of the tar paper. "What do you mean?"

"You and my dad, all quiet and cozy-like. You two are only quiet when you're mad at each other. I've watched you since lunch, and you barely spoke to each other, but you didn't seem angry. Did you call a truce? What gives?"

"Roll out that tar paper in front of you, Chase." Jack continued to staple the paper in place as Chase squared it up on the roofline. He glanced at Chase, and their eyes met. "We just had a little talk and came to an understanding."

"What kind of understanding?" Chase flattened the tar paper to prevent wrinkles.

"I think we just better understand our respective points of view. That's all."

"No agreements? No rules?"

"No. Nothing like that. Not that big a deal. Like I said, I think we just understand each other better."

Chase continued to roll out the paper on his hands and knees, and Jack followed him with the staple gun to secure a tight fit. "You told him, didn't you? You told him how I felt growing up and my struggles with my mom's death."

Jack lifted his palm and waved him off. "No. It's not like that."

Chase let up on the tar paper and it rolled back up on him. He stared at his friend. "Jack, you promised me you wouldn't go there with him."

"Well, I …"

"You went there, didn't you?"

"Sort of. But not intentionally. One thing led to another … but it's fine."

Chase furrowed his brow, and he set his mouth in a straight line. "Tell me what you said."

Jack stalled. While no words would come out, Clay ran outside after playing video games with Fernando.

"Dad, Miss Taylor is at the front door. Should I bring her back here?"

Stunned, Chase searched for the right words to not sound too excited. "Sure."

Clay ran back inside.

Jack raised his eyebrows. "Oh, and who is Miss Taylor?"

Chase smirked and considered not answering him. "Clay's summer school teacher."

Jack leaned back on his knees, and a sly smile curled at the corners of his lips. "What's she doing here? Come to see you, or Clay?"

"I'm about to find out."

When Sierra came around the side of the house, she took Chase's breath away. She wore blue jean shorts and a sleeveless blouse in a coral color. The sun had bronzed her olive skin, and her hair was in a tight ponytail. She looked beautiful—slender and fit. Her smile would light up a room.

She looked up at him on the roof. "Hey, Chase."

"Hey. What are you doing here?"

"Well, I was invited, sort of."

Chase rolled out the last corner of the tar paper for Jack to staple down. "Invited?"

"Yeah, I heard about the treehouse."

"Really? How did you hear about it?"

"Do you really think an eight-year-old boy won't tell his class his dad is building him a treehouse? He told me I should see it someday, so I took that as an invitation. Besides, I was in the area."

Jack climbed down from the roof to the platform, looked down at her, and introduced himself. "Hi, I'm Jack Simmons. Chase's single best friend—that is, his best friend, who is single."

She looked up at him on the platform and laughed. "Well, hey there, single Jack Simmons, I'm Sierra Taylor, Clay's summer school teacher."

Chase rolled his eyes. If he had been the jealous type, Jack's behavior would have annoyed rather than amused him. After all, Jack was always up for some mischief. "Never mind him, Sierra. You want to come up? Climb the rope ladder."

"We'll give you a tour," Jack said. He moved toward the ladder to greet her.

As Sierra reached the top rung, Chase beat Jack at his own game. Stepping in front of him, he gave Sierra a hand to help her onto the platform.

Jack shook his head and smiled. "Well, I think I'll call it a day.

Let me know if you need help tomorrow, Chase. Nice to meet you, Sarah."

"It's Sierra." She winked at him. "Nice to meet you too—Joe."

Jack beamed. "Touché."

As he turned to climb down the rope ladder, Chase gave him a playful nudge on the shoulder. "Thanks for the help today, pal."

When Jack was out of earshot, Sierra said, "I like him. He's funny—and he's good for you."

Chase nodded. "Yes, he is. We yank each other's chain, but we're there for each other." From the treehouse, they could view neighboring yards and the expanse of the sky and the water. "What do you think of the ocean view from up here?"

She put her hand on her forehead, like a sailor, to block the sun. "Wow. It's spectacular. This must be the special project you did to bond with Clay, eh?"

"Exactly. Actually, I think it'll be good for both of us. What do you think of the deck and clubhouse?"

She glanced at the roof and sides and stuck her head in the doorway. "Any boy would love it, Chase. You built both an open deck and a hideout for him."

"Yep. We need to finish the railing and a bunch of odds and ends on my dad's punch list, but we're almost home. Every boy should have his own fort—his own space, right? I did."

Chase found himself more attracted to her than he had first realized. Initially, it was like a gentle nudge—now it felt like a shove. "I'm really glad you stopped by."

Her deep brown eyes were gentle, and her speech was hesitant. "I hope it wasn't too forward to stop by. Did I catch you off guard?"

"No, to be honest, I've been wanting to talk with you. I have a lot to tell you, and this treehouse project is only part of it."

"Really? What have you been up to?"

"Honestly? I've taken Jennifer's advice, and yours, after our walk on the beach. And I've met with Dr. McAllister."

Her eyes widened. "How did that go?"

"Good. But it's a long story. I was hoping to talk to you over … dinner."

She smiled and looked away. "Well, I …"

His shoulders tightened, and he rolled them to diffuse the tension. "I'm sorry—now who's being forward? You may not even be available or interested. I don't know what I was thinking."

"No, it's fine. I'm available—and interested—for dinner, that is."

"You're sure you don't have other plans?"

She dipped her head and walked to the ocean side of the platform. "Actually, dinner would be nice. I'd like to hear more about how you and Clay are doing and how it went with Dr. McAllister."

His shoulders relaxed, and he stood a little taller and smiled. "Feel like being spontaneous? I know a great, casual place. Good food. Warm ambiance. Stunning view. You're dressed perfectly for it."

"Where is it?"

"Ever been to the Padaro Beach Grill in Carpinteria? It's about twenty minutes from here."

She rubbed her hands together, then slid them into her pockets. "No. Not familiar with it."

"You'll love it. Clay is having dinner and yet another sleepover at Fernando's. I'm going to have to pay back Fernando by having a ton of sleepovers here in the treehouse. Say, if you don't mind, could you hang out with the boys for a few minutes while they play video games? I need to put away some tools and take a quick shower before we go."

"I'd love to hang out with the kids. And it will be nice to talk—and have dinner—with you."

The smile on his face spoke of the memory of once being in love. She climbed down the ladder and walked to the house.

When he picked up the tools and wood scraps scattered around the treehouse, he felt his pulse quicken.

It had nothing to do with how hard he'd been working.

CHAPTER 22

Chase quickly picked up the power drill, hammers, screwdrivers, staple gun, and wood scraps, stored them in his garage, and locked the door. Sierra was fully engaged with Clay and Fernando in the house when he hopped in the shower to wash away the residue of a day's work.

The shower relaxed him, and his pace slowed as hot water cascaded over him.

Lathering his hair, he felt both a subtle thrill and a twinge of guilt. Every date he'd had since Aimee died felt empty and guilt-free, because he felt nothing. This one was different. He felt something, and that, he knew, accounted for the mist of guilt.

After he toweled off, he got dressed, slipped into a pair of white golf shorts, put on sandals, and pulled a slim-fitting navy polo shirt over his shoulders. He combed through his hair, brushed his teeth, and splashed on a dash of cologne. Gazing into the mirror, he turned his head from side to side, realizing he hadn't looked at himself like this in two years. Until now, it hadn't mattered.

"Good enough." He tossed his work clothes into the hamper before entering the living room, where Sierra was now playing a video game with Clay.

"You've got guts to take him on, Sierra. That's his favorite game."

"Tell me about it. I don't know what I'm doing."

"I should have warned you." Walking closer to the screen, he said, "Looks like you're losing—big."

"Fernando talked me into it." She glanced at Fernando with a smirk. "He said it would be easy."

"You fell for the oldest trick in the book. They set you up. These guys are con men masquerading as eight-year-olds."

She nodded. "Tell me about it."

"You're like a lamb being led to slaughter."

"And *I am* getting slaughtered."

"You sure are." Clay laughed and Fernando beamed.

Chase glanced at this eight-year-old con man. "After you put her out of her misery, I'll drop you guys off at Fernando's. Miss Taylor and I are going to have dinner at the Padaro Beach Grill."

"I love that place." Clay scored another victory at the expense of an unsuspecting rival. He set the controller down with the confidence of a gunslinger sliding his gun into his holster. "Thanks for playing with us, Miss Taylor."

"Well, I hope *you* had fun."

Chase pointed to Clay's bedroom. "Clay, do you have all of your overnight stuff packed to take to Fernando's house?"

"Yeah."

"Pajamas?"

"Yeah."

"Toothbrush? Toothpaste?"

"Yeah, Dad, and my other stuff. I'm all packed."

"Okay, just checking. We'll be leaving soon."

Sierra walked around the living room and the library. Chase followed her, stopping in the library in front of oak bookcases, twin leather recliners, and a grandfather clock in the corner.

She ran her palm over the wood trim and the glass door with gold leaf inlay that housed the pendulum. "It's a beautiful clock."

"It was my grandfather's."

She gave him a look for citing the obvious. "Is that a joke?"

"I'm serious. It was my grandfather's grandfather clock," he said with a laugh.

She rolled her eyes. "Who's the con man now?"

"It came with the house—this was initially my grandfather's house that was passed down to me."

"I love your library. Every writer should have a library in their home."

"I couldn't agree more." Chase took his keys out of his pocket while Clay grabbed his duffel bag from his room and ran to the car with Fernando. "By the way, you were a good sport with the kids. Thanks. Climbing into their world meant a lot to them—and to me."

"Wish I could have survived it."

"Don't we all?" He walked toward the front door. "Ready to go?"

After arriving at Fernando's, he and the boys climbed out of the Jeep while Sierra waited. Chase briefly chatted with Fernando's mother, Eva, and thanked her for the times she had Clay for dinner and yet another sleepover this summer.

"Eva, good to see you again," Chase said. "Thank you so much for being so good to Clay. He loves playing with Fernando."

Eva was a heavyset woman with a dark complexion and a bright white smile, and she wore her gray-streaked hair in a bun. She wore a blouse with bright colors and floral print, khaki shorts, and sandals. The lines around her eyes defied her age, but he noticed she looked older than when he had talked to her in person a while ago. Perhaps she wasn't sleeping, or the rigors of a dying relationship with her husband had aged her.

"Clay is a good boy, Chase. I think they need each other."

"Thank you. I agree."

"In the past, I've heard Clay telling Fernando to call him when he's sad. He's good about cheering him up when Fernando misses his father. You're doing something right at home."

"Thank you for saying so."

Chase looked over at his Jeep where Sierra sat waiting for him. "I have to run. The next sleepover is at our place—most likely in a treehouse."

"Fernando would love that. I'm sure they've already planned it."

"I think you're right. Good luck with these guys tonight."

"The boys are good for me. Have a nice evening."

Chase climbed into the Jeep and drove south on US 101 to Carpinteria. He turned on the radio, adjusted the station, and told Sierra how they constructed the treehouse. Traffic was light, and they arrived in about twenty minutes.

"I really think you're going to love this place." He parked and unbuckled his seatbelt.

When Sierra got out of the car, she surveyed the property. He pointed out the spectacular ocean view and the picnic tables of various shapes and sizes, complete with bright blue, yellow, or gold umbrellas that punctuated the open courtyard. Hidden landscape speakers among the shrubbery featured piped-in music to create ambiance, and lights strung between the palm trees created a warm glow.

"What are you hungry for?" Chase motioned to the menu boards overhead.

"What's good here?"

"Everything."

Sierra laughed. "That's helpful."

Chase returned a smile. "Well, they've got at least eight different burgers here, chicken sandwiches, six types of fresh salads, a fabulous fish sandwich, and shrimp or fish tacos."

She looked at him, perhaps for a little more help. "What do you usually get?"

"I like the grilled fish tacos. It's grilled snapper." He pointed to the menu. "It's right there. It has cabbage, tomato, avocado, cilantro, corn tortillas, and red salsa. I love it."

"Sounds good, I'll try it."

"I'll have the same. Soft drinks are over there. Let me know what you want."

She looked over the soft drinks as Chase placed their order. When she saw him pay the bill, she reached for her purse.

"Chase, I can get my own."

"I got this. You're with me."

The minute the words came out of his mouth, he wasn't sure what he meant by them—and he wondered what she thought he meant. Yet it was easier to ignore than explain, so he let it go. After grabbing his order number, they dispensed their soft drinks, walked to the sprawling outdoor courtyard, and found a table in the back overlooking the ocean on a raised platform next to the firepit. Sierra took a seat facing the ocean. Chase sat across from her.

Her gaze panned the environment. "This place really is spectacular. I can't believe I've never heard of it before. It's even got a play area for kids."

Chase took a sip of his cola. He pointed to the horizon. "And wait till you see sunset."

Sierra crossed her arms, placed her elbows on the table, and leaned forward. "Thanks for bringing me here. It's lovely."

"I've been hoping to reach out to you after all you've done for Clay. There are so many things I've been wanting to tell you."

She looked at him with soft eyes filled with an inner glow. "Oh, such as?"

"For starters, I wanted to tell you how my visit went with Dr. McAllister. Then I wanted to give you feedback on how your advice about opening up more with Clay is going. Plus, I had hoped to share how I've been spending more time with him working on our special project—which you now know is a treehouse."

She took a sip of her drink. "The treehouse idea was genius, Chase. What a great opportunity to bond. Talk about literally building memories."

Her choice of words warmed him.

"Yep. The treehouse has great potential." Before he could continue, his order number was called over the PA system. When he returned to the table, he handed Sierra her fish tacos and fries and unwrapped his own. Watching her take her first bite, he waited for a reaction.

She closed her eyes and nodded. "This is outstanding. Delicious."

"Yeah? Best fish taco ever?"

There was no argument from her. "Best fish taco ever."

Chase took a bite of his own.

"Tell me about your visit with Dr. McAllister," she said. "I'm curious."

"Where do I start? We briefly talked about the five stages of grief. By my babbling, we identified I'm managing my grief the way my father did—by stuffing it. Both Clay and I need a relief valve. No revelation there."

A coy smile crossed her face.

He took the bait. "What?"

"Seems to me, I intimated when we walked on the beach that you need to *stop* stuffing it. I agree with Doc. You need a relief valve. Did he mention what kind of relief valve?"

"Well, one thing he suggested was a good, hard cry, like you mentioned during our walk on the beach."

As though amused, she raised her eyebrows. "It sounds like I'm a pretty good grief counselor too." She laughed.

Chase was quiet for a moment to deny her the satisfaction. She winked at him and wore an I-told-you-so look. And he made the mistake of staring into her eyes.

"Well?"

"Yes, you are a pretty …" He caught himself.

Sierra laughed. "You can do it. Pretty what?"

"You're just, well, pretty …"

She laid her taco down slowly and looked him in the eye. Chase looked back at her, wondering if she, too, felt something. An awkward silence followed.

She broke the tension. "Did you tell Dr. McAllister about the treehouse?"

Her question felt like a diversion. Dropping his shoulders, he sat back. He welcomed the distraction because he didn't know how to define his feelings, much less trust them. "Yep. He thought that could be good for us for several reasons."

She took a long sip of her soft drink. "What else did he say?"

Chase smiled.

She looked at him and tilted her head to the side. "What? What are you smiling about now?"

"I'm not used to so many questions. I kind of like it."

She returned his grin and dipped a fry in ketchup before popping it in her mouth. "Women want details, Chase. You know that."

He knew that, and he missed it. Questions gave him an opportunity to verbalize, to vent.

"Well, Doc said something that's still rolling around in my head."

Sierra took another bite of her fish taco and motioned with her hand for him to go on.

"Doc said, 'If I feel it, I can heal it.'"

She nodded slowly. "So you will only get past your loss if you fully experience it—and talk your way through it?"

"Essentially." Chase glanced over his shoulder at the ocean. The sun was setting. As it neared the horizon, it cast a warm orange glow over the water.

"The more you talk, the more you heal?" she asked.

"In theory, that's what Doc was saying. I guess the more you release your feelings, the less power they have over you. And since I've bottled my feelings up for so long, they were in complete control."

"Makes sense. Sounds like you found your relief valve?"

"Yeah. I want to think through it, though."

"Going to see him again?"

"We left that open. We're going to see how well verbalizing our feelings and the homemade medication work first."

She tipped her head back. "Homemade medication?"

Chase laughed. "Yeah, the treehouse."

"Of course."

Chase finished his second taco and wiped his fingers. "There's something else Dr. McAllister recommended that I wanted to talk to you about."

She set her drink down and leaned toward him. "I'm listening."

"Doc mentioned another potential relief valve. He suggested Clay and I tell Aimee how we feel—at her gravesite."

"That's interesting. Are you going to do it?"

"We already did. Recently, Clay and I visited her gravesite on the second anniversary of Aimee's death. I challenged him to talk to his mom—say whatever was in his heart. I waited by the car."

She moved her tray out of the way and wiped her hands on a napkin. "What did he say? Or is that confidential?"

"I tried to give him some privacy, but I could hear him. He told her he loved and missed her. He mentioned he dreamed about her a lot and apologized for starting to forget things about her. It got to me when he told her I was doing better and he would try to take her memory with him throughout his life."

"That's powerful, Chase."

They both glanced out at the ocean. Chase wondered how he might have coped better with his mother's death if his father had encouraged him to do what Clay did today. "I wish my father had done something similar with me." He stretched his arms. "Tell me, how is Clay doing in school now?"

She looked away when young kids ran past their table to play in the sandbox across from them. Glancing back at him, she sat up straight. "I've been wanting to talk to you about that—so, I suppose

190 | James C. Magruder

if I hadn't stopped by today, I would have called you. Or more likely, Jennifer would call you since she's the social worker."

Her tone caused Chase to lean back. "Why? What's going on?"

"Well, he is doing much better. The art he drew in art therapy class is interesting and Jennifer will comment more, but I'm sure she won't mind if I give you the gist of it. Don't attach too much meaning to this yet—because it's her job to flesh it out in detail for you, not mine."

"Okay, go on."

"When Clay drew a picture of his family with stick figures, he drew a large circle with you and him in it. Your circle was in the foreground, like planet Earth. Several smaller planets surrounded it. The smallest planet, far away from the Earth, had a drawing of his mom in it. She had a smile on her face. You and he had frowns on your faces."

Chase thought about this picture before he spoke. "I would conclude if he drew his mom on a far-away planet, he feels the distance between us. I imagine he drew frowns on our faces because of our separation from her—yet she's smiling because she's in Heaven. That's my take."

"That's how I see it. Jennifer can add more."

Chase nodded, and as they talked, his mind drifted away and he recalled his grandfather telling him how he knew he was falling in love with his grandmother.

"Every time I saw her, she looked more beautiful," the old man once said. "It got to a point where I couldn't ignore it anymore. I figured it was God's way of drawing us together. Funny how I experienced this with only one person on Earth. Tells you something, doesn't it?"

Sierra's tan seemed to darken as the sun set and washed her and her coral blouse in its orange glow. They faced the sunset together now and were quiet for a moment.

She gazed at the horizon and the sun setting over the water as it dipped lower. "It doesn't get much better than this."

Chase nodded and cleaned up after himself. "Do you have time to stop by the house? I have something else I'd like to show you—and get your reaction."

"I'd like that."

~

When they arrived at his home, Chase parked in the drive, and they walked together to the front door.

"Are you going to give me the nickel tour?" She walked alongside him as they reached the door and he pulled out his keys.

"It's a small house. That may be all it's worth. And you've already seen the living room and the library."

Chase kept the living room immaculate, save for the video game controls Clay left out. Sierra seemed to notice the fine furnishings, including bookcases jammed with books. The large kitchen featured modern cabinets and the latest trends in appliances. "Newly remodeled?"

"Yep."

"And it looks like the library you showed me before was once the dining room."

"Don't have much need for a dining room. I added the bookshelves, the recliners, and this small coffee table to create ambiance to read. And of course, the grandfather clock belongs in a library."

She walked over and sat in one of the leather recliners. "And the recliners face the bookshelves."

"Precisely. I want to be tempted to read instead of watch TV."

"Cozy. Nice place to curl up with a book and a blanket."

"As a writer, I wanted a reading room to complement my writing room—a visible reminder to Clay of the importance of reading."

They walked into his den.

"Obviously, this is my home office, but I think of it as my den—because I don't just work here, I also relax here."

Chase pointed out the expansive windows and the spectacular view of the ocean and the treehouse, noting its silhouette against the orange afterglow of the setting sun.

Chase clicked on a few reading lights and opened a window as she looked around the room. "Looks like an author's home."

"How so?" He was interested in her observations.

"Well, large desk with an ocean view, two open laptops, an extensive library, crowded bookshelves, wall posters of Hemingway's *The Old Man and the Sea* and Fitzgerald's *The Great Gatsby*, looks like unpublished articles needing editing stacked on one end of the desk, neat piles of papers on the floor near the couch by the window. Sort of an organized mess. No TV in this room. It's a place to get things done."

He noticed her eyes came to rest on the wall with the quotes by famous authors displayed. She stepped closer to read them. She read a few plaques aloud. "'Description begins in the writer's imagination, but should finish in the reader's.' Stephen King. I really like that."

Walking close to the wall, she lifted one off the nail. "'For every minute you are angry, you lose sixty seconds of happiness.' Ralph Waldo Emerson. So true." Placing it back on the wall, she pointed to another. "I relate to that one by William Nicholson. 'We read to know we are not alone.' I can see why you have these displayed on your wall. They're so inspiring."

"Thanks. I refer to it as my Inspiration Wall. Each quote speaks to me in its own way. Nothing like taking advice from the masters."

Her eyes widened. "Oh, look at that one by Frank Serafini. 'There is no such thing as a child who hates to read; there are only children who have not found the right book.' As a teacher, I believe that. Kids need to be inspired too."

Chase nodded. "The secret is knowing how to write the right

book for kids. No small task. I love these quotes. They push me forward in my writing career."

She scanned the wall. "There's so many. Oh, it looks like one is missing. Was there one hanging right here in the middle of the wall?" She pointed to the space where Chase had removed his favorite plaque.

Chase bit his lip, picked up a stack of papers, and shuffled them. "Sometimes I need to change things up. But that's not what I wanted to show you."

She walked over to the couch, sat on the edge of the cushion, and folded her hands. "Oh, okay. What did you want to show me?"

"Want to see what I'm working on now? My second novel, if you're interested."

She stood and ambled closer to him. "Absolutely. What's it called?"

"It's a standalone, not the sequel my agent is pushing for. I'm working on both, but this is the one I'm passionate about. I don't have a working title for it yet, but I wanted to share the premise with you and get your feedback, if you don't mind."

"Go for it."

She appeared interested, so he shared the premise. With every word, he knew he was revealing his heart, inviting her closer to his inner thoughts than any woman since Aimee. Letting his guard down felt strange, but good.

Handing her the first chapter, he stepped back and observed while she sat on the couch with the manuscript on her lap. She quietly read without comment, but her facial expressions told the story. Her eyes widened in conflict scenes, she covered her mouth with one hand when a sudden unexpected twist surprised her, and she kept turning pages. *It's always about turning pages.*

When she finished, she looked up at him. "Can I read Chapter Two?"

"No."

"Why not?"

"I just want your initial feedback on Chapter One."

"But you left me hanging. I need to know what happens at the beginning of Chapter Two."

Stepping toward her, he reached out his hand, and she handed him the manuscript.

"I haven't given you any feedback yet."

"Actually, you did."

She looked confused and crossed one leg over the other. "How's that?"

"Your face spoke for you. Your eyes widened, you kept reading, you flipped the pages, and you asked to read the next chapter. You told me you enjoyed it—without saying a word. Thank you for the feedback."

He leaned against his desk across from the posters on his wall. A breeze blew through the window he had opened.

"Well, I have more feedback for you," she said.

"Okay."

"Adverbs. You didn't kill enough of them. And several of the verbs are ..."

"Go on."

"Several of the verbs are weak and overused."

He covered his heart with his hands. "That was painful. Any other daggers?"

She laughed. "Too much telling, not enough showing. I *am* an English teacher."

He grinned. "Fair enough. These are a few of my weaknesses, along with point of view and head hopping."

"Most writers struggle with these, don't you think?"

"I do."

Sierra crossed her arms and walked around the den. He had hoped his novel would have been a distraction to prevent her from looking around. She picked up a family picture on the bookcase.

"This must be Aimee."

Drumming his fingers on his desk, he sighed. "Yes. A few years back."

She brought the photo closer to her. "She's pretty—beautiful, actually."

"Thanks."

With her back to him, she asked, "What was she like?"

Chewing the inside of his lip, he stalled a moment. "Long story. Not sure where to begin. Maybe we should save that for another time."

Turning around with the photo in her hand, she stepped toward him as he now sat in his desk chair. "Well, what if you make it a short story? Tell me one thing you loved about her. Or if you could describe her with only one word, what would it be?"

Leaning back in his chair, he took a moment to collect his thoughts. Most women he dated got uncomfortable about Aimee. Sierra, however, didn't back away from the subject.

"Unselfish," he said. "She was the most unselfish person I've ever met in my life. Family and friends said so too. In Aimee's life, everyone came first. She came last. And that made me feel—well ..." He saw no point in finishing his sentence.

"How did that make you feel?" she pressed.

"Loved. She made me feel loved by giving me the best of every deal. Who does that?"

She glanced at the photo in her hands and a few others on the bookcase before facing Chase again, who was now leaning forward in his chair at the recollection. He didn't expect his two worlds—the past and present—would collide so soon. It was like having both of them in the same room.

Sierra inhaled, then exhaled hard. Her eyes were tender and fixed on him. "You're blessed, Chase. Aimee was a gift. Thankfully, you knew it—many guys don't."

The warmth of her tone and the sincerity of her delivery moved him again. It spoke to her integrity and respect for Aimee and his feelings about his former wife.

"Thanks, Sierra. You don't know how much I appreciate what you just said." Yet he wondered if her last three words revealed she was still carrying residual emotional baggage from a failed relationship. He changed the subject. "Say, would you like a glass of wine?"

"I'd like that."

"Look around my place. I'll meet you in the kitchen."

Uncorking a bottle of cabernet, he poured two glasses, then set a cheese board on the breakfast bar counter before slicing cheese and setting out crackers. Sierra finished looking at the family photos adorning the walls in a few of the rooms, then meandered to the kitchen, holding a copy of his book.

"Hey, look what I found on your bookshelf. Your bestseller. When we first met on the wharf by the ice cream shop, I mentioned I wished you had written *The Bridge Between Us* several years ago."

Picking up a piece of cheese, he sipped his wine. "And why is that?"

"I think this book could have helped me figure out my relationship with my father—and act on it. Honestly, I think this premise could have helped me work harder at pursuing a relationship with him, especially the way you describe the commitment between the main character and his father."

"I'm glad it spoke to you. One of my goals has been to write fictional relationships so convincingly that readers in similar circumstances find practical solutions that shed light on real-world problems. For your sake, I wish they'd published it sooner too."

She sipped her wine, then set the glass down and sat on a stool.

"May I ask how it could have been helpful?"

She placed a slice of cheese on a cracker while she answered. "Well, the premise was that there is a *bridge* between everyone involved in a serious relationship, and that bridge has the potential to bring us together if we're willing to cross it—or meet halfway. I like the way your novel explained that the secret to all relationships is finding—or developing—a literal bridge of understanding. The secret is finding that bridge."

"Good eye. I was hoping readers would pick up on that. That's encouraging."

She bit into her cracker and continued. "I liked the imagery that, in most relationships, each party stands at one end of the bridge. Yet the key to crossing—or at least meeting in the middle—is honestly understanding or attempting to understand each other."

"Thanks for your thoughts and kind words. An author needs a feedback loop with readers."

"Chase, it made sense to me the way you explained that the path to understanding each other is discovering a crucial connection, or commonality, that allows us to both see *and* feel the other's point of view. I just wish I could have figured out how to apply it to my relationship with my father when he was alive."

"I'm sorry you lost your father, Sierra. And the way you lost him." He sat now on a stool next to her. "Is your mom still around?"

"Yes, but I had a better relationship with my father despite his illness—although both relationships were severely strained. Their issues worked against each other and created the perfect storm. My father's bipolar behavior didn't help my mother with her alcoholism."

"Do you want to talk about it?"

She looked at her phone, likely to check the time, and then at Chase. "I'm sure you have neither the time nor the interest for this."

Pretending to look at his watch, he said, "What do you know—I have both the time and the interest."

She appeared encouraged by his response, so she got to the point. "The short version. I'm an only child. My parents didn't get along. My mother coped with alcohol, my father, verbal abuse, which we would later learn was bipolar disorder."

Sierra described the custody battle between her parents.

"My father won the custody battle because he could prove to the courts that he was a good provider, and his illness could be controlled—if he stayed on his medication. Your debut novel, *The Bridge Between Us,* is the first book, fiction or nonfiction, that got me thinking deeply about discovering a bridge of understanding to my father, despite his illness—to reconnect. Before I could apply it, he took his life."

Chase gasped. "Oh my. I'm so sorry to hear this."

"Maybe I'm kidding myself, but I'd like to think his illness could have been my bridge to understanding him—my bridge to forgiving him, for the way he treated me, and for how his death pulled him away from me forever. When it comes to my relationships with others, I don't know if my father's life or death affected me more."

"I'm humbled to think my novel could have potentially played any role in your restoring your relationship with him." He paused for a moment. "While it may be too late to apply to your father, since your mom is still alive, is there a bridge of understanding that could lead you back to her?"

She pursed her lips. "It's complicated. But I need to consider it— and I will consider it."

"It's just something to think about."

"Agreed." She glanced at her phone. "It's getting late. I should get back. Thank you for a lovely evening."

"Back at ya. I enjoyed your company. You're easy to talk to, Sierra. I like that. Would you be interested in meeting for coffee or having dinner again?"

She smiled. "Are you asking me out on another date?"

"Do you *want* it to be a date?"

"Do you?"

Not to be outdone, he said, "Did you think of tonight as a date?"

She stood, walked over to the sink, and leaned against the counter. "When you asked me out to dinner, did you intend it to be a date?"

"Yes, but did you accept it as a date, or as a meeting to discuss Clay?"

"I accepted it as a spontaneous meeting, but ..."

"But?" He waited for her to commit herself.

She smiled at him. "But I hoped it was a date."

He laughed. "Let's call it a date. That way, the second one won't be weird."

"I like that." She grinned.

"Text me your cell, and I'll call you."

She reached for her purse and pulled out her phone. After she texted him her number, they meandered to the front door and hesitated. A sudden urge to kiss her overwhelmed him, but he didn't trust his feelings, so he pulled back. Instead, he opened the door. She slipped her purse strap over her shoulder and walked to the car. He waved as she slid behind the driver's seat and pressed the ignition.

He cleaned up the kitchen, putting the cheese and the wine in the fridge before heading back to his den. Thinking about the conversation tonight, he felt something he hadn't since Aimee died—renewed energy to write the novel *screaming* inside him.

~

Sliding his journal off the shelf of the bookcase, he went to Clay's room and turned on the light. Glancing across the room, he noted the images of childhood—toys, games, and trucks bursting out of the toy box, stuffed animals tossed in a heap in a corner, a Spider-Man poster hung slightly askew, and open books with broken bindings on the bedside desk.

Sitting on the bed, he listened to the eerie stillness and thought Clay was much too young to be without a mom. The irony of Chase living his father's life and Clay living Chase's life washed over him. Whenever Clay was at a sleepover, the silence was both comforting and disconcerting.

Now sitting at Clay's small desk, he opened his journal and scrawled his thoughts across the page.

~

Today, I learned just how separated Clay feels from his mom—light years, according to his drawing in his art therapy class. How much farther away could she be than another planet? I understand now how art therapy helps assess how a boy is feeling when words fall short, or they cannot escape his heart and find their way to his lips.

Sitting in my son's room now, I realize more than ever how important it is to climb into Clay's world to connect with him. Jack was right when he said my twelve-year-old self must connect with my eight-year-old son. I hope the treehouse may be the secret to this connection.

Today, I reached another milestone. I went on a date. Boom. A bona fide date. (Even though it took the two of us a while to agree if it qualified as a date.) I can't deny I felt something again. A twinge here and there. I hope Sierra did too. Time will tell.

Something else happened tonight—something I thought would never happen. Sierra met Aimee—in photos. I felt like my two worlds collided. Yet I feel good about it. It makes me feel like I'm hiding nothing from her, holding nothing in reserve.

I know a man never honestly knows what dwells in the deep recesses of a woman's heart.

But what I learned about Sierra tonight is she is strong enough to cast her own shadow—rather than live in Aimee's—and confident enough to make our own memories together, without dishonoring Aimee's. I think I could love that kind of woman.

Sierra treated Aimee's memory with reverence and respect. It took my feelings for her up a notch. My "feelings." I still don't fully understand them, but I can say I suddenly feel like writing again—and living.

CHAPTER 23

It was Monday morning in early August, and Chase was already at work on his laptop. Clay was still asleep, and this was the last week of his special session at summer school.

Today, Chase was in the mood to write and felt the momentum. The coffee was on, and he got up to grab a cup. After filling it, he sipped, sat, and typed the ideas he had scrawled in a notebook last night for his new contemporary standalone novel. It wasn't the first time ideas had poked him while he slept, itching to find a home in his notebook beside his bed.

Now more than ever, Chase felt his next novel must be a standalone, not a sequel. He had tried several times previously to come up with a compelling premise for a sequel, and each time he came up dry and unfulfilled. But he didn't give up. Instead, he tried something he had never attempted before—writing two novels at the same time. If it didn't kill him first, he knew one novel would rise to the surface, and one would lag—yet both would be underway. The one that would rise would depend on which generated the most inspiration.

He'd had several recent phone calls with Ed. Although it seemed Ed felt as strongly about the sequel as Chase did about writing a standalone, he listened to Chase. And Chase knew Ed had recognized his grief required an outlet—and his writing was that outlet. His appreciation for Ed had intensified.

Chase wrote until eleven thirty. Words flowed on the page, and he had paused only to make breakfast for Clay, drive him to school, and take a shower. And for Chase, a hot shower was his idea chamber.

His mind would generate inspiration as the hot water relaxed him. Today, it was in overdrive, bringing together subplots, settings, characterization, and snappy dialogue.

Being on a roll, he didn't want to stop—so he didn't—and he accidentally missed his weekly meeting with his creative round table group. This group of writers and graphic designers shared tips to help small businesses like his find group insurance carriers, collect payment from delinquent clients, and find accounting firms and potential new business leads. Last week, one of these leads hired Chase to rewrite the copy for her website, give it a facelift, and develop a social media campaign. The work more than paid the bills and kept the dream alive of one day quitting his day job.

By lunchtime, he had added three chapters to his new standalone novel and had completely rewritten the first three chapters of the sequel. It was much further along than he had remembered. With this newfound momentum, he needed to keep it rolling.

At noon, he stopped to make a sandwich and grab a bag of chips and a soft drink before enjoying his lunch, and the view, on the deck in the treehouse. From this height and perspective, he felt like a kid again. With a few more hours of work, the treehouse would be ready for his son to christen. Clay had reserved the first sleepover for his father and himself. Fernando would be the second sleepover.

After lunch, he called the leader of his creative round table group to apologize for missing lunch. He rewrote his client's website copy, generated ideas for the social media campaign, and started curating content.

Despite the progress on his books today, he realized he should inform Ed soon of his progress. In the end, Ed may not get what he wanted, but Chase liked to think he may get more than he dreamed of. Time would tell.

～

Later that evening, after dinner, Jack stopped by. In typical fashion, he rang the doorbell and walked in. Chase was halfway to the door when Jack greeted him.

"What's shaking?"

"Not much, you?"

"Just dropped in to get the lowdown on your first date with Clay's teacher, Sarah."

"It's *Sierra*—you know that."

Jack plopped down on the couch to get the lowdown. "I know, but then I couldn't yank your chain—and what fun is that?"

"It went well. Very well—I think."

"Details?"

"Can I get you something to drink?"

"I'm good. By the way, where's Clay?"

"With his grandfather. Boys' night out." Chase sat on the other end of the couch. "What do you want to know about Sierra?"

"For starters, what did you talk about?"

"Just stuff. I told her about my appointment with Dr. McAllister, the grief counselor, which I told you about already."

"What else?"

"She talked to me about Clay's art therapy project at school."

The TV was airing news. Wedged between the cushions, with one end jutting straight up like a sinking Titanic, was the remote. Chase plucked it out and turned it off.

"Great, what else?" Jack asked.

Chase rolled his eyes. "What are you fishing for, Jack?"

"Just keep going. You'll know when you get there."

"She came by the house after dinner."

"You're getting warm. Keep going."

"I gave her a tour of the house, showed her my den. As an English teacher, she loved my author quotes on the wall. She noticed the pictures of Aimee on my bookcase and the walls."

"BINGO. Where did that go?" Jack leaned back on the couch and crossed his legs on the coffee table.

"It was interesting. She asked me if I could describe Aimee in just one word, what would it be?"

"What did you say?"

"I told her Aimee was the most unselfish person I have ever met."

Jack exhaled a low whistle. "You could have blown your chances on that one, pal. How did she react?"

"With a sense of respect, I guess. How can you not appreciate someone who treats your late wife with respect?"

"She sounds like the genuine article, my friend." Jack sat up straight and leaned toward Chase. "Be careful you don't make her feel like she has to compete with Aimee. Every woman knows she can't compete with a man's romanticized view of his late wife."

"I know, I was careful. All I can do is tell the truth."

"Anything else?"

"Not of interest to you."

"Based on the way she reacted to Aimee, I'd say she sounds like something special, Chase."

"She is."

"Sounds like you're officially back in the saddle."

"You never stop pushing, my friend."

"I'm not pushing, I'm encouraging. You know I loved Aimee. But I just want to see your life move on. You need it, Clay needs it, and Aimee would want it. Even I can tell there's something about her that's good for you."

Chase's eyes widened. "Really? How can you tell after seeing her only once?"

"It's not what I see in *her.*"

"What then?"

"It's what I see in *you* after you've been with her. You haven't felt like this since Aimee died. Every date was a dead end. Finally, you seem open to the possibility of a relationship. Am I right?"

"Most of the time, I feel open to pursuing her. Then I still get some mixed feelings. Guilt. Maybe betrayal. Confusion."

"You're not betraying Aimee."

Chase stood and walked across the room, then faced Jack. "I know. I just feel like I'm betraying her memory. It messes with my head."

"Want to talk about it—figure it out? We've got a few hours of daylight left. Let's talk while we finish the treehouse."

Chase beamed and gave Jack a thumbs-up. "I'll get the tools."

CHAPTER 24

In the garage, Chase and Jack slipped on their tool belts and loaded building materials on a cart before wheeling it to the treehouse. Chase climbed the rope ladder to the deck, and Jack loaded the pulley system he had rigged to hoist supplies up to the platform.

Once everything was in place, Jack ran up the slide, slipped, fell, slid down, then tried it again before meeting Chase on the deck.

Chase shook his head. "Really? Running up the slide. You're such a kid."

"Yep, and there's nothing like being a kid."

Jack untied the barnwood boards, slipped his hammer from his belt, and prepared to nail them on the far end of the railing to finish enclosing the platform.

"You got the nails, Chase?"

"They're in the clubhouse. I'll grab them."

When Chase returned, he passed the nails to Jack and measured an additional support beam. He wanted to be sure the treehouse was rock solid, knowing Clay would invite all the neighborhood kids over to see his fort. Chase handed him a handful of nails. Placing three nails between his lips, Jack dropped the rest into his T-shirt pocket.

"Do you want to know why you feel guilty whenever you get close to a woman?" Nails vibrated between Jack's lips as he spoke.

Chase looked up and chuckled. "Okay, love doctor, what have ya got?"

Jack put his hammer down. They both stood and faced each other.

"Okay, here it is, plain and simple. You've been through the mill, but you need to decide if you're going to live in the past or the present. The past never leads to the future—the present does. I know you respect your father and his devotion to your mother, but you're not your father. Loyalty aside, you need to live *your* life—not *his*."

Chase glanced out at the ocean then back at his friend. "I'm not trying to live *his* life."

"Beg to differ."

Chase set his hands on his hips and raised an eyebrow. "How can you say that?"

Jack pointed his hammer at his friend. "How can you deny it? Your father has modeled for you that the only way you honor Aimee's memory is by remaining single, like he has all these years. And you bought it."

"Are you sure you're not being too hard on my father?"

"I'm not being too hard on him. I admire him, but I also think he's honored your mother's memory by remaining single—and now, for all the right reasons, he's subtly pressuring you to do the same. And you're loyal to him because he was loyal to your mom. I get it."

Jack had hit a nerve.

Chase's voice cracked. "How can you not revere a man who never deterred in his loyalty to his wife? I feel the same way about Aimee. You just don't understand. Aimee and I were so …" Chase struggled to finish his sentence. Looking away, he tried to get a grip, but his emotions betrayed him. "We were so … one. She could finish my sentences."

Jack picked up another board. "I respect that. But your father made a choice to go through life alone. Your dad is a noble father. He carried you through life's worst tragedy, but you have to admit, he never gave himself permission to love again. I don't think he should make the same decision for you."

"How is he trying to make it for me?"

"By making you feel guilty about the prospect of loving again. Ask yourself, what would Aimee want? For you? For Clay?"

Chase wiped sweat from his brow, thought for a moment, and looked around at what they had accomplished on the treehouse. The platform was rock solid. The rope ladder, slide, and trapdoor were finished. The clubhouse and railing were nearly complete. And his best friend not only helped him build it, but he was now challenging him—to build his confidence. As he listened to the calming sounds of the sea, he answered, "She would want us to be happy."

"*Are* you happy?"

Chase looked away, then cleared his throat. "Jack, are you saying Aimee would want me to remarry?"

Jack held his hand out. "Hand me the tape measure. I'm saying she would want you to move on, if ..."

"Go on."

"If marrying would mean happiness for you and stability for Clay." Jack paused. "Look, Chase, no one will ever replace Aimee. But you honor her, not by being loyal to her *memory*, but by being loyal to her *wishes*. That's where I think you're getting confused. Her wish would be for you both to be happy. And you'll be happy again if you move forward. Life goes on. It did for me."

"Your wife didn't die, Jack."

Chase noticed his friend's face flush. "No. Worse. She lived. A constant reminder that she traded me in. Sometimes divorce feels like death, only you're the one who died—to your spouse."

Jack stopped and took a breath. "Julie cashed in her chips. Broke her vows. Walked out. The problem is, I'll see her again. I already have. The grocery store is never a safe place because eventually I'll turn a corner and bump into her cart." He ran his hand through his hair. "With divorce, sometimes there's no closure because you may never know how you slipped from 'I can't live without you' to 'I can't live with you.'"

Chase smiled at his old friend to break the tension. "Yeah, you're such a mess, pal. Hey, look, I'm sorry. It was wrong to compare our situations."

Jack mirrored his expression. "I was a mess—not anymore, thanks to you. But I had a choice to make too. I could live in the rubble, or pick up the pieces and attempt to reassemble my life. Ask yourself, are you going to mourn what once was, or start living for what can be?"

Jack's question hung in the breeze tonight without an answer. They resumed working together in silence. When the sun had set, they had finished the treehouse.

CHAPTER 25

On Tuesday morning, Chase loaded the dishwasher while Clay finished his breakfast.

"This is your last week of summer school and your special program," Chase reminded him. "Is your backpack packed?"

"Not yet." He yawned and rubbed his eyes.

"I have a surprise for you."

Squinting, Clay turned to him. "What surprise?"

"The treehouse is done. Jack and I finished it last night."

Clay's tired eyes widened. He bounced off his seat and ran to the window to look in the backyard. "Awesome. When can we sleep in it?"

"Hold your horses. Why don't you and Fernando play in it for the rest of the week while I'm working? Then you and I can sleep there Saturday night to test it out. You'll have the rest of August for you and Fernando to have sleepovers."

"Okay." Clay was suddenly more alert. Carrying his dishes to the sink, he handed them to his father. "Thanks, Dad."

When Chase squatted to place the utensils on the bottom rack, Clay hugged him, squeezing longer and harder than usual. Chase held him tight.

After he returned from dropping Clay off at school, and before starting his writing regimen, he picked up the house, paid some bills, put a load of clothes in the wash, and started the dishwasher. Before he sat to write, he poured himself another cup of coffee and replayed in his mind what Jack had said last night. Happiness is a choice. Aimee would want him to choose happiness. Having feelings for Sierra was not betrayal. He must *choose* tomorrow, yet *remember* yesterday—and live his own life, not his father's. Advice was easier given than applied.

As a writer, he knew these thoughts would run in the background on a continuous loop as he worked, so he started the next chapter of his standalone novel. By lunchtime, he had completed a few more chapters because he was in the zone. After lunch, he would switch gears and complete client work, check emails, return phone calls, and write a few more chapters of the sequel. It was coming along—slowly. The writing was good, but he still felt uninspired—and he couldn't shake it. He embraced the discipline required to be an author, but he also could not deny that words flowed faster from inspiration than discipline.

～

It had been a productive week. By Friday, he had written almost one hundred pages of his novel and wrapped up most of his client work, and, as an added benefit, with Clay he'd enjoyed fruit snacks, candy bars, and sports drinks and even read a few comic books after dark, by flashlight, in the treehouse.

Life felt real again, and it was feeling like *his* life. His routine was familiar, not foreign. Comfortable, not contrived. Sure, he was aware of the proverbial hole in his heart, the awkward void people were no longer comfortable talking about—but life was back on a track again. And a funny thing had happened. Fernando was becoming like a second son to him. Cute, unassuming Fernando brought balance, perspective, and a healthy diversion for Clay's life.

Most of the week he thought about Sierra, but he hadn't called her since their date last weekend. Staring at his phone, he asked himself if he should reach out to her. What would he say? When she stopped by unexpectedly last weekend, she'd caught him by surprise, and somehow it gave him a surge of courage, momentum. Now he wrestled with nagging doubt—again. It wasn't like him.

Before Aimee died, their friends saw Chase Kincaid as confident. The guy who knew precisely what he wanted, and how to get it. No doubt. No delay. Just results. "I get strength from just being around Chase," Aimee often told her mother, Joyce Thompson, when they were dating. Chase realized the death of a loved one had not only redefined his life, it also redefined his identity. *Strength had succumbed to insecurity.*

Would Sierra be expecting his call—or wondering why he hadn't called already? Self-doubt—one of the residual side effects of prolonged grief.

Chase opted to send her a text and ask if she wanted to join him and Clay on Saturday for a day of fun in the sun, paddleboarding, bike riding, and having lunch together on the beach. If she wasn't available or interested, she could let him down easily via text, he thought.

It wasn't long after he sent it that she responded. "I'd love to spend Saturday with two handsome men," she texted.

Chase was never an emoji guy, but the three smiling emojis at the end of her text renewed his confidence and made him feel more like himself again. The text he sent back said, "Date #2 confirmed. Pick you up at ten."

She responded, "I'll be waiting for you." He knew this was a standard response, but her choice of words brought home a little closer, filling the void he had felt the last two years. His upside down world was suddenly being righted, leveled. Someone was waiting for him.

He read her text again: "I'll be waiting for you." Placing his phone on his desk, he gazed out the window at the ocean. *Is this what healing feels like?*

CHAPTER 26

C hase and Clay greeted Saturday with a renewed sense of excitement as they packed the Jeep. They loved to paddleboard, and Clay had become good at it. Both enjoyed bike riding on the path along the ocean on Cabrillo Boulevard and having lunch at a beachside restaurant.

The beach had become a custom for them since Aimee died. Before that, it was a family tradition once or twice a month. It was Aimee's idea—to keep Chase from writing every Saturday away.

If he wasn't careful, he could work around the clock. Writing was like that.

"Time moves faster when you write," Joseph Kincaid, his grandfather, used to say. "Artists have their own conception of time. It's measured not in minutes and hours, but by pages written and canvas covered."

Chase's grandfather used to write poetry, often losing himself in his work for hours, like a painter with his canvas. It was true for Chase too. *An artist does his best work when he's lost in it—when the clock stops and is no longer a distraction.* Perhaps he'd inherited his passion to write from his grandfather. One more reason he admired him so much.

With several beachside restaurants to choose from, who could argue that lunch under an umbrella beside the ocean wasn't the best way to live?

Chase loaded the Jeep with towels, blankets, three life jackets, and a beach umbrella. Clay packed his snacks of choice, beverages, and a cooler. Chase grabbed the sunscreen, his baseball cap, sunglasses, and car keys.

Sierra kept her promise. She was ready at ten sharp, waiting outside her apartment. She was holding a towel and beach bag.

After Chase pulled up, he walked around the back of the Jeep. Sierra met him there. They looked at each other for a moment without a word. She touched his arm. Time stopped. He thought he felt electricity, but knew it was just the emotional connection. By the look on her face, he thought she felt it too.

"Good morning. It's nice to see you again." He opened the hatch. "Let's put your stuff back here."

Her face brightened. "Great to see you too."

His heart quickened, and he felt a surge of energy.

"Hey, Miss Taylor." Clay glanced at her through the open hatch.

"Hey, Clay. Ready for some fun today?"

"Yep. It'll be awesome."

Chase packed her things and closed the hatch, and they hopped in the front seats.

After arriving at East Beach, Chase parked and rented three paddleboards and paddles. Clay scouted out their base camp on the beach. Together, they set up the umbrella, laid out two blankets and lawn chairs, and placed the cooler in the shadow cast by the umbrella. With his swimsuit already on, Clay peeled off his shirt and sandals.

"Let's go, Dad." He grabbed his board and paddle.

"Clay, slow down. Let's wait a minute for Miss Taylor. She's our guest. And put on your sunscreen and life jacket. You know our rules."

Sierra had her swimsuit on under her blouse and blue jean cut-offs. She slipped out of them and tucked them in her beach bag before pulling her hair back in a tight ponytail with a rubber band. Once again, he found himself taken by her loveliness.

His grandfather was right. She became more attractive every time he saw her.

"Okay, guys, let's do this," Chase said.

Clay was off to the races, dragging his paddleboard toward the ocean. Carrying their boards and paddles, Chase and Sierra followed, relishing a moment alone to talk. With warm sand underfoot, the sound of waves lapping the shore, seagulls bobbing on the water, and pelicans dive-bombing unsuspecting targets, it was another picture-perfect Santa Barbara day.

When Clay got farther ahead of them, Sierra spoke softly. "It's fun to see Clay outside the classroom."

"Yeah? What do you see?"

"So far? A normal eight-year-old boy. A well-balanced kid who loves his father—and having fun. Better said, a boy who loves having fun with his father. There's a difference."

He nodded. "Kind of you to say. The door swings both ways. Truth is, I need him as much as he needs me. When I'm down, he's up, and vice versa. We stabilize each other." Chase dipped his head and looked over his sunglasses at her. "Have you tried paddleboarding before?"

"Once. I like it, but I'm not very good at it."

"What are you good at?"

"Tennis, volleyball, art, but mostly running. I ran on the women's track team at USC. I love to run, especially on Sunday mornings after church. Gives me time to think, process the sermon and how I can apply it to my life."

"Tell me more about your interest in tennis, volleyball, and art."

They pulled their boards closer to the water. "Well, I was on the tennis team in high school. I enjoy beach volleyball—for fun. And I love the arts. Painting, sculpture, watercolors, oil, anything you can put on canvas."

"Are you an artist?"

"Not particularly, but I love to paint with watercolors. I'm not talented, but I enjoy what art gives me."

"Which is?"

"Peace of mind, tranquility, and a way to express myself. I just enjoy how artists express themselves. It's exciting to see talent emerge out of pure passion. I guess I just love how creativity is born on a page, canvas, or a lump of clay. As an author, you know what that's about."

"I do. One more thing you and I have in common."

Laying his board in the water, Clay paddled out to deeper water. Chase adjusted his cap and clipped a string to the temple bars of his sunglasses and around his neck. After entering the water, he held Sierra's board until she got used to the cool water and straddled her board. "As a collegiate athlete, you should be good at this—and make me look like a rookie."

"You might look like a rookie regardless of my performance."

Chase laughed. "Clever. That's all I need—one more person taking shots at me. You're supposed to be on my side, not Clay's."

"If the shoe fits …"

Chase raised his eyebrows. "Okay, two can play at this game. And remember, you started it."

"Let's paddle out to Clay before we stand."

Clay was on his feet and paddling perpendicular to the shore.

They sat on their boards and paddled out to the deeper water near him.

"We're here, now what? Who goes first?" Sierra bobbed in the water.

Chase paddled alongside her. "In theory, you stand up and paddle your board."

"I got that part, wise guy. You want to show me how it's done, hotshot?"

"It's important to always get on your knees first. Do you know why?"

She put both knees in front of her and struggled to stabilize herself. "To get your balance?"

"No, you want to be in the proper position to pray so you don't drown before you start."

"Very funny."

Chase didn't miss a beat. "Then you slowly stand up, using the paddle for balance. I bend my knees just slightly and take my stance to maintain my balance. Finally, I alternate paddling on both sides of the board—and act like I've done this before."

"Care to demonstrate?"

"With one disclaimer. I have a fifty percent chance of demonstrating this right."

She interjected before he could finish. "Thus, a fifty percent chance of demonstrating it wrong."

"Exactly. It's sort of like writing."

She rolled her eyes as they bobbed up and down alongside each other. "Let me guess, you're going to quote a famous writer out here in the middle of the ocean?"

"Yep. There's a direct correlation."

"Oh, really? Enlighten me."

"John Steinbeck once said, 'I have written a great many stories, and I still don't know how to go about it except to write it and take my chances.' It's the same with paddleboarding."

She shook her head, and a smirk cracked her lips. "You must be the most philosophical or literary paddleboarder in the world."

"Nope. Just on the West Coast. I'll get up, then you try." Chase kneeled and slowly stood, using the paddle against the water to gain his balance. He angled his feet to get comfortable before paddling away from Sierra. "Okay, your turn."

Sierra had no problem getting to her knees. She waited for the board to settle, then she slowly stood before losing her balance and falling backward into the water. When she came to the surface, Chase laughed and struggled to maintain his balance.

"Close. Try it again."

On her second attempt, she fell sideways.

When she surfaced, Chase teased her. "You realize an eight-year-old is about to show us both up."

She laughed and played along. "I don't do this every other Saturday, Chase."

"I know, but if I didn't tease you, where is the fun in that?"

It would take a third try before she found her balance and stood on her board. Excited, she squealed as she paddled to Chase a few yards ahead of her as he kept his eye on Clay.

"It's about time," Clay yelled as he continued to paddle ahead of them.

When Chase and Sierra were side by side, she glanced at Chase, then at her feet to keep her balance. "Tell me again, why do you enjoy this?"

"You'll love it once you get the hang of it. It's like riding a bike." Their eyes met again. "You've ridden a bike before, right?"

Sierra rolled her eyes, then reached out with her paddle and pushed him off his board. When he rose to the surface, he swam to his board and said, "Hey, what was that for?"

It was her turn to laugh at him. "Now I know why you enjoy this so much. It's not about staying *on* the board—it's about knocking other people *off*. And yes, I've ridden a bike before."

She paddled off toward Clay, not noticing Chase swimming underwater toward her board.

He rocked it gently at first, so she would know her fate was in his hands.

She screamed when she saw him. "Don't you dare, Chase."

"Apologize for pushing me off my board, Miss Taylor."

"Never."

He continued to rock her paddleboard.

"Clay! Tell your dad to stop rocking the boat."

Clay shook his head and laughed at her. "No way."

Attempting to keep her balance, she tried another strategy. "Clay, I'm your teacher! Tell your dad to behave."

Chase rocked her board just enough to allow her to regain her balance. His head was at her feet.

He looked up at her. "Really? That's your strategy—play the teacher card? You may be his teacher, but I'm his father—I outrank you with him."

Chase then tipped over the paddleboard, sending Sierra shrieking into the water. When she surfaced, her hair covered her face after it came loose from its ponytail.

Laughing at her, he said, "You're right, Sierra, many people paddleboard just to push others off."

She swam to her board, mounted, and straddled it. "You've lost so many points, Chase Kincaid."

Chase straddled his board and sat up. They perched facing one another, pointing in different directions. "Okay, we're even—let's call a truce."

Clay paddled around them twice, as though showing his prowess and shaming them. Chase and Sierra lay on their backs and sunned themselves on their boards between attempts to paddleboard. The two of them frolicked in the water for another hour while keeping a close eye on Clay before heading back to shore for lunch.

After reaching their base camp, Chase tossed her and Clay a towel. They slid off their life vests, dried, and warmed up in the sun. Sierra rummaged through her beach bag for another rubber band before she combed her hair and pulled it back again.

"Hungry?" Chase asked.

Clay nodded as he pulled his shirt over his head.

"Yeah, I'm hungry too. I worked up an appetite trying to survive out there," Sierra said.

~

From the counter of a beachside restaurant, Sierra ordered a shrimp and avocado salad and a Diet Coke, while Chase ordered the Baja fish tacos and a lemonade.

"What'll you have, Clay? Let me guess, a burger or quesadilla?"

"Chicken quesadilla and a Coke."

Sierra picked out a table on the beach, shaded under a sky-blue umbrella. She slipped off her sandals and rubbed her feet on the sand. With beach toys in hand, Clay played in the sand while they waited for their food.

Sierra lifted her Diet Coke to her lips and took a sip. "So you guys used to come to the beach a lot as a family?"

"Yeah. Aimee was big on family traditions. This was one of them. She kept me focused on my family on weekends. Otherwise, I might work too much. Do you know what the toughest thing is about being a freelance writer?"

She looked at him. "Tell me."

"There is no discernable end to the workday. As long as work keeps coming in, there's no quitting time. No employees to go home, signaling five o'clock. No one to tell you to stop working, punch out, and cash in on your freedom. Thankfully, Aimee told me when to stop working, otherwise I responded to the pressure and pace of my projects—and worked too much."

A server placed their food on the table. "Can I get you anything else?"

Chase looked over the tray for their order, utensils, tartar sauce, and salad dressing. "No. I think we have everything. Thank you."

Chase called Clay to come eat, and he took his time, as usual, before seating himself at the table with the ocean to his back.

Sierra poured a small amount of dressing on her salad and took a bite. Chase sipped his lemonade while Clay devoured half of his quesadilla without looking up.

"Slow down, Clay," his father said.

Sierra was reflective, and a grateful smile curled around her lips. "Thank you guys for bringing me along on your family tradition. I'm honored."

A group of teenagers started a game of volleyball in the sand close to them.

"You should join them and show me what you can do," Chase teased.

She smiled. "Very funny. If you don't mind, I'd rather have you tell me more about Aimee." She turned to Clay. "What was your mom like?"

Clay wrinkled his forehead as he concentrated while he ate his chips.

"She was nice to everyone," he said between bites. "She loved to tease Dad, like you do. She was funny, and she would sing a lot—for no reason."

"Really? What did she like to sing?"

"Mostly songs on the radio or her phone. Sometimes she would sing and dance in the kitchen."

"This is news to me. When did she dance in the kitchen?" Chase asked.

"After school, when you were writing or not at home. She pretended a wooden spoon was a microphone."

Curious, Sierra probed Clay. "Do you remember any song she sang from the radio?"

"Sappy songs, mostly—about love and stuff. I think she liked songs that made her think about Dad—and me."

"And what makes you think that?"

"I don't know. Maybe the way she looked at me, hugged me, and danced with me."

Chase sat up straighter. "She danced with you?"

"I guess—she hugged me and moved in a circle slowly. Is that dancing?"

Sierra smiled. "Yes, that's slow dancing—and you usually do it with someone you love."

Clay finished his quesadilla in record time and gulped his Coke. "Dad, can I play in the sand now?"

"Yes, but play close by—where I can see you."

Clay scampered off to play in the sand and watch the volleyball game.

"It's amazing what comes out of a kid when you ask, isn't it, Chase?"

"It is. Just like you, Jennifer, and Dr. McAllister said."

"How about you, Chase? Tell me more about what Aimee was like. If you don't mind talking about her. I don't want it to be painful."

"Mind? No. When people ask about her, they bring her back to me. I want people to remember her—because I can never forget her. I told you some things the other day. Not sure where I would begin."

"Anywhere. I already asked you what you liked most about her. Maybe it's easier if I put it this way. As a stranger, what would I like about her?"

Chase took another bite of his taco, then leaned back in his chair while he chewed. A breeze blew through her hair as he appeared to ponder the question.

"She would like you."

Sierra nodded with a sense of suspicion. "Really? Why?"

"That's the beauty of it. She would like you because of who you are. She would see in you what Clay and I see, a confident, caring teacher who puts her students first, someone easy to like and talk to, someone who is fun to be with, and most of all, someone you can trust."

Sierra's face turned red.

He didn't wait for her to respond. "And you would like her because she would put you first, like everyone else. She would recognize your strengths and stand behind you and support your ideas.

You would notice her quiet confidence in you that would boost your self-confidence."

She sipped her drink. "The more I get to know you and Clay, I can only imagine the depth of your loss. Aimee sounds wonderful."

"You asked what she was like. Before I share a story, I never told you how she died."

"You mentioned a heart attack, but no details. You don't have to go there, Chase. I never intended to pry and ..."

He looked over at Clay, likely ensuring the beach toys kept him enthralled in the sand. "I know. But her death is not just about what happened, it's about where it happened. I'll make a long story short." He recounted the story of Aimee's death and his final minutes with her on the pavement in the middle of the highway after she slipped away.

"A couple physicians told me afterward that CPR wouldn't have helped, what with her medical history."

Sierra covered her mouth with one hand.

Sierra was stone silent. Tears cascaded down her cheeks. She did not wipe them away. They landed in the sand.

Finally, she spoke. "Oh, my. There was nothing you could do, Chase."

He covered his eyes with one hand. "Thank you for saying that, Sierra. You don't know how much that means to me, but ..."

There was an awkward pause.

"But?"

"But unfortunately, not everyone thinks so. My mother-in-law, Joyce, still thinks I could have done more, so I've avoided her by limiting my visits and not returning her calls promptly, and that's unfair to her—and to Clay." Pausing for a moment, he collected himself. "You asked what Aimee was like. May I share one story with you?"

"Please. I'd love to hear it."

"Let's walk back to our base camp first so I can put more

sunscreen on Clay. I'm sure he wants to build some sandcastles that his grandfather, the architect, would be proud of."

~

Chase watched as Clay poured a bucket of water over the sand near the shore, en route to molding the perfect castle, while he talked with Sierra. "It's not a big deal, but you wanted one example of what Aimee was like."

"I'm listening."

"It was our third wedding anniversary. We had just checked into our room at the resort. When we put our suitcases in our room, we noticed the amenities. The room was upscale, spacious, and featured a fireplace in the corner, whirlpool bath, ocean view, and skylights, so lots of natural light."

"Sounds perfect."

"It was. We were eager to enjoy the city, Huntington Beach, and Orange County, so instead of unpacking, we walked down to the front desk. We wanted to get recommendations for restaurants and local attractions, so we had to wait in line behind two couples. Turns out the first couple in line was on their honeymoon. When they tried to check in, they learned their room was inadvertently double-booked. The other party arrived first and was already in the room."

She frowned. "They had no room—on their honeymoon? That's awful."

"They asked about other rooms, but nothing was available. Crushed, the bride cried. The young groom wasn't sure what to do. You should have seen the look of panic on his face. It was a busy weekend in Huntington Beach, so finding a hotel room that night might not have been possible."

"What did they do?"

"The real question is, what did we do?"

A gull squawked overhead. Children's voices permeated the air between the waves slapping the shore. "I don't follow."

"Well, Aimee turns to me and says, 'Chase, why don't we give them our room?'"

"I hemmed and hawed because we had no backup plan. And while I agreed with her and felt compassion for the young couple, I just wasn't sure what we would do. I asked her what her thoughts were on a backup plan."

Sierra leaned forward. "What did Aimee say?"

"She said, 'We'll figure that out later. For now, if our room becomes their room, their blessing becomes ours.'"

Sierra nodded. "What did you do?"

"I said, 'Let's do it,' and Aimee offered them our room. After we handled the transaction, we retrieved our suitcases and attempted to find another room locally in our price range. When we couldn't, we had dinner in Huntington Beach and found a room on our way back home—in Ventura."

"I can't believe you two. It was your anniversary, and you gave up a gorgeous room to strangers. How were you blessed? Was your new room better?"

"No, worse. Much worse. But the evening may have been better."

She lay on her side and leaned on her elbow. "How so?"

"At dinner we talked about how we felt on our honeymoon—and how important it was for everything to be perfect. In our case, it was. She told me how she would feel if we lost our room on our honeymoon. She cried when she explained how she would have felt if complete strangers stepped up and surrendered their room for us on our honeymoon. It hit me when she said, 'Tonight, we are that couple, Chase.' It put everything in perspective for me."

"In retrospect, were you ever disappointed you had to give up your room on your anniversary because of someone else's mistake?"

Chase glanced out at Clay and the water. "No. We were one heart on the matter. Besides, Aimee would never give me a chance to feel that way. She used to say, 'Someone's mistake became our opportunity. How can you feel bad about someone giving you a golden opportunity to be a better person?' How could I argue with that?"

When Chase finished his story, Sierra sat quietly and let the air clear. Sensing she knew there was nothing she could say to compete with or complement the moment, he remained quiet.

Clay continued his masterpiece, while Sierra gazed at the ocean. After an extended moment, she whispered, "Seems you married an angel, Chase. I can see why you loved her so much."

CHAPTER 27

C hase walked up to Clay and studied his sandcastle as the waves slapped the shore.

"Impressive."

"Do you think Grandpa would like it?"

"Let's find out. I'll take some pictures, and we'll send them to him later. Do you want some help with this?"

"No, I have to do it myself."

"Okay, let me put some more sunscreen on your back while you put some on your face, arms, and legs."

Chase wandered back to Sierra and sat in a lawn chair under the umbrella again. "Can I get you a snack?"

"Like what?"

"Clay loaded the cooler. Let's see. Fruit snacks, juice packs, potato chips, water, and an ice cream sandwich that has seen better days."

"Just a bottle of water."

He tossed her the plastic bottle. "Well, now you know my story. What's yours?"

Her eyebrows narrowed. "My story?"

"Everyone has a story. What's yours?"

"My love story?"

"Only if you want to go there."

She looked surprised. "For me, I just haven't found the right person … to give my heart to. But I once found the wrong person to give my heart to—and I almost did."

Chase shot a glance at Clay and then back at her. "I don't want to pry either—but would you like to talk about it?"

"There's not much to say, really. I thought I was in love. I thought he was the right guy, but, well, let's just say, everything I thought was right—was wrong."

Chase opened his water and took a drink before twisting the cap on. "What was the turning point?"

"Turning point? I think I would call it the 'aha' moment—or the gut punch. It was when he started dating his nurses while we were a couple."

"This guy got a name?"

"Merritt Michael Patterson III. How's that for stuffy?"

"That should have been your first red flag."

She stood and stretched, then sat in her lawn chair. "I've been told."

"With a name like that, you must have heard some sirens, right?"

"Apparently, love is blind—and deaf."

"Did you love him?"

"I thought I did. Before his indiscretions. We were engaged for a while, but I broke it off because without trust, how can a relationship survive? In hindsight, maybe I loved who I thought he was rather than who he actually was. Does that make sense?"

"It does." Chase watched as a sailboat glided by as Clay diligently expanded his sandcastle kingdom. Then he turned to Sierra. "May I ask—is this relationship ancient history or a recent scar?"

She crossed her legs in her lawn chair and sat up straighter. "Let's call it recent history and a healing wound. The problem is, he's still trying to make a comeback."

"Really? Where is he now?"

"He lives and works here in Santa Barbara."

Chase raised his eyebrows. "So he can walk into your life at any moment?"

"And he's trying to. Whenever I run into him, it's awkward. And he hasn't given up calling occasionally."

"Do you feel threatened?"

"No. It's nothing like that. It just feels—well—clumsy. I have nothing to say to him."

"But he wants to get back together?"

"It appears that way, and the grapevine confirms it."

"It's not a fair comparison, even though you said you're in no danger. But Jack still feels awkward and off-balance when he runs into his ex, too."

She smiled and nodded. "Feeling off-balance is a good word. I like Jack. He takes life in stride and seems like a guy who has your back."

Chase glanced up to check on Clay and his progress on building a sandcastle with a moat around it. "Jack has always had my back. His wife, Julie, divorced him four years ago. She's local. He tries not to let on, and I know he's ready to move on, but I think he's not completely over her yet. Maybe you never are."

"As we've talked about, grief is difficult to reconcile. On a bad day, when you're feeling hurt, logic isn't a cure for pain. When I felt the pain of my breakup, I told myself I was better off."

"But that logic didn't quell the pain?"

"Right."

Chase stood, and Sierra joined him. "Do you still feel something for this guy?"

She frowned. "I don't think so. We had some good times, so nostalgic feelings create confusion sometimes, and the grief of a broken relationship can mess with your head, don't you think?"

Chase shifted his gaze to the sand so she couldn't read the disappointment in his eyes. *She isn't sure if she still feels something for this guy?* "Ah, yeah. Grief definitely messes with your head. I'm Exhibit A," he said. "I'm just glad I had a friend like Jack help me navigate through it. He's talked me off a cliff a time or two after Aimee died. It's what best friends do."

"That's how I feel about Jennifer. She's always there for me. She came alongside me when my father died and when I found out Merritt was unfaithful on my birthday."

He turned to her. "Ouch, your birthday?"

"Long story."

"What would we do without best friends, Sierra?"

Her eyes followed a kite in the sky before shifting back to him. "What would we do? Suffer more. Smile less."

He nodded. "I read somewhere that friendship divides our sorrow and multiplies our joy."

Her face brightened. "So true. You're just full of quotes today, Chase."

"It's what writers do."

"Speak in quotes?"

"No, we simply use quotes to better express ourselves. But as an English teacher, you know that."

He walked over to Clay, took more photos of his creation, and returned to Sierra.

"How goes the sandcastle construction?" she asked.

"You should see how elaborate it is. I wasn't kidding when I said he takes after his grandfather—my father."

They both stood and then lay on their blankets. He rolled toward her and leaned on an elbow, facing her.

"You've met my father, David, and my best friend, Jack, but there is one other key player in our life who I haven't said much about. I need your advice on something."

She sat up under the shadow cast by the umbrella. Folding her legs under her, she said, "Talk to me."

"Well, it's Aimee's mom. Actually, I'm not sure why I'm even talking to you about this." He stopped short.

"Chase, remember what I told you when we took our first walk on the beach—I'm a safe place. But only if you want to talk about it."

"Okay. Let's just say Joyce and I don't always get along. I don't blame her, but I'm not sure exactly what to do about it. To make matters worse, for the last month, I've just ignored the problem— and her. That hasn't been fair to her—or to Clay. He needs to have a relationship with his only grandma."

"What's troubling her?"

"Me."

"How so?"

He pulled a water bottle from the cooler and offered it to her before having one himself. Then he sat facing her. "When I've needed a babysitter for Clay, I usually ask my father. It's so much easier. I've attempted to balance Clay spending time with both of them equally, but I've avoided the pain and guilt of contacting Joyce."

"Why?"

"Two reasons. She feels I favor my father. She's partially right. I default to him."

Sierra listened intently. "And the other reason is she thought you should have done more to save her daughter—like we talked about?"

"Exactly, so I've avoided her because I can't face the guilt—or the guilt trip she puts me on."

Second thoughts suddenly swept over him, and the cycle of self-condemnation was knocking on the door.

"I'm sure you've explained this to your mother-in-law."

"Repeatedly. She doesn't want to hear it. I don't blame her. She lost her husband and her only child to cardiac arrhythmia. No one was there when her husband died, but I was there when her daughter died. I guess that makes it my fault in Joyce's mind. I'm Aimee's husband. It was my job to save her. That's what husbands do, right? Save the day."

Sierra was quiet. She opened her water and took another sip. "I'm so sorry, Chase."

Chase lowered his head. "She is right about one thing. I have avoided her. Because she's a constant reminder of how I lost Aimee, and, in her mind, it's my fault. She may force me to carry this weight for the rest of my life. So I avoid her—at least right now."

Sierra reached over and took his hand. "Don't beat yourself up about that."

"Easier said than done. I know I must move on, but I don't want her to drive a wedge between Clay and me. Sometimes I feel like I'm trapped in an endless cycle of guilt, like a train caught in a loop."

Sierra turned toward him instead of the ocean. "Have you talked to her about how you feel—or about how she makes you feel?"

"No, not yet. Like so many things in life, it's easier to ignore than confront. Remember, I'm still learning how to verbalize all this stuff. One thing at a time. Still, I know she loves Clay dearly and has a right to see him. So I wanted your opinion. What would you do?"

"I think the real question is, what would Aimee do? Was she close to her mom?"

He shot a glance at Clay to be sure he was still building his sand-castle. "Yes, despite their differences."

"What do you think she would want you to do?"

Chase looked out at the horizon and then back at Sierra. "Aimee would want her mom involved in Clay's life."

"Then we need to find a way to do that."

"We?"

She lowered her head, then looked at him. "Only if you need me."

He looked at her and smiled. "You're right. I just need the right words and proper timing."

"I'm not sure when is the right time, Chase. But if anybody can find the right words, it's an author, right?"

A breeze blew through her hair, and he watched her pull a strand away from her face and curl it around her ear. She glanced at Clay and the ocean behind him before turning to Chase. "Why is our life so different from our dreams?"

CHAPTER 28

After paddleboarding, lunch, and a long talk on the beach, the trio enjoyed biking along the ocean on Cabrillo Boulevard to cool off. Later, after they returned their rented bikes, Clay suggested they stop for ice cream on State Street at McConnell's, a popular tourist trap. He got no argument from Chase or Sierra.

In the late afternoon, Chase dropped Sierra off at her apartment and walked her to her front door. Clay watched them from the Jeep.

"I had fun today," Chase said.

"Me too."

When he stalled, she reached for her house keys in her beach bag. Chase wondered if she felt the awkwardness. She compensated for it with a comment. "I think Date Number Two was a success. Will there be a Date Number Three?" He sensed a yearning in her eyes.

"Would you like a Date Number Three?"

"I would—if and when you're ready. Take your time, Chase—I can wait."

Her comment relaxed him. She just let him off the hook, opening another relief valve—releasing the pressure of *expectations*. Her simple words conveyed so much. She could wait for him—allowing him as much time and space as he needed to figure out his feelings and his life. It drew him to her. He felt an urge to kiss her, wondering if Clay was watching from the Jeep. What would his son think if he kissed his teacher? It would require one more father/son talk.

Placing his hands on her cheeks, he gently pulled her close and kissed her on the forehead. "I'm fighting the urge to kiss you right now." He glanced toward his vehicle. "But I have an audience in my

Jeep. I should talk to him first. He and I have been in this together. I don't want him feeling alone—if my feelings run ahead of his."

He ran his hands down her arms till they reached her hands. She squeezed them.

"It's the right thing to do, Chase. Clay must come first. I don't want to risk ever coming between you—or confusing him."

"Thank you for understanding. I have to do this right—and in the proper sequence."

"I'm with you."

When Chase walked back to the car, Clay was watching him from the back seat. He knew he might have some explaining to do, but his mind was on something else. Sierra's choice of words struck him to the core. If he'd scripted it, he could not have done a better job. Everything she said was in perfect harmony with how he felt. Finally, he was on the same page with another woman.

When they returned home, Chase kept his promise to Clay to commemorate their finished project. After sunset, they would conduct the first official sleepover in the treehouse together. In the meantime, while Chase made burgers on the grill, Clay transferred more toys, posters, comic books, blankets, the air mattresses, and many of his most precious things to the treehouse to make it his own.

Near sunset, they unrolled their individual air mattresses, inflated them with a pump inside the clubhouse in the treehouse, and then laid them on the floor before placing their sleeping bags and pillows on top of them. Clay equipped the cooler with more snacks and cold water. Chase brought out a large flashlight they could point at the ceiling to create indirect light, so he could write in his journal if he was in the mood.

When the sun set, they stood out on the treehouse deck and leaned on the railing. Facing the ocean, they took in the natural beauty of a bright orange sky. And Clay talked to him the way fathers hope their sons will confide in them—with the innocent vulnerability that allows a father to see their heart.

"I loved being with you today, Dad. It felt like we were a family again."

"I loved being with you, too, buddy. There's nothing I like better than being with you."

They reflected on the day of paddleboarding, bike riding, and building sandcastles. Clay followed his father's lead—peeling back the layers—and it all happened so naturally. This had been what Jennifer, Sierra, and Dr. McAllister had been referring to—and what Chase had been praying for. Connection.

When the sky faded to black and the cool night air set in, they turned on the flashlight, slid into their sleeping bags, rolled onto their sides, and leaned on their elbows, facing each other to keep the day alive and the conversation going.

"Clay, when I was up here the other day, I noticed some of the cool stuff you have in your fort."

"Yeah. I've got comic books, posters, snacks, juice packs, your old walkie-talkie, binoculars, a small flashlight, a homemade first-aid kit, stuff like that."

Chase thought a moment before his next sentence, unsure if it would keep their conversation open—or shut it down. It was worth the risk. "I also noticed you have a special notebook with Mom's name on it. Fort A.M.Y."

Clay raised his voice. "You didn't read it, did you?"

"Calm down. No, of course not."

Clay reached for a magic marker he had stored in an old cigar box and printed TOP SECRET on the cover of his composition notebook.

"There," he said. "That should keep people out."

Chase continued. "By the way, I noticed you spelled Mom's name wrong. You spell her name A-I-M-E-E."

Clay talked over him. "I know. That's not supposed to be Mom's name."

"Really? Then what does A.M.Y. stand for?"

"Dad, that's a secret. Everything in my fort is secret stuff, you know that." He glanced at his Spider-Man poster on the wall.

Chase smiled. "Of course, sorry. Forgot it was top secret."

A look of compassion swept across his son's face. Chase wondered if Clay thought he hurt his feelings. He had seen the same look before on Aimee's face. To look in his wife's eyes once more, he had to look no further than his son's.

Clay pulled his notebook from under his air mattress, and his voice softened. "I can't tell you what's in it, Dad—but I can tell you what it's for."

"Oh, okay, I'd love to know what it's for."

Clay sat up, facing his father, and folded his legs under him. "I'm writing my secret thoughts about Mom."

"Cool. Why are you doing that?"

"Well, you write in your journal, right?"

"Yeah, and I've got it right here."

Clay opened up his notebook. "So I'm writing in a notebook too."

"What type of things are you writing?"

"That's the secret part I can't tell you."

"Right. Sorry."

Clay wrinkled the skin between his eyes. "I can tell you *why* I'm writing about her."

"Okay, go on."

"I'm afraid I'm going to forget her. That's why I'm writing down everything I can remember—so I never forget."

Chase's throat tightened. "Things you did together?"

"Yeah, and things she told me. Her favorite color. Songs and movies she liked. The times I made her laugh." Clay paused and used his palm to wipe a tear that had escaped and run halfway down his cheek.

"Anything else?"

"How good she smelled. How happy she made me feel. Secret stuff like that."

"Great idea, buddy." Chase's voice cracked. "I wish I would have done that about your grandma. I've forgotten so much about my mom."

Clay reached over and hugged his father. Chase pulled his son close to him.

Whispering in his father's ear, Clay said, "You can talk to me about your mom anytime, Dad. I know it hurts."

He squeezed his son tight, wanting to never let him go. "We'll both have notebooks about how we feel about Mom. Clay, maybe someday we can share them with each other."

Clay furrowed his brow as he considered the idea. "Maybe. But not for a few years, okay?"

"Fair enough."

A few moments later, Clay changed the subject. "Do you like Miss Taylor?"

Chase's back stiffened, and he touched his throat. "Ah, do you?"

"Yeah, but do you like her a lot?"

"Why do you ask?"

"I saw you kiss her today."

"Did that bother you, buddy?"

"No."

Sensing Clay was feeling something more, Chase paused.

"I was just wondering if you could love my third-grade teacher as much as Mom."

Chase rubbed the back of his neck and exhaled hard. He looked at Clay and stalled to let the moment breathe. "Honestly, I don't know the answer to that question. She's the type of woman I could love."

"What does that mean?"

"It means there are things about her that are easy to love. But I would never love a woman who didn't love you."

"Do you think she loves me?" Clay asked.

"Yes."

"Does she just love me because I'm a third-grader—or for me?"

Chase laughed but felt the weight of the question. "I think she loves you for being you."

Clay rolled over on his back and pulled his sleeping bag up to his chin as a cool draft swept through the treehouse.

"Remember when Mom brought home Queenie and Ginger?" Clay asked.

Surprised at the abrupt change, he nodded. "Yeah, she loved to rescue old dogs."

Lacing his fingers together, Clay slipped them behind his head and stared at the ceiling. "But why did she bring home Queenie if she was sick?"

"Well, the vet couldn't do any more, and Mom didn't want Queenie to die alone. She always loved border collies so she brought Ginger home too."

"I remember Mom taking care of me when I didn't feel good. She made me feel better, even when I was still sick."

"That's what moms do. One of their superpowers, right?"

He turned to look at his father. "Dad, did you love Queenie and Ginger?"

"Of course, didn't you?"

"Yeah, but which dog did you like better?"

Chase considered the question and where it was coming from. "I'm not sure. Queenie got most of our attention because she became so sick. But I loved to play with Ginger. Did you like one better?"

"No." His eyes narrowed. "I loved them both—but I loved them the same."

Chase squinted as he pondered his reply. "Hmmm. Really? Ginger was your dog and Queenie was Mom's. Queenie was usually too sick to play with you."

"I know. But I loved them differently."

"What did you love about them?"

"Well, I loved Ginger because we did everything together and she was my buddy—like you and me. What I loved about Queenie was she needed me. So I guess I loved them differently—but the same amount."

Chase's eyes widened at the wisdom in his words. They were profound—and spoken by an eight-year-old.

"Can I read my comic books now?"

"Sure. I'm getting tired. Too much sun today. Maybe I'll write in my journal while you read."

~

Chase stared at the ceiling for a while, listening to his son's breathing transition to a light snore. His journal lay alongside his sleeping bag. Reaching for it and a pen from Clay's old cigar box, he sat up to write. In the flickering light of dying batteries, he scrawled his fleeting thoughts across the page.

~

Today, I felt like a family again. Clay did too. I wonder if Sierra did. I sensed the urge to kiss her, but with Clay watching from the car, I held back. If I'm honest, that's not the only reason.

Every time I get remotely close to a woman again, fear seeps in.

Fear of loss. Fear that the feeling will dwindle, so I shouldn't commit. I feel an urge to pull away. Yet I think an eight-year-old unknowingly taught me a life lesson tonight. Out of the mouths of babes. He gave me something to chew on for a while.

～

When Chase had finished writing, he set his journal aside and noticed Clay's comic book resting on his face as he breathed heavily. Chase set the comic book aside, smiling at the colorful ink on Clay's oily nose.

After he tucked Clay in, he pulled up his sleeping bag to his chest before switching off the fading flashlight. Lying on his back with his hands behind his head, he stared at the ceiling under the moonlight. It was not lost on him that his son was emulating him in coping with his grief. Both had a journal or notebook to record their feelings and remember Aimee, they both were communicating more and on a deeper level, and they both had their own space—Chase his den, and Clay his treehouse. It was a safe space to relax, have fun, and daydream.

When he felt sleep grip him, he knew Dr. McAllister had been right. Of all places, they were healing together—out on a limb.

CHAPTER 29

They barely made it to church on time on Sunday morning after their inaugural sleepover in the treehouse. Even a hot shower did not relieve Chase's achy muscles from lying on an air mattress on the rigid treehouse platform inside the clubhouse. Clay moved with ease, as though he had slept in his own bed.

Another benefit of youth.

After church, they stopped at In-N-Out for a burger and fries before Chase dropped Clay off at Fernando's house. Chase noticed how often Clay desired to play with his friend and sensed it was more than just friendship—it was compassion. Both had lost a parent, and he learned Fernando had been struggling more than Clay. While he didn't know the details, he surmised Fernando's pain derived from his father *choosing* to leave him and his mother. How did a boy reconcile that choice?

Chase smiled to himself at the notion that one of the most effective ways to heal yourself was to help someone else heal. If that was what Clay was doing, it was another sign he was finding his own way through the fog of grief.

When Chase arrived home, he wanted to jot down these thoughts in his journal. Walking to his den, he looked for it on his bookcase shelf where he had kept it. It was missing.

Where did I put that thing? It took him a minute to recall he had left it in the treehouse.

When he went to retrieve it, he climbed the rope ladder and noticed how much it twisted as he scaled it. He made a mental note

242 | James C. Magruder

to fix it by adding additional support to where it attached to the platform.

His journal was not visible at first, so he lifted his sleeping bag and found it partially under his air mattress. Clay's notebook lay open across from it—he must have been writing in the middle of the night with the fading flashlight, or in early dawn.

Chase closed Clay's notebook and ran his fingers over the cover: Fort A.M.Y.

If that's not Aimee's name, what does it stand for? He was curious. Perhaps more than curious. Nosy.

A sense of guilt swept over him as he felt tempted to read it.

Maybe just one page. I won't read anything personal. After all, maybe it will tell me more about how well Clay is actually doing. As his father, I should know that, right?

Despite his better judgment, he slowly opened it. Without reading it, he flipped a few pages to see the amount of content. Clay had written several pages. Instinctively, he looked over his shoulder, remembering he promised Clay he would not read the notebook.

When he closed it, the broken binding flapped open to page one. Chase glanced at it.

It's only a few paragraphs. Looks like he already told me some of this. I'll just read the first page. Is reading just one page breaking my promise?

Pushing his guilt and his promise to the side, he read aloud in a whisper.

~

Mom, it's me. Clay.

I'm writing in a notebook just like Dad. I want to write things about you we did together and stuff you told me about yourself, so I will remember when I grow up. I want to tell my friends about you on Mother's Day or your birthday so they know I had a mother too. Don't worry, I'll tell them you were the best mom, because you are.

The treehouse Grandpa, Dad, and Uncle Jack are building in the backyard is called Fort A.M.Y., like my notebook, because when I play here I'm <u>A</u>lways <u>M</u>issing <u>Y</u>ou.

Dad sometimes wears his wedding ring on a chain around his neck to keep you close to him. Maybe my treehouse and my notebook will keep you close to me.

Don't worry, my notebook is Top Secret. So only you and I can see it.

Mom, I will always think of you when I play here. I promise.

Clay

P.S. If I forget something about you when I grow up, don't be mad at me. And please don't be sad.

His throat tightened, and he tried to clear it. He blinked hard as his eyes moistened and his vision blurred. He closed the notebook and placed it back under Clay's sleeping bag.

Glancing at the Spider-Man poster Clay had taped to the wall, he thought to himself, *My son is a superhero.*

Tucking his journal under his arm, he slid down the slide before walking back to the house.

CHAPTER 30

Another weekend arrived, and with summer school over, Clay practically moved into his treehouse with Fernando and a multitude of neighbor kids.

While Chase wrote his books, he monitored Clay and his entourage through his open den window. It was a joy to watch and listen to his son, Fernando, and more neighborhood kids than he could count get lost in their world of imagination. It inspired him and restored a sense of peace that all was right with the world.

Earlier in the week, the neighborhood kids, led by Clay, used their imaginations to transform the treehouse into something magical. On Monday, it was a pirate ship, Tuesday, a spaceship, Wednesday, a shipwreck, Thursday, a deserted island, and Friday, their own version of a Robinson Crusoe treehouse—and on and on almost every day in August. Clay finally had a healthy diversion, and right before his eyes, Chase watched his son recover.

Throughout August, Chase dated Sierra and enjoyed spontaneous lunches and spur-of-the-moment coffee breaks. She became very comfortable with his father and immediately clicked with Jack. She even loved Jack's sense of humor. Backyard barbecues on his patio became a favorite pastime, and she often invited Chase and Clay to her apartment for dinner. She was off for the balance of the summer and considered it a privilege to babysit Clay when Chase had to go to Los Angeles for business trips or meet with Ed in New York, or when he visited the Los Angeles area.

Occasionally, when Chase would travel for the day and David was not available, she would watch Clay and Fernando play in the treehouse from the comfort of the patio chairs. It had occurred to Chase that with Sierra and David occasionally sharing babysitting duties, he had phased Joyce out. It wasn't intentional, but he knew he had to make some changes soon.

Sometimes Sierra watched the kids from Chase's den window as she sat in his desk chair or perused his collection of books on the bookcase.

When Chase was home, Sierra would stop by and visit him, Clay, and Fernando. Once, when Chase was on the phone in his office and printing a draft chapter of his novel, she playfully swiveled in his desk chair until the document printed and he returned to his desk. He watched as she wandered around his office and observed the empty spot in the center of his Inspiration Wall. She walked closer to the wall and ran her fingers around the shape of a rectangle where a plaque once hung.

As August drew to a close, Chase kept Ed abreast of the status of the sequel and his standalone novel. He failed to mention the standalone was running far ahead of the sequel.

Every day, Chase had found time to write it—pouring his heart on the page with a new sense of purpose, making more progress than he had thought possible. All in all, August was a productive writing month.

Equipped with a pocket-size notebook, he jotted notes as ideas came to him after a hot shower, in the produce aisle at the grocery store, while cutting the lawn, at the car wash, in the waiting room at the dentist's office, or while having coffee on the patio at Zoe's. It occurred to him that at his current pace, he could finish the first draft of the novel by the end of September—he was in the zone. He'd also made reasonable progress on the sequel Ed requested, but the process flowed slower compared to the novel he was passionate about. He had told Sierra the sequel ran like a VW Beetle—the standalone like a Ferrari.

Now, on the last weekend in August, Chase expected Clay would ask for one more sleepover in the treehouse with Fernando before school started in September. It was a forgone conclusion and right on schedule. Fernando showed up with his backpack filled with necessities. Chase invited Sierra over after dinner, and they enjoyed a glass of wine on the patio, watching the sun begin its descent while Clay and Fernando played literally overhead.

When the sun receded below the horizon and darkness engulfed them, he hollered up to the boys. "Clay, Fernando, get some sleep now. No having fun—you hear?"

Fernando laughed, and Clay groaned. "Yeah, right, Dad!"

"We're already asleep," Fernando added.

Sierra laughed and slipped her arm around Chase's waist. He placed his arm around her shoulders, and they walked to the house.

Once inside, they settled on the couch and talked while they sipped their wine.

"Clay has made great strides since we first talked, hasn't he?" Sierra brought her glass to her lips.

"Thanks to you, Jennifer, and his art therapy program. You know, I never reached out to Jennifer again because Clay is doing so well. Maybe I should ..."

"I've spoken to her for you. I hope you don't mind. I filled her in based on how well things have gone this summer for Clay. She was delighted—and I made it clear how much you appreciated her help."

"Nice. Thank you. One less thing to circle back on, I guess. Thank you for all you've done as well. You've been so good for Clay—and for me—since we met on the wharf."

"That makes two of us. Or should I say, three of us."

He winked. "More wine?"

"Just a little."

After he walked to the kitchen, she got up and followed him.

"You know, maybe I've had enough. I really should be going.

I want to get a run in early tomorrow morning. I love to run after church on Sunday mornings—and I've got a few errands to take care of tonight."

Chase nodded and corked the wine bottle. "I understand. Thanks for coming. I enjoy your company—more than you know."

"Back at ya."

Leaning against the counter, he set his glass down and took hers as she stepped closer to him.

"See you sometime tomorrow?" she asked.

"Count on it."

His eyes were wide with desire as he slid his arms around her waist. As he moved closer, she glided her arms around his neck. He nudged her toward him, hearing her take a small gasp. She lifted her eyes till they met his and she blinked slowly. He softly brushed his lips against hers. As she closed her eyes and parted her lips, he kissed her once, twice, then in a full embrace. It was different for him this time. Today, he felt his passion rise to a new level.

From the beginning, he had wanted to be sure, to never mislead her. Before today, he had intentionally held back, trapped between the desire to kiss another woman—and the guilt of it. Aimee was gone. There was no reason to feel guilty for desiring another woman's affection. He knew this, yet every time he got too close, he felt the twinge of guilt—and pulled away. Tonight was different—finally. When they paused, she stepped back and reached for her purse. She set her phone on the counter to dig for her car keys. When she found them, he kissed her gently again.

"Till tomorrow," she said.

He smiled. "I smeared your lipstick."

She touched her lips. "Let me take care of that before I go." She walked to the restroom.

As Chase waited for her, her phone vibrated. Glancing at the caller ID, he saw a name come up: *Merritt*. He bit his lip and his stomach tightened. *It's probably nothing. I'm sure she can explain it, and he knows about us.* He knew he shouldn't worry, but suddenly he couldn't convince himself. Chase wasn't the jealous type, but he wondered. *Is this guy in or out?*

Before she returned, the call went to voicemail. When she picked up her phone, she noticed the missed call and quickly tucked it into her purse.

"I should run," she said. "Till tomorrow?" she repeated, without making eye contact.

"Till tomorrow," he echoed—wondering what tomorrow would bring.

~

After Sierra left, Chase turned off all the lights in the house except his den light. Sitting at his desk, he opened his novel on his laptop and wrote again. The hours slipped by before he realized it was after one thirty. Glancing out his window, he noticed a flickering light still coming from the treehouse. Either Clay forgot to turn off the flashlight again or they were still telling stories or reading comic books. Chase switched off the den light and went to bed.

~

It was a balmy night with only a slight breeze. In the treehouse, Clay and Fernando were fast asleep atop their sleeping bags. Clay had observed the night prior that the flashlight was growing dim, so he snuck two candles and a book of matches into the treehouse without Chase knowing. He needed a backup to the flickering flashlight for his last sleepover of the summer.

When the flashlight batteries died before midnight, he lit the candles, one for each of them, and placed them in the gap between their air mattresses and sleeping bags. They read comic books until they drifted off to sleep.

Just after three in the morning, Clay rolled over on his side, tipping a comic book off his chest and onto a candle. It ignited immediately and flames rose quickly. Clay woke amid the blaze and smoke and screamed for Fernando.

"Get out of the treehouse, Fernando!"

Fernando was groggy.

Clay screamed again. "Fernando, fire! Escape down the slide."

Disoriented, Fernando looked for his shoes first, then slid down the slide.

The flames rose, creating a wall of fire that split the clubhouse in two. Fire bloomed, licking the walls and creeping to the ceiling. The firewall stood between Clay and the slide. He looked around to save his toys and comic books, then backed up to the exit on the opposite end of the treehouse near the rope ladder.

Fanning out, orange flames spread across the platform, dancing and twisting up three walls. The fourth wall behind him provided his only way of escape.

Smoke billowed throughout the treehouse as the toys and plastic cooler caught fire. Near the rope ladder, Clay could slip out, but in the flickering light, something caught his eye across the room.

"I can reach it," he told himself. Fernando, safely on the ground, screamed at him to get out as the fire crackled and popped. Clay crawled to one side of the flames to reach for it, but the fire was too hot. Backing away, he tried another angle. His eyes burned and watered, and he coughed as the treehouse filled with dark, searing smoke.

"Clay, get out!" Fernando shrieked again before he charged into the house, likely to alert Chase.

Once Clay's haven, the treehouse was now a towering inferno. But he wouldn't leave, not yet. He thought he could reach it before the fire did, if he could just crawl around a wall of flames. There was a small gap in the firewall on the far side. If he could reach through the gap before it closed … If he timed it right, he could slip his arm in, grab it, and escape.

The wind suddenly shifted off the ocean and breathed new life into the fire. Momentarily, the flames raged away from him, and the gap widened. Lunging forward, he grabbed it and retreated. He crawled backward to the exit facing the house. Smoke burned his eyes now, and he coughed violently as he descended the rope ladder using his free hand.

The rope ladder twisted and turned, and he lost his balance, falling backward, his left ankle entangled in the fourth rung from the top. Dangling upside down and blinded by the smoke, he dropped what he had been holding.

Fernando and Chase arrived as the flames engulfed the clubhouse, support beams now cracking, popping, and splintering as Clay hung upside down six feet above the ground.

"Clay!" Chase screamed as he climbed up the ladder to free him.

Tendrils of orange flames had snaked to the ropes, igniting them like a fuse. Before Chase could reach his son, the rope ensnaring his ankle snapped, and Clay fell headfirst to the ground. Chase was swinging from the ladder now and jumped just before the remaining rope snapped and fell like a net on top of him. He yanked it off his back, preventing his T-shirt from catching fire, and threw it to the ground, where it set bone-dry grass ablaze.

~

Clay lay motionless.

Chase gently rolled Clay from his side to his back, supporting his neck. He had a pulse but was unconscious.

Hearing the commotion, neighbors gathered to help or gawk. Pete, Chase's next-door neighbor, had called 911 and rushed to assist

Chase. With the grass burning, they had to move Clay now. They couldn't wait for the EMTs. Chase ran to his garage, grabbed his surfboard, and brought it to the scene.

Flipping it over, rudder up, he laid it flat on the ground. Gingerly, he lifted Clay's head, neck and shoulders onto the board while Pete did the same with his lower body. Together, they lifted the surfboard and carried him out from under the treehouse, where burning debris rained to the ground.

When the EMTs arrived, Chase briefed them on what had transpired. Fernando shakily filled in the blanks.

"Were you in the treehouse when it caught fire?" one of the EMTs asked Fernando.

"Yes, but Clay woke me, and I got out down the slide."

The EMT kneeled beside him and looked him over, checking for burns, lacerations, and smoke inhalation. "You seem to be fine, little man. Do you know how the fire started?"

"The flashlight died, so we lit candles," Fernando confessed. "We didn't want to start a fire. We were careful, then we fell asleep."

Chase just shook his head, then buried his face in his cupped hands.

His yard was now filled with neighbors gawking—and firefighters were on the scene battling the blaze, fearing it may spread to the adjacent property.

Amidst the chaos, Chase collected his thoughts. "Pete, will you watch Fernando for me? I need to go to the hospital with Clay. I'll call Jack and have him pick Fernando up at your place and take him home. Jack will explain to his mother what happened and assure her an EMT checked Fernando out and he's fine."

Out of breath, Pete nodded. "Whatever you need, Chase."

Before he could clear his head and wrap his arms around what was happening, he was sitting in the back of an ambulance, EMTs attending to his unconscious son, while he stared at the treehouse that had been changing his son's life, but now was literally going up in smoke.

After closing the door, the driver lit up the lights and sirens, and they embarked on their way to the hospital—and another new world of uncertainty.

Wearing only his jeans, a navy T-shirt, and some sandals, he was grateful he had his keys, wallet, and cell phone.

Still in shock, he fumbled to call his father, forgetting his number and resorting to his contact list on his phone as the sirens blared. After he reached his father, he agreed to meet him in the ER. Despite the hour, he called Jack—he could always call Jack—and asked him to swing by Pete's house, pick up Fernando, take him home, and reassure his mother that he was fine.

As reality set in, he shoved his phone in his back pocket, leaned over his son—his only son—and sobbed as the thick scent of smoke filled his nostrils. It was the scent of broken dreams.

CHAPTER 31

When the ambulance arrived at the hospital, the chaos began with Clay being rolled away on a gurney to the emergency room. Following him to the exam room, Chase listened as the EMTs explained to the nurse there was a fire and a six-foot head-first fall. She immediately retrieved an ER physician who appeared the same age as Chase to lead the team.

It was like Chase was no longer in the room. Helpless. Irrelevant.

"Let's check vitals, pulse, and respiration," the physician said.

"On it," a nurse responded.

"We need a CT scan of the head and neck—stat. How long has he been unconscious?"

"Possibly twenty minutes," Chase chimed in from the back of the exam room.

"Let's get those scans," the physician said without facing Chase.

As they wheeled Clay out of the room, Chase felt alone, confused, and shocked. His heart was racing now, feeling out of control, out of his element, and out of touch. What would happen next? His breathing quickened, his palms sweating as he paced the room and tried to quell the sense of panic gripping him. He quickly talked himself off the cliff.

Can this really be happening? Again? Really? Why? Why Clay? Why Aimee? Why me? Just when my world was settling down and making sense again.

The ER physician broke his train of thought with a question. "Are you the boy's father?"

"Yes, Chase Kincaid. My son's name is Clay. Is he going to be all right?"

"We're looking into that. The nurses are taking him for a CT scan now. What can you tell me about the fall?"

Chase explained the fire and how Clay dangled six feet above the ground before the rope snapped and he fell, landing on hard, dry soil. The physician walked Chase to the waiting room. The doctor's kind, reassuring voice resonated with him.

Chase failed to catch the physician's name, but he appeared competent, sincere, and on his game. "Doctor, what will you be looking for on the scans?"

"Lots of things. We want to assess his overall condition first—brain trauma, swelling, head and neck fractures, spinal cord injury. But, Mr. Kincaid, don't get ahead of us. The scans will take about fifteen to twenty minutes, and we'll get back to you. If you'd like to take a seat here in the waiting room, we'll check back with you shortly."

"Thank you, doctor. I appreciate it."

"I'll talk to you soon. There's a coffee machine down the hall."

~

When Chase's father arrived, he found his son seated in the waiting room, leaning forward and rubbing his hands together.

"Chase, you okay?" Silence. "What do we know so far?"

Chase ran both hands through his hair. "Nothing, really. They're checking him for a head or spinal cord injury, concussion, brain swelling, brain bleed. Stuff like that. They should know something in twenty minutes. This will be the longest twenty minutes of my life."

David sat next to him and put his arm around his son. "Fill me in on what happened before you came to the hospital."

David listened as Chase recounted the story about the fire and how Clay became injured. Leaning into Chase, David said, "Let's hope for a best-case scenario—we're overdue, son. I'm sure Clay will be fine, and someday this will be one more story with a happy ending."

Chase hoped he was right, remembering how his father comforted him as a child. It was working now. Aimee used to derive strength from him, and he derived strength from her in tragic moments. He believed the beauty of encouragement was the strength derived from the one who feels certain of a positive outcome.

It was a waiting game now, and Chase found assurance in his personal faith in God and his father's confidence. Sitting in the waiting room, he remembered how safe his grandfather had made him feel as a boy. Today, his father was as calm as his grandfather—and he needed it. Chase knew sometimes it was impossible to think of best-case scenarios when someone you loved was at risk. It was easier to imagine worst-case scenarios like what it would be like with a severely injured son. He knew all too well that in the blink of an eye, life could shift from promise to precarious, from amazing to agonizing.

David appeared to notice his son pacing. He stood in his path and spoke to him in reassuring tones. "He's going to be fine. Let me worry for you. Put worry on my back. Let me carry it for you."

Chase wasn't sure how to do that, but somehow the mere thought of it relaxed him.

"Can I get you a cup of coffee? And here, put my jacket on over your T-shirt. The air conditioning in here is freezing."

David went for coffee and Chase slipped his jacket on, still warm from his body heat. It felt good. The warmth brought comfort and inspired hope. When David returned, he handed his son a cup, and they sat to talk. Chase needed a diversion. They quietly sipped hot coffee in a cold room for an extended moment before he surprised his father with a question.

Chase stared into his coffee. "Why didn't you ever love again after Mom died?"

David pulled back in his chair and squeezed his eyes shut. "What?"

Chase repeated the question. "Why didn't you ever love again—after Mom died?"

His father leaned forward. "Where is this coming from?"

"It's been on my mind for years. Why didn't you give yourself permission to love again? I just need to know."

"Chase, we've been through this."

"No, we haven't—not really—not honestly, not as adults."

David exhaled hard. "Is this really the time when Clay is …"

"When is a good time, Dad? When?"

David set his coffee on the end table, leaned forward in his chair, and buried his face in his hands before turning to face his son. "There simply was no one else for me other than your mother."

"I respect that, Dad—but you could have moved on. It might have been healthier for you." Chase paused. "And for me."

"There's no value in revisiting the past. Only pain lives there."

"I think we need to revisit the past, Dad."

"Why?"

Chase stood and paced back and forth. "Because part of me still lives there."

"That makes no sense, Chase. What part of you lives there?"

"My twelve-year-old self. The part of me that still doesn't fully understand how to grieve Mom's death—or Aimee's—or cope with what we're up against now with Clay." Sipping his coffee, he collected his thoughts. "The part of me that doesn't understand why we never moved on together—and never gave ourselves permission to recover fully."

His father looked at him with a mix of pain and anxiety. "How does one recover from the death of their soulmate, Chase? It's life. It's just the way it is."

"For you, maybe. But as a boy, I needed to love again—or at least feel loved again."

His father glanced at the floor, then at his son. "I ..." He hesitated. "Obviously, I made mistakes with you. When I was in the grip of grief, I wasn't thinking clearly. I flat out made mistakes that may be obvious now—but they weren't then. It's no excuse, but I was young too. You weren't the only one grieving."

David took a deep breath, and Chase waited for him to continue, not wanting to interrupt the moment.

"I'm not completely sure why I didn't give myself permission to love again. I dated a few times, but whenever I got close to a woman, I would eventually pull away. Honestly, I think I was afraid ... and ... I believed I could love the memory of your mother *more* than another woman."

Chase softened, seeing his own faults in his father and sensing he'd just ripped a scab off of his pain. "Dad, were you caught in the comparison trap, too?"

He nodded. "You've experienced that?"

"Whenever I dated—even with Sierra. Even now I felt it. But it may not matter because I'm not completely sure her ex is out of her life." Chase took a sip of his coffee. "I don't fault you for your loyalty to Mom—please know I love you for that. But do you see how it confused me as a boy? I felt like we couldn't move on, that it was wrong to move on—and I idolized you. You could do no wrong. You were so strong and confident."

David stood and paced the room. "I wasn't as confident as you think. I was just trying to survive. I couldn't see my mistakes then—I see them now. Sometimes a father thinks what's best for him is best for his son." Their eyes met when he stopped pacing. "Son, in life, the best thing a man can do for his children is love their mother—and be loyal to her. In death, I thought it was the best thing too.

I'm sorry it confused you. We should have talked more openly, like you're now doing with Clay. That's on me."

"Dad, it is what it is. I'm not trying to guilt trip you. I just didn't understand. And I'm still trying to find out exactly how I would go forward. It's complicated. Plus, I'm not sure where I really stand with Sierra suddenly. I think I know where her heart is, but ..."

His father offered a weak smile. "If you don't mind, Chase, I'm going to take a little walk."

"I'll be here."

Shortly after David left the waiting room, the ER physician found Chase.

"I have some good news, Mr. Kincaid. The CT scan showed a C2 pedicle fracture, but the spinal cord was intact. But—"

Before he could finish, Sierra arrived and rushed toward Chase. "There you are. I went to the wrong waiting room. How's Clay doing?"

Chase was preoccupied but was happy to see her. "I was just about to find out." He noticed she read his expression. Even he detected his voice sounded distant as he clutched his hands, glanced at the clock, and shifted his stance.

Without looking up from his chart, the ER physician asked, "Is this family?"

Chase answered on impulse. "No." It was all he offered, and she blushed. He wondered if it was because he appeared to dismiss their relationship and her role in his life.

Looking up from his chart, the physician looked surprised to see her, and Chase realized there was a strange connection between them.

"Sierra?" The physician looked her over.

"Merritt?" It was all she said.

She shuffled back a step or two. Their eyes met, and Chase felt like he was on the outside looking in. The glance between them spoke of a shared history.

Merritt turned to Chase. "Can we speak in private?"

"Sure."

As they turned to leave, Sierra touched Chase's arm. "Chase, can I help?"

He felt confused, overwhelmed by the chaos, and disillusioned by the triangle. He turned to her. "No. We've got this."

He followed Merritt to the consultation room.

CHAPTER 32

Jack arrived at the hospital a few moments after Sierra and witnessed the entire exchange. She didn't see him. Standing out of her line of sight, he watched her walk to the exit and stop. She reached in her purse, pulled out a tissue, and slipped out the door to the stairwell.

~

Chase entered the consultation room after Merritt, and he closed the door. Chase texted his father where to find him.

Merritt then wasted no time and kept it professional. "Why don't you have a seat?"

Chase sat and waited for Merritt to sit across from him. When he pulled up a chair, Chase noticed his name tag, which said, "Dr. Patterson."

"We have some good news. Clay regained consciousness after the CT scan. We briefed him because he didn't know where he was or what had happened. He was looking for you and kept asking about someone named Fernando. Clay could tell us his pain level, which was a severe headache, and he had no problem moving his extremities."

"Thank God." Chase exhaled.

"As I mentioned, the CT scan of the head and neck showed the spinal cord is intact, not bruised or severed. Vital signs and respiration are good."

Chase stopped him. "In the hallway just before Sierra interrupted us, you said, 'but.'"

Merritt continued where he had left off. "But—the brain scan revealed an epidural hematoma causing significant edema."

Chase looked at him. "English, doc."

"There is significant swelling of the brain because of the fall."

Chase jerked back in his chair and his back stiffened. "Then what do we do?"

"I've already called in a neurosurgeon, and he felt Clay needs emergency surgery."

"Surgery?" Chase stood now.

"He's being prepped. We'll need you to take care of some paperwork in the meantime."

Chase raised his voice. "Wait a minute. Why does he need surgery?"

"The neurosurgeon believes, and I concur, that we have to drill a burr hole in the skull to create immediate relief of the pressurized hematoma. This will relieve the pressure of the brain swelling inside the skull."

Chase's vocal pitch raised. "Let me get this straight. You're saying you're going to drill a hole in the skull of my eight-year-old son? You've got to be kidding."

"Mr. Kincaid, it's a standard procedure in these types of cases. Typically, patients respond well. Can we take care of some loose ends? Time is of the essence, and I've got everyone and everything lined up and in motion."

When David arrived, Chase discussed this privately with his father—he had a way of putting things in perspective. David's calm demeanor relaxed him and restored a sense of hope.

Chase spoke with Merritt again and finished the paperwork. David and Chase walked together to a post-op waiting room on the second floor. Chase texted Jack about his location and a few details about the surgery. Jack had remained in the hospital, so he quickly found Chase and his father.

262 | James C. Magruder

"Thanks for coming, Jack," Chase said. "I'm sure you've got other things to do."

"Nothing more important. Considering what could have happened, it seems like Clay's got the best-case scenario."

"If you call drilling a hole in your head a best-case scenario."

Jack smiled. "Well, there's that—but there's also some good news, too."

"Yeah, how's that?"

Jack looked at David. "Should I enlighten him, Mr. K?"

David nodded. "Tell it like it is, Jack."

Chase raised both hands to stop him. "Wait a second. You two are agreeing on something? What's wrong with this picture?"

Jack continued. "We just want to put things in perspective for you. Consider Clay's fall and the potential outcomes. You texted me he does not have a spinal cord injury, and he has movement of all extremities."

"And he's conscious," David interjected.

"And he could communicate with the doctors," Jack added.

David nodded again. "And he doesn't have much pain—and they can treat his headache pain."

It was Jack's turn. "And didn't you say the doc said the surgery is a common procedure?"

"With typically positive outcomes." David looked at Jack again.

During this volley, Chase noted the antiseptic smell and the recovering patients being walked down the corridor, tethered to IVs. "And Clay will probably have a brief hospital stay."

David chimed in, "So we can call that …"

They all finished his sentence together. "A best-case scenario."

"We have a lot to be thankful for," David added.

"So how do you feel now?" Jack quipped.

Chase smiled. "You two are quite a force—when you're on the same side."

"Wonders never cease," his father said.

Chase felt himself rally emotionally and changed the subject to keep his mind off why he was sitting in a waiting room in a hospital. "Sierra knows the ER physician. Seems to me she might have been engaged to him once. I don't remember everything she once told me."

Jack stood, crossed his arms, and then paused. "Really? Interesting. So you're suggesting there may be an opportunity for him to reenter her life?"

"Well, I don't know. What I do know is he's still trying to communicate with her. He called her when she was at my home before the fire. But she doesn't know I know that."

Jack raised his eyebrows. "No?"

"No, she left her phone on my counter, and he called when she was in the bathroom, so it went to voicemail." He thought for a moment. "And there's something else. I noticed how they looked at each other today—or at least, how he looked at her."

David narrowed his eyebrows. "This is sounding complicated."

"Yeah, and unfortunately, I think Chase just added one more complication," Jack said.

Chase scratched the base of his neck. "What? What are you talking about?"

"Based on what I saw earlier today, *you* may have opened the door to tempt him to actively pursue a relationship with her again."

CHAPTER 33

When Sierra left the hospital after speaking with Chase and bumping into Merritt again, her head was spinning—stunned by her worlds colliding. Foremost, she was worried about Clay, yet she hadn't felt this disconcerted since she'd stopped by the same hospital to surprise Merritt and have lunch together on her birthday. Instead, he surprised her by taking a junior nurse to lunch.

Although she knew she wasn't part of Chase's family, his comment sent her reeling. She knew it shouldn't have—but it did. Once again, she felt on the outside looking in. Every time she got close to the men in her life, they pulled away. First her father because of his illness, then Merritt by his indiscretions, and now Chase by his sudden indifference.

Since school was out for the balance of summer, as she drove home, she called Jennifer and asked if she would meet her at Zoe's. "I'll order for you, Jennifer. What would you like?"

Jennifer sounded coy. "It depends—is something wrong?"

"It's about Chase."

"Good or bad?"

"Possibly terrible."

Jennifer's voice became softer. "Really?"

Sierra scratched her temple. "You'll have to tell me. I'm confused."

"In that case, get me a sweet drink. I'll worry about the calories later. One crisis at a time. How about an iced white chocolate mocha, tall? Better make it a grande. Sounds like we'll be there a while."

"Thanks, Jen. I know it's only seven o'clock—and short notice."

"It's fine. I'll throw my hair up and be on my way."

~

When Jennifer arrived, Sierra was sitting out on the patio, facing the ocean again. She adored the view, and the sound of the waves brought a measure of comfort, allowing her to think clearly.

When Jennifer pulled up a chair, Sierra handed her a cup. She took a long sip. "Okay, now I'm ready. What's going on?"

"Well, let me give you some background. There was a fire in Clay's treehouse, and he's hurt."

Jennifer reached for Sierra's arm. "Oh, no—was he burned?"

"Don't think so, but I don't know for sure. I ran over to the hospital as soon as I heard."

"When did this happen, and how did you hear?"

"It happened early this morning, not sure when. Clay and his friend Fernando were sleeping overnight in the treehouse. They've been doing that most of August. Apparently, they had candles burning, fell asleep, and something caught fire."

Jennifer brought her hand to her lips. "Oh, my."

Sierra wrapped both hands around her cup and continued. "Jack texted me what he had learned from Fernando when he gave him a ride home after Chase and Clay went to the hospital in an ambulance."

"Was Chase hurt? What more do you know about Clay?"

"Chase is fine. I know little about Clay. All I know is he fell from the treehouse and hit his head. He was unconscious when he went to the hospital." She reached for her purse, pulled out a tissue, and wiped her eyes. "If anything happens to that little guy ..." She didn't finish her sentence.

Jennifer reached over and took her best friend's hand. "You really love little Clay, don't you?"

She flushed. "I thought I might love them both."

Jennifer squeezed her hand. "And I'm sure they love you too."

"Clay, maybe. Chase, not so sure."

She took another sip of her mocha. "What's going on?"

"Everything was going so well. Chase had me over for a glass of wine last night. It was wonderful and ..."

Jennifer spoke in a gentle tone. "And ..."

An ocean breeze blew a strand of Sierra's hair before she tucked it behind her ear. "And for the first time—he kissed me. I mean, *really* kissed me. There was no holding back."

Jennifer gave an understanding nod. "Interesting. It took him long enough."

"Jen, Chase doesn't do things without thinking. He's been careful not to mislead me and to sort out his feelings after losing Aimee suddenly. I respect that. But sometimes that also confuses me. And it wasn't just any kiss—for either of us."

Listening intently, Jennifer said, "Okay, now you've got my interest. Tell me more."

"Let's just say, his kiss seemed like, well, a kiss of commitment. To me, it said something like, 'I want a relationship with you—only you.'"

Jennifer released a deep breath. "Okay, and what did your kiss say to him?"

"Honestly?"

"Honestly."

"It said, 'I think I trust you. I'm ready for the next step, if you are.'"

Leaning back, Jennifer took another sip of her coffee and drew her eyebrows together. "So what problem are we trying to solve?"

"Well, let me finish. When I saw him in the hospital just now, I approached him as he was getting briefed on Clay's condition by, of all people, Merritt. I sort of barged into the waiting room and accidentally interrupted a physician/patient consultation. I asked

Chase if I could help. Naturally, he looked overwhelmed and said, 'No. *We've* got this.'"

Jennifer hesitated. "That's it?"

"Yes."

Three women stepped out onto the patio and sat across from them with their coffee. Sierra felt like she had lost her privacy until they were so chatty she knew they couldn't eavesdrop.

"Well, Sierra, who else was there that he could refer to?"

"He was in the waiting room alone—with Merritt."

"Well, maybe he meant Merritt—and the medical team."

Sierra cupped her hands around her drink. "I don't think that's what he meant."

"Why not?"

"Call it my sixth sense."

"Okay, girl, spill it. What do you think he meant?"

She chewed the inside of her lip. "I'm not sure, but maybe he meant that he and Aimee have *got this*. You know. *We*, as a family, have got this. Just the three of them. In the emotion of the moment, I felt like he pulled away from me. I know I could be mistaken, but it just felt all wrong." Sierra sighed. "Plus, I saw the look on his face when he connected the dots, when Merritt looked at me."

Jennifer raised both palms. "Wait. Let's deal with one issue at a time. Tell me about what's troubling you most."

She thought for a moment. "I think he still loves his wife. I felt like an outcast today—regardless of how he felt when he kissed me last night. Maybe their family bond is stronger than our relationship. I respect that, Jen. I never intended to challenge it."

Jennifer crossed one leg over the other. "Are you saying you think your relationship doesn't stand a chance because he still loves his late wife?"

Sierra exhaled hard. "I'm just saying sometimes I feel like he is back and forth—so I don't always know where I stand. Sometimes I think there's no room for anyone but Aimee in his life. Jen, they had something special—what every woman wants. That may not leave any room for me."

"Sounds like you're saying Chase is an island."

"At times, yes. A remote island with limited access."

"Can you talk to him about how you feel?"

"I suppose, but he doesn't need one more complication in his life right now. His mind is on Clay."

Jennifer rested her chin on her hand. "Do you love him?"

Sierra was silent and considered the question. "I'm sorting that out—but I think so."

"Why don't you find a way to tell him? When the timing is right."

Sierra pulled back. "It's complicated."

Jennifer smiled and raised her eyebrows. "The way I see it, there are two options. You talk to him—or you wait for him. What's so complicated about it?"

"Well, Merritt is trying to get back in the door. He's been calling me again. He wants another chance. Says, 'Things will be different now. Honest.'"

Sierra knew Jennifer had given up on Merritt the last time they talked, so it impressed her that Jennifer listened instead of judged. One more reason she was such a good friend. Jennifer had always been honest and spoke from observation, not judgment. "Okay. And how do you feel about that?"

"He doesn't deserve another chance."

Jennifer shrugged. "Okay, then tell him there are no second chances. Remember all the talks we've had about Merritt in the past? All the disappointments? You can't trust him, Sierra. Those are your words. Why would you let him back into your life?"

"I wouldn't. I've told him over the phone that I'm not interested in getting back together. Repeatedly. He's persistent. Wants to at least apologize in person, he says."

"Be careful, Sierra. He's out for himself."

"I know. I'll be careful. Besides, I have Clay and Chase on my mind, not Merritt."

Jennifer's index finger traced the rim of her cup, and her eyes never left Sierra. "Regarding Chase, I understand why you feel this way about what he said in the hospital, and I support you, but you want my advice?"

Sierra nodded for her to continue.

"Before you give up on a good guy, talk to him. Ask him what he meant and tell him how it made you feel—or wait for him to circle back to you. I really don't think he's pulling away from you."

"No?"

"I just think he has a lot on his mind. Look, he's trying to figure out what he's up against with his son—while he's thinking through exactly how he *feels* about you—after losing his soulmate. Besides, you're the one who said he's been careful not to mislead you. To me, that sounds like a guy you can trust." Reaching across the table, Jennifer covered Sierra's hand with hers, then sat up straighter. "Listen, why not think about his love for Aimee differently? Reframe it."

Taking another sip of her coffee, Sierra rested both elbows on the table as a gull squawked overhead. "What do you mean?"

"Look at how much he loved his wife. Isn't that the way you would want him to love you someday?"

"Yes."

"Well, isn't it thrilling that the man you're falling in love with has the capacity to love like that—to that depth? Isn't that kind of love worth *fighting* for—and *waiting* for? Besides, you would never find that capacity in Merritt—and may not find it in anyone. That's why, while I support how you're feeling right now, I wouldn't walk away from Chase unless you're absolutely sure he could never love you."

Sierra watched as Jennifer raised her cup to her lips, then

hesitated. "Ask yourself a simple question, Sierra. Are you willing to bet on this guy?"

Sierra stood, walked across the patio, leaned on the railing, and gazed out at the ocean to contemplate the question while breathing in the salt air. After a moment, she returned, sat, and faced her friend.

She used a tissue to blot away her tears, then nodded in response to the question since she couldn't find her voice.

CHAPTER 34

The neurosurgeon emerged from the operating room about an hour and a half after surgery had begun. Before Chase could challenge Jack's assertion that he may have given Merritt an incentive to reenter Sierra's life again, the neurosurgeon met them in the waiting room.

"Mr. Kincaid?"

Chase stood. "Yes."

"I'm Dr. Christopher LeBeau, the neurosurgeon Dr. Patterson referred to perform surgery on your son."

"Yes, doctor, how's Clay doing?"

David and Jack stood and approached the physician.

Chase introduced the others.

"A pleasure to meet you. The surgery was successful."

Chase held his breath. "But … ?"

"No buts. We took him to recovery. Clay will be there about two hours before we admit him to a room in the ICU for observation overnight. If he responds well, we'll release him tomorrow or the next day. That will be a judgment call tomorrow. For now, it was a very successful surgery, and I'm optimistic about a full recovery. We'll give you post-op instructions before we discharge Clay."

"Thank you, doctor." Chase turned to the others. "Dad, Jack, do you have questions?"

David stepped forward and shook his hand. "No questions. Thank you so much, Dr. LeBeau."

"Just one, doctor," Jack said. "Would you call this a best-case scenario?"

"I would say so. I've seen much worse. Essentially, this was a textbook surgery. Clay's young. He should be fine. Anything else?"

"No, thank you," Chase said to regain control of his friend. "Sounds like a waiting game now."

When Dr. LeBeau left the room, Jack echoed the neurosurgeon's words. "Best-case scenario. Textbook."

Jack's question had its intended effect on Chase. He relaxed his shoulders, felt the tension melt, and felt a sense of relief.

"And thank God for that," David said.

Chase hung his head for a moment, knowing what his friend had just done for him. It not only restored a sense of peace in him, it also ensured Chase would sleep well tonight as he replayed the doctor's last words in his head.

"If you guys got things to do, now might be a good time to go. Sounds like Clay is stable, and I'll be here. I don't want to tie up the rest of your weekend."

"Will you text me with any news?" his father asked.

"Of course, Dad."

"Okay, I'm going to run a few errands while Clay sleeps, and I'll be back this afternoon."

"Sounds good. I'll need you to be here for Clay after they assign him a room in the ICU. I need to run over and finally talk with Joyce."

"Oh, that's right," Jack said. "You haven't told your mother-in-law about the accident yet."

"Right, and I don't want her to hear it from anyone else. I've lived in her doghouse for two years."

"Whatever you need, Chase," his father said. "It's important to talk to Joyce—and this needs to be an in-person conversation. You have some lost time to make up."

When David left, Chase and Jack sat and made small talk.

"By the way, thanks for being here so much this weekend, Jack.

And for taking Fernando home and talking with his mom. How did that go?"

"Typical reaction by a mom who could have had her son 'burned alive.' She freaked out a bit before turning her attention to Clay. She wants you to contact her if there's anything she can do to help."

"Her son was almost 'burned alive'? Sounds like Fernando did the storytelling, not you."

"Fernando may have spiced it up a bit for dramatic effect," Jack admitted.

Chase sighed. "Well, the entire event was dramatic enough."

A grin cracked along Jack's lips. "I know, but you're forgetting how a kid thinks—Fernando still has his eight-year-old invincibility. Remember what that was like."

"Yep. I remember those days. Sometimes I wish I still felt that way. It's interesting to hear how a kid sees his world and makes himself the hero in almost every story."

Jack stood. "Well, how can I help you most?"

"I'll text you when my dad comes back here. Maybe you can keep him company this afternoon if you don't have anything to do—now that you guys are getting along. I need to run to my mother-in-law's place. Plus, I'm going to need her help when Clay comes home from the hospital. I hate the idea of asking her for help. Even though I work from home, I'll need someone to assist him while I work on my advertising business—and finish the novels."

"Sounds good, buddy. I can do that."

"There's something else you can do for me today."

"Name it."

Small and overcrowded, the waiting room continued to get busier.

"Fernando said Clay could have escaped the treehouse in time, but he went back for something. I know Clay had put several of his prized possessions from his bedroom in the treehouse all week. During the fire, after he had retrieved it, he dropped it when he fell backward on the rope ladder. It should be among the debris under the platform of the treehouse. Will you see if you can find whatever it was?"

"What am I looking for, exactly?"

"I don't know. Probably a toy, his favorite comic book, a new video game, or anything a boy would put in his fort. He brought all kinds of toys out there. Whatever it is, it's likely burned or wet from the firefighters. Also, I'd like your thoughts on the structural condition of the treehouse. At some point, I may have to talk to Clay about tearing it down."

Jack nodded. "I'm on it. By the way, since things seem to be stable with Clay for the moment, could I change the subject and talk to you about something else?"

"What's up?"

"It's about Sierra."

Chase raised a brow. "What about her?"

"I arrived here just after she did this morning. I overheard your exchange with Dr. Patterson. When she asked if she could help you, you said, 'No. We've got this.'"

"Okay, so?"

"When she left, you should have seen the look on her face. She wanted to help, and your comment shut her out."

"Jack, it was a stressful, chaotic moment. Everything converged at once. The fall seriously injured my son. I was nervous and confused. The doctor was filling me in on the test results. She blindsided me. I didn't realize at the time the doctor was her ex-fiancé. And I had just learned that he's been calling her again. It's not her fault, but the timing was terrible."

Jack walked over to a window for some privacy. Chase followed him. "When she asked if she could help you, what did you mean when you said, 'We've got this?' No one else was in the room with you except her ex."

Chase bit his lip and thought for a moment. "I had too much to process simultaneously in the chaos of what happened to Clay. And you know I would never hurt Sierra. But I still blew it, didn't I?"

"Big time. But answer the question. What did you mean?"

Chase looked away. "I'll be honest. In the heat of the moment, I thought about Aimee. I guess I meant we, Aimee and I, have got this. Is it such a stretch that I would think about the mother of my son when he lay critically injured? When I rode in the ambulance and arrived at the hospital, I thought about what she would say. What would she want me to do?"

He watched Jack glance at the floor before facing him. "That makes perfect sense. That's what I thought you meant. And if I thought that, Sierra likely did too. Then where does that leave her?"

Chase noticed another couple enter the waiting room. "I suppose it leaves her feeling like she's out of the picture?"

"I think so."

Chase shoved his hands in his pockets and bit his lower lip. "Okay, I hear you. Like I said, I blew it. But I'm not exactly sure where I stand with her either—or where she stands with the good doctor."

Jack glanced out the window. "I guess that's something you're going to have to find out. And it's worth finding out because although Aimee and Sierra are very different, in one way, they're much the same. And it's in a way that's important to you."

"And what's that?"

"In her own way, Sierra is also the girl next door. Unassuming, committed, and, for some unknown reason, it appears she is falling for you."

"But how do I know for sure if she has something left for Merritt?"

"I don't think that would be the problem—as much as something else."

"What else?"

"The good doctor could have something left for her, especially if

276 | James C. Magruder

you left the door open. After all, just like you noticed his interest in her, he probably noticed your lack of interest."

"You're probably right. Just the other night when she was over, I noticed he called her when she left her phone unattended in my kitchen. Obviously, something has been going on before Clay's accident. She's been honest enough to tell me he's been calling, and he is persistent, but I'm unsure if he's gaining ground."

Jack pointed at him. "I think there is some confusion on both sides of this relationship, my friend. Clear up what you can. Because as you well know, Chase, after the second chance—there are usually no chances at all."

CHAPTER 35

By late morning, the hospital assigned Clay an ICU room, and Chase was introduced to the medical staff who would care for him. When Clay was conscious, talking, and comfortable, there was nothing more Chase could do for him, so he let him rest. When David arrived, Chase wrote a note on the whiteboard in his room so Clay would know when he would be back.

After he drove home, he shaved, showered, slapped on some cologne, and slipped on a clean shirt and pair of jeans before having a late breakfast at a nearby restaurant. Today, he needed someone else to make him two eggs, hash browns, bacon, and a slice of wheat toast. It never tasted so good. Physically and emotionally spent, he felt like the day should end when it was just getting started.

After breakfast, he made the short drive to see Aimee's mother. He hadn't been there for several weeks. It was never easy going to see Joyce Thompson, especially after Aimee died. Now, as he drove, he wondered how she would take the latest news. She didn't even know he had built a treehouse. It would be one more thing that would prove how irresponsible Chase was. To her, he couldn't do anything right.

Joyce never believed in his writing. At least, that's how she acted. "A man shouldn't invest so much time in a hobby when his family needs a real job," she'd once told him.

Chase had stopped defending himself, believing there were few things harder to open than a closed mind.

When he made a west turn on State Street, he remembered Sierra had told him Joyce had a right to play a role in Clay's life—and his.

And what about Sierra? Joyce would never like her. A potential replacement for her daughter?

And what would she think now? Would she blame him for the fire and her grandson's injuries? And since Chase had avoided her for weeks—how would she react if he asked for help? Yes, there were many reasons he didn't want to make this visit. But he was determined to do things right, as Sierra had reinforced.

After parking in her driveway, he paused. If he was honest with himself, he knew she had good reason to be testy. She'd lost her daughter prematurely from the same type of heart attack that stole her husband. She lived alone. And now her son-in-law avoided her—holding her only grandchild hostage. Chase knew he was being overdramatic, but Joyce had a hard life, filled with tragedy, and now this.

Inhaling, then exhaling hard, he whispered to himself, "Here goes."

Joyce didn't answer after he rang the doorbell once, so he rang it again and waited. Footsteps. The door creaked open, and she appeared. Wearing a short-sleeved blue blouse and a beaded necklace, she wore her glasses perched low on her nose, like she had been reading. She swung the door open slowly, looking him over. Chase didn't attempt to read her mind.

"Hi Joyce, may I come in?"

Opening the door wider, she stepped back so he could enter. Once inside, he noticed how neatly she kept her quaint little home—a trait Aimee had inherited. She had positioned her brown leather couch and loveseat in a traditional L-shape with an oak end table and lamp between them. Set at an angle, the gas fireplace across the room faced the couch. The antique white walls featured colorful close-up photos of landscapes and flowers. They reminded him of how much she and Aimee loved flowers—and how they planted them to encircle sections of the house. He caught the smell of lilacs cut, trimmed, and set in a vase on the coffee table as the thought crossed his mind.

"What brings you here? And where's Clay?"

"I came to answer both questions in one sentence. I'm here because Clay is in the hospital. My father, my friend Jack, and I built him a treehouse this summer. He's enjoyed it immensely. Last night Clay and his friend, Fernando, slept in the treehouse, and there was a fire …"

She covered her mouth, then interrupted him before he could finish. "Is he …"

"All right? Yes, essentially. No burns. I came to talk to you about his condition. To make a long story short, he will be fine, but he fell backward from the treehouse and hit his head on the ground."

Joyce flushed red. She raised her chin and crossed her arms. She gestured to the couch. "Can you sit?"

"Yes, thank you."

"Can I get you a cup of coffee?"

He blinked twice. "Ah, yes, with cream, please."

Joyce disappeared into the kitchen for a moment, and he looked around the room. Pictures of Aimee still lined the mantel over the fireplace. In most of them, Chase was missing.

She returned with two cups and saucers.

Taking one from her, he stirred in the cream, took a sip, and continued. "The physicians believe he'll be fine, although he had a head injury and needed emergency surgery this morning."

She closed her eyes, took a calming breath, and placed her hand over her heart.

"The surgery went well, and he's out of recovery, and in the ICU." He read her face, noting the concern. "The surgery relieved pressure from the swelling. Although he's not out of the woods, the neurosurgeon said most patients respond well. We'll know more tomorrow. They might send him home tomorrow or the next day. I'll keep you informed."

Contemplative for a moment, she asked, "How did the fire start?"

Chase explained the story, anticipating her questions and trying to make sure he addressed all of her concerns in the first telling.

The skin between her eyes wrinkled, and she looked angry. He had expected what was about to come and kept his promise to himself to remain calm. He wondered if she was on a slow burn again.

Raising her voice, she asked, "How could this happen?"

"As I told you, they had a couple of candles they used when their flashlight—"

"That's not what I mean. Why did you let an eight-year-old use candles unsupervised?"

"I didn't know he had candles."

She snipped at him. "Why am I not surprised?"

Sipping his coffee, he tried to stall the anger rising inside him. "Joyce, it was an accident. You see—"

"What is it with you and accidents? Why would you let my grandson play with matches? Aimee would never allow that."

He took a deep breath to calm himself. "Joyce, when they release Clay from the hospital, I may need your help to take care of him for a few days. Besides my client work, I have a novel or two to finish and both have tight deadlines."

She stared at him and shook her head. "How do you live with yourself, Chase?"

"Did you hear a word I said?"

"Let me paraphrase. You need my help to take care of Clay even though you'll be in the house writing a novel while I do all the work."

"I know how that sounds, but—"

"It sounds irresponsible. But I'm not surprised. After all, you let the poor child play with matches."

"Look, Joyce, we need to call a truce. At least until Clay gets better."

"Then what? Will I not see him again—like the last several weeks, or is it months?"

Chase hung his head, stared at the floor, then inhaled. "Look, I apologize for that. That's on me. I've been extremely busy, and I never intended to overlook you or shut you out of his life."

"Have you needed a babysitter since I last saw you?"

"Yes, of course."

"Who was the babysitter?"

The house was quiet except for a clock ticking and the occasional flitter of a parakeet she kept in a cage near the kitchen. "My dad, mostly."

"Figures. Who else?"

"My friend Jack. And occasionally, Sierra."

"Who is Sierra?"

Chase paused for a moment, wondering how she would interpret his answer. Had he just walked into a trap, her judgment, her wrath, or all three? "Sierra is his schoolteacher ..."

She raised her eyebrows and tilted her head back. "Really? You would call his schoolteacher before his only grandmother to babysit?"

"It's not like that."

She glared at him and crossed her arms. "Enlighten me."

"Sierra and I are dating—or were dating."

Her eyes narrowed. "You're dating his teacher? Sounds convenient, or strategic."

"What are you talking about?"

"Next to their mother, young kids often develop feelings of affection for their teachers."

"I'm still confused. How is that strategic?"

"Well, if you and Clay love his teacher—and someday you marry—a former mother-in-law is in the way, right? Inconvenient. Irrelevant."

He squeezed his eyes shut. "Joyce, it's not like that at all. What are you thinking? You are Clay's grandmother—for life. No one will ever take your place in his life—or mine. Look, I'm sorry I haven't been able to see you recently. I'm not trying to withhold Clay from you.

But you're not making it easy for me to come over here, either. You need to consider that."

She looked away and changed the subject with just two words. "More coffee?"

"No. Thank you. I'd love to have your help when Clay comes home from the hospital in a day or two. We want you in our life, not just now—but always. All I can do is apologize for the recent past—that is, what I could control of it."

Joyce looked into her coffee, then up at him, but remained silent.

"Thanks for the coffee. I should run. I'll call you when I need you."

She stroked her brow as if to ward off a headache. When he started for the door, his last sentence replayed in his head. It was too late, but he wished he had rephrased it.

~

When Chase returned to the hospital, his father was there. Clay was awake and talkative, and asking about Fernando. All good signs of recovery. Clay asked the one question Chase had hoped he wouldn't ask.

"Dad, what are we going to do about the treehouse? Can we fix it?"

Dropping his shoulders, he let out a heavy sigh. "I don't know, buddy. Jack is going to have to check the structural integrity with Grandpa."

"What's that?"

"Structural integrity? It's checking to see if the treehouse, and the tree, are still strong enough to hold up when kids are in it. If not, it would have to be reconstructed."

"Oh."

"I haven't had a chance to even look at it yet—or the condition of the tree. Let's not worry about that now. Let's just get well first, okay?"

Clay went down without a fight and phased in and out of sleep.

When nightfall arrived, before leaving the hospital, Chase waited for Jack to show up for his shift before writing his name and cell number on the whiteboard in Clay's room to make sure the nurses could reach him.

~

Chase was exhausted, mentally and physically, when he arrived at home, so he made a cup of hot tea and stared out the window to decompress before writing in his journal.

~

Today was one of the longest days of my life. Right up there with the loss of Mom and Aimee—and now a near-miss with Clay.

I tried to take my advice from my first novel with Joyce today and build a "bridge of understanding." She's been through the wringer, and I haven't been as sensitive as I should have been. I'm sure she'll help with Clay because I know how much she loves her grandson, but I'll take this opportunity to reconnect with her too. It's the right thing to do—it's what Aimee would have hoped for—and I owe it to both of them.

I believe Dr. Merritt Patterson saved Clay's life today by how quickly and efficiently he assessed Clay's condition and ordered and executed the CT scan of his brain and neck, how swiftly he secured a neurosurgeon, and how he expedited surgery and the medical team to treat him.

He's a smart guy. A nice guy. Yet apparently a lousy fiancé. What are the chances that the guy who saves my son's life interrupts mine and destroys my girlfriend's? Or is she my ex-girlfriend?

One more thing I may need to reconstruct.

CHAPTER 36

When Chase showed up at the hospital Monday morning, his timing was perfect. His father had just arrived, and Dr. LeBeau was making rounds and examining Clay.

"Hey, Dad," Clay said when his father entered the room.

"Hey, buddy."

"Hi, Grandpa."

"Hey, sport." David nodded in acknowledgement.

They waited while Dr. LeBeau completed his assessment. "You're doing just fine this morning, tiger."

He motioned to the hallway. Chase and David followed him there.

"Mr. Kincaid, I'm happy to tell you Clay is responding remarkably. He's talking and moving well. Physical therapy has had him up and walking. Blood pressure and vitals are stable. Respiration is good. And I removed the drain. I'd like to keep him for one more day for observation, as a precaution, then he can go home tomorrow. How does that sound?"

Chase looked heavenward. "Doctor, you do not know how happy you just made me."

David let out a heavy breath. "Yes, thank you, doctor. We can't tell you how much we appreciate all you've done."

"You're welcome. The nurse will give you discharge instructions tomorrow after I check on him. I'm prescribing levetiracetam for him, an anti-seizure medicine, for a few months. I would like to follow up with him during this period. You can make an appointment with my office. There will also likely be some physical therapy for one to two weeks."

"Sounds good," Chase said.

"Well, if you have no further questions, I'll continue my rounds."

David nodded and patted him on the shoulder. "Thank you again, Dr. LeBeau."

The elder Kincaid stepped out of the room and returned with two cups of coffee, handing one to Chase.

"Thanks, Dad."

Clay was quiet and appeared to be dozing.

"Dad, you don't have to stay long. It's Monday, and I'm sure you've got some work to do," Chase said.

"I do, but I just wanted to see how the little guy was doing. Like Jack said, it's a best-case scenario."

Chase took a sip of his coffee and sat in the guest chair across from Clay's bed next to the window. "You and Jack are getting along. Why the change of heart?"

"Well, he called me on it."

"Sounds like Jack. Direct and to the point."

David sat in the chair on the other side of the bed and talked in a soft voice to not wake Clay. "He told me how he felt, how I came across, and shared his point of view."

"You already knew his point of view. What changed?"

"I listened. I really listened. And I heard him, and for the first time, I understood him and his situation. You might say it was sort of like your premise in your first book. I needed to find the bridge of understanding between us."

"I'm so happy to hear that. Jack is a good man and, as I've told you before, he's always been there for me."

David took a sip of his coffee, then lowered his head. "I know that now. I locked myself into my own way of thinking. Part of growing old, I guess."

Chase grinned. "Blaming it on old age? Sounds like a plausible excuse. I'll use it as I age."

"Feel free," David said as they chuckled together. "Well, since Clay is doing so well and is sleeping, I'll take you up on your offer and run to work for a few hours."

"Do that. I'll catch you later."

"Call or text me with any updates."

"Will do."

After his father left, Chase sat and thought about how he got here. How did a happy family of three suddenly find themselves here? Spouse passed. Son with a brain injury. Father with a broken heart—and an uncertain future.

His coffee cup was empty. Clay was still asleep. So he walked down the corridor to find the coffee machine and get another cup. His change fell through the vending machine on the first two attempts. The third time was a charm. The machine filled the cup to the brim with no covers available.

Looking out a nearby window, he sipped the coffee down to a level that allowed him to walk without spilling. When he arrived at Clay's room, a woman was sitting in his chair and gently stroking Clay's hair that stood up around the bandages.

When Chase entered Clay's room, he stopped short. His mouth dropped open. "Joyce," he said. "Thank you for coming."

"I didn't come for you. I came for him."

She softened at the sight of her grandson. Bandages wrapped around his head, dried bloodstains atop the burr hole that allowed blood and fluid to escape and relieve the pressure from the swelling. Chase briefed her on the neurosurgeon's latest report.

"He's going to be fine. He'll come home tomorrow. Isn't that great?"

"Isn't that lucky, you mean? You should have never built that treehouse."

"Joyce, he's a boy. Every boy loves a fort. We can't live like that."

She clenched her jaw. "Like what? Safe?"

"No, overprotective. Bottled up. I've been doing that for two years. Aimee would want us to live again. We can be careful, but we can't live in a bubble. You should see the joy the treehouse brought him. I haven't seen him that happy since Aimee was alive. He was alive again—and so was I."

"And now he's hurt again."

Chase ignored her. "Joyce, as I've told you, we want you in our life. I've made mistakes with you, but I love you."

She bristled and raised her shoulders.

"You don't have to love me, Joyce—you don't even have to like me. But I want you to know we want you in our lives—now and in the future."

She softened again when she saw Clay. Moisture welled up in her eyes. "Don't get all mushy on me." She palmed a tear away. "Do you have something you need to do today?"

Chase shrugged. "Well, I have a few errands to run, some client work, and I need to hit my word count to keep my novels on schedule."

"I can stay with Clay if you have something to do. I'll call or text you if something comes up, or he asks for you."

"That would be nice, Joyce. Thank you." Chase stood, grabbed a marker, wrote Clay a note on the whiteboard, then kissed his son on the cheek before walking to the door.

"Chase," Joyce said, stopping him in his tracks. Her eyes looked watery. "Aimee really loved you, you know."

Studying her, he looked for deeper understanding, then responded in a soft voice. "I know."

$\sim$

When noon rolled around, Jack drove down State Street to find a place to have lunch. After parking, he wandered through the winding streets and the upscale gift shops of the Paseo Nuevo open-air mall. The hostess seated him at an outdoor table under a shade tree. It was beautiful here with colorful umbrellas at every table and the green foliage and natural landscaping against a forever blue sky.

Across the plaza were other restaurants. At the one next to him, he noticed a tall handsome man with dark hair enter and hesitate at a table. Sharply dressed, he slipped off his sport coat and draped it over his chair. The man looked familiar, but Jack knew he was seeing him out of context. If he could see him in the environment in which he met him, he would know him. A woman arrived, and he pulled a chair out for her, and she sat. It was Sierra. She was with Dr. Merritt Patterson. Everything came into context. Clay's ER physician and Sierra's ex-fiancé. *What are they doing together?*

The server broke his train of thought. "Excuse me, sir. My name is Mia. I'll be serving you today." She handed him a menu. "Something to drink?"

"Ah, just a Coke, please."

"Very good. I'll be back in just a minute to take your order."

Menu in hand, Jack had something to hide behind to conduct his surveillance, though based on the distance and the foliage, he didn't need it. Watching intently, he wondered what they were talking about.

Why is she having lunch with her ex? And why shortly after meeting him again at the hospital with Chase? Looks like Chase gave this guy an opportunity to get his foot in the door. But Sierra wouldn't do that. Or would she?

Mia jarred him again. "Here's your Coke. Now, what can I get you?" She was young, cute, and cheery.

"I'll have the tri-tip sandwich with grilled onions, barbecue sauce, and jack cheese on a French roll. And can I get a Caesar salad on the side?"

"Sounds good. I'll put that in for you."

"Thanks, Mia."

Letting his thoughts wander, he watched them closely until Mia returned with his tri-tip sandwich, the Caesar salad, and the bill. "You can pay the cashier on your way out. You don't have to wait for me."

"Thanks, Mia."

Jack watched them from across the plaza. He had a profile view so they wouldn't notice him. Over the course of his lunch, their mood shifted. While he ate his salad, it appeared intense, but by the time he finished his sandwich, Sierra smiled and leaned into the conversation. *This can't be good. The only time you keep two guys on the string is if you're conflicted. What is she thinking?*

He wondered if her carefree demeanor signaled the beginning of the end of his best friend's relationship with her. He recalled what he'd told Chase—with relationships, after the second chance, there are no chances. And Sierra was his second chance.

CHAPTER 37

Jack called Chase early Tuesday morning. "Hey. How's it going? Sorry, I've been missing in action for a bit. I bumped into your dad, and he updated me on Clay."

"Oh, good. Then you know he is coming home today?"

"Yep. I also know what Clay went back into the treehouse for the night of the fire."

"Really?"

"Yep. I looked under the treehouse and amidst the debris, I found a red notebook. On the cover it said, 'Fort A.M.Y., Top Secret.'"

"That's all you found?"

"Yep. That's it."

Swallowing hard, Chase could barely speak. "So that's the only thing he would go back in a fire for—I love that kid."

"I wanted to let you know earlier," Jack said, "but life's been crazy for all of us—and for me at work. By the way, how are things with Sierra?"

"Not sure. I haven't seen her since, well, you know, the hospital."

Jack walked from his kitchen to his living room. "I've seen her."

"Really? Where?" Jack could hear his friend's pitch rise.

"I saw her out to lunch yesterday—with her ex-fiancé."

"Seriously? Did she see you?"

Rubbing the back of his neck, Jack continued. "No. I was at a restaurant across the plaza from them. My table had some shrubbery around it to obscure their view."

"Okay and ...?"

Jack walked to his home office and sat in his chair. "And I watched them while I ate."

"What did you see?"

"Not much. But she looked happy."

Jack waited for a reply. Silence. Finally, Chase spoke. "She once told me Merritt always wanted to get back together and attempted to phase in and out of her life. I wonder if you were right, and I gave him his opportunity."

Jack didn't let him finish his sentence. "I could see them but not hear them—but as I finished my lunch, she appeared to be leaning in."

"Leaning in?"

"Yeah."

"What does that even mean, Jack?"

Jack switched his phone to his other ear. "You know."

"No, I don't. Leaning in? Maybe she sneezed."

Jack smiled. "All I can say is she looked happy. But still—I don't want you to think …"

"What *do* you want me to think?" Chase's voice sounded impatient but empty.

"I don't want you to think anything, really. That's how you get into trouble. Chase, I'm not telling you this to tattle on her. I telling you so you *talk* to her. You owe her that."

There was another pause. "By the way, you didn't read Clay's journal, did you, Jack?"

"What makes you think I would do that?"

"Because you're Jack."

He swiveled in his chair. "Good point. But I would never violate the code."

"What code?"

"The Boy's Fort Code."

292 | James C. Magruder

"And what's that?"

Jack rolled his eyes and shook his head. "Chase, do I have to spell it out for you? The notebook clearly said 'top secret' on it."

~

When Chase arrived at the hospital Tuesday, Joyce was already there, sitting in the visitor's chair again. "What took you so long?"

"I was on a phone call." He shrugged. "Am I late?"

"I've been here a half hour, and he's almost ready to go home."

Chase looked for Clay. His bed was empty. "Where's Clay now?"

"Walking the halls. Physical therapy wants to see him moving before they sign off and let him go. The neurosurgeon already signed off after he checked the wound and changed his bandages. We should have him home within an hour."

"Great."

Chase glanced at the door and noticed the healthcare professionals scurrying in the halls.

Joyce's voice shifted to a warmer tone. "I appreciate the extended time you gave me with him yesterday afternoon. I needed to be alone with my grandson."

"Did you get bored being here when he slept yesterday?"

"No. There were plenty of people to talk to in between your follow-up visits."

Chase scratched his head. "Who stopped by in between my popping in yesterday?"

"Your father."

"Did you have a friendly chat?"

"Actually, we did. He's a kind man. It's been a while, so I really enjoyed talking with him."

Chase walked over to the closet to check on Clay's belongings. "Well, I'm glad you let me come and go yesterday, Joyce. I got a lot done, and I'm prepared to bring Clay home. I needed to set up a few 'welcome home' decorations and follow up with Fernando and his mom again."

"And then that woman stopped by."

"What woman?"

"The woman you said you were dating—or not dating. Clay's teacher."

"Sierra?"

"Yes, that's it. Her name slipped my mind."

Curious, Chase stepped closer to her. "Did she ask about me?"

"No. Well, come to think of it, she said she wanted to tell you she was having lunch with somebody. Don't remember the name."

He raised his eyebrows and bit his lip. "Really? Was it a guy's name?"

"No, I think it was a girl's name."

Chase thought for a moment and wondered what Sierra had actually said to Joyce. It wouldn't be like her not to tell the truth unless …

"She seemed more interested in Clay. We had a wonderful talk about how he had been struggling in school this summer until you set up a special program with art therapy and other things to help him."

"Well, I didn't set it up. Sierra and Jennifer actually—"

"She said you set it up. Said you were a very attentive father. Loving. Warm. Committed. She also said she has never seen a man love his wife more than you loved Aimee—and still do."

Chase rubbed the back of his neck. "Really? She said all that?"

"Yes. I told her all I ever wanted was for my daughter to marry a man who would give all of himself to her—with his whole heart."

She paused, and Chase walked to the window and glanced outside.

"She said something else to encourage me," Joyce offered.

"What was that?"

"She said, 'You got your wish, Mrs. Thompson. There is no room in Chase's heart for any other woman. You can trust him.' She was so sincere. How wonderfully kind of her, don't you think?"

Chase glanced up at the ceiling and then down at the floor and let out a breath. "Yes, she's very kind—and wonderful."

Joyce stood and walked to him. "I think I owe you an apology, Chase. Perhaps more than one. I misjudged you about Aimee—and your love for her. I'm sorry."

Chase nodded but said nothing.

They both walked to the window and stared out at another perfect day. "There's an old saying, Chase. It goes like this. 'I'm an old man, I've worried about many things—most of which never happened.' It speaks to the futility of worry. I've changed it to, 'I'm an old woman, I've worried about many things—most of which never happened.' Since Aimee was my only child, I worried she would marry the wrong man. It never happened. Forgive me."

Turning, he put his arms around her, squeezed, and felt the pain of the past flow out of him. He could only hope she felt it too.

~

The hospital released Clay late Tuesday morning. Chase and David drove him home. When they arrived, Clay asked to see the treehouse. Together, they inspected the damage, noticing the charred and black-as-coal wooden platform and clubhouse structure. The center of the platform where the fire started had collapsed and fallen to the ground. On the ocean side, the railing was intact, but the fire had consumed the remaining three sides and a portion of the slide.

"My father's old oak tree weathered the fire well—relatively speaking," David said.

Black soot ran up the old tree well beyond the clubhouse, as the flames had snaked up the branches before being doused by firefighters.

Clay got on his knees and looked through the rubble directly beneath the platform. "Where's my notebook? Has anyone seen my notebook?"

"Jack found it after the fire, Clay," Chase said. "I dried it out, cleaned it off, and put it on your desk in your room. It survived the fire but smells like smoke."

Clay pumped his fist and turned to his father. "Can we rebuild it, Dad?"

Chase looked at his father. "You're the architect. Can we rebuild this thing?"

"I don't know. I have to consult with my engineer."

Clay chuckled. "You mean Uncle Jack?"

"Yep. Uncle Jack."

Chase rubbed the back of his neck, pondering how much time and money would be involved to rebuild the treehouse. Deep down he knew it was a worthy investment, considering what the treehouse did for Clay and Fernando, his father, Jack, and himself.

Clay jumped up and down. "Uncle Jack will rebuild it. I know he will—he always finds a way, right, Dad?"

"Yes, Jack finds a way, doesn't he?" Chase replied. "Hey, it's almost lunchtime. Who wants burgers on the grill?"

Clay hesitated. "Let's not build a fire this close to the treehouse. Not yet."

Chase laughed. "Okay, buddy. Let's go to In-N-Out instead. Want to go, Dad?"

"Twist my arm," he said with a wink.

~

Clay went to bed early that night, and Chase was tired too, but he pushed himself to write a few more chapters of his standalone novel. In the zone again, his words flowed like a river, landing on the page and striking gold. Over the years, he had noticed those times when the words came easily. It was often in moments of joy—or sorrow. Funny how opposite emotions generated the same result.

"We write best out of our pleasure—and our pain," his grandfather used to say.

And tonight, Chase was feeling both—pleasure of having his son home and healing, and pain, knowing he could lose—or had lost—Sierra. Since his verbal missteps at the hospital, he hadn't talked to her, thinking it best to give her space.

His fingers danced over the keyboard. Leaning back in his desk chair, he reread a few pages. He liked it. No, he loved it. He let his thoughts wander.

My goal was to write another bestseller. Instead, I'm writing what I want to read. What I believe in. And it includes what I've learned about love from my father, mother, son, Aimee, Joyce, and yes, Sierra. What I'm writing in my standalone novel has to be said—and I believe I have to say it. My agent may not love it, but I do. Every author has to write at least one book for himself—about that one thing that is screaming inside him. For me, this is it.

The words continued to grace the pages until a knock on the door shattered his fictional dream. The knock was so light he wasn't sure he heard it. Walking to the front door, he turned on the porch light, peered out the window, and opened the door. It was Sierra.

"Sorry to bother you," she whispered. "I didn't want to wake Clay, so I didn't ring the bell."

"Come in. It's good to see you." It sounded like a cliché, but he noticed his pulse jack up a notch.

"I just wanted to drop this off for you." She handed him a small gift that was beautifully wrapped.

Does she want me to open this in front of her—or after she leaves?

"I wrapped it myself." He wondered if she said that to diffuse the awkward moment.

He chuckled, knowing she did a better job than he could ever do. "Can you sit for a minute?"

"I really shouldn't stay. Am I taking you from something?"

"I was just writing my second novel. It's almost done—except for the title." Instinctively, he started walking back toward his den to show her, and she followed.

"What was your final decision?" she asked. "Sequel or—write from the heart?"

The way she said it struck a chord in him. "It's my 'write from the heart' standalone novel."

"Good. I had hoped your heart would win. Your next book can be for your agent and fans—this one's for you."

Everything she said was what he wanted to hear. He noticed how unselfish it was, and so much like her. One more example of being on the same page.

What went wrong at the hospital? And what was her mysterious lunch with Merritt all about yesterday?

Setting the gift on his desk, he asked, "Can I get you something to drink?"

"No, I really can't stay. Just want to know how Clay is doing."

"Great. He has more energy than yesterday, and I suspect every day will be better than the day before."

She nodded and pursed her lips.

He sat on the edge of his desk. "I heard you met my mother-in-law, Joyce, at the hospital yesterday."

She looked around the room, perhaps to avoid eye contact. "Yes, she's very nice. Direct, but nice."

"That she is. Say, she mentioned you wanted to let me know you were going to have lunch with a girlfriend. I'm not sure who she was referring to or why you would want me to know that." Chase had just given her the opportunity to tell him she was actually having lunch with Merritt. All he wanted was the truth.

Sierra looked puzzled. "She said I was having lunch with a *girlfriend?*"

"That's what she said."

"Hmmm. I never said that."

Chase raised his chin and deepened his tone. "So—what are you saying?"

"I'm just saying, I didn't say that? Maybe she misheard me."

"Well, she seemed pretty clear to me, so ..."

An awkward pause hung in the air.

Sierra glared at him. "So if she is telling the truth, I must be ..." She didn't need to finish her sentence. "Is that what you think, Chase? You think I would not tell you the truth? What has gotten into you?"

Chase had committed himself. He couldn't walk it back now, but he desperately wanted to believe her. "I'm not sure why Joyce would not tell me the truth."

On the other hand, if you had lunch with Merritt—according to Jack—you would have a reason to fudge the truth.

"Chase, she must have just misunderstood me. I clearly told her to tell you I was having lunch with Merritt so you would know I was being ..." She never finished her sentence when she saw him place his hands on his hips and look down and away.

Why is she here, anyway? If she is having lunch with Merritt, is she going to give him a shot again? Did she come here to tell me that? Should I end it first to save face?

Chase rubbed his hand on the back of his neck to calm himself and gain perspective. "Should I conclude you've had a change of heart about our relationship?"

Sierra winced. "What are you talking about? Where is all this coming from?"

Chase got up from the desk, walked to the windows, then turned to face her. "Jack mentioned he saw you having lunch yesterday with

Merritt. And now you're bringing me a gift and admitting you had lunch with him after trying to cover it up by telling Joyce to tell me you were having lunch with a girlfriend. I'm not trying to make a big deal out of this. I'm just confused and trying to understand the truth. That's all."

Stunned, she folded her arms across her chest. "I don't understand you, Chase. This doesn't even sound like you. Do you not trust me, suddenly?"

"Should I?"

Her face flushed, and she rubbed her throat. Chase wasn't sure if it was anger, hurt, or both. She stepped back. "I told you the truth to your face just now. *Merritt* and I had lunch. I told Joyce the same thing. I don't know what she *thought* she heard me say. Chase, I've always been truthful with you. I would never lie to you or your mother-in-law."

She blinked away a tear, and he could tell how deeply he'd hurt her, and he dreaded it. He wondered how two people could live on the same page some days, and other days live on a different planet.

Sierra repeated herself in a soft, resolute tone. "I would *never* lie to you—or anyone. I thought you knew me better than that. It seems we misjudged each other. I should go."

Unsure of what to say, and feeling off balance, he filled the pause with an empty platitude. "Thanks for the gift." Although he was sincere, he knew he sounded cynical.

Her voice cracked, and he sensed her anger had dissolved into heartache. "I guess you should consider it a goodbye gift." She left without closing the front door.

A few minutes later, he locked up for the night and walked back to his den. He stared at the beautifully wrapped gift and the red bow for a few minutes before opening his bottom desk drawer, placing it there, and closing it.

There was no longer any reason to unwrap it.

CHAPTER 38

Chase didn't sleep well that night. How could he? It seemed whenever he gained something in his life, he lost something. After he'd gained another year of marriage on his ninth anniversary two years ago, he'd lost his wife. Shortly after gaining a treehouse for Clay, he'd almost lost his son. After writing a bestselling novel, he could lose his agent—if he didn't write a sequel. Now, as his son regained his health, he risked losing Sierra.

Life was not making sense again.

~

Later that week, David had worked on a fresh set of blueprints for a new client for two hours before he felt unproductive, distracted. After informing his administrative assistant he would be out the rest of the day, he drove home. His conversation with Chase in the hospital about why he never loved again was eating at him—and it reminded him of something long forgotten. But could he find it now?

When he arrived home, he checked his filing cabinets in case he had filed it years ago. No luck. Perhaps it was in one of his lock boxes. *I wonder if it's there?* Nothing.

Could it be in my safe deposit box?

Fortunately, he kept an itemized list of everything in his safe deposit box. Flipping through the file, he quickly noticed it was not on the list. *Where would I put it?*

What are the chances I put it in Grace's family photo album? That wouldn't make sense, but I'll look.

Pulling the photo albums from the bookcase and fanning through them yielded nothing. And then he remembered. Next to the photo albums on his bookcase was his Bible. He slid it off the shelf and opened it. It naturally parted to the middle where a letter had rested for years—since Grace had died, and his faith along with her.

Sitting in his home office chair, he opened the letter and tentatively read it. For a moment, just a moment, Grace was alive again. By reading the letter, he could hear her voice. He could sense the pain of her illness—and the strength of her will to fight. The letter conveyed her wishes—and reminded him of his failures. It was best left sealed in his Bible. A book he had once cherished and later, in a dark moment after her death, vowed to never open again.

David spent the better part of the day driving around, alone with his thoughts, rehashing the contents of the letter, rethinking what he'd lost when Grace died, and thinking about how his mistakes affected Chase and about the opportunity he had now to help his son—and his grandson.

At dinnertime, he texted Chase and then stopped by to see him. He rang the bell, then opened the door and walked into the living room, where Chase greeted him.

"Hey, Dad."

"Hey Chase, how's Clay today?"

"Better every day. He's playing in his room with Fernando. Kids—their passion for play completely diffuses anxiety. Adults could learn from them. Have you eaten?"

"Not hungry. I stopped by to share something with you. Something I never told you about."

Chase tilted his head to one side. "What is it?"

"A letter from your mother. She wrote it when we learned she had little time left."

"Have a seat, Dad." They sat on his living room couch. Chase squinted and furrowed his eyebrows. "Why did you want to revisit that letter now?"

"You'll see after you read it." David handed it to him and paced. "Read it out loud."

"Are you sure you want me to read something that's going to open old wounds?"

His father was emphatic. "Just read it."

Yellowed and brittle, the letter crinkled in his hands. He read aloud.

My Dearest David,

Thank you for being so strong for me a few days ago when the doctors revealed my bleak prognosis—and attached a timetable to it. I knew in the depth of my soul that I would never survive this wretched cancer, yet we were equally stunned with how little time I have left. I am grateful that I have placed my faith in Jesus, the Great Physician, and you're with me till the end.

The last few days have been agonizing for me, as I anticipate saying goodbye to you sooner than ever imagined. I must admit, I've seen what this cancer journey has done to our faith. Mine has somehow blossomed, and yours is dying. Promise me you won't give up on God. He owes me nothing. And has given me everything. If you give up on God, Chase will too. He idolizes his father.

Every day, I wonder how I should tell Chase this news. Or if I should tell him.

David, one side of me wants to just fade away without the risk of traumatizing our dear little boy. On the other hand, if I tell him the truth—to say "goodbye"—maybe once he's grown, he will remember this sacred moment, how much I loved him, and have closure knowing his mother attempted to say goodbye before leaving him forever.

What should I do? What's best for him?

David, there is so much we need to talk about and so little time.

Chase brings me so much joy with his energy, his questions, and his unshakable faith that I will soon be well, helping him with his homework, and allowing his friends to come over to play again. I can't imagine any of those things now, as I barely have the energy to dress myself or put on makeup.

The main reason I have summoned the strength to handwrite this letter, although it is my third attempt to complete it in as many days, is to remind you of a recurring conversation we've had over the years.

We occasionally talked about what we would do if the unthinkable happened—if one of us left the other prematurely. I never dreamed it would actually happen, and yet here we are. I must admit, I'm scared. Not of death—I've settled that with my faith in Christ—but of separation from you, my beloved husband, and my only child, who inspires me every day to keep fighting leukemia.

There are only three things I ask of you:

1) Return to the Lord. Live for him the way you did before life became so uncertain—and I became so sick.

2) Raise Chase the way we agreed. Keep him in church.

3) And live your life free of people's expectations—including mine. David, I set you free to love again. All I ask is that if you remarry, be sure she loves Chase as her own. No second-hand love for my boy.

My darling, my prayer for you is someday you both will live in our home again with the sweet aroma of love—a love like ours.

A love with "No Reservations."

Yours forever,

Grace

P.S. David, open your eyes to the possibility that a broken heart is healed, not just by time, but by daring to love again.

~

Chase looked up at his father and chewed on his lip. "I'm not sure what to do with this."

His father sat alongside him. "Let it sink in. Witness how much she loved you."

Chase cleared his throat. "She never said goodbye."

"I know. But she agonized over it. Grace wanted a special moment you would remember—a moment of closure that would answer so many questions in the future."

"Then why didn't she say goodbye?"

"Because that moment of closure in the future would be a traumatic event in the present. How would a twelve-year-old boy handle his mother telling him she was dying? In the end, she couldn't bring herself to tell you—to put you through that."

Chase's eyes were red, and he sniffled. "I wish she would have done it. I wish she would have said goodbye."

David put his hand on his son's shoulder as he stood over him.

"You say that now. Think about it. It would have been devastating to a twelve-year-old."

Chase stood and walked to the window and stared out at the ocean. His father stood behind him.

"Son, maybe this letter gives you the best of both worlds. She didn't tell you then, but she told you now. And the letter reveals her heart at the time of the decision—and it's written in her own hand."

Continuing to stare out the window, Chase said, "She asked three things of you."

"I know."

Chase turned to face his father. "You didn't honor any of them. Why?"

David looked at the floor and then in Chase's eyes. "I've struggled with my faith in God since she got sick. That's on me. I've got to fix it—and I will. I blamed God. I was angry. So I stopped going to church—and sadly, that included you. But you're wrong about the last one. I lived free of people's expectations. Everyone wanted me to marry again. I did what I thought was best for me and—I had hoped—you."

Chase fixed his eyes on him. "She gave you permission to marry again, Dad. Mom set you free. All she wanted was for us to be happy—to move on. And you missed it."

David shoved his hands in his pockets and stepped closer to him. "I didn't *miss* it, son—I *passed* on it. I made a choice. For me, I chose to only give my heart to her. The consequences for me didn't matter. The consequences for you were a different story. I was a young father, and I didn't think about how deeply you would be affected. For that, I'm sorry. I'm truly sorry."

David waited for Chase to respond, but he struggled to speak. Instead, he attempted to clear his throat, then approached his father and hugged him. David squeezed his son in return and held him for a long moment.

306 | James C. Magruder

Chase released him and took a breath. "You did what you thought was best. I accept it. Let's put it behind us now."

David remained silent.

"Dad, I'm sorry for holding this against you. I was blind—and confused. I think we can now, finally, let the past live in the past."

"Son, now it's your turn to choose. Read the P.S. again. That's the main reason I gave you the letter."

Chase picked it up from the coffee table and read it to his father.

P.S. David, open your eyes to the possibility that a broken heart is healed, not just by time, but by daring to love again.

David rubbed his hands together. "Your Mom was right, you know. Don't look to me as your only role model anymore. You need to do something you haven't done for years. Take your mother's advice now, not your father's. In the grip of grief, don't make the mistakes I made." David patted Chase on the shoulder and started toward the door.

"Dad, before you go, after all these years, where did you find this letter?"

"I had stashed it away. Honestly, I had trouble finding it."

"Where was it?"

"Right where I left it. Originally, I put it in a place I would see it every day. But when your mother died, I forgot about it, because, well, I vowed to never look there again."

"Where was that?"

"In my Bible." When he reached the door, he hesitated.

Chase walked to him and folded the letter, following the worn creases, and handed it back to his father.

David held up his palm. "Keep it. It speaks to your life more than mine now."

"Dad, it's ironic, isn't it, that even in death, Mom got you to open your Bible again?"

His father nodded, and the smile on his face spoke to the memory of the one he never stopped loving. "Maybe that's why her name was Grace."

~

After David left, Chase wanted nothing more than to speak to the one person in his life who always seemed to have the answers. The one person who knew how to live above the fray of life put everything in perspective and reduced any tragedy into bite-size, digestible pieces. He needed to speak to his grandfather—or at least revisit his Bible—where his notes could speak for him.

His grandfather had been a quiet man with a faith that defined him. Joseph Kincaid gave his Bible to Chase as a gift just before he died. It rested on his bookcase in his den, which made him wonder why he didn't reach for it and read it more.

Flipping it open, he found his grandfather's notes scrawled across the blank pages before the Table of Contents. Scribbled there in handwriting that aged with him through the years were his favorite Bible verses, pithy quotes, and personal notes. Chase smiled at the thought that this Bible had been his grandfather's constant companion for decades.

When he ran his finger along the notes, he didn't know what he was looking for—perhaps nothing more than a piece of wisdom from an old man he admired and who was always there for him. Maybe he was hoping to hear his voice once more when he read the words written in his own hand.

His eyes fixed on a verse jotted at the bottom of the page. Ecclesiastes 3:4. ... *There is a time for every event under Heaven ... a time to weep, and a time to laugh; a time to mourn, and a time to dance ...*

Below the verse, his grandfather had inscribed: *I've loved one woman for forty-five years—and she loved me. What more could I ask for? It's over now. I know where she is. I've mourned my loss enough—any more and I do it not to honor her, but to pity myself. Scripture is right. It's time to dance again.*

Chase read these words repeatedly until he absorbed the truth in them.

When he closed his Bible, he whispered under his breath, "Grandpa, thank you for your faith—your Bible—and reminding me it's time to dance again."

CHAPTER 39

C hase slept well last night, thanks to his father's visit—and the unexpected visit from his mother. It was only four o'clock in the morning, but he was up and raring to go because now, at last, he knew exactly what he had to do. Summer was almost over, and September was right around the corner. School would begin soon.

Sitting at his laptop, he typed with a renewed sense of purpose. *When the heart is full, the words flow.*

By six o'clock, he had completed his new standalone novel, and by seven, he reviewed and made final edits to the first three chapters and the last chapter, knowing Ed judged a book by the beginning as much as the end. Chase had previously edited the bulk of the book, knowing final edits would be a collaboration between the editor and him. So he emailed the entire manuscript to his agent after changing the title for the third time. Ed had expected the manuscript long before now, and it would not be the sequel he had asked for, but it was a good effort. It was a clean document, and, he believed, it was some of his best writing. The sequel he had started was nearing completion, and Chase would continue to work on it and have it ready in his back pocket if the standalone novel did not fly with Ed.

By eight o'clock, Chase called Joyce and asked if she could watch Clay for the day and possibly until his bedtime. She was more than happy to oblige and thanked him for giving her the gift of catching up with him.

Joyce arrived by nine, just after he had shaved, showered, and made breakfast for Clay. Chase skipped breakfast. Too much to do.

"Where's Clay?" It was the first thing Joyce asked coming through the door. "How's he feeling?"

"He's doing even better than expected. You can see for yourself when he comes out of his room from playing video games or whatever."

"What are you up to today, Chase? If I may ask."

"Errands. Lots of errands. I have some work to finish and review with a client. I'm going to run by the cemetery to see Aimee, and I think I owe Sierra an apology."

"Do you stop by the cemetery often?"

He nodded, and a smile curled at the edges of his lips. "Just because she left us doesn't mean we will ever leave her, Joyce."

"Sierra was right then about how deeply you loved my daughter."

"Was there ever any doubt?"

Joyce looked at her feet before lifting her head. "Sierra's a nice girl. I like her. If I may ask, how's that going for you?"

Chase hesitated, and she raised both palms.

"Look, I know it's none of my business, but she spoke so kindly about you, and she obviously loves Clay. I was just wondering if ..."

Chase held up his index finger to stop her. "I don't know where our relationship is going, if anywhere. We got into a bit of an argument the other night when I learned she had lunch with her ex-fiancé when you had told me she was having lunch with a girlfriend."

Joyce wrinkled her nose at the recollection. "I never said she was having lunch with a girlfriend."

"Yes, you did."

"No, I said she wanted you to know she was having lunch with someone, but I didn't remember the name of the person. Then you asked me if it was a man's or a woman's name, and I said I thought it was a woman's name."

Chase offered a confused look. "Well, if it was a woman's name, it must have been a girlfriend, right?"

Joyce scratched her temple. "What did you say was the name of her ex-fiancé?"

"Merritt."

"Oh, no."

Chase squinted. "What now, Joyce?"

"I remember now. Sierra told me to tell you she was having lunch with someone named Merritt. I have a girlfriend named Merritt, so I assumed …"

Running both hands through his hair and down to his neck, Chase said, "Oh, my …"

"What happened?"

"I insinuated she wasn't telling me the truth because Jack saw her with her ex, but you said you thought she was having lunch with a girlfriend."

Joyce covered her mouth with one hand. "And Merritt can be a man's or a woman's name. I'm so sorry, Chase. This is all my fault."

Chase slowly exhaled. "Don't worry about it. I owe her an apology for more than one thing. It's something I need to do today."

"Make it right, Chase. She's a special woman. Look, take as much time as you need. I'll play with Clay—when he's in the mood for his grandma—and I brought a few books to read when he's playing a video game or taking naps. And I'll make him dinner or take him out. If you're late, I'll put him to bed."

"I may take you up on that. Thanks so much, Joyce."

When Chase left the house, he ran several errands before driving to the lumberyard to place a large order before calling Sierra. She was cold at first, but he asked her if they could meet at noon for coffee, lunch, and to talk. She agreed—only after he told her he wanted to apologize.

Before picking her up, he stopped at the cemetery to visit Aimee's gravesite.

Squatting down in front of her headstone, he traced the date of her death with his finger. Relaxing, he felt time stand still. It was a moment he did not want to rush.

"Aim, it's me. Life has been tough since I lost you. Where to begin? My dad, Jack, and I built Clay a treehouse. I know Clay told you. You'd love it—because he loves it. He calls it Fort A.M.Y. because when he plays there, he's Always Missing You. I'm sure he told you. We have a great kid. He looks more like you every day. We miss you—more than you could ever imagine."

Talking to her again made him feel like he was losing his grip. Pausing a moment, he sharpened his focus.

"Clay fell from the treehouse a while ago—after a fire. It was a big deal. No burns, but he needed brain surgery—but he's fine now. 'Best-case scenario,' Jack and Dad say. Can you believe those two agree—on anything? Old Jack has kept me going since losing you, even though he still grieves his divorce from Julie. He doesn't talk much about it, but I know he's having trouble letting go too—even though she has moved on. Seems like one party always bears the most weight in a divorce. One suffers, the other lives free. Doesn't seem fair."

Hesitating, he wondered if he would ever make this statement.

"I've been wanting to tell you something." His throat constricted. He slowed his pace and took a deep breath. "Aim, I've met another woman. Her name is Sierra. And I *think* I love her. No, I *know* I love her. Yet I still love you. Can a man love two women at the same time? Is that fair to anyone?"

He thought for a moment. "Anyway, I wanted you to know—before I tell her. And she needs to know—so I'm going to tell her after I leave here."

Hesitating again, he wiped a tear away and held the wedding ring on the chain around his neck. "I needed to tell you this—but I'm not sure if I'm asking for your permission, or your forgiveness. I think you'd like her—and I know you would want me to move on. She loves Clay—no secondhand love. And I think she loves me—at least I think she did. Anyway, I wanted you to know something. While my love for Sierra will grow—my love for you will never die. I think my head and heart can finally handle that now."

He traced her name with his finger one last time. "I love you, Aim."

He walked to his car, and for the first time, didn't look back.

~

When Chase picked Sierra up at her apartment, she was waiting outside for him. *Was this to make a statement—don't come in?* If she wanted to make him feel distant, like he had lost some ground with her, it worked.

As he stepped out of the Jeep to open the door for her, she jumped in and buckled up before he could reach her side of the car. Retracing his steps back to the driver's seat, he hopped in and clicked on his seatbelt. They drove downtown in silence until he broke the tension. "I thought we'd do everything in reverse today—get an ice cream cone on the wharf first, then lunch, then coffee at Zoe's."

"Whatever."

His mind was running now. Everything he said seemed to be wrong. *Is she thinking the wharf is a great place to end our relationship because it began there?*

After parking, they walked to the Great Pacific Ice Cream Company, got cones, and wandered over to the railing overlooking the ocean. The air was warm, but the breeze was refreshing on this perfect August afternoon. She licked her cone with deliberate strokes while he struggled to find the right words.

"Sierra, I owe you an apology. I was wrong to not trust you."

"It was worse than that, Chase. You thought I lied to you. I would never lie to you."

"I know that now." He explained the misunderstanding with Joyce.

She tilted her head and savored her cone as it melted, and she listened to him.

"Sierra, I blew it. I'm sorry for not trusting you. I was wrong. It's no excuse, but as you know, for the last two years, grief has messed with my head—and heart. Now, here I am apologizing to the same person who helped me get through it. Go figure." His cone melted over his palm, and he wiped it with a napkin.

She spoke, but didn't face him. "Could you repeat a few parts again?"

"Which parts?"

"The parts about being wrong and blowing it." A smile curled at the corner of her lips, and he felt the tension melt, like his ice cream over his hand.

Licking his cone and wiping his hands again, he watched as she finished hers.

"Want to walk to the end of the wharf?"

"Sure."

As they proceeded to the end of the pier, which extended far out into the ocean, she cleaned her hands with the napkin.

Chase transitioned to what was on his heart. He knew it would be awkward, but there was no eloquent way to approach the topic. "Back to you having lunch with Merritt. May I ask what your status is with him? Are you two getting back together?"

She stopped walking, tilted her head, and stared at him. "What? No. Why would you think that?"

"Deduction, I guess. Think about it. Joyce mentioned you wanted me to know you were having lunch with Merritt. And coincidentally, that was after you saw him again in the hospital—and immediately after I blew it there too."

When they reached the end of the pier, they leaned on the railing and absorbed the spectacular view of the ocean, sailboats, and hang gliders. "Chase, I asked her to tell you I was having lunch with Merritt simply to be honest with you—so you could trust me."

"I know—and I blew that. But why did you have lunch with him? You once told me he wanted to get back together. Did you talk about that?"

"Yes, and no."

His back stiffened. "Okay, not sure what that means."

"Yes, *he* talked about wanting to get back together—and no, *I* told him I wasn't interested. I'm only interested in seeing him again on one condition."

Chase hesitated. "Okay. And that one condition is?"

She smiled. "If I twist my ankle again. And by the way, I set up the lunch. I wanted to end it in person so he would get the message."

Chase felt his back muscles relax. "Great. But Jack said he saw you 'leaning in' and you looked happy."

"Leaning in? Happy? Oh, that might be when I made it clear to Merritt our relationship is over—forever—and to stop calling me. I was happy because he seemed to get it, finally. And he actually apologized for what he did to me. But I still made him pick up the tab. Besides, I told him I'm interested in two other attractive men."

"Two other men?"

"Well, one man and an eight-year-old."

Relieved, Chase bent over the railing and shook his head over the shimmering water. "I feel like an idiot. I said so many things to you that were so wrong and so stupid. Looks like I owe you more than one apology."

"One is enough. But I would like more than one explanation."

Chase hung his head. "Yeah, about that. I'm sorry about what I said in the hospital …"

She faced him and looked into his eyes. "When I asked if I could help you after Clay was hurt, why did you say, 'No, we've got this?'"

"I've thought a lot about that since it happened. Honestly, it's complicated."

"I'm listening."

"I think the immensity of the moment overwhelmed me. Clay was critically hurt. The ER physician was your ex, and I sensed an emotional connection between you, at least on his part."

She looked out over the ocean. "Is that all?"

"No. At that moment, I felt like I needed Aimee."

"Do you know how that made me feel?"

Chase nodded. "Yes, and I'm sorry, but may I explain?"

"Please."

Chase placed his foot on the lowest crossbar and leaned on his forearms on the railing. "When Clay's life was threatened, I felt like I was losing control. In fact, I haven't felt in total control of my family life since I lost her. We were a tag team. Together, we had exchanged ideas, sought each other's counsel, and had a plan for raising him. When she died, a piece of me died too. I was no longer sure how to raise him alone."

He noticed her shoulders relax and her eyes soften.

"In the ambulance and in hospital, I felt like I desperately needed to talk with her, to get her advice, her perspective, and feel like we were both there for our son. I was in the same frame of mind when you offered to help me—so I said, 'We've got this.' Like I always said when she was alive. I defaulted to my former life."

She reached out and touched his arm but did not speak.

"I'm sorry I hurt you by shutting you out or pulling away—you've had enough of that in your life. The strange thing is, in the same moment, I also felt like I needed you—and you may not believe it, but … I really wanted you."

He waited for a reply and hoped, now more than ever, that she would find a bridge to understanding him.

There was no reply. She simply leaned into him, put her head against his shoulder, and wrapped her arms around him. She had given him what he needed. Words were optional.

His arms encircled her, and he held her tight. "I guess I owe you a blanket apology—you know, one that covers multiple mistakes and gaffes. That way, you just apply the apology to my account every time I say or do something stupid."

She laughed and stepped back. "Wouldn't it be easier for both of us to just start over—beginning today? It's a beautiful day."

"Great idea. You ready for some lunch? There's more I have to tell you."

~

Chase and Sierra enjoyed lunch at another beachside restaurant. The conversation was light, and they relaxed in each other's company. After lunch, he called Joyce to see how Clay was doing and if she needed him home.

"We're fine. Enjoy yourself," Joyce assured him. "I love having Clay all to myself. We're making up for lost time." She took a long breath. "Thank you, Chase. You're a good man."

Her words comforted him more than she would ever know, and finally, he felt a bridge of understanding being built, brick by brick, back to his mother-in-law. It wasn't complete, by any means, but it was a start.

~

They walked to the water's edge before Sierra took off her sandals. Chase left his sandals on, unconcerned about how wet or sandy they would become as they walked on the beach. He reached for her hand, and she gently grasped his.

"Sierra, I'm falling in love with you."

She turned to him but didn't stop walking. "How do you know that?"

"I know it because …"

She interrupted him. "Chase, you may *want* to love again—and you may even feel *ready* to love again—but you may not be *in* love again." Sierra wanted to believe Chase loved her, but she was frightened to be devastated by the illusion. She had demanded so little, but she didn't want him to be on a rebound. All she wanted was for him to be clear-eyed and trust his own feelings—so she could.

"Ever since I met you, I feel alive again when I'm with you, Sierra."

"That's your pulse, not your heart."

"Look, I know I've made mistakes with you and you deserve to have doubts, but I have worked through mine—and I know from the deepest places in my being that I'm falling in love with you. In fact, I'm already there."

She stopped short and listened to the surf as the wind blew through her hair.

"Chase, you need to hear me." Their eyes met. "I'm not Aimee. I'm not that beautiful, unselfish, wonderful woman who meant the world to you—who you loved so deeply, and who was lost so tragically. I'm just Sierra Taylor, a third-grade schoolteacher."

They walked again, hand in hand. "Sierra Taylor is all I want."

She stopped again and stepped back. "How can you be sure?"

"I'm sure because …" his voice trailed off, and he thought for a moment. Swallowing hard, he started again. "I'm sure because I think I've completed the journey—if it is ever really completed."

"The journey?"

"Call it a grief journey, I don't know, but what I know is there's been a desert between us. A dry wasteland we both had to cross."

They continued to walk with their feet in the water now. She held his hand and swung her sandals in the other.

"What are you trying to say?"

"You were on one end of the desert—and I was on the other. To find each other, we had to cross the desert. I had to cross through the fog of grief because of the way I lost Aimee, and you had to cross the desert of doubt. I wondered if I could ever *love* again—and because of the mixed signals from your father, Merritt, and even my pulling away from you ..."

She finished his sentence. "I wondered if I could ever *trust* another man again."

A gentle breeze blew through her hair, and he continued. "Right. I tried dating, waiting, and praying. I met with Dr. McAllister, and I even consulted with my son. I trekked through the wilderness of loneliness and finally found you—right here in the middle of this emotional desert."

He stepped toward her. She met him, their eyes locked, and he kissed her with the passion she had longed for and she knew, until today, had eluded him.

Sierra looked up at him. "I'm falling in love with you too, Chase. And how can you not love sweet little Clay? I feel like I've been standing in the center of this desert waiting for you. Waiting for someone I could trust again. Now that we finally found each other, I'm not sure what is the best way out of the desert."

"I'm not sure either, Sierra—but one thing I am sure of. We will find our way out together."

Then she said something that lit up his eyes.

"We are the compass each other needed."

"You're right, Sierra. And as my grandfather would say—it's time to dance again."

CHAPTER 40

After what Chase thought was a life-changing walk on the beach, he took Sierra out for a light dinner, followed by coffee at Zoe's. It was a purely impulsive day, and the free-flow nature of it thrilled them, reinforcing one of the best things about young love—spontaneity.

When they arrived back at Chase's home, Clay was asleep and Joyce was reading.

"How was your day?" she said in an uncharacteristically warm tone.

Sierra answered before he could. "Wonderful. And yours?"

"Same. I can't get enough of him. Clay, that is—not him." She smiled and pointed at Chase.

Sierra laughed at Joyce's playful tone. "Well, I can't get enough of Chase, so I guess we've got the two Kincaid men covered."

Joyce winked at Chase. "So you guys worked out your differences?"

"I'd say so," he said.

Joyce looked at Sierra and nodded. "I'm sorry I inadvertently misled Chase on your former lunch date. It was my mistake, Sierra."

"Don't worry about it, Joyce. We've talked it out. It's all good."

"I'm glad. You make a delightful couple."

Sierra looked at Chase, and he raised his eyebrows twice after receiving the endorsement of his mother-in-law. Joyce packed up her things and walked to the door before glancing at Sierra.

"Take care of my grandson till I get back." She walked out to her car.

"What just happened?" Chase asked.

"I think I got her blessing," she said.

"I think *we* just got her blessing," he added. "Wow, it's been a great day. I ordered materials to rebuild the treehouse, I visited Aimee's gravesite, I apologized to you—profusely—and I think I found the bridge to understanding my mother-in-law. We should celebrate. Glass of wine?"

"You apologized profusely to me? And, yes to the glass of wine."

"Yeah, when I issued my 'blanket apology' for all present and future gaffes."

She shook her head at his weak attempt at humor while he pulled out two wine glasses and a bottle of chardonnay. Pouring a glass, he handed it to her.

She swirled it and took a sip. "Can I see your finished stand-alone novel?"

"You can see the rough draft with one of the former titles, but not the finished draft with the new title I sent to my agent. Don't want to jinx it before I hear from him. He should see it first. Follow me."

They walked to his den, and she sat at his desk and scrolled through portions of the document, noting the initial draft had reached three hundred and twenty-seven pages. The working title: *To Love Again.*

"This is your working title? I like it. Why don't you?"

"It sounds too much like a romance. But it's not a romance. It's a love story. There's a difference."

"What's the difference?"

"A romance is required to have a happy ending. A love story can have a tragic ending, like a Nicholas Sparks novel."

"So what's the new title?"

"Like I said, I can't tell you. I don't want to jinx it."

She swiveled in his chair and faced his Inspiration Wall. "You didn't open my gift yet?"

"Oh, yeah. Right. I set it aside for a better time. That was a tough night, remember?"

"Open it now."

Opening his bottom desk drawer, he lifted the gift out while she rocked in anticipation. "You have an empty spot on your wall right there," she said, pointing. "It looks like you had a plaque there once. I thought you might like to replace it with this one."

Chase knew Sierra had never seen the Fitzgerald quote—the gift from Aimee. It spoke of their love, and she'd given it to him the day she'd encouraged him to write his first novel—the bestseller she never lived to see him complete. The quote played in his head as he set down his wineglass. *"There are all kinds of love in this world, but never the same love twice."*

Once again, he felt his worlds colliding, the past and the present. Yesterday versus tomorrow. It was a moment of truth for him.

She broke his train of thought. "Well, go ahead, open it."

She had folded the wrapping paper with tight creases and impeccably tied the ribbon. Sliding his finger under one end, he slipped the ribbon off in one fell swoop and peeled back the wrapping paper with care.

"It's not fragile. Just open it."

Ripping the rest of the paper, he pulled a plaque out and let the wrapping fall to the floor. Looking at her, then the plaque, he read it to himself. She stopped rocking and gazed at him. Tears formed in his eyes, but he held them back. Chewing the inside of his cheek, he tried to speak. Silence. He noticed her holding her breath and waiting for him to regroup.

Struggling to clear his throat, he sipped some wine. "It's really beautiful, Sierra. I love it."

She exhaled. "I hoped you would. It speaks to my love for you."

It was all he needed to hear, and the tears escaped his eyes now.

She stood and slipped her arms around him, and he wrapped his around her waist before he kissed her.

He hung it on the wall on the nail from the previous plaque. "He's my favorite classic author, you know," he said before they stepped back from the Inspiration Wall and he read it to her aloud.

> *"There is no remedy for love, except to love more."*
> Henry David Thoreau

~

They looked in on Clay together—he was fast asleep. Sleeping like a rock, as usual. Chase watched her as she kissed him on the forehead. "Sleep well, little angel."

After walking to the backyard, they sat in the comfortable patio chairs in the bright light of the moon, with the rhythmic sounds of the ocean in the distance. Chase raised his wineglass. "Let's make a toast."

Sierra smiled. "A toast to us?"

"A toast to whatever is on our hearts after a day like today," he replied. "Let's alternate. I'll go first. To yesterday—may we never forget our past—and how it blessed us …"

Sierra raised her glass to meet his. "To tomorrow, may we accept everything it brings …" Holding her glass high, she signaled him to continue.

"To love."

"And loss …"

"May it never stop us …"

"From loving again."

Chase continued. "To anyone who is hurting tonight …"

"May God hold them near …"

"And whisper what they need to hear."

Sierra's voice cracked. "Life must go on …"

"And so must love …"

They exchanged tears, and Chase finished the toast. "May we all grant ourselves permission … to love again—with no reservations."

They clinked their glasses together and took a sip. Chase wiped a tear from Sierra's cheek with his thumb. She did the same to him. It was then Chase knew beyond any doubt. The simple act of wiping each other's tears away was enough. It said more than words could say.

Searching her eyes, he sensed they were living on the same page. Years ago, his grandfather had once said, "Love is a universal language. It needs no interpretation, because every heart is a translator."

He sat in his patio loveseat, and she sat alongside him with her head on his shoulder. Neither spoke, each unwilling to shatter the magic of the moment. Today was their day. Now was their time. Together they embraced it, gave it time to breathe—to become theirs, and theirs alone.

CHAPTER 41

In the days that followed, prior to the weekend, Chase completed all the in-house client work and waited to hear Ed's initial reaction to his standalone novel. Agent reaction, even a gut response, gave Chase pause because agents either loved it or loathed it—anything in between was lukewarm, and no one would publish a lukewarm novel. Chase had a bad feeling about this delayed feedback and wondered if Ed would place it with a publisher—or place it in a circular file.

With the novel finished and no advertising or speech writing work on the docket, Chase cleaned his office, which he had severely neglected during crunch time. When the phone rang, he froze. Could it be Ed? Did he love the manuscript or loathe it?

It was the lumberyard, so he scheduled delivery for Friday afternoon. By then, he and Jack could have the remains of the treehouse disassembled and in a heap so reconstruction could start early Saturday.

Why not make a picnic out of it? He called his father, Jack, Sierra, Joyce, and Fernando and his mom and invited them to a barbecue at noon on Saturday—a celebration of new beginnings. Long before noon, Jack, David, and Chase would start rebuilding the new treehouse and have the gutted materials hauled away. Then, they would start from scratch with a new blueprint.

When he contacted Joyce, she surprised him with her warm response to his call. She gladly accepted every invitation he extended to her lately, and he realized how kindness helped everyone heal.

Jack would bring the nuts, bolts, specialty brackets, and

miscellaneous hardware again, while most of the tools needed were still on the workbench in Chase's garage, except the auger, which he rented. The weekend would cap off a meaningful week before school started on Monday.

~

When Saturday morning rolled around, Chase put the coffee on and called Sierra at six o'clock. "Hey, sorry to call so early, but I have an idea."

Sierra sounded groggy, and she spoke through a yawn. "Okay, what are you thinking?"

"I want you to call Jennifer Adams and invite her to our barbecue at noon today."

She glanced at her alarm clock. "We're not giving her much notice."

"I know, but you know how much she helped Clay, so I'd like her to come if she doesn't have other plans."

"Why do I think you're up to something?"

"Maybe because you're getting to know me. Just call her. I'll see you at ten."

David and Jack arrived at six thirty, toolbelts in hand and requests for coffee on their lips.

"Let's do this and make it better than the first one," Jack said as they filled their cups and walked out to the tree.

"I've made some preliminary prints," David said. "The fire significantly damaged the tree, and we lost some supporting branches, so it won't support the full weight of the treehouse, at least not like the first one."

Jack put his hands on his hips and surveyed the tree. "You mean there's no way to keep the tree involved? That's what makes it a treehouse."

David took a sip of his coffee and glanced at the prints. "I don't think so."

"What are you recommending, Mr. K?"

"The easiest option is we could just build it on the ground but make it bigger, so Clay's excited about it. What do you think? And it would be safer." He looked at his son.

"Dad, Clay's still sleeping now, but I know he was hoping for a treehouse."

"And not a dollhouse," Jack said. "No offense, Mr. K, but I think whatever we build, it's got to be up in the air—and have a slide."

"Jack's right, Dad. What if we built it on stilts close to the tree? At least it would feel like a treehouse. I ordered a few extra support beams. I could order more, but it has to be a fort, not a dollhouse."

David looked disgusted. "I would never build my grandson a dollhouse, Jack."

"Oh, oh, here we go again," Chase interjected.

David winked at his son. "On the other hand, you never know if a little girl might play in this structure someday too."

"Don't get ahead of yourself, Dad. Let's build this thing on stilts seven feet off the ground instead of ten. I'll feel better about that." They all looked at each other.

"Copy that," David and Jack said in unison.

The morning moved quickly, and around ten o'clock Sierra, Joyce, and Jennifer arrived within minutes of each other. Chase looked up from the blueprints and walked over to greet each of them. Joyce made her way to greet David while Chase focused on Jennifer. Sierra stepped off to the side, near the blueprints, with her back to Chase. She was close enough to eavesdrop.

"Jennifer, it's so good to see you again," Chase said.

"Thanks for inviting me to lunch. That's kind of you."

"Well, let's just say I wanted to thank you and let you see the fruit of your labor—after all, you suggested I invest more time with Clay by doing a special project."

She pointed to their work-in-progress. "Yes, but I can't take credit for a treehouse. That was not my idea."

"Well, let me introduce you to where the idea came from." Chase called out to Jack, who was taking a measurement. He walked over to greet them.

"Jack, I'd like to introduce you to Jennifer Adams. She's the social worker at Clay's school, and she suggested I have a special project to reconnect with him."

Jack offered his hand. "Pleasure to meet you, Jennifer."

She nodded and shook his hand. "Likewise."

Chase turned to her. "Jennifer, Jack is my closest friend—most days—and he was the one who came up with the idea of a treehouse for the special project you suggested."

She smiled and lifted her eyebrows. "Well done, Jack. Nice idea."

"Jack is an engineer, and he helped make it all happen. I just wanted to thank you both. You collaborated and never knew it."

"It's what uncles do." Jack grinned.

"I'm just happy it worked out so well the first time. I'm so sorry about the fire, Chase," Jennifer said.

"Thanks, but it could have been worse."

Jack smiled. "You might say, given the circumstances, it was a best-case scenario."

When Chase walked over to Sierra, where they could eavesdrop on them, Jack engaged in more conversation. "Tell me, Jennifer, what's it like being a social worker in a school these days?"

With their backs to them, Chase and Sierra listened in.

Sierra cocked her head. "Smooth. Very smooth, Chase. Do you think they know what you just did?"

Chase winked at her. "Doesn't matter. If it works out, it was worth it. Jack and Jennifer—it has a nice ring to it, don't you think?"

She punched him playfully on his shoulder. They laughed together and went back to work.

Before noon, the ladies set the patio table, made salads, cut veggies, and prepared the meat for grilling. Chase fired up the grill. Clay and Fernando carried supplies to David and Jack, who let them use hammers, screwdrivers, and a power drill, but drew the line at the tape measure. David adhered to the "measure twice, cut once" code of conduct. There was no hurry to finish the treehouse—or the stilthouse—since summer was coming to a close.

No matter what they called it, it was a remarkable afternoon of coming together for a common purpose. While they thought they were constructing a treehouse, it occurred to Chase they were building—or rebuilding—his family.

When Chase finished grilling and the food was ready, they sat at the patio table and enjoyed tri-tip, burgers, hot dogs, salad, chips and salsa, cold beverages, and warm conversation. Even Eva, Fernando's mom, attended, and she was not empty-handed. She brought the homemade chips and salsa.

$\sim$

When night had fallen, Chase sat on the couch in his den, gazing out the open window at the silhouette of a partial treehouse against the orange glow of the sun, now below the horizon. Opening his journal, he fingered the pages and noticed only two empty pages remained. Once again, he sat to write.

$\sim$

Life is a journey—with unexpected twists and turns. Highs and lows. Deserts—and streams.

I love Sierra. This I now know, but I must admit, I still think about Aimee—every day. Maybe I always will. I know my friends, except Jack, secretly wonder—but would never dare to ask—if I love Sierra as much as I loved Aimee. To be honest, I asked myself this question too. The truth is, I don't love one more than the other. I don't have to. I've learned I simply love them differently—but the same amount. My son taught me that.

Love is a choice—especially the second time around—and, I would argue, love after loss is blind, deaf, and dumb. Blind, because I could not see clearly through the fog of grief. Deaf, because, at first, I could not hear the counsel of family and friends to propel me forward—beyond my crisis of heart. And dumb, because I could not speak to my deepest needs or verbalize my feelings. Jennifer, Jack, and Dr. McAllister taught me that.

In this grief journey, it makes sense that nothing is the same—no two stories, no two characters, chapters, or endings. So why would my heart love two women in exactly the same way?

My father taught me there may always be a hole in my heart for Aimee. And that's okay. After all, I see her face every day when I look into my son's eyes. She will always occupy a corner of my heart reserved only for her.

Sierra will never fill that hole. She's not supposed to—she knows that. Instead, she will create her own space with room to expand. Isn't that the beauty of true love, that every love story leaves a mark all its own? Like a fingerprint—or a signature on your heart.

It took me two years to learn that if I approach love without comparisons, expectations, or reservations, it can take me to unexpected places—and fill me with hope that life goes on.

I once thought this day would never come. Healing, I mean. I didn't know what it would take to open up. Breathe in and out. And smell fresh air again. A treehouse taught me that.

Sierra and I have learned so much as we've walked through the desert between us. Those dry stretches of grief and loneliness. It was

in the desert that I learned I had been asking myself the wrong ques-
tion. The question was never can I love again? It was, will I give
myself permission to love again? Once I made this choice—I could
dance again. My grandfather taught me that.

My struggle to love again may differ from others'. But I've learned
that no matter who we are, or the circumstances of our loss, lov-
ing again, really loving again, begins with a choice. Sierra once said,
"We love best by choosing to love."

And I learned from a letter written many years ago by my mother
that I must choose to love Sierra with—no reservations.

～

When Chase finished writing on the last page of his journal, he
closed it and held it close to his heart before placing it on the bookcase and rejoining Sierra, who was sitting in the living room waiting
for him. She stood and walked to him as he entered. She slid her
arms around his neck, and he pulled her closer. He felt the warmth
of her embrace as she ran her hand gently along his face. Her lips
parted, and she kissed him tenderly. He felt no hesitation now. No
second thoughts. No regrets. Surrendering to everything that had
held him at bay, he kissed her slowly at first, and then with a passion
that finally set him free.

Hugging her, Chase whispered in her ear, "I really love you."

She squeezed him tighter, and without looking at him,
said, "I know."

～

At that moment in New York, Chase's literary agent had just finished
reading the last page of his standalone novel.

"This isn't the sequel I asked for," he said to himself.

Flipping the manuscript back to the front page, he stared at the title of this novel about a young man who had tragically lost his wife and feared he could never love again. Ed recalled Chase had told him it was a story of love after loss and that he had changed the title three times. The original title was *Reservations of the Heart,* followed by *To Love Again.*

Taking a deep breath and exhaling slowly, he brought his hand to his chin and glanced at the latest title in the center of the cover page. "I like this new title better—it fits the story."

He read the title aloud.

No Reservations, A Novel.

Standing to take a long stretch, he grinned and muttered to himself, "I think he might have done it again."

A SPECIAL MESSAGE
FROM THE AUTHOR

The theme of this novel is love after loss. Most people strive to love again after losing their spouse or soulmate. I have often wondered what I would do.

My father, who inspired this story, found himself in this situation after the premature loss of my mother when they were in their mid-forties.

Like Chase Kincaid, the main character in this novel, my father had a choice to make. Would he give himself permission to love again?

Most people eventually find their way through the emotional desert of grief and choose to love again. What did my father do?

My father chose to never love again. Instead, he focused his attention—and his life—on raising his six young children alone, just the way they planned when my mother was alive.

An incredibly strong man, my father was a committed provider, and an inspirational leader.

For the rest of his life, his modest, yet frequent, refrain was, "Not a day goes by that I don't think of your mother." After her death, he remained faithful to her memory for forty-three years until his death at age eighty-seven.

Although I deeply respect my father for his tough choice, if you find yourself in a similar situation, my hope for you is you will give yourself permission to love again. And you will love—with no reservations.

James C. Magruder

A WORD ABOUT SANTA BARBARA

S anta Barbara is a beautiful city. Can you say postcard perfect? It's called "The American Rivera" for a reason. Just ninety miles north of LA and 290 miles south of San Francisco, Santa Barbara is a self-contained paradise with spectacular views stretching 110 miles along California's Central Coast.

Some things I treasured when I traveled there during the research phase of this novel were the pristine beaches, the authentic Spanish Revival architecture with the signature red-tiled roofs, the energy of State Street, the boutiques, restaurants, and coffee shops, the picturesque Paseo Nuevo open-air mall, and the Santa Barbara Museum of Contemporary Art.

In this novel, I describe the area this way. "When God created Santa Barbara, he realized he had just created his inspiration for Hawaii." The sights and sounds of this seaside city restored my perspective. It was like pressing an internal reset button after a stressful week.

My family enjoyed the views from the top of the Santa Barbara County Courthouse Clocktower. You can take in the 360-degree panoramic view of the ocean, the Santa Ynez mountains, and the red-tiled roofs.

If you visit, don't miss exploring at least one of the four Channel Islands. Santa Cruz Island offers hiking trails, mountain paths, swimming, diving, snorkeling, kayaking, and overnight camping opportunities.

What I enjoyed most was visiting Stearns Wharf. Built in 1872, it is the oldest working wooden wharf in California. This wooden plank structure features an eclectic array of restaurants, wine tasting rooms, gift shops, and ice cream parlors that made a magnificent setting for the story. Significant scenes take place on Stearns Wharf—and the ocean view is spectacular.

Santa Barbara was the perfect setting for our main characters, Chase Kincaid and Sierra Taylor, to find each other, and later, give themselves "permission" to love again—and trust again. I hope you enjoyed this story inspired by my father's life and loss.

James C. Magruder

ACKNOWLEDGEMENTS

The theme of this novel, love after loss, has been "parked" on my heart for years. Only in the last two years have I disciplined myself to sit down and scrawl these words across the page. Yet the yearnings of my heart have found their voice on these pages.

This novel is in print today because of the people who mastered the art of inspiration—my wife, **Karen,** who not only pushed me, prayed for me, and suggested ideas for various scenes, but stood squarely behind me when I struggled to craft these words. I love you.

To **Dr. David E. Dryer** and his wife, **Judy,** my dear friends. I treasured Dave's advice, counsel, and wisdom in the development of this book, his help with research, his extra push, and his unfailing belief that I had this in me—and needed to write it down and release it to the world. Thanks for your ideas in the cabin during our winter writing retreats. You have stood by me and my writing for decades. Thank you for being a guiding light.

I would like to thank my son, **David,** and his wife, **Veronika,** for helping me write and rewrite some chapters, for catching logic errors, and for helping me write better. For my son, **Mark,** and his wife, **Natalie,** for taking intense interest in this book, helping me with the creative process, proofreading the entire novel, and assisting me with the setting they have called home for five years—Santa Barbara. For their son, **Clay,** my five-year-old grandson for, well, just being Clay, the namesake of the eight-year-old character in this novel. For **Mia,** my three-year-old granddaughter. She didn't help at all, but she sure is cute and will help me with the next one.

To my siblings and their spouses for your steadfast love and reliable support to get me past the finish line: **Kathii, Chris and Sue, Mary, Bob and Patti, Joanie and Ron.** Please know that I wrote this specifically for you. As my brothers and sisters, you witnessed our father take the unintended journey found on these pages. Thank you for helping me make sense out of life when we lost our mother together as young children and watched our resilient father trek through the *desert* depicted on these pages.

I'm so grateful to **Michelle Gross** for being willing to fit a 350+ page manuscript into her busy schedule and proofread it on an airplane and throughout her business travels.

To **Dejah Edwards,** author of *Shattered Innocence,* for being a beta reader for me and for her suggestions to strengthen this work.

To **Jon and Kathy Beggs** for allowing me to interview them on their relationship, their past, and God's provision for bringing them together. Their insights are a part of the lives of the characters in this story.

To **Dan Sessler** and wife, **Bobbie,** for their lifelong encouragement, especially for my writing.

To **Rich and Cathy Allen.** Many thanks for my extensive interview with Rich on the grief process of losing your first wife, Nancy, the mother of your five children, and your personal journey to finding love again with Cathy.

My heartfelt thanks to **Dr. Roberg Gullberg** for his advice in writing key medical scenes in this novel. And to **Don and Jeanne Tyree-Francis,** for consulting with me so I could accurately portray the social worker scenes and for proofreading them to make sure I got it right.

I'm especially grateful to **Richard Paul Evans,** #1 Best-selling Author of *The Christmas Box* and forty-five consecutive best-selling novels, for his endorsement on the front cover of this novel and for designating me as an "Author to Watch." A very special thanks to

Richard's assistant, **Diane Glad,** for coordinating this effort and being so supportive of all of my work.

I would also like to thank my agent, **Andy Clapp,** for believing in me, my talent, my discipline, and this finished work. For **Hope Bolinger,** my developmental editor, for her amazing ideas and editing skills, **Sarah Limardo,** my copy line editor for her brilliant enhancements, and my publisher, **Victoria Duerstock,** owner of End Game Press, for making it all happen so seamlessly. You all are amazing.

To **Michelle Medlock Adams,** a prolific author of over one hundred books and who introduced me to many of these industry professionals, for her endorsement and her steadfast belief in the message of this story.

And finally, to authors Eva Marie Everson, Pastor Larry Dugger, Cindy K. Sproles, Amanda Flinn, Dejah Edwards, Dr. Donna D. Kincheloe, Julie Lavender, and Peggi Tustan for supporting me with your powerful endorsements of this novel.

Thank you all.

ABOUT THE AUTHOR

 James C. Magruder writes reflective essays and contemporary Christian fiction that encourages readers to pause and reflect on the most meaningful moments in life. He is author of *The Glimpse,* an inspirational novel currently available at WestBow Press, Amazon, and most online booksellers.

He has had articles published in *Writer's Digest,* nine *Chicken Soup for the Soul* books, *HomeLife,* and several other national publications.

He is an award-winning advertising copywriter and executive speechwriter and has enjoyed a rewarding career as a Senior Marketing Communications Manager with a Fortune 200 company.

When Jim isn't breaking into a new publication, he's breaking boards as a martial artist. He has earned a third-degree Black Belt in Okinawan Karate (Wax On, Wax Off).

Visit his website at jamescmagruder.com to read his blog and sign up for his popular newsletter, PAUSE MORE. RUSH LESS., about maximizing your life—by slowing the pace you live it.

Meet James C. Magruder at

www.Jamescmagruder.com

Learn more about him, his next novel, read
his PAUSE MORE. RUSH LESS blog
about how to maximize life by
slowing the pace you live it—
and so much more.

Connect with Jim on
Facebook jim.magruder.35
Instagram: jim.magruder.35
Twitter: @jamescmagruder